The Maker

The Maker

Wes Moore

PROVECTUS

M
E
D
I
A

North Carolina

PROVECTUS
MEDIA

North Carolina

Copyright © 2010 by Wes Moore.

ISBN 978-1-4507-1113-5

Printed in the United States of America.

Second Edition.

Cover by Chris Vestal.
Layout by Tiffany Dorrin.

To those who search but are yet to find.
To those who hurt but are yet to heal.

The Maker

Sometime in our future...

"Hurry, boys! Hurry!" the middle-aged man yelled desperately into the wide hole in the ground. "We're almost out of time! It could hit any minute now—and they *can't* be lost!"

Hugh and Haddon dug with all their might, deeper and deeper into the ground, while their father, mother, and two younger sisters pulled out the loose dirt with buckets tied to old yellow ropes. In only an hour and a half, they were at almost fifteen feet down.

"How much time, Paul?" Mary asked softly as she, Drew, and Eileen pulled hand over hand to remove the heavy buckets of sandy soil.

Paul eased out of his crouch when his load slipped over the edge. "I don't know, honey," he answered. "Last I heard over the short wave, they hit Cincinnati. A couple hours before that it was DC. Then the lines went dead." He dumped the bucket onto a pile to his right and continued. "There's no more communication from back east; looks like they're all gone. It could be any second now."

Mary tried desperately to hide the utter panic boiling beneath her skin. She pulled her six- and seven-year-old girls tightly to her dirty, ragged dress and kissed each of them on the head. "I love you girls," she whispered into their red hair. "Mama loves you so much."

And then she and Paul traded those smiles parents trade when they know catastrophe is about to strike, smiles that all at once say, "Everything's going to be okay," and, "There's nothing we can do now—I love you."

Paul peeked back into the hole, sweat dropping from his forehead. "Hugh…Haddon…" he called down to his teenage boys, "that's far enough—come on out."

One at a time the boys climbed out on a third yellow rope tied to a tree in their small backyard. It was knotted every two or three feet for grip.

Once they were out, Paul turned again to Mary. "Do you have them? Are they ready?"

Handing him the two plastic bags, she answered, "They're right here."

Paul kneeled down and opened the black, metal box and gently placed the packages inside. Then he paused. "Is there anything else that needs to go in here?" he mumbled to himself. "Ah, yes!

"Eileen, run inside and grab Daddy a piece of paper and pen off the kitchen counter," he asked his oldest daughter.

Without delay, she pulled away from her mother's side and ran the twenty or so feet to the back door of their run-down, one bedroom house. And before the screen door could close behind her, she had raced across the creaky kitchen floor, grabbed the items, and made it out again.

Pen and paper in hand, Paul quickly scribbled a note on the sheet, sealed it, and slipped it under the two large packages. After the lid was closed, he pushed the box up on its side and scratched several characters on the outside with the tip of the pen.

"Help me tie these ropes around it, boys," ordered Paul. When the cords were tightly fastened, they eased the heavy chest to the bottom of the hole. "Okay, cover it up everybody. Hurry," he instructed.

They each grabbed a shovel or hoe or whatever was handy and labored furiously to fill the earthy column before time ran out on them. Just as the sun started to set behind the early spring trees, their task was complete.

"Come here everybody," he called. The entire family formed a tight pack beside the dirt mound that was the deep hole, and held each other.

"Everything's going to be alright," he assured them, fighting to hold back his mountain of tears.

Then Drew looked up and asked with clear apprehension in her eyes, "Daddy, are we going to die?"

The question nearly broke him in two. "No, no, my dear." He forced a smile and kneeled down to see her face-to-face. "This is not the end for us, sweetheart. This is our new beginning," he comforted her, taking her into his arms one last time.

As he held her tight, he whispered slowly to himself, "But I'm afraid this just might be the end…the end of the United States of America."

And then a bright light flashed in the distance, and they were gone.

Act 1

Chapter 1

Adrien Bach fell down on his hands and knees in the cold rain. A rough, desert-like landscape of sandstone boulders, course gravel, and wiry vegetation surrounded his prostrate frame. Though it was now early spring, it was hardly noticeable in this place. There were no trees, no warm spring air, no sweet smell of flowers. Hot during the day, cold at night, and always bleak—that's what this place was. Only on rare occasions did it rain, but when it did it was torrential. Like tonight.

The land was mostly flat except for a few hills that sloped slowly up and down; his path from base camp had brought him up one of those hills on this dark night. In the distance behind him, faint lights flickered through the rain while muffled sounds of atmospheric units and power generators corrupted nature's gentle melody. Outlining the camp were four bright lights that illuminated wide, square holes in the ground. Two of them sat on small hills; the other two, flat stretches of earth. Adrien had nicknamed it "X-camp" because of how it looked like an "X" from this particular hilltop.

It was not what was behind him that secured his attention on this night, however—it was the empty space before him. Over many years, the long cycles of dryness followed by intense periods of rain and flooding had carved broad, deep canyons in the land. As Adrien stared into the pitch black hollow only inches from his face, he visualized every detail.

He ran his mind over the jagged edges that marked its opening and the smoky Dakota sandstone that was its foundation four stories below. He counted the sharply contoured stones and shards poking upward from the flat bottom. He listened as the powerful downpour transformed the paltry creek into a roaring river. He admired the multi-colored rock layers that painted the opposing face many yards away.

It was all at once a beautiful and a frightening place.

The large raindrops had pounded him for almost an hour, and in that time his face had fallen so low it was nearly touching the ground. Beads of water filled his short, black hair and wrapped slowly around his cheeks forming a puddle just below his chin. And though the slick, space-age fabric that was both his work and social attire should have kept him dry, it proved unsuccessful on this occasion. Even his work boots failed to stop the advancing deluge.

He was drenched, soaked to the bone, and shivering; but he hardly noticed, nor did he care.

He opened his eyes long enough to see the slippery gold band pressed into the palm of his hand, and as his painful stare continued, he asked out into the night, "Why did you go? Why did you leave me?"

Thoughts collided in his head, gradually overwhelming him. Inside a powerful emptiness had been building for months, growing stronger with each passing day. Though he knew it wasn't a tangible thing, he had come to picture it as a malevolent dark hand that reached up from the deep and ruthlessly pulled him down into the void below.

And he hated it.

"Why is this happening?" he cried, his face now buried in his forearms. "I didn't ask for this. I don't want this."

As tears replaced raindrops on his cheeks, he lifted his head, stared out into the ravine, and asked, "Why, Sophie…why did you have to go?"

Then he lost it. The sobbing shot from within like a volcano. For months he had tried to manage his emotions, to keep them under control, to tell himself they would slowly subside as time went by, but they never did. And in that moment of savage agony, all he had stored up over the last two years finally found its way out.

He reached down into the darkness with his hand, like he was reaching for something that wasn't there, trying to grab it out of the air with his fingers. At that instant, his dark brown eyes became distant, as if he was in some other place, visualizing some dreadful, terror-filled scene.

"I'm so sorry, Sophie. I'm so sorry. Please forgive me," he whimpered.

And then his face relaxed, and his breathing slowed, and his tears stopped. He wiped his face and stood while the rain ebbed around him. Instantly a lightning flash revealed the gaping hole before him and his thin, soaked body at its edge.

He slipped the ring back onto his finger, slowly turned his eyes toward the heavens, and spread his arms wide. While the drops bounced on his cheeks and forehead, an expression of relief rippled across his face. He heard himself breathe—in and out…in and out—and felt his neck pulse as blood coursed through his veins. A gentle breeze came from the south, splashing lightly against his face and side while tiny kisses of water tickled his fingertips.

At last, he exhaled deeply and took a step forward with his left foot, and then his right. His legs tensed; his back engaged; his shoulders edged forward. He visualized himself falling, the way the air would run through his hair and how light he would feel. He thought of Sophie. He thought of peace. In only microseconds, his force of motion could not be stopped.

For Adrien Traugott Bach, his thirty-seven years of struggle and heartache were almost over, and he was glad. In only a few seconds, he would be dead.

Then a voice yelled from behind, "Hey! Are you okay?"

Adrien's entire body jerked. He lowered his arms and whipped toward the sound. Barely visible, the man was standing back on the path to the camp just where the hill started to descend.

When Adrien didn't speak, the man said, "You look pretty close there. And you don't want to fall, now, do you?"

"No, no, of course not," Adrien replied after another long pause. "I was just...um...watching the water. The creek, it's...rising so quickly."

The man was slender with dark hair and some kind of scruffy mustache or beard. Though in Adrien's position he knew most everyone at the camp, he was sure he'd never seen this guy before.

Another long silence.

Finally Adrien looked back into the canyon and then back toward the man and muttered, "Well, I guess that will have to be enough for tonight."

Walking away from the edge, he rubbed his hands on his pants and glanced back and forth between the man and the ground. Passing the mysterious stranger, he avoided eye contact and managed only a soft and nervous, "Thank you."

"My pleasure," came his short reply.

As Adrien slipped more and more into the subtle light of the camp, he felt the dark hand reach up again, and wondered how much longer he would survive if something didn't change.

And soon.

Chapter 2

Paris, France
Central Column, Global Community of Nations
Thursday, March 31
Darwin Era (DE) 523 (2332 AD)
3:53 AM

Addy, Remi, and Deston stood at the entrance of the imposing granite building. The holosign to the right of the two large wooden doors gave the building's designation: G-CoN SDC Complex. There were actually three sets of main doors to this building, but only the center allowed entry. All were recessed in a grand marble portico extending out from the main building.

Remi and Deston wore cheap two-piece suits with arms that were an inch too short. Accenting their five-and-dime Sunday morning best were dirty sneakers and clip-on fluorescent ties. Remi's slim face sported shoulder-length blond hair, while Deston, the plump one of the bunch, was cursed with frizzy, black locks and a patch of hair on his chin.

Addy Moreau, on the other hand, looked like something from a women's fashion magazine. From her petite frame fell a short-sleeved, silk red dress that finished nicely just below her knee. Flowing black hair rolled off her face, nearly covering her right eye and slightly touching the rectangular neckline of her dress.

Addy stood out in front while the boys waited a step behind. After entering an access code and waving a security medallion over the nearby reader, they waited for access. The boys scanned the entryway behind them; Addy stared intently at the holosign.

"Rad, what's the deal here? Is this thing going to open or what?" whispered Addy into her communication port implant. The "comm-port," as it was called, was a communications chip surgically implanted under the skin just behind the temple. The almost microscopic device allowed for two-way voice communication, video surveillance, and a personal, voice-activated heads-up display (known as a P-HUD).

"Cut me some slack, girl," the Chief Engineer fired back. "This stuff takes time. Don't doubt the master, baby!"

"If you don't get this door open in five seconds…" But before she could finish her threat, the holosign glowed green and the words, "Welcome to the G-CoN SDC Complex," rolled around.

"You just gave yourself another day to live," she said as she turned the knob and pushed the door open.

"Oh come on, baby! You know you still love the Rad-meister," Rad joked back.

She was about to retort when the immensity of the SDC redirected her words. "Holy smoke," she said.

"Can you see this, Rad?" Remi asked.

"Yeah, I got it, R-man." Through their comm-ports Rad could see what they were seeing on one continuous screen surrounding his tech station. He toggled between views by touching different parts of the screen.

What they saw was an enormous, open library with white marble tiles and rectangular, brown insets. Long wooden tables on each side of a main aisle preceded polished redwood bookshelves that reached thirty feet into the air and continued as far as they could see. Picketed metal gates locked down the bookshelf aisles. The faint scent of orchard blossoms permeated the place.

Just in front of the trio a contoured display console rose from a slim opening in the floor. About six feet wide and three feet tall, the screen stopped at eye-level, held aloft by its offset white base. As Addy and the boys approached, it spoke.

"Welcome to the Global Community of Nations Super Data Center Complex," said the female virtual voice. When her words ended, the screen came alive. First, a high-def graphic of a rotating earth appeared in the center with stars in the background. Then, from left to right, three phrases spread across the bottom: "One People," "One Planet," "One Community." The graphic and text formed the backdrop as the interface windows loaded.

The voice returned, "Welcome Administrator." Addy and the boys traded looks and sly smiles. The same words also appeared at the top center of the display. "Administrator controls loaded," the voice continued while a series of five squares with graphics and text appeared evenly across the panel. The center square was about twenty percent larger than the others and read, "SDC Master Controls." The other four squares, two on each side, controlled the four primary sectors of the SDC, one for each of the four government agencies storing information there.

Addy selected the center square and another large window appeared. A graphic of the SDC floor plan popped up showing the console where they stood, the tables, and the bookshelves. The shelves were divided into four sectors, two on each side of the aisle, and were color-coded— red, blue, green, and yellow— for easy identification. From the top left, clockwise, the sectors were identified and explained as follows:

Sector 1: Global Information Services (GIS). G-CoN Information Proliferation database including outlets, content, broadcast schedules, and access privileges.

Sector 2: Global Citizen Services (GCS). G-CoN Citizen Profile database including personal, family, employment, political, and spiritual data.

Sector 3: Global Financial Services (GFS). G-CoN Financial Holdings database for commercial enterprise, member states, and individuals.

Sector 4: Global Security Services (GSS). G-CoN Security Records database including organizational and individual threats, political detainees, intelligence portfolio, and military capabilities.

Below the floor plan were three options. Addy touched "Access rights" and another screen appeared. She paused to glance at Remi and Deston. "Here it goes, fellas."

She tapped the top option, "Allow access to all sectors," and, one by one, the metal gates opened: "Clank, clank, clank..."

"We're in," said Deston.

"We're in," echoed Addy. "Now let's get to it. Who knows how long before they send the Patches."

The dumpy Chief Engineer piped in over the comm-port, "Yeah, and if we're lucky, the Assassins won't come out and play tonight."

"Yeah, *real* lucky," Addy said without a trace of a smile. Then she bolted to Sector 1, pretty red dress notwithstanding.

Chapter 3

Paris, France
Central Column, Global Community of Nations
Thursday, March 31
523 DE (2332 AD)
4:08 AM

Addy's mission took her to the far left corner of the library. As she dashed down the long center aisle, she overheard Rad talking back and forth with Remi and Deston. When she reached the section with red triangles on the end of the shelves, she interjected, "I'm here, Rad. I'm looking for the files now."

Rad spoke into his comm-port. "Yeah, the one you're looking for might go by several names. Try the G's first."

"I remember," she countered, rolling her eyes. Addy walked quickly down the aisles looking for the G's. Aisle four. She touched the virtual leather book at the beginning of the G section. A holoscreen floated out two feet into the aisle. The high-resolution interface was visible to Addy but also partially transparent. To see through it, she simply changed the focal point of her eyes. It accepted touch-commands.

"P-HUD activate," she said with careful articulation. About a foot in front of her and slightly to the left a rectangular holoscreen appeared projected by her comm-port implant. Virtually any type of data could be presented on a P-HUD display, from audio and video, to environmentals, to standard data files.

"Open 'File Name List,'" she ordered. Straight away, the file opened on the screen.

"Okay, I'm here. Just a sec and I'll have it up," Addy informed Rad. While she punched in a few characters, Rad rattled off instructions to the others.

"I don't see it, Rad," she said after a few seconds. "There's no file here called 'Globalcast,' 'Globalcasts,' or anything like that."

Rad brought up Addy's feed. "We expected as much. They must have hidden it in a different directory."

"Thanks for the commentary, Einstein," she quipped. "Moving to the next file." Addy ran to the end of the aisle and turned right. Two aisles down she found the C's. "I'm at the Content files," she announced.

Meanwhile, Rad was getting updates from the guys. Remi said, "The virus is uploading now, Rad." An instant later Deston chimed in, "I've found the Threats file. Opening."

"They're beating you, Addy," Rad teased her. "You're not going to let these clowns take bragging rights, are you?"

"You know what they say, 'Don't count your chickens...'" Addy moved her fingers at lightning speed and quickly found the file. "It's here, Rad. You're not going to believe this—the Globalcast file is under a subdirectory called 'Citizen Control.' The arrogance of these guys is amazing!"

"They did try to hide it. Smart move," Rad whispered to himself. Then to Addy he said, "Why don't we force feed them a little humble pie for their efforts? Look for an update option somewhere."

"I know. I know."

As she flipped through menus, Remi screamed over the line, "Something's gone wrong, Rad! The screen is blinking red. Oh no, a message just flashed—they deployed a Patch! I'm busted!"

Rad responded, "Keep your cool, man." He spit out instructions on how to call off the Patch and activate the virus. Remi's hands were shaking.

"Deston, what's your status?" Rad asked.

"I'm good for now. Just about to upload the file to you. I guess we'll know in a few seconds," Deston replied.

"Okay, let me know, Big-D. Addy, better hurry. They may launch a sweep just for the heck of it," Rad warned.

"I'm ready," she said. "The system is expecting an updated Content file. Send it now!"

"I'm on it, baby!" answered Rad. He touched his screen and the upload marker started counting: 10%...15%...20%.

"You'd better hope this thing thinks your station is part of the G-CoN network," Addy warned. "They use Assassins to protect these files."

At that instant Addy heard a door open in the back of the library just behind her. A figure shot past the end of the aisle.

"I just saw something head your way, Remi," Addy blurted into her comm-port.

"What color was it, Addy?" asked Rad.

"Green, I think."

"Are you sure it wasn't black?"

"No, it *definitely* wasn't black."

"Okay, it's just a Patch then. R-man, you've got to stick it out. Keep doing what I told you," Rad ordered.

"Just a Patch or not," protested Remi, "I'm a sitting duck!"

"Sorry, buddy. This is war."

Suddenly Deston was back. "Rad, something's happening. The upload stopped."

"What now, man?"

"Not sure yet, but they might be on to me too."

Rad checked the file marker on Addy's screen—90%. "Addy, looks like the hounds are sniffing us out. I'm going to scramble your location while you finish. Hurry!"

Deston jumped back on the line. "My screen's locked up, Rad!"

Addy heard the door open again. Green flashes streaked by at the end of her aisle in a continuous stream, twenty at least. Best she could tell none were black.

"Looks like the sweep just started," she informed the group.

"I think I've got it, Rad," offered Remi out of the blue. "One more second…"

As he punched his final commands into the holoscreen, his anxious look gave way to a thin smile. Then he felt a sting in his chest. He looked down to see a green rod pierce through from behind at center mass. In an instant, his body disintegrated before his eyes.

Rad, who had just switched to Remi's comm-port view, saw the pointed end of the rod just before the screen went blank. "Remi? Remi!" he screamed. "I think they got him!" he yelled to all. To Deston he said, "Get out of there, man—now!"

Deston stopped immediately and ran for the end of the aisle. As he exited and turned for the front door, two Patches nailed him at the same time, one from the front, one from the back. All that made it to the comm-port was an agonizing shrill.

"Addy! Addy! What's your status?" barked Rad.

"I'm here, and I'm not running, so don't even try."

"I know better…just hurry, will you?"

The file marker stopped at 99%. She watched it, willing with all her might that final one percent. Then the numbers started to

19

reverse: 98%...95%...90%.

"Crap!" she protested. "They found me." She looked up. A green streak passed at the end of the aisle. "I think I can still make it out of here, Rad," she whispered, turning around to slip out the back.

The instant she pivoted, however, a black figure stood cold only inches from her face. She screamed. But before she could move, he pulled back his razor-sharp spear and thrust it toward her chest.

And the lights went out.

Addy jerked off her headgear and looked around in a fury. To her right, Remi and Deston sat at their stations with their helmets in their hands, trying to catch their breath; on her left, Rad stared at her through his long blond bangs.

And off in the distance, at the other end of the aisle of tech stations, a round-faced man stood at the entryway to the datacenter, his hand still on the switch marked "Emergency Shutdown."

After a short but telling glare, Addy pulled off her gloves, threw her gear on the nearby workspace, and stormed out without saying a word.

Chapter 4

Damien Addergoole reached back and propelled his hand with the force of a train. His victim's head whipped madly on its axis as blood raced from his split cheek. The room was round, dark, and cold—physically cold—and though clean, reeked of stale water. Its only light beamed directly down on the single object in the room: a scarlet red metal chair.

The man occupying the chair was barely conscious, his hands and feet bound electronically to the arms and legs of his four-legged straight jacket. This was his fourth hour there, much of which had been spent enduring virtual psychological torture—VPT—a technique for disturbing the mind through a computer-induced series of fear images and experiences, like repeated episodes of falling off a building or burning alive. Afterwards, he was beaten by unnamed men in black uniforms.

Now it was Damien's turn.

He walked slowly around the chair as the burning in his hand abated. Even at fifty-eight, his six-foot-one pitch still carried the same intimidating quality he had perfected in his youth. Not a single one of his gray hairs was out of place and only one sleeve of his long, white tunic showed the slightest wrinkle. As he turned away from his victim, the two crescent-shaped scars that were his left ear became visible in the light.

Damien spoke slowly. "So, Mr. Seger, it is so gracious of you to join us in our, shall we say, sparsely decorated yet exceedingly efficient facility. I understand you have been treated with the care you deserve."

Seger's sweaty, black hair covered his face, and although he heard every word, it took him a moment to react to Damien's statement. Finally, he looked up toward the fuzzy figure moving in front of him, spit blood on the floor, and labored as he said, "So, this is the treatment a human being deserves, huh? I'd hate to see how you treat your animals."

"You see, Mr. Seger," Damien continued in a calm voice, "this is where you are wrong. You people *are not human at all*. Of course you already know this, now, don't you?"

Then Damien's eyes filled with rage. He lurched toward Seger's face and clasped his hands on the helpless man's forearms.

"But," he screamed, "we are not here to discuss the evolutionary position of your particular group, Mr. Seger! Though I would love to engage in philosophical debate with you on this matter—supposing of course, you could even understand me—I am not here to share my wisdom with you, my friend!"

By this time, Damien's bulging eyes were only inches from Seger's swollen face. His voice slowed. "No, I am here for *you* to teach *me*."

"Yeah," Seger retorted softly, "what can an animal like me teach a big man like you?"

Damien slapped him again on the same cheek. Seger wailed.

"I lied," snorted Damien. "I will teach you one thing: I ask the questions tonight!"

Damien pulled up, laced his hands behind his back, and regained his orbit around the chair. "Why don't we start with a simple one? How long have you been a member of the Resistance?"

As Seger calculated the answer to his persecutor's question, a timid voice crackled in on Damien's comm-port and a yellow light blinked on the wall behind the chair. "Director, sir. I've got some urgent news."

Damien didn't reply. He just glared down at Seger and headed toward the back of the room.

"Think about that question, Mr. Seger...and the locations of your precious Resistance facilities in the Central Column," he said, fading into the darkness. But before the shadows had completely swallowed him, he stepped back into the light and whispered in Seger's ear, "And imagine that beautiful family of yours...in a place like this."

Damien strode into the observation room where several technicians sat at holoscreens monitoring the Interrogation Room's every facet. From Seger's blood pressure and brain waves to the temperature and humidity of the air in the room, nothing was overlooked. Some had already started manipulating video of the interrogation to mine precious intelligence treasure. Immediately, Damien was met by one of his assistants, Broderick Fuller.

"Director, sir," he said anxiously, "please forgive me for interrupting you. I would not have done it if it hadn't been urgent."

"For your sake," Damien offered quietly, "I hope it is."

"The Resistance again. They attacked the SDC!"

Damien's expression was pure ice. Walking away from Broderick toward the door, he asked, "What's the damage?"

But before the youth could answer, Damien spoke to a short man in a black uniform, "Mr. Richter, continue to prepare our visitor until I return."

"Sir!" Richter replied with a single nod and turned to two engineers seated at tech stations behind him. "Resume VPT regimen," he ordered.

"You were saying, Mr. Fuller," Damien said, rubbing his hands clean with a white towel.

"Oh, yes sir." Broderick took position behind Damien and explained. "Well, we don't have a full analysis yet, the GIS—they own the facility—"

"I know who owns the facility."

"Yes, of course, Director. They're running a full sweep to see what, if anything, was compromised. But preliminary scans show that the attack targeted several areas."

"And those would be?"

Broderick lifted his holopad and answered, "They tried to launch the Tetris virus in the Citizen Profile database, they tried to download our Threats directory, and they attempted to replace the Globalcast file with one of their own."

Damien stepped into his massive corner office. Through the two outside glass walls, the sparkling night skyline of Munich was in full view. On the hallway wall a holosign read, "Director of Global Security Services."

"These insects! Their time is coming. Their destiny awaits them, as does mine," Damien said to himself as he sat down in his chair.

"So why do you suppose they chose these three targets, Mr. Fuller?"

"Uh…I guess…I really don't know, sir." Broderick seemed to shrink right into the floor.

"Well then, why don't I give you a little education?" mocked Damien. "A clever plan, indeed. They think we use our knowledge to oppress the global population, so they try to corrupt our citizen profiles. They want to know what we know about them, so they try to read our Threats database. They want a platform to promote their weak ideology, so they try to replace our weekly information broadcast with some of their propaganda."

Damien turned in his seat toward the skyline. "This incident"—his voice grew softer—"certainly reveals much about our enemy."

After a few seconds, he asked. "When will the assessment be complete?"

"You should have it by 0700 hours. And there's one other thing, I'm afraid."

Damien rotated back toward his assistant. "And what is that, Mr. Fuller?"

"The Sovereign has been made aware of the attack. He wasn't happy about being woken up in the middle of the night. The Vice Sovereign himself called and requested your presence in Paris on Friday morning. Apparently, there is growing concern about the Resistance."

Damien clenched his teeth. "These bureaucrats! All they know how to do is talk and drink wine," he sneered. "Very well. Make the arrangements."

"Right away, sir."

"Now I must not go empty handed. Mr. Seger must ensure my trip is a success. Tell Mr. Richter I will be ready for our new friend shortly. And, Mr. Fuller…"

"Yes, Director?"

"Tell him to ensure Mr. Seger is in a mood to talk this time…or he may be the next one in that chair."

Chapter 5

"You have a visitor, Mr. Bach," the soft feminine voice called into Adrien's quarters while he stood at the kitchen counter.

After a long and sleepless night, Adrien had drudged himself into the shower at five; his clean-shaven face, neatly combed hair, and bloodshot eyes attested to this unhappy fact. Last night's drenched uniform had been traded for a clean, dry one of the same description: tan with a single gray stripe on the pants and shirt, a Global Scientific Organization (GSO) logo on the front shirt pocket, and a red, straight collar indicating his rank as Site Leader. And much to his chagrin, his cold, damp toes still reminded him of his tears.

The voice was that of his living quarter's intelligence module. Adrien had nicknamed it "Kim." Every Adaptation Living Space Unit (ALSU) deployed in the field included this technology. At about three hundred square feet, these units gave field leaders a small kitchen, sitting room with two chairs and a tech station, and bunk space with retractable sink and shower. The envy of the camp, Adrien retained the only ALSU on site; the other thirty

26

people attached to the project lived in cramped quarters with three other workers.

Kim's artificial voice caught him staring out the window toward the ravine. The warm sunlight had coated his olive skin and helped transport him to the realm of thought to which he so often retreated.

Snapping to, Adrien said, "Display visitor." A holoscreen lit up near the door. Immediately recognizing his guest, he said, "Allow entry."

Just then Journey darted from the back of the ASLU where she had been snuggling on Adrien's smartly dressed bed. Her short, high-pitched barks filled the room. Adrien barely intercepted her before the door slid open.

"Now, now, puppy," he warmly scolded the two-year-old Miniature Schnauzer. He lifted her off the floor and gently stroked her thick, dark gray coat. "It's just Nate, Journey. You know Nate."

Nate Ashby walked in out of the cold morning air. "Hi, Journey!" he said, rubbing her head. With that she let out one last bark—to assert her dominion, Adrien thought—and returned to her nap.

"Good morning, Nate," Adrien offered with a forced smile. "How are you?"

Nate pushed his fingers through his sandy hair and answered, "I'm well, Adrien. Thanks. Something smells good." He pointed to Adrien's steaming cup on the counter. "I could really use a dose of that, if you don't mind."

"Not at all," said Adrien. "Have a seat and I'll get you one."

Nate walked a few steps into the sitting room and plopped down on the armchair against the back wall. While he waited for Adrien to return, he glanced around the tiny room and surveyed its accouterments.

He eyed the pictures on the shelf just above the tech station desk, one of Adrien and an attractive blond, and another of a teenage Adrien and an older man posing in front of a government building. From there his attention wandered to a white bookshelf in the corner. The thin rack held holobooks with titles like *The World's Great Trails*, *Anthropology and Archaeology*, *The Failure of Manned Space Travel*, and *An Overview and Analysis of Modern Scientific Theories*.

Adrien returned with a strong cup of black synthetic for his friend. "Here you go," he said. After sitting down in the chair opposite the Assistant Site Leader, he asked, "So what's up? This is early, even for you."

Nate took a sip before responding. "Well, before I get out to the sites, I wanted to talk with you about the call tomorrow, the briefing with Paris."

"Yeah, I was trying to forget that one," Adrien said. "Have we made any progress at any of the digs since last week?"

"Not really. One more week but still not much to show for it. We have, however, completed the cataloging of the few things we have found. What has it been? Ten partial, badly decomposed artifacts in three weeks?"

"If that," Adrien complained. "And I have a sneaking suspicion Alejandro's going to lose it if we don't come up with something better this time around. How about the decomposed material that keeps turning up? Has Serena's team at the lab figured out what that is? I mean, that stuff is everywhere. It's like whatever was buried in the ground just deteriorated into nothing."

Nate nodded his head. "In fact, they did come back with something. I got a call late last night. Overall the chemical breakdown is consistent with wood and simple metals—basic building material type stuff—but she keeps finding compounds that shouldn't be there, traces of plastics, complex alloys, and other man-made substances that are far too sophisti-cated for any of the tribes that have ever lived around here."

"Interesting. So how'd they get there?"

"We may have just contaminated the samples. She's running the analysis again to rule out that possibility and verify her initial findings."

"And the source of the decomposition?"

"She can't say for certain about that either. Too early. But she's working on it; her team will be back in tonight to finish up. How about you? Got any ideas?"

"Not really. I'm as lost as anybody on this one," Adrien said, shaking his head. "So can we report any progress at all? How about Site 4? Didn't they see something down deep?"

"Yeah, they might have something later today. I think they're getting really close, but it's hard to tell."

"Okay. Just let me know. I'll throw whatever we've got into a file and send it over when we do the briefing."

Nate sat up and put his forearms on his knees. "Adrien, there is one other thing I'd like to talk to you about, if you don't mind."

For a second Adrien didn't know what to say. There was something about the way Nate brought it up. "Sure, Nate. I hope nothing's wrong," he said, bracing himself inside.

"Well, it's not really about the dig." He looked down at the cup in his hands, then up again. "It's about you."

"Me? What about me?"

Nate stood and walked a few steps to the bookshelves. "Adrien, we've known each other for a long time, ever since the Institute. You're probably the best friend I've got." He turned to look at Adrien, but he was staring down at the floor. Nate continued anyway. "And, well, I'll just say it: I'm worried about you. I know there's something eating away at you, something you're carrying around that you don't want to share with anybody."

Adrien felt the dark hand reach up again. His emotions went crazy, but he fought to hide them from Nate.

After an uncomfortable pause, Nate said, "You're in your quarters a lot. You look like you haven't slept in weeks. You don't come out to the sites much; you don't really know what's going on around here." His voice grew louder and more frustrated. "I mean, heck, you have to ask me if there's been any progress at the sites—and you're the Site Leader!"

Nate sat down on the edge of his chair and calmed himself. "I'm sorry, man. I didn't mean it like that. It's just, I've covered for you, Adrien, and I'm good with that. That's what friends do. But people are starting to ask questions."

Nate waited for a long moment for Adrien to respond. He didn't.

"Look, you don't talk much about it, but I know you've had your share of bad luck over the years, your father, then Sophie, and now this work thing. I thought you'd just snap out of it at some point, but you seem to be getting worse. You're turning into this loner, pulling away from everybody and everything. What's going on?"

Adrien wrestled with himself inside. He wanted to tell someone— about the anguish, about the despair, about the dark hand—but at the same time he didn't want to tell anybody—his past, his pain, his problem. Yet how good it would be to confess it all to another soul!

Finally he looked up and said, softly, "I realize I've let you down, Nate, that I've let everybody down. I'm sure you'd make a better Site Leader than I would…anybody would make a better Site Leader than I would.

"And I appreciate your concern for me. You are a good friend, probably the best friend I've ever had. It's just these things that I'm dealing with…. Let's just say I need to work through them by myself right now."

As he got up from his chair and headed for the door, Nate replied, "Okay, man. Just know I'm here if you need me."

"Thanks, man. I really appreciate it," Adrien said without looking up.

"So I'll check on that analysis and let you know."

"Great," Adrien said as he stood and walked to the door.

When the door closed behind Nate, Adrien laid his head against the cool composite frame and cried silently under his breath. Journey, again alerted by the sound of the door, trotted up behind him and put her paw on his leg as if to comfort him with her presence. After a minute or so, he forced his emotions back into place and squatted down to rub her back.

"Thanks, Journey," he said while she stood on her back legs and licked his cheek. "I knew you'd understand."

"You have a visitor, Mr. Bach," Kim announced again.

"Who could that be?" Adrien asked himself. Hurriedly, he wiped his eyes, took a deep breath, and glanced at the image on the holoscreen. "Allow entry," he said.

The door shot open. It was Nate again. He looked excited.

"They've found something, Adrien! They've found something! Site 4. And it's intact, completely intact!"

Chapter 6

Adrien and Nate sprinted toward Site 4, Journey in tow close behind. As they passed the living units, the site came into view in the distance.

Site 4 sat just beyond the lab at the northeast corner of the camp, one of two sites atop large, wide hills. Around the square hole in the ground, a crowd of tan uniforms and multi-colored hard hats had gathered. A small crane rose high above them all, cutting through the low rays of the morning sun.

Adrien and Nate pushed through the crowd and looked down into the hole. The first eight to ten feet revealed a typical dig site: layers of dirt removed to different levels, and buckets, small shovels, and brushes scattered here and there. Unlike most archaeological sites, however, there were no exposed walls or steps, no half-covered pots or bones. Instead, in the middle of the dig, an eight-foot square hole plunged straight into the ground. The cable from the crane dropped down just right of center along with several electrical wires.

Two days earlier, when almost three weeks of sifting dirt had produced less than a dozen partial artifacts, the team brought in a sub-terra imager to scan for solid items deeper in the ground. During the scan, a square object with rounded corners was discovered buried almost twenty feet below their current position. Late the previous afternoon, after the crane was anchored into place, they started digging a shaft straight down beside the object. This morning they had finally reached it.

Adrien yelled down into the hole. "Hey, Pierre, is that you down there?"

"Yeah, boss," he replied. Pierre and Manuel, two of X-camp's most experienced archaeologists, were on their knees using small shovels to dig around the object and free it from the side of the wall. "You need to see this thing, boss," Pierre called up the shaft. "It's all in one piece, one *solid* piece. We should have it out in a few minutes."

"I'm on my way down," he replied. Adrien turned to the crane operator and nodded. In a few seconds, he stepped off the crane platform onto the cool, damp ground just in time to see Pierre and Manuel pull the object from the side of the shaft.

"What is this thing?" Adrien asked as he bent over to take a look. The object was about three feet long, two and a half feet deep, and two feet tall. Although the exterior was covered with patches of dirt and a host of thin scratches, it looked black on the outside.

"One thing's for sure," Manuel offered. "This thing is heavy."

Adrien grabbed one of the lights stuck in the side wall and surveyed the object from every angle. After he wiped away some loose dirt from one side, a line appeared near the top that seemed to go all the way around, possibly indicating a lid. Just below the line on one of the long sides, a silver dial, about three inches in diameter, was recessed into the face.

"Well, let's not try to do anything else down here. Let's get it up to the lab where we can inspect it properly. I'll go on up. You guys mind getting it to the lab for me?" Adrien asked.

"Not at all, boss," they said at the same time.

With much fanfare, they hoisted the box from the hole and carried it to the lab. Once the crowd was disbanded, Adrien, Nate, Pierre, and Manuel gathered around the examination table for their initial inspection. High-tech lab equipment—bright holoscreens, hand-held mass spectrometers, miniature electron microscopes, and laser rulers—lined the outside of the room while a large stainless steel table occupied the middle. A strong overhead light shone down on the dirty object now firmly in place at the center of the table.

"First, let's clean it off," Adrien said.

Pierre and Manuel grabbed rags from a nearby drawer and delicately wiped off as much dirt as possible. The object was definitely black, and the line Adrien had seen earlier did indeed go all the way around. On one of the long sides, the dial was visible along with a short metal lever just beside it to the right.

"So what do you make of this, guys?" Adrien asked the group.

Nate was the first to respond. "Well, first of all, what is something like this even doing here? Whatever this is, the technology is far beyond any civilization that has ever lived on this part of the continent."

They all nodded.

"Yeah, but what is it?" Pierre asked.

"I don't know, but maybe we should start by figuring out this thing." Nate pointed to the dial without touching it. "It's got these short, little lines on the edge all the way around with numbers every so often."

"It looks like a primitive safe of some kind," Manuel observed.

"Yes, it does," replied Adrien. "And that dial looks like an old dial lock. You know, the ones where you'd use the dial to input a set of numbers—a combination—that would then open the safe."

"So how do these work?" Nate asked.

"Well, if I recall, you turn the knob back and forth to input a certain set of numbers—usually three—and then turn the handle," Adrien explained, pretending to turn the dial back and forth. "This is probably the handle here." He grabbed the short lever next to the dial.

"But what's the combination?" Manuel asked. "I mean, the dial goes to sixty. So that's thousands of possible combinations."

While Nate, Manuel, and Pierre debated what numbers might be used and why—birthdates, lat/lons, lucky numbers—Adrien turned and slowly walked away. Then he whipped around and whispered, "It can't be that easy, can it?"

He walked quickly back to the table and said, frantically, "Here, help me get this cleaned off...I mean, totally clean." The guys grabbed their towels and wiped away layers of dirt until there was almost none left. Adrien ran his hand over the top and then the sides, closely inspecting them for something specific. He paused when he didn't find what he was looking for.

"Turn it over," he ordered. They grunted as they carefully lifted and flipped the heavy box. Adrien grabbed one of the towels himself, wiped off the bottom, and ran his hands over it again.

"Look," he said. "Right there!"

All three leaned over the box to bring the revelation into view. Scratched faintly into the paint were three numbers: 29-41-8.

"Well I'll be," Pierre said. "How did you know?"

"We search for three weeks at this site and find virtually nothing,"

Adrien said. "Then just by chance we see an object buried twenty feet below everything else—the *only object* buried below everything else. Doesn't that seem strange to you?"

"Yeah, but what are you getting at?" asked Nate.

"This isn't some object that *just happened to get buried* many years ago. This thing was put in the ground *on purpose*, so somebody would find it later. Those numbers confirm it!"

"Yeah," agreed Manuel. "Why else would you put the combination on the outside?"

"Here, help me set it down." After it was upright again, Adrien tried to turn the rusty dial, but at first it didn't budge. Finally, it broke free and he quickly input the combination—29-41-8. After the last digit was selected, he looked up at everyone and cranked hard on the lever.

The lid popped open. He lifted it slowly until it was standing straight up.

They all gazed into the mysterious box and gasped.

"Oh my," said Adrien.

Chapter 7

Two dark objects in partially transparent plastic bags sat side-by-side on the bottom. Each of the eighteen-inch long, twelve-inch wide bags was fastened at the top with a plastic zipper.

Adrien, with his eyes still focused on the peculiar articles before him, spoke out into the room, "Computer, set humidity level to thirty percent and temperature to sixty degrees Fahrenheit."

"Acknowledged," the male voice replied.

Without moving his eyes, he instructed the others, "Clear a spot on the table."

Pierre, Manuel, and Nate each grabbed a rag and wiped the entire left side of the table clean, pushing the dirt into a pile in the far corner.

Adrien opened a drawer just beneath the tabletop and pulled out two white examination gloves. Then, ever so gently, he reached into the box, tucked his fingers under the first bag, and lifted it out with both hands.

Heavy, he thought.

"Excuse me," said Adrien, stepping sideways down the table. Pierre and Manuel, who were standing to Adrien's left, stepped back to make way while the Site Leader placed the object flat on the tabletop.

Next, as tenderly as before, he removed the second item and placed it beside the first, in the same left-to-right order in which they were arranged in the box.

"Hey, there's something else," Nate said, pointing into the container. Lying flat in the center was another plastic bag, but this one was about half the size and flat, with an off-white, rectangular sheet inside.

"What have we here?" Adrien asked as he reached in, lifted it by its top corners, and placed it to the right of the other bags.

For a few seconds they all glared silently at the neatly arranged objects on the table.

"Where would you guys like to start?" Adrien finally asked.

Pierre said, "Well that one looks like a note." He pointed to the flat bag with the sheet.

"Yeah it does," Nate confirmed. "Maybe the guys who planted this thing have something to say?"

"Let's find out." Adrien slid the bag just in front of him and carefully zipped open the top. He held the mouth open wide and slid a finger above and a finger below the thin sheet of paper. Like a surgeon, he pulled the sheet from its holder.

The stiff sheet was a light, golden color and was folded in half. With a pair of soft-tipped tweezers, he slowly lifted one half of the fold until the sheet was completely open. Inside was handwritten text.

"Good call, Pierre," said Manuel.

"Indeed," Adrien confirmed, laying the note flat on the table.

They all squeezed around to get a better look.

Adrien read out loud, "'March 31, 2182.'"

"Hey," Nate said, "2182—that's pre-Darwin Era dating."

"Yeah," Adrien said. "And 150 years ago to the day." They traded knowing glances until Adrien resumed his reading. "'We're not sure anyone will ever find this, but we wanted to leave record of that which is most important to us. We do not have long now. May he spare us.'"

Nate threw up his hands. "Whoa! Whoa! Whoa! This is nuts," he said. "Not only should there not be technology like this buried here, but something like this dating itself to just 150 years ago? There's no record of anyone *even living in this region*, or the middle half of this continent, for more than 300 years!"

"Yeah," Pierre agreed, "the last recorded inhabitants of this continent were the Indians back in the third century after Darwin."

"And they were all wiped out in the Gaia Catastrophe of 218 DE," Adrien said. "Up until about a year ago, this whole continent has been under complete quarantine—nobody could even step foot here."

"Let's see what other mysteries they've left for us," said Manuel.

As he placed the note on top of the plastic bag and slid them both toward the back of the table, Adrien replied, "Yes, let's do." He reached for the first bag and zipped it open. Turning to Nate, he said, "Grab the bag while I pull this out." Nate grabbed the ends of the bag with his fingers while Adrien slid out a large black leather book about three inches thick. The back cover folded over the front and was bound with a leather string tied in a loose knot.

"Wow, that's a *real* book," Pierre said. "I've only seen a few of those in my entire career."

"Most people haven't even seen one," Adrien added. "Everything's digital now. Actually, this looks more like a journal than a book—

there's no title on the cover." He carefully loosened the knot, eased the flap over, and opened the front cover.

"That's strange," he said. "It is a book." The first page was the title page. All it said was "The Writings of the Maker." The words *the Maker* were in large, bold text.

The next page contained a table of contents with names of main headings: The Beginning, The Choosing, The Battle, The End—there were a total of ten listed. Under the main headings, chapter names were listed, more than fifty in all. The written content started on the next page. He turned and read a few words out loud:

> *Before there was anything, there was the Maker. He has no beginning and no end. He was not created; he has always been. In his being resides the power of life, the power upon which all other life rests.*
>
> *When it pleased him, he spoke and created the universe, the vast galaxies and stars, the earth and its life systems, and, last of all, he created man.*
>
> *Through creation he is the Father of us all, and in him mankind finds its ultimate purpose.*

Adrien had read the mythological accounts of countless ancient civilizations—he had studied them, dissected them, compared and contrasted them—and every time he felt as if he was reading a fairy tale. Nothing connected. Nothing seemed real.

Until now.

"Sounds like a primitive deity myth," Nate interrupted. "Two thousand years ago, yeah. But 150 years ago, in the age of science? No way." He looked to Adrien for affirmation.

"Yes, it's crazy, isn't it?" Adrien said in an unconvincing whisper.

He flipped quickly through the rest of the book. "Let's see what's in the other one."

The second bag contained a book also, of the same design as the first except it was reddish-brown and about two-thirds as thick. When Adrien opened it, the title page read, "Evidence for the Maker." Adrien read a few section titles from the table of contents: The Existence of the Maker, The Reliability of the Writings, Science and the Maker, When the Maker Walked the Earth.

He quickly thumbed through about half the book and stopped. Again he read aloud. "Science is the process whereby man understands the world the Maker has made. However, it comes with the same limitations as man himself—it can be deceived and manipulated, and it can make errors and be forced to change. The Maker has no such limitations, so his word should be taken over science when the two conflict."

"Wow!" Nate said. "So these clowns actually *believed* this fairy tale and then wrote a book about why *others* should believe it. I think we've got a bunch of superstitious nuts on our hands here, guys."

Pierre walked behind Adrien and looked over his shoulder. "We're archaeologists, Nate, not philosophers. Our job isn't to say whether they were right or not, but to answer the questions *how* and *why*. *How* did this box get here and *why* did they put it here in the first place?"

"And of all the things I've unearthed in my twenty years in the field, I've never wanted to answer those questions more than now," Manuel said.

"Yes, but what if they were…" Adrien started, as if he'd not heard a single word his fellow archaeologists had just said.

"What if they were what?" Nate asked.

Adrien locked eyes with his friend. "What if they were right?"

Chapter 8

They hadn't spoken since the events of early morning. After being up most of the night and the stress of the mission—the failed mission—all they wanted to do was lay low for a while and get some sleep. One at a time they trickled into the eighteenth floor lounge for the mission debrief.

The lounge, in addition to hosting two cushy sofas, a gray, overstuffed chair, and a round mahogany cocktail table, offered large rays of sunshine through its oversized windows, one of which was cracked open slightly, leaking in the warm, sweet air of newborn spring.

Except for Addy, the entire team was now assembled. Rad and Remi sprawled out on one of the couches while Deston sat in front of the window on the arm of the easy chair, and Rene, who had called the meeting, looked in from the kitchen doorway.

Addy rushed in and made her way to the empty couch. As she settled in to her seat, the afternoon sun fell on her like a gentle spotlight. Its brilliant rays not only drew out the luster of her silken, dark brown hair, but also the simple curves of her face, and the shimmer of her olive skin and golden-brown eyes. And though her ponytail and casual clothing fought desperately to hide it, Addy's authentic beauty could not be subdued.

Neither could her fire.

"So what happened, Rad?" She launched the first salvo. "I thought the 'Rad-meister' had it all worked out?"

"Wait a minute." Rad sat up and glared toward Addy. "Are you blaming *me* for this?"

"Well this was *your* mission, *your* plan, *your* techno-wizardry," she barked.

Rad leaned in toward Addy and retaliated, "Hey I'm not perfect, Addy! Maybe if you would have…"

Before he could list her failures, however, Rene broke in. "Alright. Alright. That's enough," he said calmly in his baritone voice. Rene was one of those men who instantly commanded both love and respect. His graying black hair was combed back from his forehead, revealing kind brown eyes; his round face was buttressed by a thick, salt-and-pepper beard.

When the ruckus subsided, he continued. "We're all part of the same team here. It's nobody's fault; these things happen even with the best planned ops." Rene eased over and sat his five-foot-seven frame on the couch next to Addy.

After a long silence, Addy's countenance softened. "You're right. I'm sorry, Rad. It's not you I'm mad at—it's those jerks we're after. We almost had those guys."

Rad was not one to hold a grudge, especially with a beautiful woman. "Don't sweat it, Addy-girl," he said, falling back into the hefty cushion. "And yes, we were *this close* to sticking it right in their ear." He measured out "this close" with his fingers.

"But Dad, why did you shut me down?" Addy asked Rene. "I

told you I could get out of there on my own."

Rene started to answer, but Rad took over instead. "He did the right thing, Addy. Remember what I told you about those Assassins? The Patches just fix what you've done and kill your connection to the virtual datacenter; the Assassins, on the other hand, work backwards and find your physical location. It only takes a few seconds and they're in *your* system hacking *your* files."

Rene picked up the explanation. "He started tracking you as soon as he saw you. The only way to keep him from finding us was to shut the whole system down. Sorry, honey."

Deston had just finished a sip of hyper-espresso, or hyper-e, when he asked, "So what happened? How did they find us so fast?"

"Well, as you know, the plan was for Addy to load the Trojan so we could get in from the outside," Rad said, "which of course she did a couple of days ago. Then we'd hack the virtual datacenter from here and do our business—plant our bugs, read their database, and most importantly, replace the Globalcast file with our own. The Trojan sits idle until we activate it to gain entry into their system. The one we used last night was a new one I got from a guy in Delhi. He said there's no way the GIS network would recognize it for several minutes, maybe up to thirty.

"But apparently my guy was wrong, and when you swiped the medallion at the door"—he looked at Addy—"the Trojan sent up a red flag. It took the system a few minutes to launch the sweep, but they were alerted right away. We were actually doomed from the get-go. We just didn't realize it," Rad finished.

"So what's the fix, Rad?" asked Remi. "If we can't get to them, we're out of business."

Rad shook his head. "To be honest, I don't know. I'm thinking it'll have to be a combination of things, probably a zero-day Trojan and—you're going to love this—an inside access job."

Addy's face came alive with surprise. "You mean actually accessing the system from *physically inside* a GIS facility?"

Rad's head cycled up and down. "Yes, that's exactly what I mean. But I'm not sure exactly which facility yet or exactly how to do it. We might be able to do it through a remote facility, or we might have to penetrate GIS headquarters."

"Okay, Rad," Rene said. "Keep working on a way back in. Most importantly, find a way to access the Globalcast. Everything else is secondary. I'll give the Council an update tonight.

"And there's one other thing you all need to know." Rene leaned back on the couch, slowly unbuttoned his sheen, gray tunic, and breathed out a long sigh. "Seger's been captured."

The group erupted. "What?" "How?" "When?" Questions popped out like bees from a beehive.

"Security Services snatched him last night about ten," Rene explained. "Our sources say they took him straight to GSS headquarters in Munich."

"That's not good," said Addy. "Seger knows things…about our facilities and people and who knows what else. *Whatever* he knows, those GSS thugs will beat his brains in until they get it."

"Isn't that the third guy we've lost in the last few weeks?" asked Rad.

"Yes it is, I'm afraid," Rene answered. "But the others weren't as highly placed as Seger. Apparently we're getting more attention at the upper echelons of the G-CoN. The word is Addergoole is handling his interrogation personally."

"Oh no," Addy moaned. "He's a dead man…and so are we. If they get the right information from him—and they will—we're done for."

The three young men joined Addy in expressing their frustration.

"Ah, man," Rad complained; Deston just frowned and slid deeper into his puffy chair; Remi kicked his feet onto the table and said simply, "Not good." The melancholy reaction was unanimous, except for Rene.

"This isn't the first time we've faced setbacks," he offered warmly as a father comforting his children. "All of these men knew the risks, and they'll fight to protect our secrets. And what should we expect? This means we're getting somewhere; otherwise they wouldn't pay so much attention. Most importantly, for them and for us, is to remember that we're not in this fight alone—we've never been. While things seem to be getting darker, we must keep our faith."

They all nodded. Everybody, that is, but Addy.

"We've got to hit them, hit them hard, hit them now!" she ordered.

Her father looked at her and did what he had learned to do whenever she felt so strongly about something: sit quietly and listen.

"I know we've got to have faith, Dad, but we've also got to *act*. If I know the Council, they'll sit on this until it's too late. They'll let these guys—Seger and Jonathan and Dmitri—suffer for nothing. I just can't do that."

"I understand how you feel, Addy. But we've got to think this through," Rene implored. "We'll act...*at the right time*. I'll talk to the Council. They'll authorize another attack when it's wise, when we've got a solid plan. I know this seems all wrong to you, but the one above has a plan and we can't rush ahead of him."

"I can't wait anymore, Dad," she said with finality. "Ahead of him, behind him—I don't know. But what I do know is somebody's got to stop these guys." Before Rene could say anything more, she grabbed her things and rushed out the door.

A few minutes later, Addy popped out of the Resistance headquarters building, her casual attire now a dark blue pant suit and silver purse, and her dark hair now a bleach blond wig. With clarity of purpose, she stepped onto Rue de Salut, called a Personal Autonomous Vehicle, or PAV, and hopped inside.

In no time, she stood gazing upward at a towering blue-glass skyscraper parked at river's edge in the heart of the city. The building's wide base curved inward as it rose into the sky, and then curved outward again to a sleek, three-pointed peak 100 stories above.

Addy strode into the open lobby and toward the armed guards stationed at both sides of the main building entry. Wearing black battle uniforms and matching plasma rifles, the intimidating soldiers paced back and forth as they scanned the crowd for any sign of trouble.

Just before reaching the station, Addy eased her hand into her purse and held it there for the final steps up to the checkpoint. Her suspicious movement caught the eye of one of the guards, who slowly raised his rifle from his side and spoke into his comm-port.

Their eyes met, but Addy continued undeterred. When she was within only a few steps of the gate, he motioned to his counterpart, who moved in unison with him toward Addy.

As she pulled her hand from her purse, the first guard started to speak. But before a sound could escape his lips, she lifted her arm quickly from her side, flashed her identification medallion to the security reader, and continued quickly past them both.

"Welcome, Miss Devin," the first guard said as he repositioned his rifle.

Just above their heads, a holoscreen displayed Addy's picture and position: "Amia Devin—Network Support Analyst, Global Information Services."

Chapter 9

Surrounded by three armed GSS security escorts and two assistants, Director Damien Addergoole walked into the grand entrance hall of the Global Capitolium. At 2,600 feet in height, this pyramid-shaped skyscraper was the tallest and most expensive building in the world. Its metallic-gold exterior shot up from the center of the G-CoN One Planet campus, a collection of twenty-two buildings spread over 1,000 acres which housed the headquarters of most major government branches. The one exception was Global Security Services, which remained in Munich at Damien's insistence.

The G-CoN extended its power to all three major divisions of the planet: the Central Column, comprising what used to be Europe, the Middle East, and Africa; the Western Column, made up of North, South, and Central America (though all names including the word *America* did not exist in twenty-fourth century vocabulary); and the Eastern Column, consisting of Asia and Australia.

Each branch had major field offices in the two outer columns—Eastern and Western—in Beijing and Rio De Janeiro respectively, but all understood that real global power emanated from the Central Column and this building in particular. Not only did most Director-

48

level ministers of the Global Government call this building home, but also the Global Sovereign and his staff, who occupied the top three floors, and Vice Sovereign Rurik Pulgate, who took residence just below on floor 247.

After Rurik's assistant opened the double doors, Damien forged confidently into the Vice Sovereign's office, leaving Broderick and his remaining entourage behind.

Wide and open with gleaming, black floors, the space looked more like a large ballroom than an office. Opposite the door, the Vice Sovereign sat at his desk in front of a monstrous sheet of solid glass that was the back wall.

"Ah, Damien," he called as his visitor approached. The second most powerful man in the world stood, walked from behind his desk, and lifted his hand from beneath his long burgundy cape.

"Vice Sovereign," Damien replied, shaking Rurik's hand and bowing insubstantially. "How pleasant to see you this morning." He forced a narrow but unconvincing smile.

"Please sit down," said Rurik. Two black chairs were spaced equally in front of his desk. Damien pushed his official white cassock out of the way and settled into the chair to his right.

Rurik's smile continued. Walking to the nearby bar, he said, "I trust Collette is well."

"Yes, she is. It is so nice of you to ask. And Tasya?" Damien replied.

"Tasya and the children are well. Thank you," the skinny Russian informed him. "A drink?"

"Of course, Vice Sovereign. Of course."

With the refined moves of a lifelong politician, Rurik poured Damien a Vodka, eased it into his hands, and sat down.

49

"I have a problem, Damien," he started.

"And what is that, Vice Sovereign?"

"I cannot sleep."

Damien raised his glass for a sip. "Perhaps you should see a doctor," he guilefully extended the metaphor. "They have medicine for these things, you know."

"Yes, they do. Maybe you could be my medicine man today. You see, I have this pain in my side. I thought I had the right doctor for the job, but he can't seem to take care of it. And it's troubling me deeply."

The two men locked eyes in battle.

"Yes, I can see how that would trouble you, Vice Sovereign."

"This pain I have, it's getting worse every day, and it must be stopped. To the person who brings it to an end, I will be *very* grateful, Director...as will the Sovereign. However, to the one who lets it continue...let's just say, he will experience a little pain of his own."

"But be careful," Damien warned coolly, "the difference between *medicine* and *poison* is not always so easy to detect. You should learn to trust your doctor, and never, ever make him unhappy."

"Indeed," Rurik said with a sly grin. Then his demeanor soured as the pace of his voice increased. "Damien, I do not need to tell you the trouble these people could cause all of us, including you, if their plans succeed! If what they know gets out, chaos will ensue for the entire global government. Imagine the damage to the Global Sovereign!"

"I am well aware of the seriousness of the matter, Vice Sovereign!" Damien yelled.

Rurik leaned forward in his chair and raised his voice several more decibels. "Then do whatever it takes to crush these people before it is too late!"

"Do not tell me how to do my job, Rurik!" Damien screamed, nearly coming out of his seat.

The Vice Sovereign sat back in his chair and calmed himself. "Of course, Damien," he said eventually, in pretended humility. "It is not my place to do this. I am simply trying to communicate the gravity of our situation as the Sovereign himself has directed me." And then, as if he had not just about come to blows with the man sitting opposite him, he said, "I understand you have several prisoners. Have they provided anything of value?"

Damien straightened his tunic, eased a deep breath into his lungs, and calmly replied, "In fact they have. Last night I extracted information regarding the location of Resistance facilities in the Central Column. This information will allow us to mount a counterstrike, but only when I am satisfied we are ready."

"Very well," Rurik said. Then he stood and raised his hand toward the door. "Now that we understand each other, let me ask you something else," he said as they walked. "The Sovereign is interested in their intentions. What do you think their next move will be? Will they continue their cyber attacks, or will they try something more...aggressive?"

"These people do not have the courage to come out of their caves," protested Damien with disgust. He stopped and turned toward Rurik, all the while fixing in on his eyes. "Like many in our midst, they are cowards of the lowest order, the *defaveur* of all nature."

"Ah, disfavored, indeed," Rurik replied with an edgy smile.

As the two reached the door, Rurik's serious expression returned.

"Director, you have one week to finish this, or I may have to change doctors. Are we clear?"

Damien glanced at him and walked out of the room, not saying a word.

After the elevator doors closed, Damien commanded Broderick, "It is time for the lion to awaken, Mr. Fuller. Contact Othman and Helmut; I want a plan on my desk Monday morning. This time next week, I want all of them dead!"

Chapter 10

I thought I might find you up here," Rene said, walking up behind Addy. Poised against a round, silver rail, she stared out over the city, blissfully soaking in the bright, warm rays of the midday sun. The top of the building had been transformed into a living eco-garden with real trees, soil, and soft grass. A clear composite fence protected its occasional visitors from the 200 foot drop to the street below.

Addy looked back. "Yeah, I like it up here. It's so quiet."

Rene put his arm around her. "It is quiet up here. I should come more often."

"You could use more times of peace, Dad. We all could."

"Indeed," he replied. "I remember when they were building that thing," he said, pointing to one of the many hundred-plus story skyscrapers in a long row in front of them.

Addy tilted her head up and then down. It was the only building within sight with a courtyard around it. All the rest were packed so tightly it was difficult to get a single PAV between them. She spied the splotches of grass separating the lanes of paved walkways, and the faceless figures moving about like ants below.

"The Global Health building. Long time ago, huh?"

"Yes, I'm afraid so," he answered. "You know, before they built all these, we'd actually get some sun up here during the winter. Now we have to wait until spring before it swings high enough. And then it only cuts through for a few minutes." He glanced up into the sky and squinted.

"You were pretty upset yesterday when you left for work. Are you okay?" he asked, changing the subject.

Addy didn't answer right away. "Sometimes it gets to me. I mean, lately it's really getting to me."

"What's that, Addy?"

She kept looking straight ahead. "This war, Dad. I'm tired of it."

"I know, my dear. We're all tired of it."

"It's all I've ever known," she said with a heavyhearted grin. "Did you realize that? Since before I knew how to read, all I've ever known is the G-CoN and the Resistance and the battles…"—her voice trailed off—"…and the losses."

"And you've always fought so bravely," Rene encouraged her. "You were born for this. I've always told you that."

She turned to face him. "But I want more for my life than this, Dad. I know what we're doing is important, but there's so much I want for my life that is…slipping away."

"You want a family?" Rene asked mildly, but it wasn't really a question.

"I didn't use to think so. But I think about it more and more. I'm thirty-two now. I guess I'm running out of time."

"Oh, my dear," Rene sighed as he wrapped both arms around her, "I'm so sorry I dragged you into this! You deserve a life of your own, a life away from all this."

"It's not your fault, Dad. Besides, I chose to be a part of this, to fight these monsters, this evil. And a part of me wants to keep fighting because I know the truth about them and the things they do, to our people and our family. But there are just other things too."

"I know, Addy. I know," he consoled. "Your dreams will come true. I'm sure of it. Just give it a little more time. He knows of your desires, and he won't make you wait forever." Rene kept one arm around her as they walked along the edge of the garden.

"I want to believe that. I do." Then after a pause she said, "I miss Mom."

"So do I, my dear."

"It's only been two years, but it seems like so much longer. I know she'd understand what I'm going through." Addy caught herself and quickly added, "Not that you don't understand, Dad. It's just…"

He smiled to ease her concern. "I know. She's your mother, *and* she's a woman. She would understand better than me; she always understood *everything* better than me. I could use a little of that understanding myself right now."

"I know you could. It's a stressful time for everybody," she said. "That reminds me, have you talked to the Council about Seger?"

"Yes, we met briefly last night. We cataloged and prioritized what he knows. Now we're trying to figure out how to limit the damage he might cause if—or should I say *when*—he breaks."

"You think he will?"

Rene pinched his lips together and shook his head. "He's a tough guy, Addy. But nobody can last forever in there. We've got a few days, maybe a week at the outside, before they break him.

"But enough shop talk. When was the last time you and Gabrielle got together?"

Addy thought about it and answered, "It's been a while. Ever since she moved over to Alex's team, we don't see each other much."

"Will she be at the party Sunday night?"

"She usually is."

"Why don't you make it a point to spend some time with her then? You could use it. It might help take the edge off."

"Yeah, you're right. I'll do that." Addy started to pull away and then leaned back and kissed him on the cheek. "Thanks for talking, Dad," she said, now smiling. "It really helps."

"You're welcome, my dear."

As she headed for the elevator at the center of the roof, Rene realized how proud he was of the person she had become, how she meant more and more to him with each passing day, and how he longed for her to have the life of which she dreamed.

When her ears were safely out of range, he murmured to himself, "I just hope I'm right, my dear. I hope you don't have to wait forever."

Chapter 11

What was Omaha, Nebraska
Friday, April 1
523 DE
9:03 AM, Local/4:03 PM, Paris

Tell me you have more for me** this week than last, Adrien,"
Alejandro Vargas, the Assistant Director (AD) for Western
Column Projects, sneered through the holodisplay in the lab. "I'm
starting to think I didn't demote you far enough."

The weekly sight of Alejandro was a constant reminder to Adrien
of how far he had fallen. Though Alejandro was a few years older,
he and Adrien had joined the GSO at the same time, some sixteen years ago. For many years, Adrien was promoted faster up
the GSO ladder than his counterpart, a fact not overlooked by the
super-ambitious—and vengeful—Alejandro. Through the years,
he had looked for any way possible to sabotage Adrien's career and
propel his own.

After the tragic death of Adrien's wife, Alejandro got the chance
he had always wanted. Periods of deep depression, bouts with alcohol
abuse, and a growing apathy for work and life in general caused Adrien's
performance and standing to suffer greatly. His GSO supervisors,
known for their cut-throat style, and helped on by Alejandro's constant
complaints about Adrien, eventually promoted Alejandro to AD and
gave him license to deal with Adrien as he pleased. Seeing it as a fate

worse than death, he demoted Adrien back to the field and sent him to the farthest corner of the planet, the forgotten desert of the Western Column.

Adrien glanced to the floor and said, "Yes, Alejandro, we hope we have."

Alejandro leaned back in his chair, sighed, and meshed his fingers together in his lap. His perfect bald spot shimmered in the light of his Paris office. "Alright," he said, unconvinced, "let's hear it."

"We believe we've made an incredible find," Adrien started as he looked across the exam table to Nate. "And this is it." In perfect sync, he and Nate lifted the black box up on its side to give Alejandro a full view.

The AD leaned forward in his chair and squinted. "What is that?" he asked.

"Pictures are coming your way now, Assistant Director, along with the rest of our report," Nate said. "It's a primitive safe. And unlike the rest of the artifacts we've found, it shows no signs of structural decay or, really, decay of any kind."

On Alejandro's holoscreen, images of the box appeared from several angles, as well as a file entitled, "The Maker Find."

"A safe?" he asked, disbelieving. "How can there be a safe out there?"

"We asked the same question ourselves," echoed Adrien.

His curiosity sparked, the AD peppered them with questions: "Have you determined an age?" "Were you able to open it?" "What are the contents?"

Adrien took the first stab at answering. "Our teams are trying to verify a date as we speak; we should know something later today. And the contents—yeah, we opened it, and that's where it gets even more interesting."

"How do you mean?" Alejandro asked.

"The box contained three items," Nate said. "First, there were two large books—actual paper books—sealed in plastic bags." He lifted the books up, one in each hand. "Images of the cover and a few internal pages are in the file.

"They're an ancient deity myth about a being called *the Maker*. A synopsis is included in our report."

"But even more fascinating," continued Adrien, "is that the box contained a note. That's the third item, here." He held it up for Alejandro's inspection.

"A note?" the AD asked. "What does it say?"

"I'll just read it to you," Adrien said. "'March 31, 2182'—that's the actual date on the note— 'We're not sure anyone will ever find this, but we wanted to leave record of that which is most important to us. We do not have long now. May he spare us.' That's all.

"We digitized it and sent it over with everything else," Adrien finished.

As he processed Adrien's words, Alejandro rubbed the thin strip of black hair on the back of his head over and over. "How do you explain this?" he finally asked.

"We can't as of yet," replied Nate.

"Alejandro, does that date mean anything to you?" asked Adrien.

"Now, now. I thought the GSO golden boy knew everything," he answered with a sarcastic smirk on his face. He paused to make sure the rib didn't go unnoticed, and then said, "No, that date doesn't mean anything to me, especially in the context of that location.

"Nate, maybe you know more than your fearless leader. Why is it so well preserved when everything else you've found has been so damaged?"

Nate and Adrien traded looks before Nate answered. "It's buried deeper, about twenty feet lower than our deepest dig point and about thirty feet below ground level. That's the only thing we can think of. Whatever caused all the damage to everything else around here didn't penetrate deep enough to harm this particular artifact."

"Okay," Alejandro said with finality. "I'll read your report and, if it merits, report it to Dr. Advani. In the meantime, you'll keep me—."

Suddenly the lights surrounding the lab blinked red and an alarm sounded from overhead. "Fire Alert" flashed on the holodisplay over Alejandro's image. A loud but steady voice blared from every corner: "Fire Alert. Fire Alert. Evacuate the building immediately. Discharge imminent."

"Alejandro, we've got an alarm here," Adrien hurried to say. "We've got to evacuate."

They didn't wait for their boss to answer, but ran for the open exit door.

Once outside, they saw people rushing from every building: living quarters, stock rooms, social areas. Even the techs at the four sites left their shovels and headed for the emergency rendezvous point in a field at the southeast corner of the camp.

When the entire team was assembled, Adrien quickly took roll and then scanned the campus for fire or smoke. But none could be seen.

Fifteen minutes after the initial alarm, a man in a dark blue uniform made his way from the camp toward the assembled mass.

Adrien and Nate met him halfway back.

"What's the word, Max?" asked Adrien.

"Well," the squat, overweight maintenance man answered,

"looks like a false alarm, boss. The sensors that activate that type of alert sometimes get clogged with dust and go off when nothing's wrong."

"So they can discharge when there isn't even a fire?" Adrien asked.

"That's not good. That suppressant's poisonous," Nate quickly added.

"Yeah, it is. But the system has a built-in fail-safe," Max told them. "The circuitry for the alarm and the circuitry for the suppressant are two separate systems. So the alarm can go off, but that doesn't trigger the gas. The discharge system initiates its own, much more complex check before it discharges. It's pretty much impossible to fool.

"I guess the bottom line is that there was never any real danger," he concluded.

"So we can go back to work then?" asked Adrien.

"Yeah, you're good to go."

Turning to the crowd, Nate called out loudly, "Back to work everybody. False alarm."

As they walked with the pack back to camp, Nate asked Adrien, "So do we need to call Alejandro back?"

"Nah," he answered. "Knowing him, he's already home by now. And I don't think I can take any more of that guy today."

"I don't blame you. Say, you got a few minutes to talk?"

"Yeah, but I've only got a minute right now. I'm due at Site 1 at ten."

"That's okay. Go ahead. I've got to run too," Nate said. "But I'd like a chance to talk to you later if that's okay."

"Sure. Is everything alright?" asked Adrien.

"Yeah, yeah. Everything's fine. Just got a few things I'd like to talk with you about."

"How about eight at my place?"

"Eight sounds good. See you then."

Chapter 12

With eyes half open, Cassy meandered into the overcrowded living room and asked, "I guess you didn't even make it to bed, huh, Grandma?"

"Well," the silver haired woman replied, "I tried to lay down for a few minutes at about 11:30, but your mother's monitor went off. And seeing as how we all have to be up anyway, didn't make much sense to go back to bed." She slid a thin, white blanket up to her daughter's neck and checked the IV in her arm.

Cassy eased herself onto the nearby couch and pulled her robe closed over her pajamas.

"Has she been awake any?" she asked.

"No, I'm afraid not," Grandma replied without expression. "She doesn't do that too much these days." She stroked her patient's forehead with the back of her wrinkly fingers, smiled a tender mother's smile, and said, "She just sleeps. Now, don't you, Abbey."

"I'm sorry I wasn't able to leave school to go with you to that doctor yesterday. You know the rules. So how'd it go?"

Her grandmother walked around the secondhand, rusted hospital bed and sat in the only armchair in the room. "It was awful," she

62

sighed. "I never should have taken her there."

"What happened?" asked Cassy.

"Well, it's just…. It wasn't a good place. It was all dirty, and the doctor—if he could even be called that—didn't seem to know very much. In all fairness, the way they have to go underground and all. It's just no wonder." She laid her hands one over the other in her lap and exhaled deeply. "And I was scared to death the whole time. If somebody finds out…. But there really was no other choice."

"Did he tell you anything new? I mean, how long does Mom have?"

"Not really. He didn't say anything different than the government doctor told us six months ago. If they don't let her into a GHO hospital soon, it could be only a few weeks."

Cassy scowled. "That's just so wrong!"

"I know, dear," Grandma acknowledged. "I've petitioned the government every way I know how. They've made their decision and we just have to learn to live with it."

The two of them sat closed-mouthed until Grandma asked, anxiously, "So where's your brother?"

The young woman shrugged. "I know he worked until one. Sometimes he hangs out with Mark. Sometimes, who knows? He's getting more and more unpredictable, and I'm really getting worried."

"So am I," said Grandma. "Is he drinking again?"

"I think so. He never comes home until dawn. The other night I heard him fumbling with the medallion; it took him three or four times to get it right. There's only one explanation for that."

"He's turning out like his father," complained Grandma as she glanced at the clock on the wall. "He can't be late again. They're watching him, you know. They're watching all of us. If he's not careful, he'll end up like Mr. Harris."

"I know. He's supposed to come home directly from work. He only gets an exception to curfew because he's working. I'm surprised they haven't grabbed him yet," offered Cassy, shaking her head.

"Speaking of Mr. Harris," she went on, "did they ever find out what happened to him?"

Grandma stood when Abbey's monitor buzzed. She stepped over and pushed a blinking red button and started to explain. "They're saying the GSS got him. According to Kate, a good friend of Mildred's, he missed a bunch of broadcasts and then tried to organize. Mildred hasn't seen him since he went out to walk their dog three weeks ago. She found Lucy the next morning sleeping on the front porch, her leash still attached. That poor woman's a real wreck now. But the government's still not saying anything."

Cassy's face filled with apprehension while she processed Grandma's words. "It's scary, what's going on now."

"Very," Grandma agreed.

"And speaking of scary things," Cassy said, "did I tell you about Professor Mann, my government teacher at the university?"

Grandma rubbed a cold, wet cloth over Abbey's forehead and replied, "I don't think so."

"Okay. I couldn't remember if I told you or not. I just found out myself yesterday."

"Found out what?"

"He's missing too."

"Oh, my! What happened?"

"Mr. Mann teaches what the government tells him to teach," Cassy started. "They all do; they don't have a choice. But lately

I've seen him in the halls with some men who usually aren't around school. I don't know why, but it just looked suspicious.

"Then Kelly said she heard he asked a few students—Bobby, Alex, Glenda, basically his best students—to meet him after class to talk about some kind of new group he wanted to start. It was supposed to be all hush-hush, but you know how that is. Anyway, we don't know what the group was about, but it was scheduled to meet at five on Tuesday. Mr. Mann didn't show up. Ever since then we've had subs for his class."

Grandma took in a quick breath. "You don't think…?"

"I don't know, Grandma. Next thing you know they'll be ringing our doorbell in the middle of the night and taking *us* away."

"You know that did happen a few years ago," Grandma said. "When I lived over off Milburn, before the Consolidation and they moved me in here with you all, Sarah Griffin's husband got involved with some underground group. She said one night the doorbell rang in the middle of the night, and when Charles answered, three men in black uniforms pulled him out and took him away. He's been gone ever since."

Just as she finished the doorbell rang.

Frightened, they looked to the door and then back to each other.

"You said Jack has the medallion, right?"

"Yeah," Cassy whispered.

"Then who is that at the door?"

Chapter 13

Lismore, Australia
Central Column, Global Community of Nations
Saturday, April 2
523 DE
1:42 AM, Local/4:42 PM, Paris (Friday)

Cassy stood up from the couch and crept toward the front door. Before she opened it, she glanced at Grandma and back again. Holding her breath, she pushed the button.

"Jack! I thought you had the medallion," his younger sister objected. "You scared us to death!"

"Sorry, Sis," he offered, walking past her. "Lost it." Over his white nursing uniform, Jack donned a matching white jacket with red stripe. He smelled of alcohol but wasn't drunk.

"I'm glad you made it," his grandmother said, breathing out her anxiety. "It's not good to give them a reason to come after you, Jack. You know they're watching, especially us."

Jack threw himself on the couch beside Cassy and retorted, "I don't care if they come after me or not."

"*Jack...*" Grandma protested.

"So how's Mom tonight?" he asked, ignoring her.

"She's about the same," Cassy answered.

"And that doc?"

Cassy looked across the room to Grandma who had just returned to her chair.

66

"Nothing new. They can't do anything for her," Cassy said, her voice cracking.

Jack almost exploded. "I'm sick of this!" he yelled as he shot up from the couch. "This is unbelievable! What right do they have to say she isn't worth saving? Huh?" His voice dripped with sarcasm as he mocked, "'I'm sorry, Mrs. Livingston, at fifty-one you just don't provide the return on investment the Global Health Organization requires. If only you were forty, maybe we would save your life!'

"What a joke! Then after making us wait six months just to get in and bow before their presence, they cut us loose and force us to these back alley loons just to get a shot from some rusty needle!" With that he reached down and threw his hands across the top of the chest opposite his mother's bed, just beside the living room window. Bottles of white pills, holopads with family pictures, and an old stained glass lamp crashed to the floor right in front of Cassy.

"Jack! Jack! What's wrong with you?!" Cassy screamed, glaring up at him. But she could tell by the look on his face he already regretted his rash, angry act.

It only took a minute for him to calm down and apologize. "I'm sorry, Sis," he spoke softly as he knelt down to help pick up the mess. "I just don't think I can take any more."

"I know you're upset about Mom, Jack. We all are. But this isn't helping. You're normally not like this. And the drinking—you hate that. That's Dad, Jack, not you. Are you sure there's not something else going on?"

He stood up, forced his hands through his thick hair, and paced around in front of them.

"It's everything, you know. This thing with Mom. This isn't coincidence. They target us; they've always targeted us. And these stupid Globalcasts. We're controlled like animals. The people who disappear. I mean, did

Grandma tell you about Mr. Harris?"

"Yeah, I just heard."

"There are stories like that everywhere. People are afraid. I can't even imagine what's going on that we *don't* know about."

From the corner chair, Grandma asked confidently, "What's happened, Jack? Something at work?"

Ever since Jack was a little boy, Grandma always had the ability to read him. No matter how hard he tried to hide what was going on inside, she saw right through his disguise, right into his heart. Over the years he learned it was futile to try to hide anything from her, and tonight was no exception. So he didn't even try.

"For the last six months we've had a lot of suicides come in," he said evenly. "I mean *a lot*. A hundred and sixteen in March alone. Overdoses. Jumpers. Plasma pistols. It's like everybody just wants to die.

"So we report these things in our GHO database, hoping the higher-ups will address the issue in some way. But we don't hear a thing. We keep logging the reports; they keep ignoring them. No memo. No requests for more information. Nothing.

"So I'm at work last week, right. I go to enter another suicide into the system and I notice that all the reports we've already logged are gone. So I check the Health Information Database to see if the numbers have been reclassified or something. No dice.

"Then I go ask my supervisor about it. You know what he tells me? *I must be mistaken.* There were no suicides last month in our service area. And then he closes his door and says, 'And if you know what's good for you, Jack, you won't report any more.'

"It's wrong, what they're doing! And then we see these holosigns along the Superway and these Globalcasts where they proclaim their goodness and how much they're helping us, giving us our homes and free medical, and how they're 'perfecting society.' Look at this place—it's a hole in the wall! And look at her." Jack pointed to his mother. "And I wonder what Mr. Harris thinks about their perfect little society?"

As Jack turned and stared out the living room window, he said in an eerily calm voice, "Somebody just needs to expose these people for what they are."

Grandma and Cassy sat quietly and thought about what Jack had just said. In a way, they were glad he had said it—that somebody had said it—and they were proud of him, for his courage to utter what few dared even think, much less say. But at the same time, they were afraid for him, afraid because the few who braved to speak out did not speak out for long.

"Jack," Grandma finally said, "they will be exposed in time. But for now, we've just got to stay quiet and survive."

Jack turned and stared hard into her eyes. "I hope you're right, Grandma."

Just then the holodisplay lit up and a high-def graphic of a rotating earth appeared in the center. From left to right, three phrases spread across the bottom: "One People," "One Planet," "One Community."

A feminine voice spoke through the display, "Welcome to your G-CoN Globalcast," after which a small box with the words "Identifying Participants" appeared on the bottom, left-hand side of the screen. A sensor built in to the government-mandated system activated and scanned the room.

In a few seconds, the sweep ended and the feminine voice returned. "Thank you for joining the Globalcast Sadie, Jack, Cassandra, and Abigail."

Shaking his head, Jack threw himself down on the couch. "I really hope you're right, Grandma," he said under his breath. "I really do."

Chapter 14

D id you see the look on his face when we told him what we'd found?" Nate asked, laughing out loud.

"Yeah, the words sounded strange coming out of my mouth," Adrien replied from his tech station chair, hot synthetic in hand. "I can only imagine how they sounded to him."

"I'd love to be a fly on the wall in that place tomorrow morning. I'll bet they'll be racking their brains to solve this little mystery."

"I'm sure," agreed Adrien. "So what did the guys find this afternoon?"

Nate took a long swig from his silver water bottle. "Well, according to Manuel's research, the technology of that safe is from between two and three hundred years ago. And Pierre said the carbon dating of the paper gave a range of one to five hundred years. But you know how that stuff is.

"So I guess the bottom line is we're definitely in the ballpark. There's no evidence the note isn't authentic to the time period indicated."

"But how did it get here?" asked Adrien. "I spent some time on the database this afternoon, and it's just what we thought. None of the indigenous people groups of this area have ever had that kind of technology. The primitive Indian tribes lived here pretty much technology-free for hundreds of years. I checked several G-CoN databases, and they all say the same thing. But database or not, that box is real. Something just doesn't add up."

"Yeah, it's not making a lot of sense, is it?" Nate said.

"No, it isn't," Adrien agreed. "And you know this isn't the first strange thing that's happened on this dig."

"What do you mean?"

"Well, back when we decided to study the upper Western Column peoples, the Indians, I spent some time researching possible dig sites in the database. I looked for known settlements based on historical records, places where we might find the best artifacts. I found a few in this area and scheduled a scouting trip to finalize the site.

"But when I came out here, I didn't find any evidence of settlements in the areas mentioned in the records; even some of the natural landmarks referenced were nowhere to be found. It was like the places in the database didn't even exist."

"So what did you do?"

Adrien walked into the kitchen for a refill. "Since I was here, I spent some time looking around. Maybe the database was just off? I thought. Then I found this site, and here we are."

As he got up and walked to the kitchen entrance, Nate asked, "So if there was nothing down there but the decayed remains of building materials and artifacts, why did you ever recommend this site?"

"Two reasons. One, the mounds at Site 1 and 4 indicated that something was buried under them at one point. And two, the initial scans showed some partial pieces buried below. I mean, it wasn't exactly the tomb of King Tut or anything, but when you combine

the mounds, the settlement references in the database, and the preliminary scans I took, it seemed like a good bet. We've pitched a
shovel on less."

Nate thought for a second and said, "Makes sense. But if the
databases were so off, why didn't you say something then?"

Adrien shrugged. "At the time it didn't seem like that big a deal.
It's a big database—you can't expect everything to be perfect."

"But now it seems pretty strange, doesn't it?"

Returning the tall synthetic replicator to its stand, Adrien replied,
"Yes, it does."

"Adrien, earlier today you said something, something I wanted
to ask you about."

"Yeah, what's that?"

"We were talking about the deity myths in those books, and you
said you thought they might be right. You don't really believe that,
do you?"

Adrien stepped over to the kitchen window and looked up toward
the ravine. In the bright moonlight, the outline of the hill and a
faint trace of the path from the camp were visible. Somewhere down
below, the dark hand stirred.

He spoke slowly. "I don't know. Maybe."

"What do you mean 'maybe'?" Nate asked.

"I mean, I don't know enough to say for sure if they're right or
not. I'd need to study their writings more. But I'm not so sure we're
right either, the way we view the world." He kept staring out the
window.

"What's wrong with the way we view the world?" Nate asked,
unable to hide his agitation.

"Have you ever asked yourself what's the meaning of all this?"

Adrien turned to Nate and asked, spreading his arms wide.

"All of what?"

"Life, Nate. Our existence. Why are we here? What's the point of it all?" Adrien walked past Nate, back into the sitting room. "So we just work and suffer and then grow old and die? And some of us don't even grow old!

"Think about it. The work we do, studying the past. At the end of the day, what are we really studying?"

Nate looked confused. "I don't know. History, I guess."

"*Death*, Nate, that's what we study. We study people *who have died*, some through famine and some through war, some through floods and some through disease. But they all die! In fact that's all this life is, Nate—it's just *death*." Adrien's voice cracked and his eyes glossed over with warm tears.

"So what's the point, Nate?" he asked again, this time in barely a whisper.

Nate answered loudly, "There is no point, Adrien! *That's* the point! I know you want an answer; I know you want someone to tell you why Sophie died, or your father. You want it to be alright; you want there to be some fairy tale ending. But that's just not the way it works! That's just the hard, cold scientific truth."

Adrien turned and pointed at Nate. "Is that really good enough for you? So she was nothing more than random chemical reactions? Her smile, her laugh, the feeling in my chest when she was near me, the touch of her lips—all just natural, material responses to physical laws, huh?

"And my father? His pride in me, his embrace—not real, just simulated emotions from some biological process?

"And think of the places we've been and the things we've seen, the beauty of this world, even in the most remote places. Do you remember the mountains in New Zealand, on the South Island? Remember the fields of Lupins in the valleys there? The colors, Nate—they would take your breath away. Was all of that just chance? There's really nothing more to it than that?"

After a few seconds, Nate collected himself and said deliberately, "Adrien, I don't make the rules. If I could change it, I would. But we've both been taught the truth about these things. The science is solid. You can't let your emotions overcome your brain."

"The science is *solid?*" Adrien asked as if Nate had just landed from another planet. "What science is that, Nate? The science about the dinosaurs? How many times have we changed our story about them? Or maybe the science about the Maya? Or the science about the fossil record? Or the science about our origins? Remember the Big Bang? Whatever happened to that?

"We change our story all the time, Nate! Open your eyes. We're like drunken children walking down a mountain in the dark. We can't decide what happened 100 years ago, much less a billion."

His passions reignited, Nate yelled back, "Come on, Adrien! You can't be serious!"

Adrien ignored him. "Yes, we've been taught alright. Indoctrinated, more like it."

"I can't believe you! You've completely lost it," Nate said, throwing up his arms.

"And you know what, Nate. They never gave us a chance. They only taught us one side of the story. If they were so 'open-minded,' why didn't they lay it on the line and let us decide for ourselves?"

For what seemed like a month, neither of them said a word. At last Adrien spoke in a conciliatory tone, "Look, Nate, I'm sorry I yelled. I know you're just trying to help, but I just can't keep my eyes closed any longer. I've got to check it out."

"Okay, Adrien," Nate sighed. "I guess there's no convincing you otherwise. Just do me one favor—don't check your brain at the door. Please."

"You know I can't do that, Nate. I'm a scientist. I'll follow the facts. You can count on it."

"That's all I can ask. Well, I've got to look over the Site 2 results before I turn in. So I guess I'll run." With that, Nate turned and headed for the door.

"No problem, buddy. I understand," answered Adrien. "I'll see you tomorrow."

When Nate was gone, Adrien returned to his chair, sat quietly, and let the heated conversation tumble around in his head for a while.

Eventually Journey moped in from the bedroom and jumped into in his lap. As he rubbed her tummy, an image of the moonlit ravine flashed in his mind. Once again he heard the canyon calling, and like many nights before, he could not resist its wordless invitation.

Though he knew the dark hand would certainly meet him there, at almost midnight, he pressed for the door.

Chapter 15

Vallée Blanché
Chamonix France
Wednesday, January 1
521 DE
7:04 AM, Local/7:04 AM, Paris

Sophie walked to the high-top table where Adrien was sitting and put her hand on his shoulder. "Good morning, honey," she said and kissed him on the forehead.

"Good morning to you," he replied, smiling. "I ordered you some juice."

She patted his hand. "Thanks! Did you order breakfast yet? I'm starved!" Sophie laid her red beanie on the table and grabbed a menu. "So when is John supposed to meet us?"

"He said seven," Adrien answered. "And it's barely that. He'll be here any minute, I'm sure."

Adrien looked past Sophie and surveyed his surroundings. This resort, like many in the valley, had the feel of a rustic log cabin with its wood beam walls, stuffed and mounted wild animals, and smattering of ski paraphernalia placed here and there. Through the windows, the jagged peaks and snowy valleys of the Alps completed the perfect postcard image now before him.

"So are you ready for the big day?" he asked.

Sophie looked up from her menu and tried to force some cheer onto her face. It didn't work. "I think so, Adrien. But I've never

76

gone off-pisté before. Are you sure it's safe?"

"Honey, John has done this a million times," he reassured her. "He's a professional. And I'm bored with the typical ski runs, anyhow. You know that."

"Yeah, I know. And I realize you've wanted to do this for a long time."

"I have, but I don't want to do it alone," he begged. "You're still coming with me, right?" For some reason her crystal blue eyes stood out more than usual that morning. Maybe it was the white sweater she wore or just the bright morning sun that brought them into such clear focus. He reached his hand toward her face and pushed a single blond strand from her eyes.

"You're so beautiful," he said in a whisper.

"Thank you," she replied, leaning over to gently kiss his lips.

At that moment the world disappeared for the smitten archaeologist, as it always did when his new bride drew near.

"Am I interrupting something?" John called from behind them both.

Without taking his eyes off Sophie, Adrien answered, "Not yet. But it's nice of you to join us. Is this how you treat all your best clients?"

John lifted himself into the tall chair. "Well, in the first place, you guys are *friends*, not *clients*. And in the second place…I've got some bad news."

"Don't tell me…" Adrien started.

"Yes, I'm afraid so. I just got off the phone with Quinton's assistant. Apparently, he's decided to stop by Chamonix for a little ride down Vallée Blanché with a bunch of his rich buddies. They land in about an hour, and they called me first."

"And one rich guy's worth two good friends any day, huh?" Adrien asked. "So where does that leave us?"

"They're only in for the day, so I can definitely take you out tomorrow." John looked back and forth between Adrien and Sophie.

"That's okay, John," Sophie consoled. "We can wait."

"Actually we can't," Adrien cut in quickly. "Remember, that storm is supposed to blow in tomorrow. Near blizzard. Nobody will go anywhere tomorrow. And we leave the next day."

"Look, Adrien," said John. "I know you want a guide and all, but the reality is you really don't need one. I mean, you guys are great skiers and it's not like that glacier's never been skied before."

"You're saying go up there alone?" inquired Sophie.

"Yeah, it's no big deal. Get on the transport with everybody else and take your turn. Piece of cake."

"Oh, no," Sophie complained. "There's no way I'm going up there without a guide."

"Honey, he's right," Adrien said. "We can do this. You're one of the best skiers I know, and we've done steep grades before."

"Yeah, but these are *off-piste*, Adrien. No markers. No ski patrol. If you fall, nobody's there to save you. You just lay there and die."

Adrien let out a slow, frustrated breath. His voice lowered. "Okay, if it bothers you that much, I can wait. But just remember, it might be years before we get back here again."

Sophie glanced at John, who was nodding his head, and then back to Adrien. It only took a minute for her scowl to fade. "Okay," she said, now grinning. "But only because I love you."

"Thank you," Adrien said, smiling widely. "You won't regret it. I promise."

With a mischievous look, Sophie warned, "But I'm still going to beat you down!"

"Think so, huh?"

"Alright, before you love birds start taking bets, let me give you a few pointers." John looked down at his watch. "I've got to run in just a minute."

"Shoot," Adrien said.

"First, keep a lookout for upslope fog. As you know, it forms when the wind blows up the slope. It's higher than typical fog and is usually pretty dense. It's not uncommon on this face and there's a chance of it today. If you see it, turn away if you can. Dangerous stuff.

"Then, that glacier has some nasty crevasses in it. Those holes can go down hundreds of feet. Watch out for cracks ahead and dark blue lines, or it could be the last time you ever put on those ugly boots." He pointed to Adrien's boots.

Sophie laughed.

"And whatever you do, stay on the main pass coming down the mountain. About half way down, there's a fork in the slope. Stay left. It's the larger of the runs anyway. To the right is what the skiers call *Chemin Noir*, the Black Path. It's a blast, but it's also very dangerous. You guys would probably do fine on it, but I wouldn't recommend it on your first trip."

"You don't have to worry about that," Sophie promised John as she looked at Adrien. "Does he, honey?"

"No, we'll play it safe today," Adrien promised. "Now let's eat. The transport leaves in half an hour."

Chapter 16

Vallée Blanché
Chamonix France
Wednesday, January 1
521 DE
9:25 AM, Local/9:25 AM, Paris

The transport landed at 12,700 feet above sea level. Thousands of feet below, the tranquil village was barely visible through a thin layer of clouds. At their altitude, however, the sun shone brightly against the gray-blue mountain peaks, which nosed through thick layers of snow and ice like spikes.

Adrien and Sophie stepped out of the transport door and walked slowly down the thin ridge to the launch site, a flat opening where skiers gathered before tackling the glacier. A thick cable attached to the ridge served to steady them until they reached more level ground a few hundred feet away.

"Can you hear me?" he asked through his comm-port.

Sophie, who at the moment was staring down the thirty-degree slope below, looked over to Adrien and said, "Yeah, I hear you fine. How about you? Hear me?"

"Crystal," he answered. "So, are we ready?"

"I don't know, Adrien. I'm really scared…" she started.

"Scared of what?"

"*Scared you're gonna lose!*" With that she pulled down the tinted visor on her helmet, and took off.

"Is that right?" Adrien cracked, propelling himself forward on his ski poles. "I wouldn't count on it!"

In a matter of seconds they reached sixty miles per hour, cutting and turning to slow their pace and buy time to scan ahead. The first thousand feet were wide open, but then the space narrowed and banked hard to the right, then left. Ice walls and rocks formed the tight borders of the snake-like course down the mountain.

"So how does it feel back there?" Sophie teased.

"Not too bad, actually. You can have the lead. I'll just hang back and enjoy the ride for a while." Just then the pass opened and Adrien slipped by on her right.

"You devil!" she yelled. "Don't get too comfortable up there."

As their decent continued—10,000 feet, 8,000 feet, 6,000 feet— they traded lead a few more times.

Not long after the 6,000 foot mark, Sophie spoke up, "Adrien, is that fog coming up the face? It doesn't look like cloud cover."

Adrien looked down the mountain. "Yeah, it might be, but don't worry about it. It's not that thick, and it doesn't look like we're headed that way anyway."

"Okay, but you know what John said."

"Yeah, I know. Just keep going. The great Sophie Bach isn't looking for an excuse, now, is she?"

Then the fork appeared up ahead, Chamin Noir. Adrien immediately took off and started working right.

"Adrien, what are you doing? That looks like that fork John told us about," Sophie warned, panic in her voice.

"Oh, come on, honey! We're doing great, and John said we'd be fine," Adrien replied, still pressing right.

"No, Adrien. I don't want to. It's too dangerous! You promised."

But Adrien didn't listen, and in a split second, there was no turning back. They were now on the Black Path.

When catastrophe did not instantly overtake them, Sophie's fear slowly faded and her edge returned. "Okay, Mr. Big Shot. You asked for it!" Making her move, she whisked by Adrien on the outside just before a tight curve to the left.

As soon as she made the corner, she saw it—a thick cloud of fog swallowing the entire path ahead.

"Oh, no! Adrien!" Sophie called. "We'll never make it!"

"Don't panic, Sophie," Adrien said calmly. "Try to slow down and let's talk our way through this. I'll back off you just a bit so we don't run in to each other."

"But I won't be able to see, Adrien!"

"Yes, you will. It just looks that way from here. When you get inside, you'll be able to see fine. Stay focused. I'm right here. I won't let anything happen to you."

A moment later, the thick, cottony mass absorbed them both like tiny raindrops in the sea.

"You okay, Sophie?" Adrien asked.

"Fine for now," she said, cutting a path in the snow left and right. "I can see light up ahead. I think we're going to make it."

"I see it too," said Adrien, relieved. "Just stay focused. We'll be clear in a second."

Then Sophie screamed.

"What? What is it, Sophie?!" he asked as a dark blue line appeared up ahead, slicing across the entire width of the slope. He worked to slow himself and yelled, "Sophie! Sophie!"

"Adrien!" she answered, horror in her voice. "Help me! Help me! I can't hold on!" But this time the sound didn't come from his comm-port; it was out in front of him, somewhere down low.

In energized panic, he threw off his helmet, disconnected his boots, and ran toward the wide-open hole in the ice. As he came closer, a gaping ravine some thirty feet wide and just as long materialized through the fog. He threw himself on the snow and slid to the edge, arms outstretched. There, just a few feet below, Sophie clutched, with just one hand, a short plank of ice poking out from the wall. Her free hand and both feet waved wildly in the open air, and her helmet was gone.

He stretched down and struggled to reach her. Sliding closer and closer to the edge, she finally came into range. "Reach up with your hand and grab mine," he said as calmly as he could.

"I don't think I can do it, Adrien," she grunted. "I'm slipping!"

"No, honey, you *can*! Just hold on tight and reach up to me. I'll pull you up."

Her hand slipped a fraction of an inch, causing ice chips to break off and fall beside her into the crevasse. She screamed and started to cry. "I don't want to die, Adrien! I don't want to leave you!"

Tears filling his eyes, he said, "You're not going to die, sweetie. You're not going to leave me. Just stay focused and give me your hand."

"Okay," she finally agreed.

Adrien stretched as far as he could while Sophie threw her free hand upward. When she did, her other hand slipped off the ice, provoking another piercing scream. Just in time, Adrien clasped her wrist and squeezed tight, but his grip was weak.

"I've got you, baby," he lied.

Her trust completely in him, she broke into a narrow smile. But immediately her gloved hand started to slip and terror replaced the grin on her face.

Then peace.

"I love you, Adrien. I always have," she told her husband one last time.

"I love you too, Sophie. I love you so much…"

Drops of sweat fell slowly from Adrien's face. He heard himself breathe—in and out…in and out—and felt his neck pulse as blood coursed through his veins. A breeze came from the south, splashing lightly against his face and side. His fingers tingled as her hand slipped from his. Her eyes widened. Her arms and legs waved in the air. A few small shards of ice tumbled off the ledge.

And then she disappeared into the darkness.

"Nooooo!" he howled. But it was no use. Sophie was gone.

His body was completely rigid with fear when his eyes opened wide in the darkness. He tried to move, but the adrenaline had paralyzed him. All he could do was sweat, jerk his eyes from side to side, and breathe like a sprinter.

Within a few seconds he could move again; first his head, left and right, and then his arms and body. He threw his blanket to the floor and swung himself upright to the side of the bed. To be sure the dream was really over, he smacked both sides of his face with his damp palms and scraped his fingers across his scalp.

He had relived it again, and, like the countless times before, it was as real as it was 822 days ago.

Finally, he stumbled into the sitting room and turned on the light. When his senses finally revived, his mind ran immediately to the black box, and a wild idea popped into his head.

It only took him a few seconds to throw on his boots and coat and walk to the lab in the cold. As he expected, the books were lying in the same place he had left them the day before, only the dirt and debris had been cleared away.

In hopes that the old writings would give him some much needed comfort, he scooped them up, trekked back to his quarters, and read until dawn.

Chapter 17

Paris, France
Friday, April 1
523 DE
10:14 PM

Addy held her tray and perused the nearly deserted breakroom landscape. She had all but given up hope when she spotted him sitting alone in the back corner. Innocently, she made her way over.

"Do you mind if I join you? There isn't much room in here tonight," she asked.

He looked around at the rows of empty seats and up to Addy. "Sure," he answered in a weak, squeaky voice, and then his eyes dashed back to a thin holopad lying beside his tray.

Addy slipped off her suit jacket and dropped it on the back of the cafeteria-style chair. One of three large breakrooms in the GIS main headquarters building, this was the only one open during the nightshift.

After Addy sat down, she asked cheerily, "So, Walter, is it?" The name on his ID medallion read Walter Waite.

"Yes," he answered in the same chafing voice.

As he peeked up, she got her first good look at him. In his late-thirties, Walter combed his short, black hair flatly to the left and buttoned his white shirt to the very top. His small brown eyes were set in a thin face, which, in turn, was wrapped in a wiry, unkempt beard. In spite of all this, with a little work he might actually be a handsome guy, she thought.

"I think we've been in a few meetings together," Addy said, pushing aside her fake blond hair. "You're the one who always has those great holodisplay charts. You really make all those numbers easy to understand."

Walter grinned and turned a thin shade of blush. "Thank you," he said. "I didn't know anyone noticed."

"Well, I did," Addy said, smiling. She held out her hand. "Hi, I'm Amia, Amia Devin."

Walter looked up and tried to smile back, but what came out was more like a distorted, uncomfortable scowl.

"Hello," he said, feebly shaking her hand. "I'm Walter."

"You're in Assimilation, right?"

"Yes, I am. And, you're in…Support Services, right?" he countered, his face relaxing.

She sighed loudly. "Yeah, unfortunately."

"Oh…is something wrong?"

"Well, I shouldn't really be talking about it. We just met and all. Besides, it'll just bore you anyway."

"No, no," Walter said. "I don't mind. Really."

"Well, okay. Thanks." Addy looked down the long, empty table and back to Walter. "You know, I really like my job," she started in a low voice. "But some of the things that go on around here are starting to get to me. I mean, the things that come across my desk sometimes, I'm not so sure about anymore."

Walter mimicked Addy's suspicious look down the table and whispered, "Oh? What kinds of things have you seen?"

"Have you ever actually looked at what goes out on those Globalcasts, Walter? I mean, some of that stuff just isn't true. I hear after they get it from the departments, they change it if it doesn't say what they want it to. That really bothers me." Addy took a bite of her dinner. "Have you seen anything like that?"

"Well, maybe," he mumbled.

"Oh, yeah? What did you see?"

Walter looked down the table again before answering. "I'm not sure, but one day I did see my supervisor do something strange."

"Is that right? What happened?"

"Well, he—that is, Mr. Tosh—had the news report up for the week from the Eastern Column. I walked in his office and stood there for a moment waiting for him to turn around; I didn't want to interrupt him, you know, and his door was already open. Well, while I was waiting, I saw him delete a part of the report and change some words in another part. When he turned around, I acted like I wasn't looking. He got very mad at me and screamed," Walter admitted, full of fear. "I thought he was going to kill me."

Addy reached across the table and touched his hand. "That was very brave of you, Walter," she consoled. "Most people don't have that kind of courage."

"Well, I don't know. I was really scared."

"Somebody ought to do something about this. Don't you think?"

"Do something? Like what?"

"I don't know, but the people have a right to know the truth. Don't you want to know the truth, Walter?"

"Well, yes," he replied, nervously. Then he started to pick up his tray. "I'm sorry, but I've got to go now. My break is over. I hope things get better for you."

"Thanks, Walter. I'm sure they will. Have a great night," she said, trying to sound upbeat. "Maybe we'll see each other again soon."

"Okay. See you later."

After dinner, Addy returned to her department on the twentieth floor. When the door opened, she noticed a group of coworkers standing in front of the office informational display, an office bulletin board announcing everything from department meetings to work schedules to GIS directives. In the center of the display was a document titled, "GIS Globalcast Protocol Changes."

Addy slipped into the crowd and read the directive:

From:	Director Amisi Dakarai
To:	Globalcast Implementation Team, Assimilation Group, Network Support Services
Subject:	Confidential Memorandum— Change in Globalcast Data Storage and Transfer Protocols

Due to recent security threats to the Globalcast database, weekly update files will no longer be transferred to the SDC via the global network. As of 1 April 23 they will be delivered via GSS courier directly to the Assimilation team for input.

Department leaders will communicate with individual teams forthwith to ensure compliance with the new directive.

As Addy finished reading, she heard a co-worker say, "That's fine with me. Less work for us."

Yes, Addy thought. Less work for us, but now we have no choice. It looks like Rad was right. This may have to be an inside job after all.

"This is not good," she said to herself. "Not good at all."

Chapter 18

After pouring a cup of strong, black synthetic, Adrien slipped into his thin sitting room chair, perched his feet on its small matching ottoman, and opened *The Writings of the Maker* to the table of contents. One by one, he worked through its sections and read or thoroughly scanned each of its fifty detailed chapters. As he went along, he verbally dictated notes to his tech station on the nearby desk.

What he learned over the next few hours both captivated him and severely challenged his assumptions about the world around him. And even life itself.

He was fascinated to read more about creation *ex nihilo*—how the Maker created the world from nothing by simply speaking it into existence. If true, this meant that each part of this fantastically vast and complex universe had a specific purpose from the very beginning.

One of the examples given in *The Writings* was the heavenly bodies: stars, star clusters, galaxies, nebulae. Whereas modern cosmology taught that their very existence was random, and without any preconceived purpose, *The Writings* argued that the Maker had designed them to serve several important functions from the outset.

First, they provided a constant pattern for navigation on the earth and a continual means for man to mark the seasons, a celestial map and clock so to speak. As he meditated on his studies of ancient man, he realized the human race had always used the stars for these important purposes. While scientists assumed this was an after-the-fact use, what if it was the other way around—that man was using the stars this way because *that's what the original designer intended all along?*

In fact, the thought led him to another anthropological epiphany of sorts—that in spite of evolutionary assumptions to the contrary, humanity *had always been a highly intelligent race.* The advanced ways they studied the stars long before the "scientific age" was clear evidence of this.

"Pull up graphic of the Antikythera Mechanism," Adrien called out to his tech station. Immediately an image of a circular device partially encased in hardened sediment appeared. Then a larger, clearer image traced onto the screen, a re-creation of what the original Mechanism looked like and how it worked.

A series of golden brass dials interlocked with tiny, sophisticated gears, levers of different lengths, and detailed scale calibrations moved in unison on the holoscreen. This fascinating device was a 2,500-year-old precision computing instrument that tracked the movements of the moon and sun, and was even used to predict some planetary orbits. From its discovery nearly 600 years ago, it had been a constant challenge to the common assumptions about man's intelligence in the past.

Not only this, but there were many other things ancient people groups had accomplished that bewildered the greatest of modern scientists. The ancient city of Tiahuanaco, for example, in the lower Western Column, displays remnants of immense statues and buildings that defy even the creativity and building power of contemporary engineers. And thousands of years ago, the Mayans built astronomical observatories that are strikingly similar to their modern incarnations.

Yes, the heavens gave man a way to navigate and tell time, but these were not their only purposes. More than this, they demonstrated the sheer magnitude of the Maker's power. Just like in everyday observation, the larger the creation—building, bridge, ship, whatever—the greater the power required to create it. So it is with the world.

"Note," Adrien ordered, reading from the text itself, "*The Writings* state the following: 'The night-time sky tells every person the immeasurable power of the Maker. The deeper you reach into its depths, the more powerful you will see he must be.'"

Adrien called to mind a seminar he attended at a global science conference in London a few years back. During this particular talk, an astrophysicist—Dr. Lisle?—described the size and scope of the known universe. Using incredible 3-D animations, he showed how a million earths could fit inside our small sun. Furthermore, if you tried to drive to the sun at a speed of 200 miles per hour, it would take more than fifty years to get there; if you drove the same speed to Pluto, it would take more than 2,000 years to reach your destination; and it would take more than 6,800 times longer (more than thirteen million years) to get to Alpha Centauri, the closest star system to earth!

By the time the seminar was over, Adrien was overwhelmed with a profound sense of his own smallness as the gargantuan size of the universe—the *known* universe—came into focus.

But the books explained more than the heavens above. In another section, he read about the Maker's plan for ecology, how he had created each component—land, water, atmosphere, and their constituent microscopic elements—specifically to provide an environment for life, and how life had not evolved at all, but was generated directly by the creative power of the Maker. Mankind was made last, not because he was the end result of millions of years of evolution, but because he was the Maker's crowning achievement, the only creature in the universe with the capacity to truly know, experience, and love the Maker.

Furthermore, claimed *The Writings*, the Maker—far from a distant bystander—had interacted with mankind many times since creation. He read in detail the firsthand accounts of the Maker's spectacular acts of deliverance that defied the seemingly fixed laws of nature, and how the Maker himself had actually walked the earth long ago to personally carry out his most important work for the human race.

These acts, and the knowledge gained from them, were written down in a book, the very book he was reading, so that all humanity would know the truth about him. Intended to tell mankind of the Maker's love and law, these writings were treasured by many throughout history, and fiercely hated by others.

After almost three straight hours of reading, Adrien set the black book on the small table beside his chair and stood to stretch his tight muscles. As he did, Journey hoped off her seat and lifted her front paws up the side of his leg. He rubbed her on the head for a second, and then walked slowly around the room, processing what he had read while also sensing a complete paradigm shift in his thinking.

Though the body of knowledge set forth in *The Writings* reverberated deeply within Adrien's heart, his thoughts were driven not first to the facts and alternative explanations they presented, as powerful and logical as they were. Instead, he kept coming back to something less intellectual, but to him much more important: the very meaning of life itself, his in particular.

By now he had memorized a statement buried in the middle of the old book's stale pages. He repeated the words out loud to himself, "You were made to know, experience, and glorify me, your Maker, to do the good I have planned for you, and to find eternal life when life for you has ended."

Inasmuch as the data satisfied his mind, this teaching filled his soul.

And yet his sense of reason, trained for so many years to seek evidence and challenge conclusions, burned with more and more questions: What about science? Are supernatural "acts of deliverance" even possible, especially when they must defy the laws of nature? Is there any other evidence the Maker exists? Can these writings be trusted?

What was new with this set of questions, however, was that he asked them not as one bent on disproving the propositions he had just been given, but as one whose mind was now truly open, ready to be convinced if the evidence led him there.

While his brain filled with interrogatives, his eyes tracked to the dark red text hidden under the first book. Though it was now almost four in the morning, his spirit revived with freshness as he plopped back in his chair, pulled out *The Evidence for the Maker*, and continued his late night quest.

For the remaining hours of that long night, exhaustion wielded no power over him. He consumed the pages like life-giving water and dozed off just when the sun started to rise.

Chapter 19

Adrien was yanked from his sleep when Journey bounced into his lap and started licking his chin. "Not now Journey," he complained, trying to push her away without waking up. But she could not be persuaded. Finally, he gave in, opened his heavy eyes, and glanced at the clock.

When the time finally registered, his eyes flew open. "Oh man, nine a.m.!" he let out in a raspy voice.

After a quick shower, he threw the books in his bag and rushed to check in with the site teams and play down his late start. When that formality was satisfied, and he had hung around long enough for the techs to wish he would go away, he said goodbye and made his way to the lab. Just as he expected, Serena Burton was hard at work and all alone.

Serena was the senior lab scientist at X-camp. A short, pudgy black woman in her late forties, she had been on Adrien's team since his demotion back to the field almost six months ago. Although her specialty was chemistry, as a support scientist for archaeological digs, she was also well-versed in many other sciences, including biology, geology, and anthropology.

When Adrien walked in, she was standing at the center table with her back to the door. She turned to see him, smiled, and quipped, "Well, if it isn't the man himself."

"Serena, how are you this morning?" Adrien set his bag on the floor and stood beside her at the table.

"Couldn't be better if I was sipping Chateau Lafite at Fouquet's," she joked.

"Tell me about it," he replied. On the table before her were several small, badly decomposed pieces from the dig.

"So what do we have here?" the Site Leader asked.

"Well, more partials from Site 1 and 2. I'm logging the data and running the analysis, but looks like more of the same to me." She picked up a fragment and rotated it in the air.

"Yeah, strange dig, huh? And thanks for your help with those documents we found a couple of days ago. I know you guys were up late getting that done."

"No problem. I hope it was what you wanted."

"Yes, it was. Actually, that's what I'm here about, not the analysis but the documents themselves."

"Well, they're not here. I was hoping to look through them a little more this morning, but I noticed they're gone. I guess that was you?"

"Yeah, it's easier for me to study them in my quarters."

She sat back on her high stool. "I see. Those things are the talk of the town, you know. So, any answers yet?"

"No, not yet." Adrien pulled a stool from a nearby counter and sat down. "As you know, it looks like the technology is from about two or three hundred years ago. We checked all the databases and something like that shouldn't be found anywhere near this site.

But my question isn't so much about how they got in the ground to start with as it is about some of the content of the documents themselves."

His words intrigued her. "What's on your mind?" she asked.

"Well, I'm not sure how much time you were able to spend with them…"

Serena interrupted. "A little. They're basically an ancient deity myth, not unlike others I've seen over the years. One tells the basic story of the deity and the other attempts to support that story with science, logic, and philosophy. Now that part *is* different."

"Yeah, no kidding," Adrien said. "But the most intriguing part is that…" He paused and looked down at the artifacts on the table.

"Is what?" Serena asked.

He kept his head down but lifted his eyes. "Is that they actually make sense."

"Make sense? What do you mean?" she asked, skeptically.

"Well, let me ask you a question. Can science say definitively that there is no intelligence overarching our universe, no person beyond nature who made all that we see?"

Serena thought quietly for a moment.

Before she could say anything, Adrien answered for her. "Actually, we can't. First of all, that being, by definition, would be outside of nature and not subject to the scientific method. Second, in order to say with absolute certainty, you'd have to be in every part of the universe at the same time. In other words, you'd have to *be* that being to say that being didn't exist."

"Yes," said Serena, "but that's a far cry from saying there *is evidence for* such a being. You could just as easily argue that a group of fairies made the universe, but without proof the claim is empty, if not absurd."

97

"Right. But what if that evidence has been staring us in the face all along and we just didn't see it because we've been conditioned to interpret it another way or eliminate choices others didn't want us to have?"

Serena puckered her lips. "Evidence? Like what?"

"Where did we come from, Serena?"

"What do you mean? Where did we as humans come from, or where did the universe come from?"

"The universe. Where did all of this come from in the very beginning?"

"Well, there are several solid theories out there. There used to be the Big Bang theory, but that's fallen out of favor. The Pierre Wave Unity has gotten a lot of attention lately, but presently I don't think another view has really emerged as a preeminent one," she answered. "But again, the theories that do exist are based on *facts*, not speculation."

"Okay, let's talk about those so-called facts in just a moment. Right now, let's just focus on the big picture. I know it's not the most popular right now, but take the original Big Bang concept as an example. According to the theory, billions of years ago there was an infinitesimally small speck of matter—a singularity—that exploded. From that explosion, eventually, over time, everything we know came into existence.

"The problem is this: that's really not an answer to the question at all *because it doesn't explain where the mass came from in the first place.* If there was a gigantic explosion from a speck of mass billions of years ago, where did the mass come from? It's a question of causality.

"Everything in science is built on causality. We assume that everything in our world has a cause, that's why we study things in the first place, to learn the chain of causality. So we just throw that out when it comes to the biggest thing of all—the universe itself?

"Doesn't it make sense that something had to put that mass there in the beginning?" he asked.

"Okay, let's say something put that mass there to start with," Serena replied. "Who put that something there?"

"That's just it, Serena. Something has to have the power of simply existing; otherwise we'd keep going back one step forever. Let me illustrate it like this. Your mother gave birth to you, and her mother to her, and her mother to her. And so on. Now, is it logical that you can go back in time forever like that? Of course not. It only makes sense that at some point someone did not have to be born. They simply exist. They have the power of life within themselves.

"It just doesn't make sense any other way. Does it?"

Serena glared suspiciously at Adrien as she slipped off her stool and walked slowly around the table, contemplating an answer to his reasoning. Finally, she stopped opposite him on the other side and leaned over onto the tabletop.

"I guess not," she admitted reluctantly. "I guess not."

Chapter 20

Her uncertain concession proved only momentary. "But how do you explain a self-existent being?"

"You don't have to; it's logically necessary. That's what these documents are saying. Let me show you." He reached down into his bag, opened *The Evidence for the Maker*, and flipped about a third of the way in. "There," he said, pointing to a heading entitled, "The Necessity of a First Cause." "Read that."

Serena read in a whisper, "'The law of causality, which scientists and laymen use every day, demands a first uncaused cause of the universe. Inasmuch as an infinite regression is logically impossible, a First Cause is necessarily and inescapably inferred.'"

She raised her head and stared off into the distance. "Fascinating," was all she said.

"It gets better. Not only must he exist, but we can also learn things about him by studying the world around us. We do this all the time with our artifacts. We deduce things about the people we study based on the things they made.

"In this case, we can deduce the power of the First Cause based on the enormity of the universe—you have to be powerful to make something this big. And then, we can deduce intelligence—super-intelligence—because of the complexity of the systems in the universe, like the biological ones," he went on.

"Now wait a minute. Aren't you forgetting a little something called *natural selection?*" Serena objected.

"No, I haven't forgotten it at all," Adrien said. "In fact, I've been thinking a great deal about it, and the books have a lot to say about it as well."

She sighed. "I'm listening."

"I don't think natural selection explains half of what we say it does. Think about some of the mechanisms we've discovered that can't be explained by natural selection. Take the bacteria flagellum, that little tail that propels the bacteria cell along. It has more than forty working parts and each must be in place *from the beginning* for the system to work.

"Natural selection just doesn't work like that. If you've got a part that doesn't serve a purpose, it would be eliminated over time. No chance to build up forty useless parts until they could finally do something productive, right?"

"But Adrien, hundreds of years of science and the entire scientific community say you're wrong. There may be small problems here and there with the theory, but eventually we'll find an answer. We always do."

"Serena," Adrien said calmly, "if it was just one or two simple questions, I would say you're exactly right. You've got to put your faith in something, right? But it's more than just a few small issues. The problems brought up in these writings are numerous and foundational in nature.

"Let me ask you another question," he continued. "For evolution to be true, somehow information must be added to the genetic code that isn't already there, correct?"

"Correct," she said. "The addition of more complex systems to life, say wings for instance, requires that information be added to the DNA to provide for those wings."

"And according to biologists, that information is added by genetic mutations guided by natural selection, right?"

"Right. When the genes are copied, there are sometimes mistakes, mutations, that cause changes in that life form. Over time these changes build on each other and new systems develop."

"But have we ever documented an example of natural selection or mutations actually *adding* information to the genome?" he asked.

She looked at him as if he'd gone mad. "Of course, Adrien! Didn't you take biology at the Institute? We see changes in life systems all the time, sometimes over very short periods of time."

"No," he shook his head, "not just *change*, but change caused by *additional information?* According to this—look here—" Adrien pointed to another page, "there have been no documented cases of information-adding mutations. Whether a virus becomes resistant to a vaccine or a beetle is born without wings, in each case the information in their genes is either lost or reshuffled, but no new information is added. The whole thing is going the *wrong way!*"

Serena read for a minute and then flipped the page and read some more. Finally, she looked up, walked purposefully to a tech station, and typed in a few words.

When it looked like she was about to comment, Adrien said, "Let me lay one more thing on you while you're thinking. Have you ever thought about how the evolutionary model of the world doesn't explain the fact that we can do science at all?"

"How do you mean?"

"For science to work, certain other things must be in place beforehand. There must be uniformity in nature, otherwise we couldn't predict future events or make inferences about the past. Then, for us to draw conclusions from our work or identify flaws in our test methods or processes, the laws of logic must exist and apply across time and space. And, to be certain we could even understand what we were observing—in the world or in the lab—our senses would have to be reliable.

"Without these three things in place up front, the scientific method would be a waste of time.

"But if the evolutionary worldview is true, none of these three pre-conditions should even exist. Why should uniformity come out of the chaos of the Big Bang or any other model? Since when did an explosion ever produce order? And how would we know we had understood or applied the laws of logic correctly if our minds are nothing more than the result of millions of years of chance, chemical processes? The same holds true for our senses, which supposedly are the result of the same biological card game.

"So how can this whole system be true when it can't even explain why these most basic principles exist?"

"I don't know, Adrien," Serena said. "But they do exist and they work. So I don't see the problem."

"Of course, they exist and they work, Serena. I'm not saying they don't. I'm asking *why*. *Why* do they exist and *why* do they work? Evolution can't give an answer."

"I'd need to think about it for a while. But how does the existence of this deity explain it any better?"

"It explains it because the world was built by him and reflects his nature and attributes. He is orderly, so he made his world orderly; the laws of logic reflect the way he thinks, so they're built in to the universe; he made us to understand the world around us, so he made us with senses that are trustworthy."

"So what conclusion do these books draw from all this?" she asked.

"That this whole thing we've been sold is smoke and mirrors designed to cover the truth: we haven't evolved; we were created. And the being who made us is still out there."

"But there's got to be more than just pure deduction and inference, Adrien," Serena observed. "If this being is out there, he wouldn't stop with that. He'd do more than send us on some supernatural treasure hunt, wouldn't he?"

"Yes, he would. And *he has*. The books also talk about his direct acts in time with humanity, many of which suspended the laws of nature for a while.

"These acts were seen by eyewitnesses and then recorded in these documents." He tapped his finger on the black book. "You know what this means, don't you?"

She paused for a moment. Her eyes opened wide when the answer finally scrolled through her mind.

"Yes," she said, "it means we can evaluate their accounts for authenticity just like we do with all the other written accounts that have ever been found."

"And I have a funny feeling about this," he said with a smile.

"I never thought I would say this," she muttered, her expression now serious. "But so do I."

Chapter 21

Paris, France
Sunday, April 2
6:51 PM

When Addy arrived, the large, rectangular room was still almost empty. About fifty people talked in dispersed huddles around the rows of black, contoured chairs filling the room. On the raised platform at the other end of the meeting hall, several techs worked to adjust the light cores and reposition the podium.

Suddenly, a short redhead emerged from one of the huddles. "Addy!" she almost screamed, stretching out her skinny arms for a hug.

"Gabrielle! It's so good to see you," Addy said, smiling widely.

"Hey, come this way." Gabrielle pulled Addy's arm and headed for the back of the room. As she walked, she turned to Addy and said, "These tarts are to die for! You've got to try one." They reached the dessert table, snatched up a few treasures, and found two chairs in a nook where the staircase turned into the meeting hall.

"These are great," Addy said, looking out into the room. "Where is everybody, anyway? This place is usually packed."

"I'm not sure, Addy, but I think everybody's just scared. I've been here for about fifteen minutes and all anybody's talking about is Seger. They're all wondering who'll be next."

Addy's eyes fell to the clear glass in her hand. "Yeah, I know what you mean. I'm worried too."

"So, any word on Seger? Has your Dad told you anything? I heard Addergoole has him."

"That's what he told me," replied Addy. "Dad said they were interrogating him in Munich, right in Addergoole's building."

"Oh, Addy, I'm so sorry. I know you guys used to be close."

"It's not that, Gabrielle. I mean, that was a long time ago. It's just…he's a good man, and he's got a family."

"Yeah, I know. They're getting closer, aren't they? The G-CoN. That's what everybody's saying—that we're fighting a losing battle."

Addy didn't say anything. She simply stared at Gabrielle for a long moment, hoping she was wrong.

Out of the corner of her eye she saw her father walk out onto the platform in his blue tunic. "It's about to get started," she informed Gabrielle. Before Rene reached the podium, they were comfortably in their seats on the back row.

"Everyone, we'd like to get started please," Rene said as he reached the stand. He watched while the attendees quickly seated themselves, including the members of the Council on the front row. Once the room was settled, he paused and looked around at the sad, fearful faces spread across the meeting hall.

"My dear friends," he began, "it is a rich gift to be gathered with you on this important occasion, an occasion that marks the beginning of our most beloved festival of the year, Anticipation. It is during this time of year that we focus not on our present difficulties, but on what he will do for us in the future." As he said this, he motioned his finger toward the heavens.

Pushing his baritone voice an octave lower, he continued, "And we all know what difficulties we face at this hour. Do we not? I know you all know about Seger, and Jonathan, and Dmitri. And I know you're all praying. And I know you're all worried and many of you are frightened." He leaned in toward the crowd. "What does this mean for us, you ask? What will happen to us now? Will I be next?

"Need I remind you," Rene offered, now fully animated, "that we did not start on this path by ourselves, and we have never been in this battle alone! He showed us this path, and he has shown us our victories thus far! Do not lose your faith now, at this hour, when we need it most.

"I realize there are some who disagree with me, even on the Council." Rene glanced at the four men dressed in identical blue tunics on the front row. "And I respect that. But I must tell you now what I have told you many times before. There is someone coming, someone he is sending to us, who will lead us to hopeful days, days when this war will be over, days when no more of our sons will be taken from us in the dark of night.

"So I say to you tonight—things are not what they seem to be. Things are *not at all* what they seem. Therefore, let us discard our fear and celebrate this festival with the same joy we have for the last seventy years. Let us eat tonight and enjoy each other's company while we *anticipate* the deliverance that is soon to come to our way." And with those words, he pulled back from the podium and slowly walked off the stage.

But the people didn't stand up. They didn't smile. They didn't rush for the dinner tables or pick up their conversations as they always did after Rene's opening comments. They just sat quietly and solemnly and waited…until something special happened.

As if out of nowhere, Addy saw a woman rise from the crowd. From the back row, she was nothing more than a dark silhouette breaking the bright view of the stage ahead. Then she did something no one had ever done before on this occasion, but the one thing they all needed.

She started to sing.

She raised her voice until the entire room echoed with her powerful, soothing melody. And as if a fire had been ignited, others joined in until all the sad and worried voices in the room leapt from their cold cages and flew into the air. Propelled, as it were, by an unseen force inside, every person ascended to their feet and pushed their hearts into the warm brightness just beyond the dark clouds that had buried them.

In the middle of it all, Addy saw her father step back onto the platform. As tears rolled down his face, he lifted his arms back to the heavens and did something she had never seen him do before either: he sang with all his might!

Powerful waves of joy and hope overtook her anxious heart. And for once in a very long time, she thought her father was right. Things are not what they seem to be, she assured herself. Things are *not at all* what they seem.

So she closed her eyes and bathed in the power pouring down on her from above. And as the joy overcame her, she breathed out in barely a whisper, "Thank you. Thank you."

Chapter 22

We have completed our analysis of the Resistance technical capabilities, Director Addergoole," said Eric Helmut, Assistant Director for Information Security at the GSS. "Surprisingly, they demonstrate very advanced technology and techniques. However, we believe we can penetrate their intrusion prevention systems and replicate the attack they levied against us last week."

"I don't want to *replicate* their attack," Damien sneered. "I want to obliterate them!"

"Yes, Director. That is what I meant to say," Helmut replied submissively before continuing. "The attack will be three-pronged in nature, as was theirs. However, unlike their attack against us, ours will prove devastating to their electronic capabilities."

"Go on," Damien ordered.

A graphic appeared on the holodisplay that covered the entire back wall of the GSS main conference room. The large, bright room seated up to twenty participants around a horseshoe-shaped, glossy black table. Each position at the table was seamlessly equipped with a state of the art tech station, interactive holoscreen, and P-HUD synchronization interface. In essence, when a participant joined a meeting, he or she became an interconnected part of the room itself.

Damien, along with everyone else in the room, turned to see Helmut's presentation on the main display.

"We believe the Resistance stores their assessment, surveillance, and attack programs in a hidden subdirectory on their main computer. By hacking this database, we can not only learn the limits of their systems, but also wipe out their ability to wage cyberwar against us.

"The second prong of our attack will be their G-CoN records," he continued as a second bullet appeared on the screen. "We believe they have amassed a wealth of information about us. Our personnel, our facilities, our electronic means—they have files on every part of our organization."

"I am well aware of what they know about us, Mr. Helmut," Damien countered calmly.

"Yes, Director. Our plan is to retrieve this data and replace it with false information. We will know what they know, and they will know what we want them to know."

Damien nodded his head. "Very well. And the last prong?"

"The last prong of our attack will be to disable them through a catastrophic viral attack," Helmut continued. "Our team is near completion of a new virus we call *Kopfen*. As the name implies, it is designed to decapitate the enemy's electronic ability to fight. Once launched, this virus will first go after their defensive applications and then randomly delete files all over their network until their entire system is gone."

"And how long before this new virus is operational?" Damien asked.

Helmut turned to his chief technical advisor, Ronald Gaius.

"By Monday, Director," Gaius answered.

"You have seventy-two hours, Mr. Helmut," Damien informed him. Then he turned his attention to the man sitting opposite Helmut, Mauritz Othman. "Mr. Othman, what is your plan for the Rue de Nullepart facility?"

The Assistant Director for Special Operations sat up straight in his chair. "Director, we have confirmed the intel you gathered from the Resistance prisoner. The location he provided is definitely a Resistance location, quite possibly their main headquarters. According to our surveillance, the facility is twenty stories tall with Resistance offices on the eighteenth floor. They are not aware of our knowledge of their location."

"And how will you proceed?" asked Damien.

"When you give the order, we will make our primary thrust through the top of the building; it is equipped with an eco-garden which will provide perfect cover for our entrance. We will also cover the front and rear exits at the main floor."

At that instant, the communication panel lit up and an image materialized in the bottom, left-hand corner of the main holo-display.

"Director Addergoole," the young woman said, "I'm sorry to disturb you, but Dr. Mahish Advani, Director of the Global Science Organization, requests to speak with you immediately. He says it's urgent, sir."

With a cross look, Damien turned to Helmut and Othman and nodded. The two men and their associates immediately left the room.

"Very well. Put him through," Damien said without looking at the screen.

An Indian man of about fifty appeared sitting at a large desk, fidgeting with his fingers. His yellow vestment identified him as the GSO Director.

"Director Addergoole," he said in a distinctly Indian accent. "I am glad to finally speak with you. Your reputation is well known, even at the GSO."

"Thank you," Damien said with some condescension. "What can the GSS do for you today?"

"Are you alone, Director? Can anyone else see or hear this transmission?" the man asked in a hushed voice.

Damien's eyes narrowed as he looked around and said, "No, Director...Advani, is it? Please speak freely."

"Yes, Director. I received a call this morning from my assistant for Western Column projects, Alejandro Vargas. Alejandro was briefed on Friday by a team in the upper Western Column."

"The upper Western Column? What are they doing there? That area is off limits to research of any kind."

"Yes, Director Addergoole," Advani said. "As you know, the Level 3 quarantine was lifted a year ago to allow mining for much needed natural resources."

"Yes, but a Level 2 quarantine doesn't permit research, Mr. Advani! So how did your team even get there?"

"I'm afraid Mr. Vargas was a bit overzealous, and...well...he interpreted the mining exception as permission to dig."

"He 'interpreted.' I see," Damien replied, sarcastically, before asking, "But how did you *physically* get there? How did you penetrate the GSS blockade?"

"I'm not exactly sure, Director. Maybe they slipped through a weakness in the blockade without realizing it, or maybe your men assumed they were part of the mining expedition. I don't know."

"Are you saying this is my fault, Mr. Advani?"

"No, not at all, Director. I…"

But Damien didn't let him finish. "So your people are somewhere they're not supposed to be, doing something they're not supposed to be doing. Just get them out of there. I will deal with my men in my own way. Is there anything else?" Damien asked, leaning back in his chair.

"They found something." Advani just threw the words out.

"They found what?"

"They found documents buried in the ground, documents about someone called *the Maker*."

Damien, who was looking away, jerked his head back toward the display. "The Maker? What else did they find?"

"There was a note as well."

"A note? What did this note say?"

"Let me read it to you." Advani picked up a holopad and read the note from the site out loud.

When he finished, he said, "Oh, and there's one other thing, Director. It's dated *March 31, 2182*. I assume you know what this means."

When Damien didn't reply, the GSO Director added, "So you can see why I called, Director. I need your help to contain this situation. This knowledge cannot get out to the population. And if the Global Sovereign finds out…. Well, let's just say it would not be good for either of us."

Damien stood and walked away from the screen, down the long table, scratching his chin with one hand. Finally, he turned to Advani and said, "Of course, I know what this means, Mr. Advani. Who else knows about this?"

"Just you, me, Alejandro…and my team on the ground."

"Has anyone left the site?" Damien asked quickly.

"Not to my knowledge. What are you thinking, Director?"

"I'm thinking the GSO had better learn to control its people, Director Advani! Send me the project file right away, including the exact location and personnel roster. Do you understand?"

"Yes, yes, of course. What are you going to do?"

"I am going to do what I do, Mr. Advani. You want the situation contained? Yes? Then go back to your white gloves and reports, and spare yourself the gory details. But whatever you do, make sure no one leaves that site!"

Damien pushed a button on the commlink station and Mahish disappeared. He clicked another button. Broderick answered.

"Mr. Fuller, send the team back in. It seems we have another target to add to our list."

Chapter 23

By the time Damien stepped out of his sleek, bulletproof security vehicle, his three armed bodyguards had already taken their stations, two on opposite sides of the driveway and one near the front entrance.

When he and his leather briefcase had safely exited the vehicle, his driver quickly returned to his seat and pulled into the secured garage just west of the house. As Damien strode toward the front door, he noticed his son's dark blue PAV parked in a space just up the hill from the main driveway.

"In for the night, Director?" one of the soldiers asked when Damien had almost reached the front door.

"Yes, Mr. Thomas."

"Very well, sir." At once he ordered the two other guards, "Take your night watch positions, gentlemen. The Director is in for the evening." Without a word or an instant's hesitation, one of the men jogged to the front gate and began a constant sweep of the perimeter, while the other took a permanent post at the rear of the residence. Mr. Thomas maintained his position at the main entrance.

Damien walked in the door a little after seven. As he hung his coat in the foyer of his three-story, 10,000 square foot acropolis, a little brunet sprinted from the family room to his right and greeted him.

"Papa!" she cried, her feet tapping up the four shiny stairs to the foyer.

Damien set his briefcase on the table and bowed down with open arms. "My dear, Priscilla," he said, grinning. "How's Papa's little girl today?"

The three-year-old held a doll in her hands. She fiddled with its hair while she informed him, "I'm sick, Papa."

"Is that right?" Damien replied in a gentle voice. "Well, you look well to me." After a few more seconds, she squirmed out of his arms, ran back through the spacious family room and library, and disappeared into her playroom.

Damien turned left out of the foyer and headed toward the sound of voices in the kitchen. He entered to find his wife, Collette, his son, Tobias, and his daughter-in-law, Kara, talking quietly around the hefty, teardrop-shaped island.

"Damien…" Collette started, but the words never came out. She placed her hand over her mouth and turned promptly to check the stove.

"Dear," Damien greeted her, noticing the drab mood in the room.

"Hello, Father," Tobias said.

"Son," he answered, and then shifted his eyes to Kara. "Good evening, Kara."

"Good evening, Mr. Addergoole," she replied.

"Priscilla is sick, I hear," Damien said to them all.

Tobias laid his hand on Kara's. "Yes, Father. We didn't want to say anything until we were sure, so we haven't mentioned it until now. But today we got the tests back." Tobias tightened his lips and looked at his wife.

"Well, out with it," Damien said flatly.

"There's just no easy way to say this—she's got Malvin's Disease."

Damien pulled in a short breath through his nostrils as alarm flashed across his face. Before anyone noticed, it was gone.

"Malvin's Disease. I see. And how long has she had the disease? How far along is it?"

"She's had it all her life," replied Tobias. "It's caused by a genetic defect in the brain."

"I thought the prenatal genetic tests were negative," asked Damien.

"They were, but it's not a perfect science, apparently."

"And the prognosis?"

"We don't know yet. But we talked to the doctor about it and did some research ourselves this afternoon. It's not good. The disease deteriorates the central nervous system and eventually leads to catastrophic organ failure. Basically the brain stops telling the organs to function. The global survival rate in children is only three percent." Tobias started to cry. "And the worst part is…it runs its course quickly. From the onset of symptoms to death can be as little as six months."

Damien walked past Collette, who was still hovering over the stove, rubbing the tears from her eyes. He poured himself a Scotch and turned back toward Tobias and Kara. "When will you know more?" he asked.

"She goes back to the doctor tomorrow for more tests, but it could be next week before we know for sure," Tobias replied.

Damien didn't say anything else. He simply walked past them, down the stairs, and into the recessed library.

Tobias looked at his mother as if to say, "I told you so," and then back toward the library archway.

"Father, did you hear what I said?" he yelled.

But before he could launch the second wave of his verbal assault, Priscilla pranced into the room. In short order, he traded his angry look for a fake smile and said, kindly, "Prissy, go back to the playroom, sweetie. Kara, will you take her back for just a few minutes?"

When Priscilla was out of earshot, he marched into the library and renewed his attack. "She's dying, Father, and you show no emotion, no expression!"

"She will survive," Damien said calmly. "She is one of the favored ones."

"Oh, yes, I've heard you say that before. Your beloved *natural selection*."

Damien cut his youngest son a sharp look.

"Let me ask you, Father, would you love her any less if she were not? Would you attend her funeral if she is—how do you call it?—one of the *defaveur?*"

"Watch your words, my son," Damien warned with fire in his eyes.

Tobias stormed out of the room and called for Kara and Priscilla; they left without saying goodbye.

A few moments later, Collette walked into the library to find Damien staring out the tall library windows, toward the swimming pool, quietly sipping his whiskey.

"Damien, he's right, you know," she said from the doorway. "But you also know he's not just asking for Priscilla—he's asking for himself. Would you love him if he were not one of the favored?"

"Hmm," was all he said, and Collette walked away.

Damien stood alone, glaring long into the night and struggling with an unfamiliar and troubling feeling: a sharp pain in his heart, and a desperate fear that he might soon lose his dear Prissy.

Chapter 24

So you're certain** this must be done from the inside?" asked Leroux, a bald man in his mid-sixties, the longest serving member on the Council. All five Council members, along with Rad and Addy, were seated around a conference table in the Resistance main headquarters building.

"Yeah, there's just no other way to do it now," Rad said to the group.

Then Addy weighed in. "Since our last attack, they changed the Globalcast policies. Now, instead of uploading the data from off-site, it's loaded and posted from within the main site itself. It's delivered there by a contingent of GSS guards each week. I saw the directive myself."

Rollan asked from the other side of the table, "Addy, I'm afraid I'm not following you. Could you explain exactly how this whole process works?"

"Sure," she answered. "In the past, all the G-CoN departments loaded their data for the Globalcast from the G-CoN SDC—that's their main datacenter—to a group called Assimilation, right down the hall from my office at GIS headquarters. Those guys took that data, sanitized it the G-CoN way, and sent it over to the Nest, the control room for the Globalcast located in the center of the building. The Nest is where they broadcast the Globalcast each week."

"But after we hit them last time," Rad picked up the explanation, "they took the data out of the SDC so we couldn't get to it again, and instead of sending it over the network, they save it to a quantum drive at each department and send it via GSS courier directly to GIS headquarters. Basically, they've cut off any way to get to the information except from inside."

Eduard, the youngest member of the Council, asked Addy, "But you don't have access to the Assimilation area?"

"No," she replied. "And that's the biggest problem. Access to any area within GIS is strictly controlled, and though I've been able to expand my access over time, high security areas like Assimilation are very hard to get into, especially now."

"So how do we get in then?" Gerard asked from beside Rene.

"Well," answered Rad, "the only way we can figure is to get to somebody inside Assimilation."

"What do you mean 'get to somebody'?" Rollan cut in.

"Well, ever since I started there," Addy said, "I've been sniffing around to find people who might be sympathetic to what we're trying to do; basically, talking in the lunch room and on breaks to coworkers, sort of feeling them out. That was part of the plan all along. Get in. Gather intel. Work sources.

"Anyway, I've met several people who might be valuable to us, from various departments in the building. And one of them just happens to work in Assimilation. His name is Walter Waite."

"So what's your plan? Just walk up to him and ask him to join the Resistance?" Leroux asked.

Addy glared hard at him. "Not exactly," she said. "Don't worry about *how* I'm going to do it, just let me see if I can get him to help me with access at the right time."

"She's going to try some of that Addy-charm on him!" joked Rad.

"Don't push it, Rad," she sneered.

"Addy," Rene asked, "do you really think you can turn him, get him to help us?"

"I can't say for sure, Dad. But I give it a pretty good chance. Give me a couple of days to see what I can do."

"Okay," said Rene. "Addy will try to turn this Walter Waite guy, and Rad, you'll make sure when she gets in she can do what she needs to do." Rad nodded silently in affirmation. "And we'll meet again to discuss this in a few days.

"However, before we adjourn, we need to discuss one other issue. Rad and Addy, you can stay if you'd like."

They answered at the same time, "Sure."

"As you all know, Seger was taken five days ago now. According to our sources in Munich, they've been interrogating him on and off since then, but haven't gotten much. At least that's what they say. But given what he knows, we need to decide how to nullify any information they might get from him."

Gerard sat up in his chair. "If they'd gotten anything significant, don't you think they would have hit us by now?"

"Not necessarily," replied Leroux. "The G-CoN is so big they're sometimes slow to react even when a rapid response is called for. And sometimes they just delay to get you to let your guard down."

"Then hit you with a sledgehammer," Rollan added, pounding his fist in his hand.

"Well, as we discussed before, Seger didn't know a lot of our technical secrets, but he did know about our locations," offered

Eduard. "And he certainly knew about this facility."

"Yes," said Rene, "but he'd die before he gave up our location. However, if he was pushed, just to give them something, he might give them the west-side office, the one in the Roselin building."

"So let's evacuate that location, at least for a few weeks," suggested Rollan.

"I agree," said Leroux. "Bring them all over here for a while. Then when this passes, we can send them back."

"But what if they *do* know of our location?" Addy pointed out. "What if Addergoole got it out of him and Seger just couldn't help it? If they take us here, we're done for."

All the Council members except Eduard shook their heads in disagreement.

Then Rene said, "I don't think that's going to happen, Addy. But just in case, why don't we post extra guards on the roof and at the elevator."

"I'll send out a couple of guys to scout the area for surveillance," Gerard added.

"And I'll have my guys check the firewalls and update the defensive applications. Give them a little heartburn if they try to hack in here," said Rad.

"That settles it then," Rene said. "Meeting adjourned."

As they filed out of the conference room, Eduard grabbed Addy's arm and whispered in her ear. "I think they're underestimating this Addergoole guy."

"Me, too," she turned and said. "A few guards? That's all. They're betting Seger will be able to keep his mouth shut. I hope they're right."

"If they're not, we won't be around to tell them about it. We'll all be dead."

Chapter 25

Unable to concentrate, Adrien left work early to spend more time reading the books. In what seemed like only a minute, an hour passed, and the low rays of the sun beamed through the sitting room window onto his feet as they rested on the tech station desk.

"Journey," he called, "want to go for a walk?" Instantly, she jumped off her chair and headed for the front door. After slipping on his boots, he grabbed his coat and followed her out.

As he strode out of camp, the quiet solitude of the lonely wasteland brought him a sense of peace that was almost tangible. In a strange and ironic way, it felt more like home than anywhere he'd ever been.

A hundred feet from his quarters he turned left to follow a trail he often shared with desert vermin and the occasional downpour. When he had almost forgotten the whole world, Journey darted out from behind him almost causing him to trip over his own feet. For a split second he thought of scolding her, but then he remembered how Sophie always loved that about her—her spontaneity, her energy for life no matter how dismal the circumstances.

Adrien had resisted getting a puppy; he hadn't wanted the extra work or responsibility. But Sophie had insisted, and her charm—not to mention lavish promises about how she would do all the work—finally won him over. One day she asked him to go for a drive with her out into the country. She had something she wanted him to see.

"I know what you're up to," he said as she wore a guilty grin. "You've got some animal you want me to see."

She grabbed his collar with both hands and leaned against him. "Oh, come on, Adrien," she said, her hands sliding out onto his shoulders. "We don't have to get one. Just come take a look with me. It'll be fun." Then she gave him those sad eyes he could never resist, and the battle was over.

"Okay," he said, trying to look disagreeable. "But don't be mad when I say no."

It took nearly two hours to get to the small house out in the farmlands. Adrien waited in the PAV while Sophie knocked on the door. After the front door opened and closed again, Sophie walked back toward the PAV and waved for Adrien to follow. When they reached the kennel area behind the house, they saw the old wood and chicken wire cages atop a series of rusty metal tables. Thin blankets covered one side of the pens.

Mrs. Maxine, the old lady breeding the Miniature Schnauzers, pulled back the blankets to reveal the little brown and gray pups snuggled tightly around their mother. Sophie picked one out right away, a dark gray tyke hardly bigger than two hands cupped together.

"This is the one," she said, beaming.

He didn't want to admit it, but the puppy was adorable, and he saw the happiness in Sophie's eyes.

"How much?" he asked Mrs. Maxine.

"Four thousand global."

Sophie turned quickly to Adrien. "You're going to buy her for me?" She grabbed him with one arm and kissed him on the cheek.

"How can I say no to you, Sophie?" he said. "So, what are you going to call her?"

"Let's call her *Journey*."

"Journey it is."

So they put Journey in the cage, which they also bought from Mrs. Maxine, and headed home.

After about an hour, the tiny pooch finally stopped crying and dozed off on one of Adrien's old shirts they had spread out on the bottom of the cage. Sophie sat quietly in the passenger seat for a while, and then into the silence she said, "Can I ask you something?"

Adrien looked at her. "Sure."

"Have you ever asked yourself what's the meaning of all this?"

"The meaning of what?"

As she turned away and looked out her window, she said slowly, "The meaning of our lives, our existence."

"My, aren't we the philosophical one today."

Sophie hit him on the arm, playfully. "I'm serious, Adrien. Look at those fields. They're so beautiful, but they're just fields. Nothing special about them, and yet there is.

"And that puppy. She's so perfect. She loves. She plays. She's happy. Isn't there some meaning to her life?"

"I don't know, Sophie. I'm a man of science. These aren't my kind of questions."

"But they are. You're a human being with a personality and a will, and you make choices and think and create," she said. "Is there no meaning to you, Adrien Bach?"

She paused for a moment and then asked, tenderly, "And what about us? Is the way we feel about each other just simulated emotions from some biological process—nothing more?"

"You tell me, Sophie," said Adrien. "What is the meaning of it all? I guess next you'll tell me you believe in some benevolent deity who gives meaning to life and one day will swoop down and save us all."

"And what if I do?" she replied.

As Adrien approached the ravine, Journey shot from behind him again, barking at the top of her lungs. The sun shone brightly on the side of his face as he walked parallel to the small creek below. When he reached the ravine, he glanced down briefly and then turned east toward X-camp, into the setting sun.

"Maybe she was right after all," he whispered.

They never talked about it again; he never learned what she really believed deep inside. But today he wondered. Maybe there were others in his life who found faith but he just never noticed. He thought of his father, how gentle he was, and how kind. Maybe he experienced something like Adrien was now experiencing. But he would never know because his father was gone.

At that instant, a face popped into his mind, an old friend of his father, Banan O'Shea. He hadn't thought of him in years. Where did he live now? Was he even alive? If he was, he might be able to tell him about the faith of his father, if he ever had any.

"Come on, Journey," Adrien called. "It's time to go—we've got someone to find."

So off they went, back toward X-camp, in search of something that is sometimes more valuable than gold, and often much more difficult to mine. Answers.

Chapter 26

That night Adrien searched for Banan in every database he could think of. Since he hadn't seen him in more than twenty years, finding him was not an easy task. At long last, he tracked down a Banan O'Shea not far from London who was the right age to be his father's old friend. But by the time he left a message, it was four a.m. in England.

The following day, Adrien rushed home when Kim notified him through his comm-port of a call at his tech station. After he let Journey out to play, he sat down at the console and played the call. It was Banan.

Just after the message ended, Adrien said, "Return message," and the word "Calling" blinked on and off on his holoscreen. In a few seconds, O'Shea's image appeared.

When Banan saw his old friend's son, his face lit up. "Adrien, my boy, I can't believe it! It's actually you!" His Irish accent gave his speech a delightful, poetic rhythm.

"Banan, it's been a long time. How are you?" Adrien asked, sitting out on the tip of his seat. He remembered Banan as a skinny man with a full head of strawberry blond hair, light green eyes, and thick eyebrows. But twenty years of Irish living had taken not only his skinny frame but his thick head of hair as well.

"I'm very well, thank you. So what are you up to these days?" he asked. "Last I heard you had graduated from the GSO Institute in Greece, in archaeology if I recall. Then I lost track of you."

"Your memory serves you well. Yes, I did. Now I'm a field archaeologist for the GSO."

"Ah, I see." Banan smiled again. "Did you see your mother, Clarice, while at the Institute?"

"No. I think she had some family on one of the islands at one time, but as far as I know, she never returned there to live."

"So you haven't seen her in all these years?"

"No, I'm afraid not."

"I'm sorry to hear that, Adrien," Banan said.

"Don't worry about it."

"My, how you remind me of your father. Traugott did love you so, Adrien."

"I know he did. Actually, that's why I'm calling."

"Oh?"

"I have some questions about my father, some questions that may seem a little strange, and I didn't know who else to talk to. As far as I know, you were my father's only real friend."

"Yes, your father and I were very close. I think of him often, and I'd love to talk to you about him. So fire away."

"Well, like I said, this may sound a bit strange, but did my father believe in any kind of…higher power?"

His tone now serious, Banan replied, "What do you mean?"

"I mean, did my father believe there was something beyond us—something beyond what we see—that gives some kind of ultimate meaning to life?"

Banan answered slowly, "Do you mean *a deity*, Adrien?"

"Yeah, I guess. Did my father believe in a deity?"

Banan stared at Adrien for a moment and pursed his lips. At last he asked, "Adrien, may I ask why you want to know? What's going on?"

Adrien bounced back and forth in his chair before he finally answered. "We found some documents a few days ago, actually about a week ago, buried in the ground at a dig I'm running. These documents are about a deity called *the Maker*. I've been studying them and, well, I'm starting to think there may be something to them, that they may be telling the truth."

Banan's eyes opened wide with surprise. "Is that right? Tell me more about the books. What do they teach?"

Adrien reached over to the end of the desk, grabbed the books, and set them in front of the screen where Banan could see.

"Here they are," he said as he lifted one in each hand. "Basically they teach that this being, the Maker, is a self-existent deity who spoke the world into existence, has acted in time with confirmed miracles, and even walked the earth himself at one point to bring about some kind of deliverance for mankind. The book calls this deliverance *vita eternus*, life that is eternal.

"That's the first book," Adrien said, lifting the black book up with his right hand.

"Then there's the second book, this one." He lifted it with his left. "It sets forth facts and arguments that support what the first book says, and refutes many of the scientific and philosophical arguments we take for granted today. I know this sounds crazy, but they make a lot of sense."

"Unbelievable," Banan said, chiefly to himself. "Where did you find these books? Where's this site you spoke of?"

"That's going to sound a bit strange too. The site is in the upper Western Column, in the middle of the continent. They were buried in an old, dial-type safe. We still can't figure out how it got here.

"Oh, and there's one other thing—there was a note in the box. It basically said whoever buried it wanted to preserve the documents because of their importance to their culture. It was dated March 31, 2182. Anyway, we haven't been able to figure out the significance of that date; there's nothing about it in the historical databases anywhere."

"No, there wouldn't be, now would there," Banan said, slipping deep into thought. He scratched his cheek and looked away from the screen.

"What do you mean?"

Banan didn't respond. He stood up and walked away from his desk, out of view of the tech station.

"Banan, what's going on? Where are you? Do you know something about this?"

Suddenly, Banan came back into view, his face filling the screen. He spoke quickly. "Adrien, who else knows about this? Have you reported this to anyone at the G-CoN?"

"Yes, yes, I have a progress briefing with GSO every Friday. I told them all about it last week, at my last briefing. Why?"

"Adrien, listen to me carefully. You don't have much time," Banan warned with panic in his voice. "Is there any way you can get out of there, quickly, maybe even tonight?"

"Why? Get out of here—what do you mean?"

"I mean leave the dig, leave the site!"

"Well, there are no personnel transports for a few more days."

"Is there any other transport off site, perhaps a supply ship or equipment transport?"

"Yeah, there's a supply ship that leaves tonight, back to Paris."

"What time?"

"In about ten minutes."

"You've got to take that transport, Adrien! Grab your things, and the books, and get on that ship now!" Banan yelled into the holoscreen.

"But, why, Banan, why?"

"They're going to kill you, Adrien!"

"Kill me? What?"

"No time for answers now—just get on that transport!" Banan's eyes were now red. "Now Adrien! Now! Please!"

"Okay, okay," Adrien said while he stood up and looked around frantically.

"And, Adrien, one more thing. Whatever you do, don't tell a soul where you're going. Not a soul."

Act 2

Chapter 27

What was Omaha, Nebraska
Wednesday, April 6
4:17 PM, Local/11:17 PM, Paris

Adrien ran into his bedroom and jerked an overnight bag from the storage compartment over his bed. In less than a minute it was overflowing with shirts, pants, socks—whatever he could find. He pressed them down to make room for the books, which he placed on top, and zipped it shut. Once he was back in the sitting room, he paused for one last look around, to make sure he wasn't missing anything, and raced for the door.

As he turned in the direction of the scramjet pad, a sudden realization stopped him cold in his tracks. "Journey!" he said out loud.

Instantly, he reversed course and ran back past his living quarters to the open space on the other side of the camp.

Pacing back and forth, he called, "Journey! Journey!" But there was no sign of her anywhere. He checked his watch—only three minutes left—and yelled even louder, "Journey! Journey!" cupping his hands around his mouth. He gave her one more minute and begrudgingly grabbed his bag and ran for the pad, looking over his shoulder the entire way, hoping she would dash out of some bush and escape with him. But she never did.

She'll be okay, he told himself. Kim will feed her until I get back.

When he came around the central storage building, he heard the scramjet engines come alive and saw a man in a white helmet closing the personnel entrance on the side. "Hey wait!" Adrien yelled. At the last second, the co-pilot saw him, lowered the door, and waved him in.

"Got room for one more?" Adrien asked, out of breath.

"Sure, Mr. Bach. But this isn't a personnel transport. It's a freighter. Not too many comfortable seats in here."

"No problem. They need me in Paris first thing tomorrow. Last minute meeting. Can't wait for the next run."

"Suit yourself, sir," the co-pilot replied, motioning toward the lone seat in the crowded bay, a thin metal plate sandwiched between a small window and large cargo container.

Adrien quickly buckled himself in and looked out the window while the freighter lifted straight up into the air. When they passed over the site, Adrien saw Journey standing near his living quarters, watching the metal bird fly overhead, barking as loudly as she could.

"Journey!" he called out, though he knew she couldn't hear him. "I'll be back for you, puppy. Don't worry. I'll be back for you soon." As the scramjet gained speed and altitude, Journey's small form disappeared from sight.

And the man who said he never wanted a dog missed her already.

Chapter 28

Addy had been looking for him for two days. She had taken long dinner breaks on both nights and loitered in the hallways around Assimilation whenever she could. But Walter Waite was nowhere to be found.

She had almost given up hope when she came back to her office for the last stretch before shift change. Walter was coming out of Sherry McCann's office, the office right beside hers. As he turned out of Sherry's doorway and headed for the exit, Addy caught his eye. Instinctively, he looked away.

"Walter," she said in a long, drawn out sort of way. "Is that you?"

He looked up at her, all at once uncomfortable and delighted with the attention of a beautiful woman. "Hi, Amia. Nice to see you again," he offered without losing a step.

"What brings you to this part of the world?" she asked.

Holding up a holopad with columns of numbers on it, he replied, "Just reviewing some packet analyses with Ms. McCann."

Addy turned to join him. "Can I walk with you back to your office?" she asked. "I've been wanting to talk with you."

"Me? Okay."

When they turned into the hall, she asked, "Walter, I was wondering if we could have a synthetic or something sometime?"

"Synthetic?" he asked, sheepishly.

"Yeah, you do like synthetic, don't you?"

"Oh, sure. Sure, I like synthetic. What…uh…what for?"

"Well, I was just hoping to get to know you a little better." She pulled at his arm and stopped him in the middle of the deserted hall. "I really enjoyed our talk in the breakroom last week," she looked him in the eyes and continued, "and I have some ideas I'd like to share with you."

Walter's face lit up. "Uh…yeah…yeah, we could do that. Um, when?"

"I don't know. What do you have going on in the next couple of days?" she asked.

"Um…Saturday morning I have to leave for a big project. I'm not so crazy about it, but I have to go to Moscow for a month. I may come in to work on Friday, but I don't know."

"Oh…well…how about tomorrow morning then?" she threw out on the fly. "Say nine at Chandler's? It's not far from here. Do you know where it is?"

"I think so. Isn't that the old, rundown place off Rue Cachée?"

"Yeah, yeah, that's it. I know the owner, Mike. Good guy. And it's never that busy. It'll give us a little privacy."

"Sure, I guess. I can meet you there."

"Awesome. I'll see you then," she said as she started back to her office. "Oh, and Walter," she turned to say, "thanks so much."

"You're welcome, Amia. You're very welcome."

The next morning Addy was waiting when Walter showed up

just before nine. She stood when Mike walked through the narrow hallway into the empty back room with Walter.

"Hi, Walter," she greeted him brightly.

Still unable to maintain eye contact, he replied, "Hi, Amia."

"Would you like something to drink?" she asked, glancing toward Mike.

"Sure, sure," he said, nervously. "A regular will be fine."

"And a hyper-e for me, Mike," she said.

"Sure." Mike nodded and turned back toward the front. In a few moments, he returned with Addy's hyper-espresso and a regular synthetic for Walter.

"This place is darker than it looks from the outside," Walter observed.

"Yeah. It's dark, but homey."

"Was that the owner, Mike, the guy you know?"

"It was. He's an old friend of my father. Never charges me." She smiled. "Walter, thanks so much for meeting me this morning."

He squeezed his cup with both hands and replied, "Sure."

"So how long have you been at GIS?" she asked.

"About eight years, I guess. It's the only job I've ever had. I used to live at home and just go to school all the time." He played with his ear and glanced around behind Addy as he talked. "Then my parents said I had to get a real job."

"I know how that is. Parents are so demanding sometimes," she agreed. "Do you like your work?"

"I guess it's okay. I like numbers and everything. And everybody leaves me alone. Do you like…? Oh, I forgot, you said you really don't like your job."

"It's not that I don't like my job," she started to answer. "I just want to make a difference. You know. And that's sort of what I wanted to talk to you about."

"Okay."

"Like I said when we talked last week, I think some bad things are going on at GIS, and it bothers me." She looked away and let out a frustrated sigh. "It *really* bothers me."

"Is there anything I can do," he asked, genuinely concerned. "I don't want you to be unhappy."

She paused for effect, then looked at him and said, "Maybe there is, Walter. But first I need to tell you something, something important. It's a secret. Can you keep a secret, Walter?"

He looked left and right and replied, "Sure."

"Okay." Addy leaned in toward him and whispered, "I'm a part of a group that believes the government isn't telling us everything. In fact, the government is hurting a lot of people. This group, Walter, the group I'm a part of, is trying to show the world what the truth is. And we need your help."

"My help?" his voice squeaked with his high pitched reply.

"Yes, Walter. We need *you* to help us. Will you do that?"

"Help you...work against the government? I...I don't know, Amia. What do you want me to do?"

"I need you to help me get into Assimilation. I need to access the system for just a few minutes."

"Access the system?" Walter started to fidget with his hands. "No one is supposed to come in there without permission," he whispered. "I could get in *a lot* of trouble."

"No, I'll make sure you don't, Walter. I only need to be in there for just a few minutes." She put her hand on his and said, "It would be for me, Walter. Won't you do it for me?"

140

With that Walter's resistance began to melt and his demeanor soften. "Okay," he finally consented, "I guess I could do it for you."

Addy was overjoyed. "Great! I'll just need access to your supervisor's station for about ten minutes."

Walter's eyes opened wide. "What? Mr. Tosh's station!" He was almost yelling. "Oh, no, I'm not doing that again. He screamed at me! He said he'd fire me if I even stepped into his office again!"

Walter stood up and rubbed his hands on his pants wildly, his eyes bobbing all over the room. "No, no, I can't help you. I'm sorry. I just can't." And he took off for the corridor leading to the front.

"Wait, Walter! Wait! Maybe we don't have to use the supervisor's station. Maybe...maybe there's another way," she said running down the hallway after him. "Please...Walter!"

But Walter didn't respond. He cut through the tables in the front of the cafe, barrelled through the front door, and disappeared into the crowd.

Chapter 29

Addy **turned the corner** from the café and slipped into a nearby alley. She commanded her comm-port, "Call Dad," and in no time his face appeared on her P-HUD.

"Dad, Walter balked," she said coolly. "He won't help us."

"What happened? I thought you said you could turn this guy?"

"I know—I did. And I almost had him. He's just too scared."

"So what now?" he asked. "Is there anybody else?"

"No, he's the one. I don't know anybody else in his department."

"Well give him the weekend. Maybe by Monday he'll soften up."

"We *don't have* until Monday," Addy said emphatically into the air. "He's going to Moscow for a month, leaving Saturday. We don't have time for the cat and mouse game; we've got to try something a little more risky if we're going to pull this off."

"Risky? Like what?"

"Send Trip and Tony after him. They're both former GSS, right? They could bring him in and we could talk to him at our office. Help him see the light. Worst case, maybe we can get some access codes from him and do this thing ourselves."

"I don't know, Addy. Tony and Trip mean well, but.... And,

you're talking about *kidnapping*."

Addy fired back, "They're on to us, and if we don't do something soon, they're going to nail us, kill us all! Tony and Trip will just have to do." Then she calmed a bit. "Dad, you said I was born for this, and this is what I think we should do. Anyway, we don't have to hurt him, just talk to him, encourage him a little."

"I don't know, Addy."

"Do you have a better idea? They might hit us tonight, and while we're debating, they're planning our destruction."

"Okay, I'll talk to the guys. But we're just going to talk to him," instructed Rene.

"Exactly. Just talk."

Chapter 30

Tinsley, England
Thursday, April 7
7:10 AM, Local/8:10 AM, Paris

Adrien's scramjet flight took just over two hours, arriving in Paris a little after midnight. After landing, he immediately took an aero-shuttle to London just as Banan had instructed. At the shuttle station, Banan met him and brought him to Tinsley, a small village northeast of London that Banan now called home.

They arrived just after two-thirty in the morning and chose to forgo serious conversation in favor of a few hours rest.

Just after seven a.m., Adrien walked into the kitchen to find Banan sipping a cup of hot synthetic at the small kitchen table.

"A good morning to you," Banan said. "Seems you forgot your jammies."

Adrien looked down at his wrinkled work uniform and laughed. "Well you didn't exactly give me a lot of time to pack, now did you?"

Banan returned the chuckle and said, "I guess not. But you're alive."

"The jury's still out on that," Adrien joked. He sat down while Banan poured him a cup, and then took his seat at the table.

"Sorry to do that to you, son," Banan said. "I wouldn't have done

144

it if I hadn't thought you were in real danger."

"So, let's hear about that danger. How can some old books found in the middle of the desert be dangerous?"

"Where are the books, Adrien? Can I see them?"

"Sure." Adrien walked into his room, brought the books out one in each hand, and laid them on the table in front of his father's old friend.

Banan didn't speak; he just stroked his fingers over the books, inspecting them inch by inch. "May I open them?" he asked.

"Of course," answered Adrien. "I've been reading them for days now. They're in pretty good shape. You can't hurt them."

Banan opened them with the care of a mother with her newborn baby. He gently turned the pages and let his eyes savor every word. Adrien noticed the old man's eyes were beginning to water.

"I cannot believe what my eyes are seeing," he said as he continued to adore the pages before him. "Do you have any idea how long we've waited for this?"

Leaning forward on the table, Adrien asked, "Waited for what? Who's 'we'? Banan, what's going on?"

Banan gingerly closed the book and looked up to Adrien.

"Adrien, what if I told you that everything you've ever been taught about the world was a lie?"

He thought about the question for a moment and answered, "After what I've learned over the last week, I think I might actually believe you."

"Well, I'm glad to hear that…because it's true. Long ago, before there was a global government, many people in many nations believed in a deity of some kind. And there was one group whose belief system stood above all others. Their beliefs made the most sense out of reality and were confirmed by science and archaeology and good old common sense."

Banan stood up and walked toward the back door, the floor creaking underneath his feet. "Their claims to truth were anchored in real historical acts which were recorded and confirmed by many eyewitnesses. Unlike the fables and myths of the past, or those of that time even, these teachings stood the test not only of the heart, but also the intellect.

"The being this group worshiped was known as…the Maker."

Adrien's eyes opened wide while his head slowly pulled back in disbelief. He took a deep breath and processed Banan's words. By finding those dusty books in the desert, he'd just done what every archaeologist always dreamed of and hoped for—to discover some unknown truth or hidden culture and make it known to the world.

His professional amazement soon gave way to more questions, however. "So what happened to them? I've studied history for twenty years and have never even heard of them."

"Now that's the question, isn't it?" Banan said. "Over time the power in the world shifted, and the new powers hated them. They saw them as weak and unnecessary in a modern, scientific world. Though, ironically enough, it was these very people of faith who discovered many of the scientific principles the world now embraces.

"In the end, millions of them were eradicated and all history of them purged from the world's databases. All their hard copy writings were burned, like these," he tapped his finger on the books, "and any electronic versions were permanently erased."

"You mean they were killed? All of them?"

"Yes. At least that's what the government thought. But they weren't able to get them all. Many survived all over the world, but their fear of the G-CoN forced them underground. And though their source documents were destroyed, some secondary documents persevered. In fact, there are some who still believe today, though they hardly know what to believe given the dearth of information they have about the Maker."

Banan reached down, picked up the black book, and lifted it into the air. "What you have found here, my dear friend, is the only primary source document for this ancient faith in existence. What I hold in my hand has not been seen in more than 150 years!

"That's why you're in danger—you just dug up their secret, their genocide."

Adrien sat quietly and took it all in. After a moment, he asked, "So how did they die? And how did these books get buried in the middle of the desert?"

"Why don't we save those questions for later? I've got some folks I want you to meet soon that can satisfy that scientific mind of yours far better than I can. Can you hold your curiosity for a day or two?"

"Sure, I've got plenty to process anyway," answered Adrien. "Ever since we dug up those things, my whole world's been turned upside down.

"But there is one thing I've got to know now. When I called you last night, I asked you if my father ever believed in any kind of higher power. You never really answered me."

"No, I didn't, did I. Well, the answer is yes, he did, Adrien. He was going through an awakening much like yours just before he died." Banan looked like he wanted to say more, but stopped there. "You look tired and, like you said, you just got a huge load dumped on you. Why don't you get a shower and then rest a while longer?

We can talk later."

"Sounds good," Adrien said, forcing a weak smile. As he walked out of the kitchen, he stopped at the door and turned back to Banan. "You said there are some folks who believe today. Are you one of those folks, Banan?"

He paused for an instant, and then looked directly into Adrien's eyes. "I am, Adrien. I most certainly am."

Chapter 31

When Adrien walked into Banan's study that afternoon, the old Irishman was seated at a large wooden desk, completely immersed in the documents from the site. Scanning the room, Adrien saw wall-to-wall books—real books, with paper and binding and ink—dark stained wood floors, and cherry bookshelves that reminded him of pictures he'd seen of old, dusty libraries from days gone by.

Banan's desk was centered on the wall opposite the door just in front of a window that reached almost to the ceiling. At that moment, he sat in his chair reading *The Writings*. A host of other books littered his desktop.

When he was aware of Adrien's presence in the doorway, he turned, smiled gently, and said, "Well, well, what do we have here? He lives."

"Indeed," Adrien said, echoing Banan's grin. "Amazing what a few hours of sleep and a hot shower can do." He walked over and sat down in a brown leather chair to the right of Banan's desk.

Banan closed the book and sat up. "I'm glad you're rested. Would you like a cup of tea? It's the real thing."

"No, thank you. Maybe in a bit." He pointed to the book in

149

Banan's hand. "So what do you think? Anything to it?"

Banan smiled like a schoolboy. "Fascinating, Adrien. Absolutely fascinating."

"How so?"

"Well, first, *The Writings of the Maker* isn't written like a typical book, by one author at one time. It's really a collection of writings written by different people at different times in different places, but with an overall theme and coherency, as if it flowed from one mind.

"We've had bits and pieces of what's contained in them for many years, and some of the writings we have refer to documents included in the books you found. But we had all but given up on finding a complete set. We assumed they had disappeared forever."

"What other writings do you have?" Adrien asked.

"Well, several," replied Banan. He reached onto his desk and picked up a book. "Like this one. It gives a synopsis of the creation of the world and some major miraculous acts of the Maker, but no way to fit the whole story together. Based on the books you found, what it records is accurate, but it's missing a tremendous amount of detail.

"And this one." Banan grabbed another book. "It discusses a concept called *reconciliation*. It's about how to be right with the Maker. Again, it gives us a high-level overview, but lacks important details: the specific instrument for returning to the Maker's favor, and how we take advantage of that instrument. In other words, this book tells us there's a problem in the relationship between the Maker and mankind, but it doesn't tell us what to do about it."

Adrien leaned forward in his chair and, with a confused look, said, "Yeah, that's a part I was a little unsure about. From what

I was reading, the Maker describes himself as our father, in the sense that he made us all. And he cares for us as a father does his own children, right?"

"Yes, that's right."

"But there's a problem. And that problem is our immorality?"

"Correct."

"Exactly how is that a problem, though? If he's our father, shouldn't he just overlook our moral failures?"

"An excellent question indeed," Banan said. "To understand the answer to that question you first need to understand that all of our problems in life—death, depression, hopelessness, evil— stem from our broken relationship with the Maker. He is the source of life in every sense: moral, physical, emotional—you name it. So if we were separated from him in any way, obviously, life in every sense would suffer. Do you follow?"

"Yes. Go on."

"Now, the Maker presents himself in several ways in the writings, all of which are designed to show us who he is and how he relates to us. He's our father, as you've said, but he's also described as our friend, brother, and helper. These descriptions give us intimate and loving pictures of who he is to us, but they don't *exhaust* who he is to us.

"In addition to these affectionate images, he describes himself in a more formal way, as our *judge*," Banan explained.

"Judge? Like a courtroom judge?"

"Exactly." Banan stood and walked over to a small table in the corner and poured two cups of hot tea.

"But whose law is he judge over?" Adrien asked. "Human laws change over time, and rarely does one group's laws perfectly mirror another's. Archaeology's proven that."

Banan handed Adrien a cup and looked down into his eyes. "That's just it, Adrien. He doesn't use our laws or our standards to judge us—he uses his own. He is judge over *his own law*."

Adrien paused for a moment and took a sip from his cup. "I see," he said.

"The Maker has given mankind a moral code, a set of moral laws to live by. That law is specifically laid out in the writings you dug up, but we already know its basic parameters. All of us."

"What do you mean?"

"The conscience. You know, that sense inside that something's right or wrong."

"Yes, but, again, not all humans agree on what's right and wrong," Adrien objected.

"Actually, if you think about it, there is a core set of moral truths on which we all agree. Murder, rape, genocide, for example. But more than this, have you noticed how we all try to justify ourselves when we do something we know to be wrong?"

"How do you mean?"

"Do you remember those terrorists from a few years back, the ones who executed those prisoners in Chongqing?"

"Yes, how could I forget? They threw several of them off a building. What about them?"

"The videos they put out on the underground network, did you notice what they spent most of their time talking about?"

"Not really," replied Adrien. "They weren't up for that long. I think I only saw a few minutes of one of them. As I recall, the government took them down after a day or two."

"Yes, they did—and that's another subject altogether. Nevertheless, in all the videos they put out, the majority of the time was spent not stating demands or bragging, but *justifying* their actions. 'Killing civilians is justified in war,' they said. Their logic was insane, but still, they felt a need to be right in what they did. Why did they do that, Adrien?"

"I don't know, but it doesn't have to be from a deity, does it? Doesn't science explain that in some way, maybe some kind of inherited survival mechanism?"

"How, Adrien? Why would we expect in a world of chance—which is what we have if evolution is true—for every single person to have this same inner compass? Why wouldn't there be some with it and some without, some with one kind of compass and some with another?"

Adrien sat quietly and contemplated what Banan was saying.

"Back to the point—the Maker as judge. Every person ever born has disgraced his moral code: lying, pride, deceit, greed, murder, adultery, pornography, lust. You name it. And perhaps worst of all, we've denied he even exists! He has given us life and a world to live in and food to eat. Minds and opportunity and sunny days. And what have we given in return? A denial that he is even real!"

Banan turned and walked toward the window. "And we fancy ourselves *good*," he chuckled sarcastically to himself. "Nothing could be further from the truth."

Adrien didn't say a word. He knew Banan was right. About everything.

Chapter 32

Adrien felt a sting inside his chest. As Banan spoke, images floated through his mind, memories from his past, things he'd done and tried to forget. More than that, the fact that he had lived thirty-seven years on the Maker's earth and had never so much as given him a second thought. The guilt covered him like hot, black tar. His entire life was now open for view, and it scared him to death.

"And like any other law," Banan went on, "when it is broken, a punishment is required. Our real problem is this—we've already been found guilty and sentenced for our crimes."

"What's the sentence, Banan, according to the writings?"

"*Death*, Adrien. The writings call it *Gehenna*, the place of eternal darkness, the place where men and women are removed from the Maker's life completely and permanently. It is described as a place where we burn forever, never dying, yet never finding relief. The partial death we experience here bears not the faintest resemblance to what awaits us in that place." With that sober proclamation, Banan turned and stared out the window in silence.

To Adrien, it was as if a part of him had entered into another

154

world. Though to the human eye, the room was empty save for himself and Banan. Yet now it was alive with a supernatural, invisible presence.

Finally, he asked, "How can he do that, if he truly loves us?"

"He doesn't want to," Banan replied, awakening from his thoughts. "He is *forced to*. The Maker is perfect in every way. He is perfect love, strength, wisdom, *and* he is perfect justice. Think of it this way. If you had a perfect sense of justice, could you let any crime go unpunished? No. Otherwise your justice would not be perfect.

"But the Maker is also perfectly merciful. He desires to show us mercy. So instead of giving us what we deserve—Gehenna—he has made a way to satisfy his justice and mercy at the same time," Banan said.

"How?"

"By taking our punishment himself."

"You mean when he lived on the earth?"

"Precisely. He became a man and, as a man, took the punishment for all of us. Because he loves us, he took our place. And the writings give a beautiful picture of this act." Banan moved the books around on his desk and found the red one. He flipped to a specific page and read silently to himself. Then he handed the book to Adrien.

"In this section here," Banan said, pointing to the middle of the page, "it gives an illustration from our world that helps explain what the Maker has done." Adrien put the book in his lap and read while Banan pressed on.

"The illustration is that of a judge hearing a capital murder case. A man is accused of raping and murdering a woman, and, if found guilty, the law requires he be put to death. The judge hears the case and, based on the evidence, finds the man guilty. Then, as required by law, he sentences the criminal to death. He has no choice.

"However, the twist is that the murderer *is the judge's own son.* So you can imagine how hard it must have been for him to hand down this sentence to start with. He doesn't just let his son die, however; the love of the father inside him is so great, he stands up, takes off his robe, and is executed in his son's place.

"This is the picture the writings give us of the Maker."

"Wow," Adrien offered softly, "what a picture." After a few seconds, he asked, "So no one goes to Gehenna now?"

"I'm afraid not. The Maker has made the way, but now it's our turn. We must make a choice. We can continue to pretend he isn't real and that we aren't guilty of any wrong against him. If we make this choice, we suffer Gehenna when we die—his sacrifice will not apply to us.

"Or, we can acknowledge his reality, mourn our crimes against him, trust that he died for us, and use the rest of our lives to serve him. When we make this choice, his life counts for ours and we are forgiven for our crimes. It's as if they never even happened."

Adrien stood, walked across the room, and stared at the bookshelves. After a pause, he turned around and said, "So what happens to us when we're forgiven? Where do those who believe go when they die?"

"They go to be with the Maker. They leave this life of death and worry and pain and experience the full life of the Maker forever."

Adrien's face softened, and then he looked away as if reflecting on something important.

"But that's not all, Adrien," Banan said. "Not only do we receive the promise of a better life in the next life, but he also promises to give the one we're living now real meaning and purpose. He promises a reason to live *today.*"

"Why would he do this for us?"

"Because he loves us. He truly and freely and completely loves us. That's the only reason he gives."

Adrien sat down again, speechless. The weight of guilt that seemed impossible to remove only a few moments before, now seemed as light as a feather. The sweet elixir that was Banan's words gave him hope he could be forgiven for it all. There was no way to express it, but he was overcome with a sense that he was loved in spite of his wrongs. He knew it was the Maker.

At last he started to cry. Finally, he spoke again, his voice coarse and strained, "It's been so long, Banan. And so hard. I'd lost all hope. I almost took my own...."

"Took your own what?" Banan asked after a second.

"Nothing. I just wasn't sure I was going to make it. That's all." After a long silence, Adrien lifted his head and looked deeply into Banan's eyes. "I want a reason to live," he declared. "I want to believe."

"So do I," Banan said smiling. "So do I."

So at three-forty in the afternoon on Thursday, April 7, DE 523, Adrien Bach and Banan O'Shea got down on their knees, mourned their failures, and put their faith in the Maker.

Chapter 33

Damien watched from his plush office chair while the faces of Eric Helmut from Information Security and Mauritz Othman from Special Operations appeared on the large holodisplay just in front of him.

"Good afternoon, gentlemen," he said. "Are we ready to squash this little bug that has been annoying us?"

"Yes, Director," they answered.

"Very well. Then let us proceed."

The images of the Assistant Directors' were replaced by three live feeds from the field. The far left image was split in two, top and bottom. The top image was a set of five tech stations in a remote GSS datacenter; Ronald Gaius sat at the center position. The bottom image tracked the progress of the three cyber attack goals.

The center and right images were from inside two different military transports, each filled with soldiers dressed in black uniforms and helmets, gripping plasma rifles. The center image was labeled "Paris" and was led by Captain Jaeger, while the right image, labeled "Western Column," was led by Lieutenant Vasilii. Jaeger's team arrived first.

The back of his transport opened just above the eco-garden at the Resistance facility. At once the men leapt into action, dropped to the terrace below by automatic nylon cables. Two men served as lookouts as the other eight made their way down the gravel path past trees and plants to the entrance at the center of the roof.

When Jaeger arrived, he nodded to the soldier nearest the door who then waved a thin, silver medallion over the access port. The door opened and one by one the assassins entered with the stealth of bats in the night.

"Paris team in," he updated the Director. "Targets imminent."

Meanwhile Gaius spoke up from the datacenter. "Breaking firewalls now." His team was busy typing in commands and speaking into their comm-ports. Their holoscreens were alive with windows and command lines and flashing red and yellow icons.

The tech to his left said, "Searching for cyberwar programs," while a tech to his far right called out, "Planting Trojan for remote virus initiation." To his immediate right, a female voice interjected, "Files found. Extraction commencing."

"Director," Gaius said, "we have completed the first phase of each of our attack goals."

On his holodisplay, Damien saw the progress indicators turn green and slide to the right, confirming Gaius' report.

"Excellent," he replied.

The last to reach their target, Captain Vasilii's team landed about a mile south of X-camp. Immediately the men separated into two teams, one to take the living quarters and two westward dig sites and the other to the lab, technical areas, and the two eastward sites.

When they had reached their predetermined rendezvous positions, Vasilii instructed both teams over his comm-port, "Men, remember, kill everyone, but do not damage any equipment or tech stations. Engage targets in 3…2…1…go!"

Back at the Resistance headquarters, Rad was screaming commands like a madman. "They're bringing it, guys! Remi, keep that firewall up, man! Deston, they're hacking our files—break that connection or move those files. Now!"

In the stairwell, Jaeger's team gathered just inside the door to the eighteenth floor. "Team two, have you secured the lobby and security stations?" he asked.

Two hundred feet below, a soldier replied, "Yes, lobby has been neutralized. Security is down. Exits are sealed."

"Very well. We're moving in to main target areas. Kill anyone who tries to leave."

"Got it," the soldier replied.

Jaeger opened the door and stepped into the main hall followed closely by the rest of his men. With their rifles drawn and ready, they crept down the long corridor toward the Resistance offices. As they passed a breakroom on their left, Jaeger pointed without looking and a single soldier peeled off to attack. Next they passed a large meeting room. With another quick motion, two soldiers paused at the doorway and rushed the room. At the end of the hallway, Jaeger's team stopped just outside the main workspaces, and then invaded, firing at point blank range.

In the bright desert of the Western Column, Vasilii's men sprang from their positions and assaulted the site, firing and killing at will. The first victims were walking between the dig sites and camp buildings; the super-hot spherical rounds from the plasma rifles burned instantly through their soft bodies.

From there, team one spread out and slaughtered everyone at the westward sites and moved rapidly to the regular living quarters; team two eliminated the eastward sites and pressed toward the technical areas.

Each team lead reported in, "Dig sites clear. Pressing inward."

Back in the GSS datacenter, Gaius stepped up the attack. "Initiate second phase," he ordered. Again, his techs issued updates through their comm-ports. One tech said, "They're trying to counter our attacks. Compensating. Defensive efforts repelled." The female tech said, "Extraction complete. Replacing files with reproductions."

"How about Kopfen? Is it installed yet?" Gaius asked.

The third tech replied, "The Trojan has been planted, and the Kopfen virus has been installed."

"And the cyberwar files?"

The third tech spoke up again. "Cyberwar files have been located."

Meanwhile, the Resistance datacenter was in chaos.

"They copied the files, Rad!" Deston yelled.

"I thought you broke the connection!" Rad howled back.

"I thought I had, man. But they rerouted the connection, and before I could find them again, the download was complete."

"Did they delete the file?"

"No, it's still there, but they got it," Deston answered.

"Are they trying to get anything else," Rad asked.

"No. Doesn't look like it," replied Deston.

Rad walked over and stood behind Remi's console. "How about you, man?"

"I think I stopped them," he said. "They were trying to load something onto our system, but when I reloaded the firewall, it cut off the upstream and terminated the transfer."

"Great! Close one," Rad said, breathing out a heavy sigh. "Looks like they're done. At least for now."

Chapter 34

When Jaeger and his men stopped firing, no one was in sight over the open office compartments at the Resistance building. At his command, the men split up and inspected every station in the area. But found no one.

Jaeger called downstairs. "Team two, have you engaged the enemy? Has anyone tried to escape?"

"No. No one has come our way."

"They must be hiding somewhere; maybe their security system tipped them off. Break up and search the other areas," Jaeger ordered a group of his men. "You two, come with me. We're going to the datacenter."

Team two kicked in the door at the X-camp lab and found Serena working at the center table with several other technicians. She turned and started to scream as a plasma round cut her down. Before she even hit the floor, everyone in the room was gone.

Team one, at the other end of the compound, had just finished the living quarters and common areas. The team lead announced, "All areas secure except Site Leader's quarters. Moving in now."

The men blasted the door open and moved quickly through

Adrien's ALSU. But no one was there. Just then, Journey ran out of the bedroom, in full attack mode, barking and growling. One of the soldiers kicked her away towards the couch. She shrieked and ran for the front door. As she turned the corner to escape, a second soldier fired a shot in her direction, causing a plume of dust to explode into the air. The helpless puppy squealed, tumbled head over heels, and rolled out of sight.

The team leader stepped out of Adrien's bedroom and confirmed: "Team one, all clear."

"Initiate phase three," Gaius called out to his crew.

On his right, a tech keyed in a command line and pressed enter. "Trojan enacted. Kopfen deployed," he said. "Resistance cyberwar files being destroyed." The third attack goal progress indicator started inching toward the right and the words "Goal Complete."

Vasilii pushed open the door to the lab storage building and quietly walked into the room. Just when he was about to leave, a noise sounded from a metal cabinet in the far corner. While he trained his rifle on the contents, he signaled his men to get the door. When they jerked it open, they heard the high-pitched scream of Nate Ashby as he pushed himself to the back of the cabinet. Vasilii was not moved, however; he located his laser sight between the eyes of X-camp's last living target and whispered, "Goodbye, my friend."

As the pressure of the attack passed, Rad, Remi, and Deston were sitting at their stations surveying the damage and trying to relax. Windows with lists of copied files and defensive applications littered their holoscreens.

All of a sudden Deston said, "What's happening? Do you guys see this?"

"See what?" asked Rad.

"I don't know, but the files I was just looking at are all gone."

"Yeah, something's up," said Remi. "My analyzer just locked up. Rad, you might want to run a meta-scan and see what's going on."

Rad punched in a few commands and a file diagram of the entire Resistance network came up on the main display. One by one, files within the tree vanished.

"Oh, crap! They're back!" Remi cried out.

"No, no. *They never left!*" yelled Rad. "They're getting everything. Launch the sweep, Deston. We've got to stop them before they erase it all!"

Deston touched a button on his holoscreen, but nothing happened. "The sweep won't work, Rad! They must have destroyed the program already!"

The files were deleting much more rapidly now. "Oh, no. They've got us!" Rad said, punching commands into his holoscreen. "Nothing's working. Cut the system, Remi! Cut it now!"

"But it might have a power override on boot up. When we turn it back on, we might never be able to turn if off again... until everything is gone!"

"It's a chance we have to take—hit the kill switch now!" Rad ordered.

Remi leapt from his chair and slammed his hand against the red power cut-off switch. Everything but the emergency lights went dead.

Just then Jaeger and his two men crept up alongside the datacenter main door. As they settled into position, they heard sounds coming from inside. Jaeger whispered, "They must be hiding in there. They might be armed. Go in low and eliminate them all."

The two men nodded back. And after a silent countdown from Jaeger's fingers—3...2...1—they blasted through the door and rolled into the half-lit datacenter, flashes of plasma rounds lighting up the room.

But no one fired back, and no one screamed out in pain.

In a few seconds, Jaeger realized what was going on. "Lights activate," he called out into the room. When the light cores ignited, their full brightness revealed an unbelievable surprise.

There was no one in the room.

Damien, who had just seen the whole thing on his holodisplay, sat astounded in his office chair. "What's your status, Mr. Jaeger?" he asked.

"Director," the GSS captain replied. "There's no one here. Not a soul."

"What?!" Damien yelled into the display. "Where did they go?! What happened?!"

"I can't answer that, Director. But one thing I can say for sure. We've been had."

Chapter 35

Trip and Tony waited outside GIS for Walter to leave. As people came in and out at shift change, they scrutinized every face for the man Addy had described to them earlier, the man whose image now floated in the air on their P-HUDs. At exactly five minutes after one, a nerdy figure with black hair and a wiry beard pushed his way through the throng, turned right on the sidewalk, and headed east.

It was Walter.

The covert Resistance team stepped out from the large bushes behind the walkway and followed. So as not to be noticed, they stayed back thirty or forty feet, and as the bright lights of GIS faded, their black shirts and pants made them nearly invisible.

The plan was not complicated. First, grab Walter at the park tunnel just before his apartment. Then, while one subdued him, the other would get the PAV, and together they'd take him back to Addy and Rene.

Suddenly, Walter stopped and turned unexpectedly at a street crossing. Tony and Trip tried to act natural, but when Walter glanced their way, they froze. Walter spotted them right away and panicked. Without hesitating, he darted out into traffic. PAVs screeched to a halt and horns blared while he cut and slashed his way through the lanes and sprinted down the sidewalk leading away from GIS. Tony and Trip immediately took off after him.

At the next corner, Walter turned left at Rue de Soif, into the bistro district, and quickly pushed his way into the mass of lovers, drunks, and party-goers. When he glanced back to spot his pursuers, however, he slammed into a short, fat man in a leather jacket, and crashed to the ground. The angry man cursed and reached out to grab Walter, but the frightened GIS analyst was too fast. Barely missing a step, he sprang to his feet and resumed his desperate getaway.

But the delay had cost him. By the end of the bistro district, Trip and Tony had closed the gap to less than fifty feet.

Still in a full sprint, Walter cried out, "What do you want? Leave me alone!"

"Hey," Trip yelled back, "we just want to talk to you Walter! Wait up!"

Walter turned and disappeared into a long stairwell leading to the street below. Just as he started his descent, he tripped and fell, tumbling down the stairs. His right eye smashed against one of the cold stone steps, pouring blood into his eye and blurring his vision. But he had no time to tend to his wound; hearing footsteps rapidly approaching, he forced himself up and limped hurriedly to the bottom.

The Resistance team made the corner and skipped down the stairs; by the bottom half they had again closed to within a few feet of their target.

As Walter stepped off the last stair, he looked back and screamed, "I didn't tell her anything! I'm not helping her!" Then he turned left and rushed down the sidewalk.

He was now on Rue de Diable, a large, multi-lane freeway leading to the Global Superway, a magnetic repulsion transport system that accelerated vehicles to more than 200 miles per hour. The stairs dropped him off at the intersection of Rue de Diable and Global Superway 7.

Trip jumped off the stairs and yelled, "Walter, we're not with the government! We won't hurt you!" But Walter could not be persuaded. At the offramp junction, he veered left and ran up the offramp itself, PAVs buzzing by him like lightning bolts.

"This guy's going to get us all killed," Trip said to Tony.

When Walter turned to look back, he stumbled at the edge of the roadway and fell into the offramp just as a large, brown PAV was decelerating. He never had a chance; the PAV slammed him head on and bounced him down the road like a rubber ball.

When Tony and Trip got to Walter, they found him unconscious, his face bloody and grated and his head cracked open and bleeding.

"Oh, no! What have we done?" was all Trip could say.

They slid Walter off the road while a few PAVs slowed to watch and two stopped to help.

"We've got to get him out of here, Tony," Trip said. "Help me." They picked up Walter's body and slipped through a crack in the roadway fence as a small mob of bystanders yelled and screamed. When they made it to an alley just off Diable, Trip sent Tony for the PAV.

In a flash, Tony turned the corner into the narrow corridor and screeched to a halt. They threw Walter's body into the back seat and sped away. Trip tried CPR, but it was no use.

"Ah, crap!" he yelled, slamming his fist into the back of the seat.

He activated his comm-port and waited. When Addy's face appeared, Trip said, "Addy, I've got some bad news."

"What?"

"Walter Waite is dead."

Chapter 36

Adrien woke up to the dim glow of the rising sun in his small bedroom window. And, unlike most every morning for the last two years, he didn't feel tired; by some miracle, he had actually slept. In a matter of minutes, he headed out the back door for the dusty gravel road that was Banan's long driveway. The cool air focused his mind while his ears tingled with the call of skylarks from above.

Not far from the house, the road was joined on both sides by trees and grass and dry leaves as far as the eye could see. When he slid into the forest's cover, he noticed a thin path worn in the brush on one side. He eased off the driveway, pushed back the small branches blocking the way, and disappeared.

The winding path led him into the heart of the woods, and eventually vanished altogether. As he drifted farther and farther from the common province of men, he freed himself to enjoy more of the wonders around him. To the treetops overhead he panned, admiring their height and strength, and the full, bright green leaves springing from their branches. A sweet vanilla fragrance floated faintly in the air.

Then a sound up ahead—the rustling of leaves, and crunching,

169

like light, quick footsteps. He locked in place until two red squirrels bounced across the opening just in front of him and scurried up a nearby tree.

"Journey!" he called. "Go get…" And then he caught himself—she wasn't there. A sad, heavy pain filled his heart and helped him realize how much she had meant to him since Sophie went away. "I'll come back for you, Journey," he whispered to himself. "Don't worry."

Pushing aside his sorrow, he continued on, deeper into the woods.

Adrien was no stranger to nature's glories. Through his work as an archaeologist, his eyes had seen virtually every postcard image in the world. From the shimmering oasis at Chebika, to the otherworldly peaks of Cerro Chaltén, to the fantastic colors of the Caño Cristales, no natural wonder had eluded his gaze.

On this occasion, however, in this nameless, inconspicuous wilderness, he saw more than he had ever seen in those spectacular places. Before, nature was simply there, a purposeless expression of time and chance. But today it had a meaning; today it spoke. And its singular report? *I am not random. I have been made for a purpose.*

He saw beyond the vista before him to the beauty of the being who made it all; beyond the complexity of nature's design to the intelligence of its designer; beyond the soul of man to the heart of his Maker.

He found himself praying. It was a strange thing to him, to talk to someone he couldn't see. And at the same time, it was only natural now. He didn't bow his head or close his eyes. He just spoke out into the morning, as if the Maker was walking right beside him.

He gave thanks for the books and for what he'd learned from Banan. For the hope he now felt deep inside and for the absence of the torturous dark hand. He gave thanks for the forest and the squirrels and the tall, strong Sessile oak trees.

Before long, his mind wandered back to Sophie. For the first time since her death, his foremost impulse was not to cry, but to rejoice in her. He chuckled when he remembered her laugh, the way she twirled the same strand of hair over and over, her irrational competitiveness.

And as nature had spoken to him that morning, so did she: *I am not random*, she whispered gently from the recesses of his mind. *I have been made for a purpose.* And what compliments her Maker deserved, for she was indeed a rare and exquisite creation.

"Is she with you?" he spoke out loud. "I hope she is. I *believe* she is."

When he crested a small hill, the fragrance of vanilla, once only faint, now packed the air. Within a few steps, the curve of the land gave way to a sea of lavender-blue flowers, a natural carpet for the picturesque clearing ahead. The soft rays of the sun beamed through the surrounding branches onto a single tree in the center.

Adrien eased his way through the blanket of thin, green stems and sat down at its base. The warm light energized his body and a profound thought crept into his mind. *I am not random either. I have been made for a purpose.*

"But what is my purpose?" he prayed toward the brightness.

For the next hour, he sat quietly and mused the answer to that most important question. And when his mind was satisfied he could not on that day mine the answer, he grudgingly decided it was time to return to Banan's, and the real world outside.

When he walked in the door, Banan was busy cooking breakfast.

"Did you enjoy your walk?" he asked, smiling. "I saw you leave—I couldn't sleep either."

"Yes, it was wonderful."

Banan scooped the eggs onto Adrien's plate. "Eat up. We've got to get ready."

"Ready? For what?" asked Adrien, picking up his fork.

"For Paris."

"Paris? Isn't that where the bad guys are?"

"Yes, but that's where the good guys are too."

"Oh, yeah? And who might that be?"

Banan turned from the stove and walked to the table. "The ones I mentioned yesterday morning," he said, setting his plate down. "Adrien, have you ever heard of the Resistance?"

Chapter 37

Paris, France
Friday, April 8
3:09 PM

Once again, Addy found herself in a Council meeting. This time, however, she knew she wasn't there to offer advice. As before, Rad sat next to her at the long conference table, but unlike the last time, Trip and Tony now joined in, hunkered quietly at the other end.

Rene started off. "Everyone, thanks for joining us on such short notice. Why don't we talk about the attack first and then we can discuss the situation with Walter. Rad, give the Council an overview of what happened yesterday."

"Yeah, no problem," Rad said. "Basically they threw everything they had at us. Viruses, Trojans, file corruption, file obliteration—they tried to wipe us off the map."

"And did they succeed?" Gerard asked.

"They came close. Let's put it that way. At first it just seemed like a hack job. You know, trying to get in and nose around our system for a while. But then they tried to upload a file—I wasn't sure what it was until later. We thought we'd stopped them and then they dropped the bomb on us—boom!" Rad made a mock explosion with his hands. "That file I wasn't sure about turned out

173

to be a Trojan they'd planted in our system that would let them remotely launch a mac-daddy of a virus on us. Once they hatched it, we were toast."

"So what's left?" asked Leroux.

Rad turned his head to the other end of the table. "Our internal systems are pretty much intact. Remi got the firewall back up this morning, and we're running a complete system inventory now to see what else has been compromised or destroyed. It's early yet, but looks like most of our cyberwar systems have been wiped out. Hitting back will be all but impossible for a while. But I'll know more in a couple of hours."

"And I understand they copied some of our confidential files?" Eduard inquired from in front of Rad.

"Yeah, looks that way. Best I can tell at this point, they now know *everything* we know about them," Rad replied.

Eduard threw his pen on the table and exhaled loudly.

Rollan complained, "I can't believe this."

"Let's not lose our heads, gentlemen," Rene said evenly and then looked at Rad. "Well, the most important thing is to get our defenses back up, then identify the full scope of the damage and make the needed repairs."

Everyone at the table nodded.

Leroux asked, "Rad, exactly how vulnerable are we now?"

Rad glanced at Addy and replied, "Given the ease at which they breached our system when it was at 100%, very. If they try again anytime soon—and if they're smart, they will—it'd be lights out for us."

"Can we keep critical systems off the network for a while until our defenses are back up?" asked Addy.

"Yeah, sure. But being blind is almost as bad as being out in the open."

"Very well," concluded Rene. "Get back to it and give us an update as soon as you can."

"Will do."

"Now, I guess we need to talk about Walter," Rene said.

It only took a second for Leroux to say, "What in the world were you thinking, Rene?"

Rene started to reply when Gerard interrupted. "Kidnapping? And murder!"

"You've violated everything we stand for!" Rollan called out loudly. "You've got to stop listening to your hothead daughter," he continued, pointing at Addy, "and exercise a little wisdom!"

"Hothead?!" Addy fired back. "At least we *did* something instead of sitting around and *talking* about it all day!"

"Watch your tone, young lady," Leroux warned.

"Now wait a minute, everybody," Rene said. "Let's just calm down here. We didn't murder anybody; we only wanted to talk to him. Addy tried to turn him, but he wouldn't go for it." He leaned back in his chair and spoke softly. "We're running out of time, brothers, as last night's attack so clearly demonstrates. We felt more aggressive action was necessary."

"But at the cost of the man's life, Rene?" asked Gerard.

"Yes, a tragedy I deeply regret. And we have asked for forgiveness for this, all of us." He pivoted to Addy, Trip, and Tony. "We were rash and we were foolish, and we ask for your forgiveness as well."

The room was silent for a while. At last, Leroux glanced around at his fellow Council members and said, "We forgive you, Rene, all of you. We've acted foolishly in the past ourselves, and have learned the value of forgiveness the hard way."

"So where does this leave us?" asked Rollan.

"Not to change the subject," Eduard cut in, "but let's not forget they came after the Rue de Nullepart facility as well. We got them out just in time. They hit only an hour after our people slipped out through the tunnels."

"Indeed," Gerard agreed. "Let's be thankful we made that decision. We saved forty lives with that move."

"Yes, that was a close one," added Rene.

"So where does that leave us?" Rollan asked again. "At our last meeting we talked about hitting them back from the inside. Obviously, that's not going to happen now."

"I'm not sure if hitting them is the best course of action at this point," Leroux said.

Gerard concurred, "I'm not so sure myself."

"But if we did," Eduard pressed, "how would we do it now?"

"We still might be able to do it from the inside," Addy informed them. "Rad and I talked about it this morning. Yes, Walter is dead, but we still have his security medallion and we think we can hack his bio-ID implant, the chip the building sensors use to identify him. We can load that data onto another chip in one of us."

"You're saying sneak in and *pretend* to be Walter?" Eduard asked.

"That's it exactly," Rad quickly confirmed. "Look, from what Addy's saying, the guy's pretty much ignored by everyone in his office, and there are only maybe ten people in his entire department at any one time."

"Plus," noted Addy, "I've seen into his office area through the hallway door. It's a pretty dark environment. If we can get somebody who looks like him, they probably won't even notice."

Rollan objected. "Yeah, but still, whoever pretended to be Walter would really have to *look* like Walter. I mean, *a lot* like Walter. If just one person discovered he wasn't the real Walter—a janitor, cafeteria worker, somebody from another office—the whole mission would be over. And they'd kill his imposter."

"He's right, Addy," Rad agreed. "It would pretty much have to be a clone for this to work."

Addy reached down into the bag by her chair and pulled out a holopad. "I scanned Walter's ID. Rad helped me alter the image to remove the beard. Here's what he looks like without it." She plugged the pad into the conference room holodisplay and transferred the image to the larger screen.

"Well, who do we have who might look like him?" she asked.

They all stared at the man's face, but no one mentioned any possibilities.

After another long, uneasy silence, Eduard spoke up. "Addy, you're going to think I'm just trying to be difficult, but I don't think we've got anybody in any of our groups who looks like that guy."

"I think he's right, Addy," said Leroux.

Addy looked around the room. Everybody was shaking their heads no. "Then we have to find the closest we've got and send him," she said, "or I'll just go myself and try to sneak in. We don't have any choice. We've got to do something!"

"I don't know, Addy," Gerard muttered, reflecting the growing skepticism in the room.

After a few moments, Rene said, "She's right, gentlemen." He stood and walked toward the large, open window at the back of the conference room. When he turned back, he said, "Brothers, our enemy is now awake. And if he hits us again, we will not survive. So it's time to decide who we really are.

"Are we the kind of people who can only go halfway, the kind who run and hide when the battle goes against us?" He turned and stared out the window for a few more seconds. "Or, are we the kind who fight until the end, the kind who find a way to prevail?

"No, this plan is not perfect. And, yes, it is risky. But it's all we have, unless, of course, you have something better."

No one said a word.

"The Maker has brought us to this place. We've tried everything else; this is all we've got left. And by his design, it requires the exercise of our faith. We must do whatever we can to make it successful, and then leave the rest to him."

One at a time, Rene's gaze found each of them. Finally, he asked them all, "So, what will it be?"

For the longest time no one looked up or even traded a glance. Aware of this particular moment's uniqueness and significance, they all looked away, or stared down at the table, or simply closed their eyes. Each was searching inside, deciding for themselves if they had the courage—and the faith—to step out into the dangerous chasm now before them.

Eduard was the first to speak. "Let's nail them," he said softly.

"I agree," said Gerard. "We'll never know if we shrink back now."

"Faith, my friends. Faith," Rollan encouraged from his chair.

Leroux was the last to voice his feelings. "Yes, there are more with us than there are with them! Are there not?"

Addy, Trip, Tony, and Rad looked back and forth at each other with grins on their faces. An intangible but overwhelming energy filled the room as every heart swelled with confidence and hope.

"Very well," Rene said, tears filling his eyes. "Let's take it to them!"

And then they all stood and embraced—and cried—certain that victory would be theirs at last, though each knew it would take no small miracle to secure it.

Chapter 38

Let us start with the good news**, Mr. Helmut," Damien said from his seat in the GSS main conference room. "It appears you fared better than our other teams."

"Certainly, Director," Helmut replied. "Overall our efforts were very successful. We now have all G-CoN intelligence files held by the Resistance, and they hold fabrications. Furthermore, their cyberwar systems have been completely destroyed."

"And the Kopfen?" asked Damien.

"We believe the Kopfen caused irreparable damages to their internal communications and networking capabilities," Helmut explained. "Electronically, they are on their knees."

"You said you *believe*. Do you mean you do not know?"

"Ah...yes...we...know, Director," he said.

"And you, Mr. Othman? Do we have any theories about what happened at Rue de Nullepart?" Damien asked.

"We're not sure how they got out, or how they knew we were coming. We had surveillance there around the clock. They all went in that morning like usual, but when we hit the place, they were gone. And there isn't the first clue as to where they went."

179

"I see," said Damien.

"But I don't believe it was their headquarters, Director, as we were led to believe," Othman continued. "It was simply too small. They only used about half the space on that floor, and their datacenter was the size of a large closet. You can't run an operation like theirs from a place like that. The real headquarters is still out there."

Damien turned to his assistant Broderick, who was taking notes on his holopad.

"Mr. Fuller, Mr. Seger played me for a fool. It's time he learned to respect his elders. Have Mr. Richter put him back in his favorite chair."

"Yes, Director," Broderick replied.

"Mr. Othman, prepare plans for a final attack on the Resistance headquarters," Damien instructed. "Use what you learned from the Nullepart facility to postulate the most likely facility types and security measures they will have in place. I'll get the location from Mr. Seger soon, and I want you ready to strike within twenty-four hours. Do you understand?"

"Absolutely, Director."

"And the Western Column site?" Damien asked.

"The site has been completely neutralized and an inventory of documents, personnel, and artifacts has been taken. We're going through the tech station data as we speak. Although no books were found, the case in which they were buried has been located."

"And Site Leader Bach, has he been found yet?"

"No, I'm afraid not, Director," Othman replied. "One can only assume he was able to escape somehow. There is no record of him leaving on any personnel transport, but according to the logistics manifest, a supply transport left late Wednesday afternoon. It's possible he was on that plane."

"Where did they land?"

"Paris. I've dispatched two agents to interview the pilots. I hope to know more soon," explained Othman. "However, I received word just before our meeting that during a search of Bach's living quarters, it was discovered that he spoke to a Mr. Banan O'Shea a few minutes before the transport departed."

Damien looked surprised. "I haven't heard that name in many years," he mumbled to himself.

"You know him, Director?" asked Othman.

"Quite possibly," he answered. "An adversary from a different time, Mr. Othman. Where is Mr. O'Shea now?"

"A village not far from London."

"Dispatch a team there right away. Kill them both on sight," he ordered. "I want to be rid of these traitors for good."

"I'll send them right away," Othman answered. "And, Director, there's one more thing?"

"Yes."

"There is one survivor."

"Survivor? From the site? I thought my orders were clear."

"You were clear, Director. But I think you know him."

"Well, who is he?"

"He says he's your nephew."

Chapter 39

Luciana took the stand in the front corner of the raised VIP platform. The Italian beauty's long, full brown hair, tight, one-piece dress, and knee-high black boots captured the full attention of the six men sitting before her.

"Gentlemen," she called out to her regally adorned guests, "welcome to the Nest. On behalf of the Sovereign himself, I would like to thank you for joining us for this display of one of the Global Government's greatest achievements—the weekly Globalcast." As her greeting ended, she lifted her long arm and turned toward the large, open room behind her.

"What you see before you are the technical and human assets necessary to deliver the weekly information broadcast to the entire global community."

As they gazed out into the busy room, they saw, just below and in front of them, the Conductor's station elevated five feet above the main floor. Below the Conductor were three rows of tech stations, seven stations in each row, separated by a thin aisle and metal rail. Every seat was filled. And center stage before them all, a giant holodisplay covered the massive front window that was the Nest's outer wall.

"As you know," she continued, "each member of the global community is required to view the Globalcast live wherever they are in the world, and personally review the information files downloaded to the holodisplay station in their family unit. The Globalcast and its corresponding database are the only sources of information for the global population."

She stepped down from the stand and walked along the front of the platform. When she reached the opposite corner, she pivoted on one heel and resumed her memorized speech.

"When it comes to maintaining and expanding the Global Government's power, the importance of the Globalcast cannot be overemphasized. Through centuries of human experience, we have learned that the key to controlling a population does not simply lie in brute force, as important as that is. The lowest-cost and most efficient way to master the masses is to control the *information they receive*—what they are allowed to know about the world around them, what they are allowed to know about their government, and what they are allowed to believe. By doing this, we can master *their minds*."

She paused for effect.

"Given this truth, the Globalcast is the most effective, ongoing, human control instrument in the history of mankind. And when combined with the power of the GSS and complete control of the global educational infrastructure, the boundaries of the power it can produce cannot be measured or imagined."

The six high-level G-CoN ministers all nodded in agreement.

"In just a moment, you will see Conductor Naggai start the five minute countdown, and you will watch as he orchestrates the individual elements of the Globalcast: the video address, the information file dissemination, and the citizen response directives."

She returned to her seat and concluded, "Enjoy the show, gentlemen. And every time you experience the spoils of your power, do not forget the day you saw how that power is maintained. And, more importantly, do not forget the loyalty you owe to the one who provides this power for you. Do not forget the debt you owe to our Global Sovereign."

Chapter 40

There's only one possibility," Cassy hysterically informed her grandmother. "They've got him—they've got Jack!"

"Oh, no!" Grandma called out through the handkerchief covering her mouth. "I just knew this was going to happen. Why did he have to fight them? Why couldn't he just keep quiet?"

"We've got to find him!" Cassy demanded. "It's only been two days. Maybe he's…maybe he's just being held in one of the security stations until someone claims him." But she quickly corrected herself when the appalling reality settled upon her. "No, that…that never happens," she whispered. "We might as well just face it—we'll never see him again."

"Don't talk like that, Cassy," Grandma said. "Are you sure he's not just out with his friends somewhere?"

"No. No. I already talked to his best friend Mark. He said they haven't seen him. Apparently he was supposed to come by Wednesday night after work, but never made it. And then Aiden from the hospital said he saw some guys in black uniforms come up to him when he walked out of the building Wednesday night.

"What do we do, Grandma? What do we do?" she asked, blinking

185

back tears.

Through the awful understanding of her grandson's fate, a peace poked through and descended upon Grandma. Finally her calm answer came. "I don't know, my dear. I'm not sure there's anything we can do for him now. But we've got to be strong for your mother."

Grandma stood and walked over to the bed where Abbey's frail, atrophied body lay motionless. She pulled the blanket up snugly beneath her chin and checked the readings on her antiquated monitor. The light sound of pings echoed with each flutter of Abbey's weak heart.

"She can't take this kind of stress around her," Grandma warned quietly. "She can still sense it; it affects her. And we can't have that now, not so close to the end."

"I know. I know, Grandma," Cassy acknowledged as she walked up to the bed, put her arms around her grandmother's waist, and rested her head on her bony shoulder.

"It's okay, my dear," the old woman encouraged her. "Tomorrow is a new day. Tonight will soon be over."

Suddenly alarms rang out from the patient monitor. The steady pings became a single, long, shrill pitch.

"What's happening?!" Cassy screamed, terror in her eyes.

Grandma hurriedly pushed buttons and turned dials, but nothing changed. Then she looked at Abbey and knew what to do next.

Slowly, she reached around to the side of the monitor and pressed a small black button. The disturbing tone stopped; the flashing lights went dark.

"She's gone," she said to her granddaughter. "My Abbey's gone now." While plump, round tears carved valleys in her cheeks,

Grandma reached down and rubbed her only daughter's lifeless face. "Ah, my sweet girl. Rest well. Your pain has finally come to an end."

As they stood beside the bed and cried, the holodisplay lit up behind them, and the feminine voice spoke once again, "Welcome to your G-CoN Globalcast." After the sensor performed its sweep, the lifeless voice returned, "Thank you for joining the Globalcast Sadie and Cassandra."

And for the first time in fifty-one years, it did not mention the name of Abigail Livingston, a fact not lost on Grandma, who wailed out loudly at the terrible realization.

Chapter 41

Banan and Adrien stood on the front porch of a small villa on the outskirts of Paris. Through the door they heard the intelligence module announce their presence. A split second later, the outer door slid open revealing a small anteroom just before a second entrance.

They stepped in and waited, and, after the alcove was secured behind them, Rene activated the door and welcomed his visitors.

"Banan," Rene said, his brown eyes gleaming with joy.

"Rene, my dear friend," Banan replied as they embraced.

"Come in, please. And I suppose this is Adrien?"

"Yes, Adrien Bach," Banan answered, and turned to Adrien and said, "Adrien, this is Rene Moreau, an old friend of mine."

"Nice to meet you, Rene," Adrien said. "Banan has told me many wonderful things about you."

When Rene reached out for the young man's hand, his expression stiffened as if he'd just seen a ghost. He recovered quickly to his former smile and joked, "Well, he'd better. If he shares any of my secrets, I'll share his."

They all laughed.

"Please, sit down," offered Rene. Banan and Adrien sat down in the living room, Adrien on the small couch in the middle of the room and Banan one of two armchairs opposite the couch.

"May I offer you something to drink? A synthetic perhaps?" Rene asked.

"Yes, if you don't mind," replied Adrien.

"Why not make it two, Rene," said Banan.

Rene stepped into the kitchen and returned with a serving tray and three steaming cups. After supplying his guests, he took his portion and sat down in the chair beside Banan.

Adrien took his first sip just as Addy eased down the stairs and walked into the room. Their eyes met immediately. Adrien lost himself for a moment, spilling synthetic on his chin; Addy paused with an expression much like Rene's from a moment earlier, and then blushed slightly before continuing into the room.

"Gentlemen, I've asked my daughter, Addy, to join us this morning. I told her about your visit, Banan, and about your interesting guest, and she was curious," Rene explained. "Addy, this is Mr. Banan O'Shea, a friend of mine, and Mr. Adrien Bach."

"Hello, Banan," she said, shaking his hand. "And Adrien, good to meet you."

Adrien stood and gently took her hand. "It is a pleasure to meet you, Addy," he said softly.

She smiled and took the only seat left in the room—the one beside Adrien on the couch.

For the next few moments, Banan and Rene made small talk about the good old days. But their voices faded into the background for Adrien. Only Addy existed. He fought it, but her presence had seized him. Her smell. Her skin. Her hair. The touch of her fingers. While the old men continued, he was certain he saw her glance his way and then back again, but she didn't say a word. And neither could he. He was frozen in place, praying with all his might his synthetic would not run dry.

"Well, Adrien," Rene said at last. "I understand you're an archaeologist."

It took a second for Rene's words to register. "Yes, yes, I am. I work, or *worked*, for the GSO as an archaeologist for a number of years." He felt Addy looking at him, but resisted looking back.

"Banan also tells me you made a discovery recently, something important."

"Yes, I did, Mr. Moreau."

"Please, call me Rene."

"Sure. How much did Banan tell you, Rene?"

"Not that much, really. He just said I'd want to hear your story, that it would be very important to us."

During the next half hour Adrien told them about the dig in the desert and the strange way the materials they found had decomposed into almost nothing. He recounted the discovery of the safe buried deep in the ground, and the books it contained about the Maker as well as the cryptic note from 150 years ago. And, lastly, he explained how he'd come to believe what was written in the books was actually true, and how that new faith had given him a fresh sense of hope.

Rene and Addy listened in stunned silence. Every so often, at pivotal points in his story, their eyes met as if to say, "Can you believe this?"

"Do you have those documents with you, Adrien?" Rene asked.

"In fact, I do," he replied, reaching into his bag. "This one is called, *The Writings of the Maker*, and this one, *Evidence for the Maker*. Together they contain a large body of sacred writings and a defense of the teachings contained in them."

Rene delicately flipped through the pages while Addy eased off the couch to peek over his shoulder. "Have you read them?" he asked Adrien. "All of them?"

"Yes, I've read them all, some parts more than once," he answered. "So, Banan said you're part of the Resistance, and you believe in the Maker and fight the G-CoN?"

"That's right."

"But, if you don't mind me asking, why fight the G-CoN? I was always taught the G-CoN was a force for good in the world. Now Banan tells me they committed genocide 150 years ago. What do you know about that?"

"Worthy questions, Adrien," Rene said, standing from his chair. "Why don't you follow me downstairs? I've got something I'd like to show you."

Adrien stood and accompanied Rene and Addy into an oversized pantry just off the kitchen. Rene reached behind a box marked "Olives" and pressed a small, silver button. The back wall of the pantry slid sideways revealing a roomy elevator.

Once inside, they descended into a space about the size of the sitting room upstairs, but this one was filled with tech stations and holoscreens.

"Addy," Rene said with a slight nod.

Without answering, she took position at one of the stations and pressed several keys.

"Have a seat," Rene said to Adrien and Banan. Then he leaned back against a table and started to explain. "You ask what we know about the genocide carried out by the G-CoN. Why don't I just show you, and, in the process, tell you about the greatest crime mankind has ever perpetrated."

Rene began his explanation with these words: "There was once a great nation called the *United States of America.*"

Chapter 42

This nation, also referred to as simply America, occupied most of the land you and I know as the upper Western Column. During the second and third centuries after Darwin, it was the most powerful nation on earth, with great cities, vast farmlands, and fantastic wealth." While Rene talked, Addy put up corresponding images and video on the large holodisplay on the back wall.

"These are images we've found over the years." Rene pointed to the display. "Millions of its people believed in the Maker. And for this reason, among others, the rest of the world hated them. But, as time went by, America's power faded while her enemies grew stronger. Eventually, in spite of the Maker's influence, her greed, arrogance, and corruption led to her military and economic collapse. In only a few generations, she went from the world's only superpower to nearly a third world country.

"As much as they wanted to, however, America's enemies were not able to act on their hatred until the formation of the Global Government, the G-CoN. The G-CoN was the brainchild of a group of nations known as the *European Union,* now located in the upper Central Column." A map of the world appeared on the display.

"They, along with other powers spread across the globe, like China, Russia, Saudi Arabia, and Iran, used the political framework of an organization called the *United Nations* to centralize power and eventually form what you and I know as the G-CoN.

"Though America sustained the United Nations during its early years, and at one time or another supplied economic and military aid to many of the countries I just mentioned, these powers refused America a place in the new government.

"Over time, the G-CoN gained control of global military forces and all global communications: satellite, radio, electronic, print, and the Global-net, what used to be called the *Internet*. And that's when the true depth of their evil was manifested.

"The Global Defense Force, the precursor to the GSS, had developed a weapon that could destroy human and animal life, but leave structures, equipment, and plant life intact. So they put a plan in motion to annihilate every man, woman, and child in America on a single day: March 31, 2182."

"But something went wrong," Addy said from her chair. "The original weapon, called a *neutron bomb*, was developed several hundred years ago, ironically enough, by the Americans. Basically, it was a nuclear weapon, similar to the ones we have today, but modified to kill through the release of high levels of neutron radiation instead of a massive heat and blast wave. So it didn't destroy all the infrastructure of the enemy, just its people and animals.

"It was abandoned back then because it had a relatively low effective radius and was expensive to maintain—the tritium core had to be replaced in each device every ten years or so."

"Not long after its establishment, however," Rene said, "the G-CoN launched a massive project to revive the neutron concept and perfect it, increase its kill area and extend its shelf life. The project was a monstrous success. The new weapon could spread lethal doses of radiation up to 200 miles from the detonation point and the core only needed to be replaced every fifty years. They called it *Heaven's Dagger* because it was, at least in theory, the perfect weapon—it killed the enemy, but preserved his treasure.

"But their new design was much more effective than they had anticipated," Addy continued. "Instead of destroying buildings and infrastructure just around the immediate blast area—a characteristic of the old bomb they thought they'd maintained in the new design—the radiation generated from these devices was so high that most structures within 100 miles of the blast became brittle and structurally unstable. Concrete, wood, and metal literally started falling apart.

"Within a few weeks of the G-CoN takeover of America, buildings, highways, and equipment began collapsing under their own weight. Here are some classified G-CoN photos we took from their main datacenter." A series of before-and-after images of ancient cities dropped onto the screen. A title appeared on each image: New York, Chicago, Seattle, Omaha.

She turned from the display back to Adrien. "And remember those vast farmlands my father just mentioned? Well, when the country's infrastructure was destroyed, the ability to plant, water, and manage those millions of acres of rich agriculture, already greatly reduced by the nation's financial condition, was devastated." A second set of before and after images came up. These were of vast fields of corn and other crops labeled Nebraska, Idaho, and Indiana.

"Combine this technological and logistics collapse with the natural, cyclic change to warmer temperatures the planet has endured over the last five centuries—not the manmade global warming nonsense the eco-alarmists preach—and you've got the perfect recipe for extensive, prolonged drought, and massive dust storms. The periods of torrential rains and flooding that followed made things even worse. When all was said and done, the G-CoN spawned one of the largest ecological calamities in world history.

"By the end of the first year after the attack, almost nothing was left. Office buildings became piles of rubble; fields of corn became barren deserts," Addy concluded.

"One other thing you need to know, Adrien," Rene said. "Heaven's Dagger didn't kill everybody instantly; those on the outskirts of the blast didn't die right away. Yes, their radiation exposure was lethal, but for tens of millions of people it took several days, in some cases weeks, to die. The G-CoN cut off all communication, sealed the borders, and watched as women and children died of radiation poisoning. No help. No medicine. No mercy."

Video of masses of people attacking border checkpoints played on the display, along with still images of children covered with sores and swollen limbs, crying in terrible agony.

"It's ironic," Banan added, "the G-CoN's plan was actually more successful than they ever could have dreamed. In the end, they not only killed *the people of America,* they obliterated *the entire nation*—people, buildings, land, everything."

"What you dug up at your site," Addy went on, "—all that mysterious decomposed material—was actually the dusty remnants of one of the greatest nations the world has ever seen. You didn't know it at the time, but you just resurrected the bones of the United States of America."

Chapter 43

Adrien's face registered complete shock, as if his entire psyche had just suffered a massive earthquake.

Finally he asked, "But why is there no record of this? How'd they keep it a secret from the whole world?"

"Well remember," answered Rene, "America was virtually a third world country by that time. Their destruction didn't have the political or economic impact it would have had in the past. And the G-CoN controlled *all* the information on the planet. They told the world it was a natural disaster brought on by manmade climate change—remember those eco-alarmists Addy told you about?—and they were none the wiser. How could they find out any differently?

"They even put out fake pictures and video and declared a global day of mourning. They took donations for relief and said they were using—let's see, how did they put it?—'every resource at our disposal to save our American brothers.' But they did nothing. And no private groups were allowed anywhere near the continent.

"Even so, it was complete pandemonium for almost a year. People with relatives there, corporations with factories and workers—they were begging the government for access. But they never gave in; they kept up the lie and weathered the storm. Then, over time, they just erased America from the global databases, and rewrote history without her."

Addy said, "To keep everybody away from the evidence, the G-CoN declared a quarantine of most of the continent and charged the GSS with enforcing it. Nobody's set foot on that land for almost 150 years. Until you guys."

"So, the Gaia Catastrophe of 218 is a lie too?" asked Adrien.

"Yes," Addy confirmed. "That whole story is a fairy tale concocted by the G-CoN as a smoke screen. The Gaia Catastrophe is the name they gave the supposed 'natural disaster' that destroyed America. After a couple of generations, they moved the date back a couple hundred years to really throw people off. Eventually, they want to get the date back to before America was even discovered to make sure no one will ever make the connection."

"But why did they let us go there in the first place if they were trying to cover up this secret?"

"The G-CoN is so big," Banan spoke again. "Somebody in some office in the middle of nowhere probably authorized it and is now dead. You can believe me—there won't be any more digs in America. Ever."

"Where exactly was your dig site?" Rene asked. "Do you remember the coordinates?"

"Yeah, how could I forget them? I wrote them a million times in my project requests. 41° 15' N, 95° 56' W."

"That's it," Rene said to Addy.

He turned back to Adrien. "Earlier this morning we got word from our people inside the GSS that there was an attack carried out on a site in the Western Column two days ago. We didn't get a lot of details, but here's the location of the attack." He nodded at Addy. Another map materialized on the holodisplay, a large map of the Western Column.

The image focused in on a small dot in the middle of the continent and the coordinates 41° 15' N, 95° 56' W traced across the screen.

"Adrien, Thursday morning the GSS attacked your dig site. I'm sorry to have to tell you this, my friend, but your entire team has been murdered."

Adrien sat in stunned silence. His mouth gaped open but not a word escaped. Faces shot through his mind: Pierre, Manuel, Serena. Then he thought of Nate, his best friend in the world—his only friend. All of them, murdered in cold blood. And then Journey. It didn't seem fair, but in some sense his heart ached most of all for her. If she wasn't dead already, she would never survive in that desert alone.

He stood from his chair and walked slowly past Addy toward the other end of the room.

"Adrien," Addy said tenderly, "I'm so sorry."

"This is why we fight them," Rene said. "They look so righteous on the outside, but they're evil!"

"I'm really sorry," added Banan. "But you've got to know your friends are just the latest victims. They've been hunting us for years."

"He's right, Adrien," Rene confirmed. "They oppress the general population, and they hunt us down all over the world. They refuse our families medical treatment; they grab us off the street in the middle of the night. They're holding three of our men now. They usually torture them for information and then kill them. But they always make sure we get the body back."

"So why don't you tell someone about it?" Adrien said, exasperated.

"That's exactly what we've been trying to do all these years, Adrien," replied Addy. "We've been collecting data and searching for a way to get it out to the world, but it's almost impossible with the way they control information."

"The only hope we have is to hack the weekly Globalcast," Rene said.

"You mean the G-CoN information transmission?"

"That's it," Addy replied. "Although we like to call it the 'weekly brainwashing transmission.'"

"So, what's the problem?"

"It's more difficult than it looks," she said. "Both the data and process are tightly controlled."

"Adrien," Banan interrupted, sensing the young man was about to overload, "you've had a lot dumped on you in the last hour. Why don't we take a break for a while? We can continue our discussion later."

"Yes," Rene affirmed. "Come on upstairs and I'll show you both to your room. Banan's right—we can talk more later."

Though his mind was still full of questions, Adrien didn't fight the suggestion. "That sounds good," he said, eventually.

While Banan and Adrien walked toward the elevator, Rene pulled Addy aside. "Did you see who he looks like?"

"I couldn't believe it when I saw him."

"Call an emergency meeting tonight," Rene ordered. "Make sure everybody's there. Tell them we're going to hear from the Maker."

"You mean Adrien's going to talk to them?"

"Exactly."

She looked at him in disbelief.

But before she could voice her doubts, he said, "Don't worry. I'll talk to Banan. He'll do it."

"Okay."

"And, Addy…"

"Yes?"

"Our miracle has started."

199

Chapter 44

This time the auditorium was filled to capacity. Every chair was occupied and people lined the room on all sides. Even the back entrance stretched to overflowing.

As Addy and Gabrielle watched from the front row just down from the Council, a long line of teenagers trickled up from the back and sat on the floor in front of them. In a matter of minutes, there wasn't enough room to squeeze a holopad in the space between them and the platform.

While they waited, the constant buzz in the room was of Adrien and his special books. Though Addy had called the meeting just as her father had instructed—giving away no juicy gossip in the process—somehow word had gotten out about the unassuming archaeologist and the otherworldly items he had discovered.

Like last time, Rene entered wearing his blue tunic. When he took the platform, a rapid hush blew through the crowd.

"My dear friends," he began. "It is a rich gift to be gathered with you on this important occasion. Thank you for coming on such short notice. When you hear from our guest tonight, I'm certain

200

you'll be more than glad you made the effort.

"This morning an old friend of mine, Banan O'Shea, brought a very special man to see me. His name is Adrien Bach, and he has an amazing story. I've asked him to share that story with you tonight. I hope it moves you as much as it has moved me. Everyone, please welcome, Mr. Adrien Bach."

Amid cordial applause, Adrien stepped out into the spotlight and walked deliberately toward the podium, his eyes focused securely on the path before him, the black book held tightly in hand. As he placed it on the podium, the room swelled with anticipation.

Adrien looked up and forced a smile. The first face he saw was Addy's.

"Good evening to you all," he said nervously. "My name is Adrien Bach."

Adrien had spoken from time to time at conventions and office briefings, but only when the necessity was laid upon him. Though he was a good speaker and always received compliments from his peers, he was always thankful when the ordeal was over. Tonight's crowd was the largest he had ever addressed, and Addy's presence only made it worse.

After a brief pause, he continued. "I'm an archaeologist with the GSO. Or, I should say, I was an archaeologist with the GSO. The events of the last ten days have brought that relationship to an end. And for me personally, those ten days have been the most enlightening and, in some sense, frightening of my life. In that brief time, like a pendulum, I have swung from the edge of suicide to the center of a life filled with hope." His voice cracked as he tapped the book and said, "And I owe that change to these books, the books I found when I myself was in a deep, dark hole in the desert."

201

He took a moment to compose himself and pressed on. "By the strangest of circumstances I find myself here with you tonight. And, as I am starting to understand, what appears to me as chaos and randomness is to the one above all according to plan.

"It seems the one I have found in these books is the one you've been searching for all these years. The one you have only known in part is set forth with clarity on these pages. So then, let me tell you about him. His name, as you know, is the Maker, and this is his story."

So Adrien told them all the books had revealed. He shared how the Maker created everything at the beginning of time, including man. He told them about the group he chose to reveal himself to thousands of years before, and that he had instructed them to record his words and acts so that future generations could know him.

He recounted how the Maker had walked the earth long ago to bring peace between himself and mankind. And he detailed the love and justice of the Maker, the problem that separates humanity from him, and the solution to that separation the Maker himself has provided. Finally, he did not forget to proclaim the Maker's great promise of vita eternus, life that is eternal.

They were rapt. They shed tears. They tasted guilt. They felt love and forgiveness.

And that very night, when Adrien's words had ended, they all—the Council, and Rene, and Addy, every one of the 263 souls gathered in that auditorium—got down on their knees, mourned their failures, and put their trust in the Maker.

And Adrien Bach could not believe his eyes.

Act 3

Chapter 45

After the hugs, kisses, and tears had ended, the gathering broke up for the evening. While Adrien answered questions and talked with a crowd of curious spectators near the podium, Rene collected Addy and the Council and led them into the hallway.

When they had formed a huddle away from the exiting masses, Rene asked the men, "So what do you think, brothers?"

Leroux said, "I've never seen anything like it."

"I'm still in shock," replied Gerard.

"Me too," said Eduard.

"Did you notice the resemblance?" Rene asked. "Did you see how much he looked like Walter?"

They all nodded.

Then Leroux spoke. "It was just like you said, Rene; the resemblance is truly uncanny. I know I doubted you in the past—I just didn't have the faith to believe you were right. Please forgive me."

"All of us," Gerard added.

"You're forgiven, my dear brothers," their leader replied.

"Have you said anything to him about joining us?" asked Eduard.

"Not yet," responded Rene. "There just hasn't been any time, and

I wanted you all to see him first."

"Why don't we go talk to him now?" asked Leroux.

"I really don't think now is a good time," Rene answered. "We need more of a private setting."

"How about tomorrow night?" suggested Addy. "Doesn't the Council have a meal on the second Sunday of Anticipation? Maybe you could have it at our house instead of here?"

"That's a great idea," said Gerard. "Let's do it."

"Okay," replied Rene. "It's settled then. I'll ask him to join us there. See you all tomorrow night."

Chapter 46

As Seger's swollen, bloody face fell to his chest, the flashing yellow light caught Damien's attention once again. Scowling, he walked briskly to the exit at the back of the room.

His young assistant spoke up as soon as Damien pushed through the darkness into the observation room. Broderick chose facts over apologies.

"It's your son, Director. He says it's urgent."

Damien grabbed a towel from a medical station just outside the door and wiped his hands.

"Very well," he said to Broderick. And then to Mr. Richter, "You know what to do, and you know what I want."

"Yes, Director," he responded.

A few seconds later, Damien sat down in his office chair and commanded, "Viewer on." Tobias' red face and puffy eyes appeared on the screen.

"Son, what is it?" Damien asked calmly.

"It's Priscilla."

The very mention of her name filled every pore of Damien's body with anxiety. "And?" he asked.

"We got the tests back early," said Tobias. "They just came in over the Global-net. They've given her three months. I thought you'd like to know."

The hysteria shot like electricity through Damien's cold skin.

"I'm very sorry, son," he said placidly.

"Just thought you'd like to know," Tobias said again. "I've got to run." And the screen went blank.

As the image disappeared, a small tear cascaded down Damien's cheek, and a heavy groan rushed from his soul. "Close door," he spoke to the building intelligence system. "Darken windows."

Alone in his office, he sat in unhinged silence, a bystander in his own internal war between love for his dear Prissy and the single driving principle of his life—survival of the fittest.

Just then, a message popped up on the holoscreen: "Call from Dolf Richter." Damien rotated himself and looked toward the window, placing his back to the holoscreen.

"Allow call."

"Director, I thought you'd want to know," the man in the black uniform said.

"Know what?"

"The prisoner—he broke. We've got the address."

Damien swiveled quickly in his chair and looked into the holoscreen, his sadness forced aside by his bloodlust. "Very well, Mr. Richter. Send it over. Now."

"Yes...and Director..."

"What is it?"

"The prisoner is dead, sir."

"Rejoice, Mr. Richter. Our gene pool has been purified."

"Very well, sir."

Damien ended the transmission and dialed Othman.

"Yes, Director," he answered.

"Your target is 1281 Rue de Salut," Damien said, reading from the screen.

"But...that's only a few blocks from the G-CoN campus!"

"I know very well where it is, Mr. Othman," Damien replied. "I want your brief by eight tomorrow morning and the attack within twenty-four hours. I want them all dead by the Tuesday morning synthetic break! And to be sure they don't slip away this time, you will lead the attack personally."

"As you wish. There as good as dead," he answered.

"One more thing, Director," Othman continued. "Our men raided O'Shea's home near London. There was no one there. Bach is still on the loose; we're not sure where."

"If my guess is right on this, when you're cleaning up at Salut, you'll find them among the dead."

"Yes, sir."

"But, Mauritz..."

"Yes, Director."

"If you do find them there alive, make sure they know I sent you before you kill them."

Othman smiled. "My pleasure, Director. My pleasure, indeed."

Chapter 47

As dinner wound to a close, Rene lifted his wine glass and stood to address his guests. Around the large, oak dining room table sat the Council, Addy, Banan, and Adrien.

"Thank you all for helping us celebrate this festival tonight," Rene said. "And a special welcome to my old friend Banan, and to you, Adrien, not only for your company, but also for the hope you have brought us through your words."

Adrien smiled and nodded uncomfortably. And then Rene went on.

"So, let us raise a toast to the goodness of the Maker, and to his great acts we *anticipate* on our behalf."

"Here, here," they all said cheerily, lifting their glasses high.

After they got up from the table, Adrien caught Addy's eye and made his way to her side of the table.

"Addy," he said, "I was wondering if I could see some of those files on America again sometime, the ones you and Rene showed me yesterday."

"Sure, anytime," she answered. "Would you like to take a look now? The old guys will never miss us."

210

"That'd be great," he said. Like children sneaking away to the playroom, they eased out of the small dining room and took the elevator downstairs.

Addy sat down at the same station she had the day before. "Here you go," she said, pulling up another high-backed, black chair beside her. "You should be able to see everything from here."

While she accessed the files, Adrien asked, "How long have you known about this? I mean, the whole G-CoN conspiracy thing?"

"My father first explained it to me when I was five."

"Wow," he said. "So you've been in this a long time, huh?"

"Yeah, I guess I have. My whole life, really."

"Does it get old?" he asked.

She looked at him and took a second to answer. "Sometimes. Especially lately. I don't know. I guess I'm starting to want some other things for my life. It's complicated."

"I understand," he said. "So, is your boyfriend out of town or something?"

Addy laughed. "My boyfriend? You remember what I said about those 'other' things?"

"Oh," he said and grinned.

"Yeah, well, it's hard to have much of a social life when you're fighting a war. How about you? Is that a wedding ring on your finger?"

"Well, I still wear it, but I'm not married anymore."

"What happened? She get tired of you dragging dirt in the house from those holes you dig in the ground?"

They both laughed.

"Not exactly," he said, his countenance falling. "She passed away two years ago. Her name was Sophie."

"I'm so sorry, Adrien. I didn't know."

Twisting the gold band on his finger, he replied, "It's okay."

"She was special to you, wasn't she?" she asked, delicately.

It seemed like forever before Adrien looked up from his hand and said, "Yes, she was. Very special."

Just then the elevator door opened.

"Sounds like we've got company," she told him.

"Maybe we could talk again sometime," Adrien suggested.

"I'd like that," she replied. "I'd really like that."

Chapter 48

Paris, France
Sunday, April 10
7:47 PM

Rene, Banan, and the rest of the Council turned the corner into the basement ops room just as Adrien and Addy's long stare came to an end.

"We thought you guys might have sneaked down here," said Rene.

"Yeah, I wanted to get a look at those files you showed me yesterday. Addy was helping me pull them up," Adrien said. "Is everything okay?"

"Yes, everything's fine, Adrien," Rene replied while the other men gathered around. "We were hoping to talk with you about something though."

"Sure," he said, uncertainly.

Rene paused, searching for the right words, and said, "Well, Adrien, I really don't know how to ease into this, so I'll just come right out with it. For years we've sensed the Maker would send someone to help us in our fight against the G-CoN, someone who could really turn the tide. Lately, as times have gotten worse for us, we've sensed it even stronger. After talking with you yesterday morning and hearing you last night, we all agree that you're the one we've been waiting for—the one sent to us."

Adrien was stupefied. His lips started to mouth a response, but his mind didn't send the words. "Rene," he said at long last, "you can't be serious. I don't know the first thing about fighting the G-CoN. I couldn't possibly be the one—you must be mistaken."

"We know how this must sound, Adrien," Leroux commented from behind Adrien's chair. "We can hardly believe it ourselves. But it's more than just a feeling. There's evidence that can't be overlooked."

"Like my father told you," Addy said, picking up where Leroux left off, "we're reaching the end game with the G-CoN. We've got to hit them soon or we'll all be dead. Friday, the night before you came, we met to plan our last attack. Our only shot—and it's a long shot to be sure—is to get inside GIS and plant our files directly into the Globalcast system.

"To make a long story short, the only way we can do that is if we can find a man who looks like this." She turned, tapped a button, and a picture of a clean shaven Walter Waite appeared on the screen. "He's got access to the part of GIS we need."

Adrien immediately recognized the similarities between himself and the stranger on the screen, but didn't comment. Instead, he asked, "Why can't you just use him then?"

"Because he's dead," said Eduard from beside Rene.

"He died Thursday night," explained Addy. "We've checked with everyone we know. Nobody in the Resistance looks anything like this guy."

"At our meeting, we prayed for a miracle, Adrien," said Rene. "Then you walked in my door on Saturday morning, and you look just like him! There's only one explanation for that."

"But there's got to be another way. I'm just an archaeologist"—

214

his voice faded—"and barely that."

"We wish there was another way," admitted Rene. "But we're out of time. It's this or nothing at all."

"So I'm supposed to waltz into GIS and pretend I'm somebody I'm not and access some sophisticated system that I don't know how to use and load some special files I've never even seen? Guys, I'm just a scientist. I'm not a GSS operative."

"The Maker needs you," Addy pleaded. "*We* need you."

Adrien turned to Addy. Having her look at him that way was intoxicating, but his doubts overwhelmed him. "I'm sorry, guys. I really am. But you've got the wrong guy. I'm no soldier, and I'm no spy. I've brought you the books. I've done all I can do."

Then he stood, slipped between Rene and Eduard, and left the room.

A few minutes later, Banan stepped out onto the back porch with a holopad in his hand. Adrien was sitting in a corner chair, staring up at the stars.

"Sorry about that, Adrien," he said. "We didn't mean to…"

Adrien interrupted, "It's okay, Banan. I know these are desperate times for you, and I want to help. It's just…"

"I know," he said. "I realize you must feel like this isn't your fight, that you're a bystander being pushed into someone else's war."

Adrien just shrugged.

"You may be surprised to know this, but you've actually been in this thing a lot longer than you think. For more than twenty years, in fact." He handed Adrien the holopad. "I'm sorry, Adrien. I just didn't have the courage to tell you before." Banan didn't explain further; he simply turned and walked back inside.

Adrien looked down to see an image of his father on the screen along with the words "Traugott Bach: Communication File." The file contained documents related to Traugott's meetings with the Resistance during the summer of 502, the same year he was killed.

His father had met Rene while working as a government liaison stationed in Paris. Rene sought him out when he got word Traugott was secretly researching G-CoN oppression in the Western Column territories. A week after their second meeting, Traugott was found dead. Adrien was told it was an accident, but the file said it was murder. According to the documents in the file, Traugott Bach was killed because he was about to discover the truth about the Global Government.

Adrien flipped from screen to screen reading every detail of his father's interaction with the Resistance and the details about his murder. On the bottom right of the last page an icon appeared entitled, "Confirmed Assassin." Adrien paused and pulled in a deep breath. Then he tapped the link and a picture and name popped onto the screen.

The image was of a young GSS operative. His name: Damien Addergoole.

Chapter 49

Vice Sovereign Pulgate waited anxiously while his holoscreen blinked, "Connecting to Global Sovereign." When the blue screen and text disappeared, a busy image rolled across the screen.

Seated in his chair with his back to the screen, the Sovereign's wavy black hair fell just over the gold laced collar of his royal robe. Two voluptuous women, dressed in shiny, tight red dresses slipped off the screen to each side. Rurik's eyes were drawn immediately to their exposed midriffs and the heavy incense that floated up from each side of the long, dark table behind them.

The Vice Sovereign bowed his head. "Global Sovereign. Please forgive the interruption."

"Yes," the Sovereign replied without turning around.

"Damien has failed you again, my Supreme."

There was a long pause before the Sovereign said callously, "Kill him."

"And his second attack? The one he is planning as we speak?"

"Pull his team. Send them somewhere."

The Sovereign slowly turned in his chair.

For the few seconds Rurik dared to gaze upon him, he saw the thin face of a man in his early thirties, a long, black goatee hanging from his chin. But his young face did not bear the look of innocence and goodness its outward form would suggest. On the contrary, it was only a thin veil covering the austere and serpentine intentions of some ancient, evil king.

Just before Rurik looked away to offer his bow of humility, he caught a glimpse of the Sovereign's eyes. He was certain, if only for an instant, that they glowed with a bright red center. And then they didn't.

"Keep him in the dark," the Sovereign ordered. "By the time he realizes what is happening, he'll be dead. I'll take care of the Resistance myself."

"Yes, my Lord," replied Rurik. But he was too afraid to lift his head a second time.

When the screen finally went blank, Rurik could breathe again.

Chapter 50

Paris, France
Monday, April 11
11:48 AM

Adrien **stepped out of the basement** exit and headed toward Rue de Salut. Addy had warned him about going out in public, but he had to get away. His mind worked better when he was moving.

While he wandered the city streets, he thought of his father, and how knowing he had been murdered collapsed the fickle house of cards that was his past. His death when Adrien was just sixteen was traumatic enough, especially since his mother was long out of the picture; but knowing he was murdered in some political power play revived demons he had struggled to put to rest for more than two decades.

And then his mind drifted to Addy, how being near her made him feel so much excitement inside, and how dreadful it would be to disappoint her. These good people needed someone to help them, but how could it possibly be him? They had chosen the most unqualified man in the world.

Again he found himself praying. From deep within the words and phrases just popped out, like bubbles from simmering soup. "Will you show me what to do?" he breathed upward. "Is this my purpose?" he offered a few steps later. "It just doesn't make any sense."

Soon his prayers were interrupted by the aroma of breads, soups, and sandwiches. The tantalizing smells quickly convinced him it was time for lunch. He followed the scent, and in only a few blocks turned onto Rue de Compromis, a short street between Rue de Vérité and Rue de Menteur, filled with restaurants, bars, and boutiques.

As he walked, he glanced left and right at the signs on each side of the street. About halfway down, just past a dirty jewelry store called Monique's, he spotted a pub that reminded him of Banan's village. He turned into Sauveur's and took a seat at the bar.

The place was empty, except for Adrien and an overweight, crude bartender named Max. After looking over the menu, he ordered a thick ham sandwich called a *Jambon Fumé* and a cup of strong, black synthetic. In no time, Max plopped the plate down on the bar.

"That's 100 global," he gnarled. "Pay when you're done. And don't even think of skipping out on me."

"No problem," Adrien assured him. "A hundred global …plus a tip." And he ate until he thought he would bust.

About the time he finished his last bite, a man walked in and took a seat two stools down. Adrien glanced toward him and mouthed a simple, "Hello." After that, he all but ignored the new patron until the sound of metal clanking on the stainless steel bar renewed his attention.

He looked to see the stranger dumping several ancient gold coins on the counter. They looked like Persian commerce coins from about 2,500 years before Darwin. As the man inspected them, Adrien noticed the imprint of a king's face on one side, but didn't recognize it.

"Are you a collector?" he said to the dark-haired young man.

"Of a sort, I guess you could say. And you?"

"I'm an archaeologist. So I guess I just like anything old," he offered, grinning.

The man returned the smile. "An archaeologist? That must be interesting work."

"Sometimes," Adrien answered. "So tell me about your coins."

"They're a rare set of coins from an ancient Persian king who was famous for his wisdom."

"Ah, wisdom. Don't we all wish we had more of that," Adrien said, disheartened.

The man rubbed his fingers over the thick strands falling from his chin. "I hope you don't mind me saying, but you look like a man with a lot on his mind."

Adrien eyed him cautiously, trying to decide how much to share. "You could say that," he said. "How did you…?"

"A gift, I suppose." He turned to face Adrien. "Let me guess: You have a big decision to make and you're not sure of yourself. You may have to do some things you don't think you can handle, and it scares you."

"Wow! You really do have a gift." Adrien wanted to say more but strained to put his feelings into words. Finally, he said, "You know, when you're a kid, you think you're going to grow up to be something special, do something important. You're not going to be just another Joe like everybody else. But life has a way of taking that dream from you. You fail. You compromise. You surrender. Before long you don't know who you are anymore.

"And then when an opportunity comes along to revive those

hopes, you just can't seem to get off the stool and walk out the door." Adrien glanced toward the front door. "You say, 'What if I fail again?' 'What if I just don't have what it takes?' 'What if I never had what it takes?'"

"I know exactly what you mean," the man said. "Your heart wants to follow the wind, but your mind knows the weakness of your sail."

"Yeah, something like that."

The young man picked up a coin and tossed it to Adrien. "You know there's a story about this king. Apparently he had a magnificent garden outside his castle. And though he himself was a master gardener, he decided to have someone else tend it so he could be about other business in his kingdom. So he put out the word that he wanted to hire the best gardener in all the land.

"After a long search, he found and hired the most skilled gardener in the entire kingdom.

"But in a few seasons, the king became very dissatisfied with his garden. The expert had completely changed it; everything the king had worked so hard to build, this man cut down and rebuilt it in his own way. And when the citizens came to admire the king's new garden, the expert took all the credit for himself.

"So the king fired the gardener, and searched for a new one. But this time, he looked for a man with no experience at all. The only requirement was a willing heart and a teachable spirit.

"Eventually the king found such a man. He was not brilliant; he was not experienced; in fact, he didn't even have a garden. But over the years the king taught him everything he knew about gardening, and the man learned. He didn't destroy the king's garden, but expanded and increased what the king had already planted.

"And when it was time to show off the garden to the citizens of the land, the man said this: 'At one time, I knew nothing of gardening, but now I am a master. Yet I cannot thank myself for the beautiful scene now before you. Instead I must thank my great king for calling me to this task and teaching me all I needed to know to accomplish it. But most of all, I thank him for the great privilege of knowing him and learning to love him.'

"So you see, my friend," the stranger finished, "perhaps, as with everything else in your life, you should not look within yourself for the capacity to perform what you feel called to do, but, like the second gardener, to your wise and loving king. Then, when your task is complete, he will be honored through your work, and you will receive the great reward of loving him."

Adrien paused in silence and contemplated the man's powerful words.

The befuddled archaeologist saw himself so clearly in the stranger's story. He thought he had to be skilled and experienced to carry out the Maker's task. But perhaps the Maker just didn't work that way. Maybe he didn't call those who were qualified; instead, he qualified those he called. If this was the case, then he was *the most qualified man* in the world for the job before him because *he was not qualified at all.*

All of a sudden, Adrien's doubts faded away, and he knew what he had to do next. He slipped off his stool, turned to the stranger, and said, "Thank you so much for sharing that with me. You have no idea how much it helped."

"My pleasure," came his short reply.

"Here's your coin back," he said, reaching out to return it.

"No, no, you keep it," the stranger insisted.

Adrien inspected the coin for an instant, and dropped it in his pocket.

"Thank you," he said again. "For everything." And he hurried out the door.

As he walked briskly back to Vérité, his once tense and concerned face softened to a relieved smile. Then he stopped cold.

"Max! I forgot to pay!"

He swiveled on his toes and hustled back toward the pub, staring at the ground the entire way, his mind still spinning from the stranger's words. When he passed Monique's again, he raised his head and looked for the door, but there was none. In fact, there was no pub at all—not even a building.

At the exact spot where Sauveur's had been only seconds before, there was nothing but an empty lot.

He grabbed a passerby and asked, "Where's the pub that was here, Sauveur's?"

"What?" the woman said with a grimace. "There's no pub there. Never has been. What's Sauveur's?"

"What do you mean? It was just here! I had lunch there!"

The woman looked at him like he was mad and pulled away.

Adrien stared at the empty lot for a full five minutes, baffled. Finally it dawned on him—he knew just what had happened.

Energized by the realization, he sprinted full force all the way back to Rue de Salut to tell Addy and Rene. And though he could hardly believe it himself, he knew they would not doubt him for an instant.

Chapter 51

Before the datacenter door could fully open, Adrien squeezed his way through and ran for the pod of tech stations at the back of the room. Rene, Addy, and Rad were huddled over a holoscreen, deep in conversation. Their heads jerked as they heard the commotion that was his hurried entry.

His disheveled hair and sweaty brow elicited looks of distress until, between heavy pants, he grinned and announced, "I'm in!"

"You're in?" Rene asked. "*In* what?"

"Yes, yes…I'm in. In the Resistance, I mean." Noticing their confusion, he slowed down to clarify his meaning. "I want to join the Resistance," he said, purposefully.

Addy beamed, jumped from her seat, and ran to Adrien. She threw her arms around his neck as he lifted her into the air.

When she finally let go, Rene smiled, held out his arms, and said, "Welcome aboard, my son." Then he hugged Adrien too.

And though he had never actually met Adrien, Rad slapped him on the back and, like they were old friends, said, "Welcome to the team, buddy!"

When the euphoria had subsided, Rene asked, "So what made

you change your mind?"

"Well, I've been thinking about what you guys said last night—about needing me—and about my father. But I still wasn't sure until I went for a walk this morning. I just had to get out and clear my head. While I was out, I stopped by this place to grab a bite over off Compromis, and you'll never guess what happened."

So with contagious enthusiasm, Adrien told them in great detail about the vision he had just received. When he was done, he pulled the gold coin out of his pocket and showed them all.

And then they all rejoiced together, and cried...again.

Chapter 52

Damien stared into the night sky from his library chair. Though he had walked through the door at eight, in the three hours that followed he had only managed to shed his long cloak, pour himself a half dozen drinks, and ignore Collette's many attempts to get him to talk. She had offered him dinner for the last time an hour before, and then retired to the bedroom on the other end of the main floor.

He flinched when the tech station on his desk announced a call.

Rotating to face the screen, he said, "Receive." Mauritz Othman's countenance burst onto the display. His image was grainy; his voice, uneven.

"I assume they're all dead," Damien said flatly.

"No. No, not at all, Director," he let out in short bursts. Judging from the large containers and Othman's swagger back and forth on the screen, he was in the cargo bay of some kind of military transport. "The mission has been cancelled."

"Cancelled? What?" Damien sat up in his chair and raised his voice. "By whom?"

"About ten minutes ago, the Vice Sovereign himself called me

227

and axed the mission," Othman continued. "He didn't give me a reason; he just said we were all being reassigned. Then, not a minute later, this transport landed and took us away. According to Captain Jaeger, who's here with me, they pulled our surveillance of the Rue de Salut facility before noon today. I'm not sure where that team is now. As for us, we're headed to the Eastern Column. Or at least that's what they say. But I don't know. I smell a trap."

"As do I." Damien pivoted in his chair and tapped his fingers on the desk. "Rurik—that pompous bureaucrat," he spoke in a whisper to himself. "He thinks he can throw me aside like some cockroach. I will not be denied by that worm."

His attention now refocused, he turned back to Othman. "Go along. But find a way out. You and the whole team. You remember my emergency comm-port code?"

"Yes."

"Get the team back to Paris and call me on that number," Damien ordered. "I'm not done yet."

"Yes, Director."

Immediately, Damien ended the call, ran to the other side of the library, and yelled down the long hallway toward the first floor bedrooms. "Collette! The safe room! Now!"

"What?" she replied.

"The safe room! Now!" He heard her scurrying as he ran back into the library and touched a sensor just below a painting of the Galapagos Islands. The picture disappeared and a slick metal door opened to reveal a rack of guns and ammunition. Damien grabbed a black plasma rifle and a spherical canister and snapped them together in one smooth stroke.

Then the lights went out.

As Damien turned back into the room, both the library windows and front door exploded inward. He ducked while shards of glass sprayed him from behind, slicing small cuts in his back and legs. Unshaken, he sprinted for the kitchen as five men in black battle gear, three from the window and two from the front door, crashed into his home. Instantly, they opened fire in all directions, their bright plasma rounds flashing down the hallways, cutting through doors and walls.

When Damien entered the kitchen, he saw Collette in the far corner keying in the code for the door to the underground safe room. It slid open instantly, but just as she started down the stairs, a plasma round burned through the kitchen wall and blazed through her chest. She fell forward and tumbled down the short stairwell to the safe room entrance below.

Damien crawled quickly to the open door and called down to her, but she was already dead.

His time to mourn was cut short when his wife's killer invaded from the library door. Through his helmet display he spotted Damien and touched off three quick bursts in his direction. The Director dropped behind the island, narrowly escaping the rounds, and crawled toward the other side. Inch by inch, the two men circled the island, one hunting his target, the other struggling to stay alive.

When the soldier reached Damien's former position at the far corner of the island, the savvy GSS leader popped up from the front and launched a double shot into his torso, hurling him through the safe room door and down the stairs on top of Collette.

Just then a second man entered from the adjacent hallway and opened fire. Damien jumped toward the foyer hallway to dodge the white-hot rounds, but one nicked him on his way out, burning a two-inch gash in his left calf. He shrieked as he hit the floor, but remained focused, rolling over with his rifle aimed at the doorway.

The man hurried through the opening in pursuit. When he stepped into view, Damien pulled the trigger and held it down. But nothing came out. His fall had dislodged the plasma canister and jammed his rifle. The soldier pulled up and coolly trained his gun on the Director's chest.

But before the soldier could finish him off, a white streak zipped past Damien, just overhead. He watched as the faceless assassin was thrown back into the kitchen. But before he could process his attacker's sudden demise, something crashed to the floor behind him.

He turned to see Mr. Thomas, his only living bodyguard, standing on the broken remnants of his front door, and the body of the third soldier lying flat on the floor just inches from his face.

"One shot, two defaveur," Mr. Thomas said, holding his rifle in his right arm, his left hanging gingerly beside him.

"Indeed, Mr. Thomas," said Damien. "So nice of you to join me."

"My pleasure, Director. That's three down, right?"

"And two to go."

As he finished those words, rounds came blazing from the direction of the bedrooms. Damien jerked himself into the hallway between the kitchen and foyer while Mr. Thomas leapt down into the living room, crawled between the table and couch, and aimed his weapon toward the oncoming fire.

The barrage finally stopped as the two remaining soldiers worked their way toward their targets. Through a fresh hole in the wall, Damien saw one of them taking position beside the doorway to the living room.

He twisted his plasma canister back into position and whispered, "Mr. Thomas."

"Sir," he replied, just as quietly.

"Fire into the wall just right of the doorway."

Mr. Thomas let loose a flurry of rounds at various positions along the edge of the doorway wall. Smoke rose from the scorched openings, and a split second later, the fourth assassin fell out onto the floor.

Mr. Thomas, his rifle still on target, lifted himself to ensure the assassin was dead. When satisfied he was no longer a threat, he turned to the Director and whispered, "Got him." Before the words had left his mouth, however, a single plasma round burned through his heart, killing him instantly. The soldier he thought was dead had managed to raise his rifle one last time and deliver his final kill shot.

Enraged, Damien leapt to his feet, darted into the foyer and screamed as he sprayed rounds into the fallen soldier's body. He was about to release the trigger when the last commando barreled into him from the side, hurling them both down the stairs onto the living room floor.

The motion of the fall landed the soldier on top of Damien, propelling the two rifles and the assassin's helmet out of reach. As if by instinct, the soldier pushed himself up, grabbed Damien's shirt, and nailed him in the cheek with several quick blows.

When Damien was almost unconscious, the soldier looked up and quickly spotted his gun only a few feet away. As he reached out for it, Damien regained his senses, bent his fingers to the first knuckle, and shot them into the man's throat with a single, deadly motion. His larynx and esophagus now collapsed, he gasped out for air.

Damien pushed the choking man onto the floor, grabbed his rifle, and took up a slow, limping orbit around the dying man's body.

"So, you are the best Rurik can do?" he sneered. "You thought I would be an easy mark, didn't you? Just another bureaucrat who would wet his pants when you stormed through the front door."

Damien stepped over the man's chest, centering his twitching frame between his legs. He pushed the warm barrel of his gun hard into the soldier's forehead and asked, "Now what do you think?"

Then he pulled the trigger three times.

Before the smoke from the barrel had dissipated, the rumble of an approaching transport vibrated the walls around him. Reenergized, he turned and sprinted for the safe room door.

At the bottom of the stairs, he paused to say goodbye to Collette. "Get off of her," he said as he pushed the dead soldier to the side. Taking her head in his hands, he brushed her hair back and gently caressed her cheek.

"I'm sorry, my dear," he muttered. "They will pay for what they have done to us. They will *all* pay."

After his one-way goodbye had ended, he entered the access code and ran to the back of the safe room chamber to another door; there he punched in a second code and the narrow door opened to the threshold of a dark, underground tunnel. Feeling the cold, stale air on his face, he looked back to Collette one last time, and launched out into the darkness.

Chapter 53

The first thing we've got to do is make sure you look like Walter," Addy said to Adrien while Rad listened in over the hum of servers in the datacenter, "which won't be nearly as much trouble as hacking your bio-ID."

"Don't worry about that," Rad assured her from his tech station. "It's not easy, but hey, that's why I'm here, right?"

"So you're saying this bio-ID contains some kind of identifier code?" asked Adrien. "They can tell who I am by scanning this chip?"

"Not only can they tell who you are, Adrien," Rad answered, "but with some of the newer chips, they can tell where you've been, who you've been with, and what you talked about. Basically, you can't go to the bathroom without the G-CoN knowing about it."

"But I thought this chip was just for medical stuff, some kind of emergency information file in case something happened to you."

"That's what the government told us years ago when they started implanting them in everyone," explained Addy. "But that was just a line they used to get the people to go along. Now it's just another tool they use to control us."

"Don't sweat it, Adrien my boy. I'll make sure you're good to go," Rad pledged.

"Okay. I trust you. You are the Rad-meister after all," Adrien joked.

Rad grinned and said, "Finally, somebody gets it around here."

"So the basic plan is to go in a little before shift change on Friday," Addy said, ignoring Rad. "The Globalcast goes live at exactly five, so we need to be in place by four. They start the transfer from Assimilation at four thirty. When we get there, we'll go straight to your department and duck in to the supervisor's office."

"But what if he's there?"

She looked at Rad and smiled. "Well, Rad is making sure he won't be."

Rad grinned back from his swivel chair. "The guy from the earlier shift will think his house is burning down, and the guy from Walter's shift will have a massive water leak just before he leaves for work. Either way, you're clear."

"But, how...?" Adrien started to ask.

"He hacked their home intelligence modules," Addy horned in.

Rad's guilty smirk gave away the subversiveness of his intentions. "Amazing what you can do today with a few pass codes and the right equipment."

"Now, before we get too much further, are you comfortable with the floor plan? Feel like you can find your way around if we somehow get disconnected?" Addy slid a holopad of the schematics toward Adrien.

He picked it up and looked it over again. "Yeah, I think I've got it down pretty well. And Rad said he'd load it to my comm-port just in case. So I should be fine," he answered and handed the holodisplay back to her.

"Okay, as I was saying, that supervisor station is where the final upload to the Nest takes place. So we'll jump on his machine, put this"— she handed him a thin, square black drive—"in the external interface, and replace their files with ours."

Adrien rotated the flat object in his hand and said, "Interesting. I've never seen one of these before. How does it work?"

"It's a mini-quantum drive," explained Rad. "It's thin so you can put it in your pocket, but when it nears an input drive on a tech station, it automatically expands vertically, and the connection port extends from the side. Check this out." Rad moved the small drive to within about a foot of the front of his tech station. The drive expanded upward in his hand while a small door opened on the face of the tech station. Then a slim platform extended out to accept the drive. When he placed it in the square slot in the platform, it retracted back into the station and the door closed again.

"Wow," Adrien said. "Cool gadget. So why does it expand like that?"

"Cooling. When you're running the amount of data that thing can run, you've got to give the chips some room to breathe," Rad said. "When you want to take it out again, just touch the door with your finger." Rad tapped the nearly invisible door and the drive magically appeared. He handed it back to Adrien and it collapsed again to a thin square.

After he looked it over for another minute, he asked. "So what files will we load?"

"First they'll see a video of Rene," Rad answered. "He'll expose the G-CoN for their atrocities against America, and their oppression of people across the globe. He'll also tell the world about the Maker, and how the G-CoN has destroyed his writings and suppressed the knowledge of his existence.

"While they're taking all that in, we'll be downloading a series of documents, images, and videos supporting our claims to every station on the planet. We've digitized the Maker documents you brought us—they'll be included, as well as secret G-CoN files about America, the attacks, and the cover-up. Basically, they'll get everything we have."

"We'll wait around until Rad tells us the upload was successful and then we'll bolt," Addy said. "We'll be out of there before they even know what hit them."

"Yeah," said Rad, "I'll be in touch via comm-port the whole time. Their attack hurt my system pretty bad, but I can still do a few things. If you run into any trouble loading the data or anything else, I'll be there to back you up."

"So why won't they just stop the transmission when they see it's us?" asked Adrien.

"Because they can't," answered Addy. "A few months ago, we hacked a Globalcast mid-stream and tried to put our video up instead, real time. We only got off a few seconds before they regained control, but one of the safeguards they put in as a result was to code the transmission so it can't be interrupted once it starts."

"So all we've got to do is get it over to the Nest, and by the time they figure it out, they'll have no way to stop it," Rad said. "Pretty sweet, huh?"

"Yeah, sounds like a great plan," Adrien replied. "But since when has anything ever gone according to plan?"

"Right. Thanks for the encouragement, man."

"Anytime, Rad-meister."

"One more thing," Rad said, leaning forward in his chair. "Just in case something goes wrong, here's a little backup plan." He handed Adrien another small drive. This one was red.

Addy rolled her eyes. "That's not another Trojan program, is it?"

Rad only glanced at her. Then he continued with Adrien. "This drive has a file on it that will allow me remote access."

"You mean *should* allow you remote access, right?" she interrupted.

"Yeah, *should*. Like I said, it's a backup plan," Rad offered in his defense. "When you get in, if you run into any trouble, plug this in. Once it loads I'll be able—*should* be able—to do the dirty work from right here."

"What's the problem, Addy?" asked Adrien. "Is there something I should know?"

"Well, we tried Rad's famous Trojan plan about a week ago and nearly lost our entire system. If they detect it as fast as they did last time, we won't even finish the upload before they nail us. I just think we'd better make Plan A work or we're in for trouble."

Rad eased back in his chair. "Have it your way," he murmured. "But take it anyway; it's not the same file I used last time. You never know."

Adrien slipped it in his pocket. "Will do Rad," he said and smiled. "Just one more question. So I have some idea of what to expect, how long will each of these take to load?"

Rad thought for a second. "The black one? There's a lot of data on that one, probably eleven exabytes or so. Hmm…three or four minutes tops. The red one? Only about ten seconds."

Just then Rad's display lit up with a call from a technician named John.

"Rad," John said, "you'd better come down here. Those files we're trying to restore—they're just not coming up. We need your help."

"Be right there," the Chief Engineer replied. "I guess I'll leave you two to wrap up," he turned to Addy and said. "Let me know if you need anything else."

"Sure, Rad," Addy replied.

Once Rad was gone, Adrien and Addy just looked at each other, unsure of what to say or do now that they were alone again.

Chapter 54

Addy spoke first into the uncomfortable silence. "I've been waiting to tell you...I'm glad you changed your mind. I was hoping your face would become a staple around here."

Adrien looked down at his boots and then to Addy. "Yeah, I'm glad too. I have to admit—for a while there..." but he didn't finish his thought. "I'm just happy things turned out the way they did. And I was hoping to see you again too."

Those embarrassing words came out without Adrien's permission. "Maybe I should just look over these schematics one more time," he said, nervously, as he leaned past her to grab the holopad on the desk.

His reach brought his face very close to hers, but she didn't pull back. Then everything but her presence went blank—no surroundings, no sound, no mission to accomplish. Just her. It felt so good to want her, and to think she wanted him too.

They both paused. And moved closer. She laid her hand on his, and eased toward his mouth. He looked into her golden-brown eyes and felt her sweet breath on his face. Their lips had almost touched when Adrien suddenly pulled back.

Guilty thoughts exploded in his mind: What about Sophie? How would she feel about this? Just a week ago he was on death's door for her; now he was about to betray her. But it wasn't wrong—was it? She was gone. She would want him to…or would she?

"I'm sorry, Addy," he said in barely a whisper. "I just can't."

"It's Sophie, isn't it?"

"No. No, it's not that at all. It's just me. Like you said the other day, it's complicated."

Addy sat quietly trying to think of something to say.

"I've got to go," he said finally, saving her. "I'll see you later."

Her mouth opened and closed several times before she realized there was nothing she could say that would help him resolve what was going on inside. So, at length she convinced her burning heart to calm, and said simply, "Okay. I'll see you around."

In the midst of Adrien's confused emotions, he remembered something important.

"Oh, and Addy…" he offered on his way out, pausing at the door.

"Yes?"

"I've been thinking about sneaking back to my apartment and picking up a few things, clothes and some other stuff. What do you think about that?"

"I wouldn't, Adrien. Who knows who's looking for you out there? They killed your entire team. If they find you, they'll kill you too."

"I thought you might say that. Odds are they think I'm dead, anyway. And if I'm only there for a few minutes…"

"Adrien, please don't."

"There are some things there I need, Addy. Important things."

"I understand." Although he didn't say as much, she knew it had something to do with Sophie and with what had just happened. "I still wouldn't, Adrien. But if you have to, you should have Trip and Tony check out the place before you go, and then go in with you. They're former GSS."

"Good idea. I'm sure it'll be fine," he replied and turned and walked away.

Forcing a smile, she said, "No problem."

As Adrien left the datacenter and headed down the hallway, he felt his heart pulled back toward Addy like they were connected with a giant rubber band. The farther he got from her, the harder the rubber band pulled, and the more he wanted to go back and hold her.

"What am I going to do?" he asked out into the empty corridor. "I think I'm falling for her."

Chapter 55

Hello, uncle," the man on the other end greeted Damien. "I've been meaning to call and thank you. You saved my life."

"Good day, nephew," Damien said calmly. "Yes, you are fortunate you mentioned my name. If you hadn't, *you* would be an artifact for someone to find in 500 years."

"I know you're right, uncle," his nephew said. "I'm calling as you instructed. When I was released from confinement, the officer said I should right away. I guess I owe you for that one too."

"Yes, you do. Now for what you can do to repay me," said Damien. "Do you remember Adrien Bach?"

"Of course. He's a friend of mine. But he's dead. He was killed in the desert like the rest of them," the man replied.

"Well he wasn't. And that's a problem for me. I think he's back in Paris. Can you find him?"

"I think so. I know of a few places he might go."

"Very well," the Director said. "Find him as quickly as you can and call me when you do."

"Okay. What do you want with him, uncle?"

"Don't worry about that. Just find him. Understand?"

"Yes, of course."

As soon as Damien hung up, his comm-port chimed with another call. It was Othman.

"Receive," Damien instructed. "Do you have your team back in Paris?" he asked without a greeting.

"Not yet, Director," Othman answered. "We need your help. We've got a plan to slip away from our new unit, but we need transport back to Paris. Got any strings you can pull to get us a lift?"

"Yes. When do you need it?"

"Looks like the earliest we can get away is Thursday night. They're sending us out on maneuvers. Have the transport land about a mile north of Shenyang at midnight. If all goes according to plan, it should be a few days before they realize we're gone."

"Very well," Damien replied. "You'll have it."

"Director, what do you want us to do when we get back to Paris?"

"Finish the mission. Take out the Resistance. Kill them all," Damien ordered coldly.

"Yes, sir. Once we get back, we'll have to secure a few additional weapons and a small transport. But I can handle that on my own. We'll hit them as soon as we can."

"Excellent."

"What are you going to do in the meantime, sir?" Othman asked.

"Clean up some unfinished business...from twenty years ago," Damien said, and hung up.

Chapter 56

Paris, France
Wednesday, April 13
6:15 PM

After Trip checked out the apartment, he called down to Adrien and Tony who were waiting discretely a few blocks away.

"All clear," he announced. With that Adrien and Tony slipped from their hiding place, walked briskly to the building, and took the elevator to the thirty-second floor.

When Adrien opened the front door, he saw his entire life strewn across the floor. Clothes, utensils, sofa cushions, dog toys. The walls had holes smashed in them, and his tech station was missing along with his desk drawer holofiles.

What he couldn't step over, he pushed out of the way as he hurried back to his bedroom. Tony and Trip followed him down the hallway, peeking in the second bedroom, the hall bathroom, the closet.

Adrien walked around to the bedside table on the far side of the room. The top drawer lay broken on the floor a few feet away, but the large bottom drawer was still in its slot. He touched the top edge, and the drawer opened automatically.

"Yes, it's here," he said, barely audible. He reached in and pulled out an old holopad. After he fingered through several images, he slid it into his pocket.

Next he walked over to the large dresser and tapped open the drawers, picking out pieces of clothing and tossing them in a pile on the bed. Quickly, he pushed the small pile into a blue canvas bag and proceeded back up the hall to the bathroom.

As he dropped a tooth sanitizer in his bag, he heard the hiss of the front door, and then the sound of footsteps crunching slowly through the living room.

His heart raced when Addy's warning echoed through his mind—*If they find you, they'll kill you too.* He eased himself toward the door and listened for Trip and Tony to come marching out from the back, but they didn't make a sound. In fear for his life, he pushed himself against the wall, nestled against the door frame, and waited.

The footsteps became faster, like running, but not human feet. Closer and closer they came. Adrien braced himself inside, his body full of adrenaline. Then the small gray form turned the corner and leapt up at him, barking wildly.

"Journey!" Adrien called over and over as he reached down and took her into his arms. "I didn't think I'd ever see you again! How on earth did you make it back here?"

He stepped out into the hallway and immediately found his answer.

"Nate?" he asked, disbelieving. "Is that you?"

With a wide smile, he replied, "In the flesh."

Just then Tony and Trip came barging out of the back bedroom with their plasma pistols extended.

"No, no, no!" Adrien cried, waving his hands to stop them. "It's okay! It's just Nate. He's an old friend of mine." They pulled up abruptly, and each blew out a heavy sigh.

Adrien turned, met Nate between the bathroom and kitchen, and threw his arms around his old friend.

"I thought you were dead, man!" Adrien said with a big grin. "I thought they killed you along with everybody else."

"I almost was. I barely made it out."

"What happened? How'd you get out?"

"Fortunately for me, I was curled up in one of those small tunnels at Site 2 when all the shooting started," Nate explained. "I didn't know what was going on; I heard people screaming, and then Linda dropped dead right in front of me. I was scared to death. So I just stayed there until the noise stopped."

"So how did you get back?"

"Later that night, I came out of the hole and saw these guys in black uniforms walking around everywhere. I knew if they saw me, I was a dead man, but I had to find a way to get back. So I made my way to the landing pad and slipped in the back of one of their cargo transports. Journey here jumped in with me just as the door was closing. When they landed, I hid in one of the containers and sneaked out after the off load. I've been hiding out ever since."

Adrien's face was alive with joy. "I can't believe it. I'm so glad to see you."

"And I'm glad to see you. I never figured I'd actually find you here. Just had to take the chance," he said. "How'd you get out?"

"Well, I was warned before the fact. I mean, I didn't actually know they were going to do what they did, but someone told me I should get out of there as fast as I could. So I did."

"Looks like you got some good advice," Nate replied. "Saved your life."

"Yes, indeed."

"Adrien, we really need to go," Trip said.

"Okay," he replied, grabbing Nate by the arm. "Come on. I've got some folks I want you to meet. You'll *never* believe what's happened."

Chapter 57

Nate relaxed on the couch in the breakroom while Adrien talked. He explained why the documents they found in the desert were there in the first place, and walked Nate through the story of America and the G-CoN's great cover-up. Finally, he told him how he had come to believe the books were true and that the Maker was real.

Nate listened with great interest without comment; but Adrien was sure he was holding something back. Although Nate was hiding it well, underneath Adrien discerned the same disgusted disposition he had the day the documents were found, the same day he called the people who believed in the Maker "a bunch of superstitious nuts."

"So what do you think? Am I crazy?" Adrien asked, opening the door for Nate to say what was on his mind.

Nate took a deep breath and slapped his hands on his pants. "So, you're telling me that not only is this deity myth true, but the entire history of the world as we know it is wrong? And the government is behind it?"

Adrien didn't flinch. "That's exactly what I'm telling you, and they've got the facts to back it up."

To Adrien's surprise, Nate's countenance relaxed and a hint of a smile stretched across his face. "Okay, Adrien. Maybe you're right. Maybe it's true. I've never known you to go anywhere the facts didn't lead you." He stood, took a few steps, and turned around. "Do you think I could see some of that evidence?"

"I don't see why not."

"And those documents about the Maker…I'd really like to read through those if you don't mind," Nate added. "Maybe it's time for me to open my mind to new possibilities after all."

"Absolutely, Nate," Adrien said happily.

"So the folks you met up with, the ones who work here, they fight against the G-CoN?"

"Yes. They're trying to expose what's happened, the genocide the G-CoN has committed and, in fact, still commits today."

"And you've joined them?"

"Yes, Nate, I have. I've got to help them. The world must know the truth about all this."

"What exactly are you planning?"

Addy walked through the door before he could answer. She smiled at Adrien, but her demeanor quickly dimmed when she saw Nate sitting on the couch.

"Addy," Adrien said as he stood to greet her. "I'd like you to meet someone. This is Nate Ashby, a friend of mine. He was at the site with me in the desert."

Addy extended her hand, but her concerned expression remained. "Hi, Nate. Good to meet you."

"Nate was there during the attack on the site and barely escaped," he explained. "He came looking for me at my apartment."

"I didn't know if he was dead or alive," Nate said. "It was a shot in the dark, really. Adrien's been filling me in, about America and about you guys here."

With that innocent disclosure, Addy's look of care became one of absolute panic.

"Adrien, can we talk for just a minute? *Alone.*"

"Uh, sure," he replied. "Excuse us, Nate. Refill your synthetic or something, and we'll be right back."

Addy led him out into the hallway. When they were a few steps away from the door, she turned with murder in her eyes.

"Just what do you think you're doing?" she whispered.

"What do you mean?"

"You just can't bring in some stranger off the street and give him the VIP tour. How do you know he's not a spy?"

Nate slipped off the couch and headed for the synthetic replicator.

"He's my friend. I trust him," Adrien said. "He almost got killed himself."

"But he *didn't.* Those GSS guys don't miss, Adrien. So he just *happens* to escape execution and just *happens* to come by your apartment and you just *happen* to be there? Don't you find that a little too convenient?"

"Don't be so paranoid, Addy."

"I've learned to be paranoid. You can't trust anyone outside these walls. *Nobody.*"

"Alright. Alright. I still think you're wrong, but I see your point. I'm sorry. What do you want me to do now?"

"Whatever you do, don't tell him anything else, especially about Friday at the GIS."

"Okay."

"Let's get him to a room, and we'll figure out the rest later. Just act like everything is okay."

As they walked back into the breakroom, Nate bolted from the door so fast he spilled his synthetic on the floor; he stopped nonchalantly and covered it with his boot.

"Sorry, Nate," Adrien said.

"It's okay. Hey look, I'm pretty tired. Do you think I could crash somewhere for a while?"

"Sure," Addy answered. "I'll have someone show you to our guest quarters."

"Great," he said and walked past them and out the door.

When Nate was out of sight, Addy looked down at the puddle of synthetic on the floor and shot Adrien another sharp look.

"What have you gotten us into?" she whispered.

But she never gave him a chance to answer. She just walked out and left him standing there all alone.

Chapter 58

Adrien opened his eyes to a light so bright it burned. Immediately, he raised his hand to block the brilliant surge and forced his eyelids open to scan the space around him. What he saw was pure white in every direction—no boundaries, no borders, no defining lines—just a continuous encasing sheet of brightness broken only by a single point of powerful intensity just ahead.

He started to press forward until a form appeared in the distance and slowly came into focus.

"Sophie."

She was just as he remembered her: Her straight blond hair, her strong blue eyes, her warm smile. She was just the same, except for the long, white robe she now wore. But he hardly noticed it.

He stood petrified as she floated toward him. Something inside his chest began to swell. When she had almost reached him, he pulled a finger across his wet cheek and reached out for her.

"Adrien, my dear!" she barely got out, her emotions overwhelming her.

Adrien's smile broke through his tears as he squeezed her tight in his arms. "I've missed you so much, Sophie."

"And I've missed you!"

"Where are we? Is this real?" He waited before asking, "Are *you* real?"

She laughed. "Yes, I'm real. You're touching me, aren't you?"

"Yeah, I guess I am. But in my dreams I've touched you many times."

"Well, this time I can promise you—I'm the real thing."

"And this place?" He looked around but still found only brightness.

"It's a place for us to meet. Just you and me. Come on, walk with me."

As they walked, the brightness mysteriously gave way to a deserted, tropical beach, and Sophie's clothes began to change. Before his eyes, her white robe became a thin, yellow summer dress, and her hair, which only a few seconds before fell perfectly onto her shoulders, now tossed freely in the salty breeze. He felt the smooth sand between his toes and the warmth of her hands around his arm.

"I'm so sorry I had to leave you, Adrien," she said. "I know how hard it's been for you."

"It has been hard, Sophie. I've felt so alone, so empty; it's been so dark without you." The tears, which the wind had almost dried, dripped down his cheeks again.

As she stopped along the shore and took his face into her hands, she said, lovingly, "I know. I know. It won't always be this way, Adrien. Things will get better."

"I'm sure you're right." After a second he said, "There's something I've got to say, just in case you vanish on me."

"Yes?"

"I'm so sorry about what happened. I never should have forced you to go on that glacier, and I never should have taken us down

253

that path. I was so selfish, and such a fool. I cost you your life! Please forgive me," he said, squeezing her tight again.

"It's okay, Adrien. It's okay. I forgive you." She looked him in the eyes. "It wasn't your fault. I'm a big girl. I could have said no. So stop blaming yourself. There's a reason for all of this."

"Okay," he said as he tried to calm himself. And then he asked, "So how about you? Are you okay now?"

"Except for missing you, I couldn't be better. I'm with him now, and the life he gives is more than you can imagine."

"I knew it!" he let out. "That time we talked in the PAV and you asked me about the meaning of it all. You believed something then, didn't you?"

She smiled gently. "Yes, I did."

"Well, I believe now too, Sophie. You'll never guess what has happened to me..."

"I know, Adrien. I know," she said before he could finish.

"You know?"

"Yes, I know, and I'm so happy about it. But that's not why I'm here." She stepped back from him, took his hands in hers, and looked at the ring on his finger. "It's time for you to move on, my love. It's time for you to box up what we had, put it in a secret place in your heart, and close the door."

There was nothing she could have said that would have been more of a surprise than those words. He pulled away, walked down to where the waves rolled up on the sand, and looked out at the puffy clouds hovering over the horizon.

"But I don't want to move on!" he turned and said over the sound of crashing waves. Then for a second he couldn't speak. "I want you, Sophie," he finally muttered. "You're all I've ever wanted."

"And I want you, my love. But our time has come and gone; we can't be together now. He has something else in mind for me… *and for you.*"

"For me?"

"Addy, Adrien."

"*Addy?* What do you mean?"

"I know how you feel about her, and it's okay. She's yours now."

"But Sophie…" he protested.

She walked out to him and eased her arms around his waist. "Your life here must go on. I want you to be loved and I want you to feel love again."

Adrien looked away for a moment and then long into her eyes. "But it doesn't mean I don't love you," he reassured her, the tears welling up again. "I'll never love anyone like I love you. You know that, don't you?"

"Yes, I know, and I will always love you, my dear Adrien—that will never change. But you will love her in a different way than you love me, and in a special and wonderful way. And that's alright. I want that for you—*he* wants that for you."

"He? You mean…?"

She nodded.

"Besides," she added, "we'll be together again soon. Everything will be made right in the end, and you won't cry anymore." She wiped his cheek one last time and pulled away.

Letting her go was the hardest thing he had ever done, something he swore he would never do again if he ever got the chance. It was like opening a wound whose pain ran so deep the only way to ease it was by death itself.

And yet it all seemed right somehow.

As her white robe returned and the paradise that was their final meeting place faded, he said tenderly, "Thank you, Sophie. Thank you for loving me so much."

"Be strong, my dear," she said through tears, floating backward into the light.

When it had just started to burn again, he woke up.

Chapter 59

Paris, France
Thursday, April 14
3:10 PM

The next day Adrien woke up at ten. After a late lunch with Nate, he hurried off for a meeting with Addy, Rad, and Rene, the last one before the final attack on GIS on Friday. Nate was not invited.

Although the gathering was important, he found it almost impossible to concentrate; he kept trading looks with Addy and fighting a mischievous smile. After the long parley finally broke, he caught up to her in the hallway.

"Hey," he said, pulling up beside her.

She grinned. "Hey. What's with you today? You seem so…chipper."

"I don't know. Good night sleep I guess."

"Well I hope so, considering you got up at ten!"

They both laughed.

"How'd you know about that?"

Playfully, she answered, "You'd be surprised what I know, Mr. Bach."

"Is that right?" he asked, smiling. "Anyway, I was wondering if you'd like to get out of here for a little while this afternoon. Maybe go somewhere and talk. You're not working tonight, are you?"

"No, I took the night off to prepare for the mission. And yeah, I'd love to get out of here for a while, but at this point I don't think prancing down Rue de Soif would be the right play. Might not come back in one piece, if you know what I mean."

"Good point." Then he got an idea. "Hey, I've got the perfect place! You ever heard of the Great Falls?"

"Yeah. I've never actually been there, but I've seen pictures. The ones down south, right? The manmade falls."

"Exactly."

"Well that's not exactly secluded," she complained.

"The part I know is!"

Addy arched her eyebrows and donned a crooked grin. "I don't know what you've got up your sleeve... but I'm game."

"Well let's go!"

"Now?"

"Now!"

After an hour drive, Adrien exited the Superway just north of Toulouse and eventually turned left onto a winding gravel road. When the main road was no longer visible in the rearview display, he eased the PAV onto the greening grass on the roadside, and parked.

"We're here," he announced.

Addy looked confused. "This doesn't look like the Great Falls to me."

"Patience, my dear. Patience," he encouraged her, stepping out onto the loose rocks. "Follow me."

Snuggled on each side by wild grass and budding flowers, the road rolled up and down into the distance.

As they started down the path, Addy turned to Adrien. "So what is this place?" she asked just before the warm air fluttered her bangs into her eyes.

"When I was a teenager, my father was friends with the man who did the maintenance at the Great Falls. From time to time I would spend the day with him, fixing broken bridge supports, replacing pumps, changing light cores. In the process, I learned all the back alleys and secret places at the Falls. This road is one of those secrets. It used to be one of the main maintenance roads, but it doesn't look like they use it much anymore."

"So where does it lead?"

"That's a surprise."

After a few more steps, Addy said. "You just mentioned your dad again. You must have been close to him."

Adrien kicked a rock off into the grass. "I guess I was. But I don't think I realized how close until he was long gone."

"I know what you mean. I lost my mother a couple of years ago. Breast cancer. You know they say that disease has been around for hundreds of years, but they've never been able to cure it. But she may have lasted longer if it wasn't for the G-CoN."

"How's that?"

"Getting sick as a member of the Resistance is a death sentence. We have to get medicine on the black market, and we've got some good doctors, but they never have the right equipment. Anyway, they couldn't stop it. She just faded away, and one day she was gone."

"I'm so sorry, Addy," Adrien consoled her. "More of that evil you were telling me about, huh?"

"I guess."

"You must really miss her."

She glanced at him. "I do. I do. You know, it's funny. I thought as I got older I wouldn't need my parents as much, that I would outgrow their advice, that I wouldn't need their hugs anymore. But it's just the opposite. As time goes by, I seem to need them even more."

The roar ahead was becoming more noticeable. As Adrien and Addy peeked over the final hill, the Falls slowly came into view. From their perch on the crest, they could see and experience the full power of this manmade wonder. Down below, the raging water launched over the face of the rock and cascaded downward 200 feet onto the large, moss-covered boulders below. The mist rose like explosive fog into the air.

Addy's mouth fell open and her steps slowly ceased.

"It's so big...and beautiful," she said. "And so much different than the pictures."

"It's awesome, isn't it?" Taking off toward the Falls, he charged, "Come on! You haven't seen anything yet."

The sun was starting to set when they reached the bottom of the hill and the base of the Falls. Addy looked up to see a burgundy metal stairway zigzagging up the face of the rock just to the right of the descending water. At the top of the stairway, a door was set into the profile of the rock.

Addy pointed to the top of the stairway and asked loudly, over the roaring water, "We're not going up there, are we?"

"You got it!" he yelled back. "Trust me—you don't want to miss this!"

By the time they reached the peak, it was almost dark. The

stairway seemed so strong from the bottom, but Addy felt it wobble and give as they stepped onto the top platform. Her fear quickly gave way to amazement, however, as she leaned against the rail and stretched her hand out toward the rushing falls. Every so often she looked back to Adrien and smiled as the water splashed against the palm of her hand.

Adrien squeezed the doorknob and cranked it hard. The old door, which had not been touched in years, opened with the sound of a hundred rusty gates pivoting on their hinges. When he had pushed it wide, Adrien tapped Addy on the shoulder and beckoned her inside. With a hint of reluctance, she turned from the water and followed him into the darkness.

As the door closed behind them, the faint lights of the tunnel took over and the smell of stagnant water filled the air. In a few minutes, another door appeared. Adrien grabbed the knob and paused. "Are you ready for this?"

Before she could answer, he pulled it open.

Lights of all colors flickered through the clear glass tunnel on the other side. Overhead the water rolled by and turned to descend down the falls. From every angle, the colored lights—red, white, blue—shone up through the water. On each side of the large, open tunnel, tourists stared intently at the fish and rocks and long grasses on the bottom of the river.

"It's the underwater tunnel," she whispered, enthralled.

"Yeah, it comes out about two thirds of the way and then circles back. We're about twenty feet down here."

Addy smiled like a little child as the rays of light bounced off her face. "It's so beautiful," she whispered.

For a long time, she walked silently through the tunnel, her head bobbing from side to side, oblivious to the hoards of people, and even to Adrien. All the while he followed closely behind, and though it had been many years since he had experienced the spectacle around him, he was unable to see anything but her.

When the tunnel finally ended, they stepped out onto a rocky path and the light of evenly spaced lampposts.

Tugging at her arm, he said, "One last thing," and headed down the walkway. Within a few steps, they turned left onto an overgrown path that led back toward the Falls. At the end of the path, a large tower appeared rising twenty stories into the sky.

"What is that?" she asked.

"The Great Falls Observation Tower."

"Another secret?"

He just looked at her and smiled.

When they stepped out onto the small, empty platform at the top of the tower, the full glory of the Falls broke through, overwhelming them both. Lights from the tower and points all around illuminated the thick mist and foam spraying up from the bottom. From beneath the river, red, white, and blue rays shot up like bright, glowing candles. And off in the distance, the sparkle of Toulouse made the entire scene look like an immense, petrified fireworks display.

Adrien and Addy leaned against the railing and quietly took it all in.

Then Addy turned to Adrien. "Thank you," she said.

"For what?"

"For bringing me here. I needed this. You don't know how much I needed this."

"I needed it too, Addy."

Her face now serious, she asked, "So what's going on, Adrien?

You seem different today."

Adrien eased closer and laid his hand on top of hers. "I guess I've been thinking...about us."

"Us? I thought you weren't ready. I thought..."

He put his finger over her lips. "The other night I said it wasn't about Sophie...but it was. I knew I had feelings for you, and yet I felt so guilty, like I was betraying her or something. But I'm past that now. I know it's okay. I know *she's* okay. And I..." He couldn't get the rest of the words out.

"You...?" she helped him along.

"I think I'm falling in love with you, Addy."

She reached up, placed her hands on his cheeks, and pulled his lips toward hers. They both paused, and then moved closer.

"And I you," she said.

And they kissed.

Chapter 60

Nate Ashby edged out onto Rue de Salut and spoke a command into his comm-port. In a few seconds, a voice came on the line.

"Yes?" Damien answered.

"I found him. Yesterday actually. I would have called earlier, but I couldn't get away. I spent the night with some group called the Resistance."

"And what did you learn?"

"I know where he is. But there's more. They're planning something big, something against the G-CoN. Tomorrow at GIS. They're going to hit GIS."

"How? You mean actually at the GIS building? What are they going to do?"

"Yes, at the building. It's not a military operation, but some kind of technical attack. I'm not sure exactly what. I overhead some of them talking. All I could get was that something's going down tomorrow around five at GIS in Paris."

"Excellent work nephew," Damien said. "Hang around and see what else you can learn. If you get any more information, call me right away. If nothing else develops, meet me at GIS tomorrow at three."

"Yes, uncle. I'll be there."

Chapter 61

Adrien tried not to follow Addy too closely when they approached the main entrance of the GIS headquarters.

"Everybody still hear me?" Rad asked.

"Loud and clear," whispered Addy.

"Yeah, I'm here," Adrien said nervously. With Addy's help, Adrien was a spitting image of Walter Waite—the white shirt buttoned all the way to the top and even the wiry beard. "I hope you got my bio-ID right, Rad."

"What? You starting to doubt the Rad-meister already?"

"Can we please stay focused, gentlemen," Addy said.

Upstairs in the main security room, Damien, Nate, and Security Chief Snead scanned the images of the incoming workers as they passed through the main entrance. When Damien and Nate arrived an hour earlier, they searched the GIS employee roster for Addy's name, but none matched, not that they were surprised. On one of the holodisplays, Adrien's GSO picture was posted as well as an older image of Addy.

The mere sight of the armed guards at the main security checkpoint caused a cold chill to reverberate through Adrien's body. He watched

266

intently while Addy made it through without a hitch, and couldn't help but notice how the guards gawked when she walked by. His momentary jealousy was quickly eclipsed by alarm when the guards laid eyes on him. As he passed the station, a buzzer went off; he nearly screamed. Immediately a guard grabbed his arm and jerked him out of line.

Addy paused at the elevators and looked back in panic. In a vehement whisper, she said, "They pulled him out of line, Rad. Oh crap! We're dead!"

"Keep your cool, girl," Rad responded.

"Let me see your medallion," the taller guard grunted. But he didn't wait for Adrien to offer it on his own; he plucked it rudely from his shirt pocket and turned away.

The shorter guard said, "You new here? I don't remember seeing you before."

"Ah...no...I just...usually keep to myself."

"Yeah, I guess so," the guard replied.

Upstairs Nate said, "Look—what's going on there? That security guard just pulled someone off to the side."

Chief Snead tapped a few buttons on his screen and a series of cameras focused in on the guard station. Instantly four separate high-resolution close-ups of Adrien burst onto the screen. Damien and the Chief bounced back and forth between Adrien's GSO picture and the images from the cameras. But Nate just stared at the screen.

"Nate, you know him better than anyone. There's certainly a resemblance there," Damien said.

"He definitely looks like Adrien, but..."

"I don't think that's him," the Chief interrupted. "He looks familiar. I think he's a regular."

"Don't worry," the short guard said to Adrien. "We've been having some trouble with the system the last couple of days. Your bio scan was good. Sometimes we just have to enter the medallion data manually."

Adrien's blood pressure dropped twenty points. "No problem."

The tall guard handed him his badge back. "You're good. Move along."

He walked away from the guards and eased over to Addy. "Just a problem with the system," he whispered, without looking at her.

Upstairs the Chief said, "Here it is. They just posted his data from the floor. Walter Waite." The picture of Walter crawled across the screen. "Like I said, he's a regular."

"Okay. Keep looking," Damien ordered. "We've got a little less than an hour before five. They've got to pass through here at some point."

Nate stared at Adrien's face until Chief Snead pulled the image. "I swear that guy could be his brother," he whispered to himself. "Easy."

While they waited for the elevator, Adrien's attention was drawn to a large, clear wall about thirty feet to his right. Behind it was a wide, open space as deep and tall as an entire building. Without realizing it, he walked over and gazed upward into the expanse above. Spread out before him was a massive, round room in the middle of the building that extended up twenty floors. Around the edges, alternating layers of black glass and blue granite compassed the room at each level. An enormous image of a world map was etched in blue across the marble floor.

A three-story, fully-enclosed structure hung some fifty feet from the ceiling like a giant chandelier. Behind the ten-foot window that encircled the disk-shaped structure, the faint images of people moved about. Just below the window, a thin maintenance balcony and short guardrail stretched around the perimeter. Metal bars and supports fell from the bottom like protracted icicles.

As he crept closer to the door, the frigid air emanating off the glass brushed against his skin.

"That's the Chamber," Addy said from behind. "And that up there," she pointed to the disk high in the air, "is the Nest. About thirty people work up there. Nobody gets in without the approval of the Sovereign himself. And the only way to access that space is by a single, highly secure elevator from the top down. That's why we've got to access the system from the outside."

After a second, Adrien said, "I see."

"And those black layers," Addy continued, "they're floor after floor of Magnatium servers, the all-knowing brains of the global government. It's about thirty degrees in there all the time."

"Why?"

"Cooling. Those servers pass so many electrons, they'd burn up without it."

The elevator bell rang. "Let's go," she said. "We don't have much time."

When the door opened, Addy walked out first and led Adrien to Assimilation. At the door to his department, she turned and made eye contact. "You ready?" she asked.

Without a word, he put his medallion up to the reader under the holosign. "Checking bio signature," the voice said as they waited. At last, the screen glowed green, the shiny metal door slid open, and they both walked in.

Just like Addy said, Walter's department was mostly dark, and the ten or so workers there were settled in to their private cubicles unaware of anything or anyone around them.

"Go about twenty more feet and turn into that office on the right," she said.

"I remember the schematics," he assured her. When they had both entered the supervisor's office, she closed the door behind them.

"You did it, Rad," Addy congratulated the Chief Engineer. "The office is empty."

"Sweet! Now let's get down to business," he replied.

Adrien sat down at the station, pulled up the holoscreen, and flashed his medallion when the security scanner beeped. Then he gave way to Addy. When she brought the black drive near the station, it expanded to a full cube and a platform slid out to receive the drive. After the drive was installed, an access window appeared on the tech station screen. Addy tapped a series of buttons and brought up a second window entitled, "Globalcast Transfer Protocol."

"We're in," she told Rad. With another short series of taps, she opened the file called "Globalcast Broadcast 4.15.32," accessed the Resistance video and data files, and pulled them from the Resistance drive to the Globalcast window. Immediately, a progress bar rolled out onto the screen with the words, "Transferring data."

"It's working, isn't it?" asked Adrien.

Addy smiled. "Yes, just like we planned."

Suddenly, the transfer stopped and an error message beeped: "Improper Command Sequence."

"What?" Addy objected. She read the error details out loud. "'Globalcast files cannot be loaded from this station. Per Directive 4.3.551, Globalcast files can only be loaded from Globalcast

Command Room.'"

A look of dismay and panic washed over her face. "Oh, no!" she cried. "We're done."

"What? What is it?" Adrien asked.

"We can't load our files from here anymore."

"What do you mean? Then where do we load them. Let's move!"

"No, no, you don't understand. They can only be loaded in one place now."

"Where?"

"*The Nest!*"

Chapter 62

But you've already said there's no way to get in there, right?" protested Adrien.

"Yeah. I mean, it's impossible."

"So what do we do now?" asked Rad.

"Wait a minute," Adrien called from behind Addy's ear. He reached into his pocket and pulled out the red drive. "Rad, you said you might be able to hack the system if the files from this second drive were installed, right?"

"Yeah, but like Addy said, that's a long shot, man."

"Well now's the time for long shots." Adrien touched the panel and the platform released the drive. He quickly replaced it with the red one and said, "See if you can hack your way into the Nest now and load the files."

"Okay. Let's see if the Trojan will load first." Rad said, staring intently at his screen.

"Got anything?" asked Addy.

"We should know in a second," he replied. "It's programmed to find me once it loads. If it worked, I should see something right about…"

Before he could say the word "now," a window popped up on his screen.

"Bam, baby!" he yelled. "You're the man, Adrien!"

Adrien and Addy beamed at each other. Rad punched several keys and opened three additional windows. But after a few seconds, his expression changed from joy to frustration.

"Bad news, guys."

"What is it?" asked Addy.

"Well I'm definitely in—I can see the entire GIS network. But I can't see the Nest. It's just not there."

"How can that be? It's just across the hall?" she asked.

"It's got to be on its own stand alone network. I mean, it's not physically connected to the GIS system. There's no way I can get to it; there are no roads between here and there."

Addy threw up her hands in exasperation while Adrien turned and walked to the back of the office.

"What are we going to do now?" she complained. "There's no way into the Nest. It's impossible."

"Maybe not," Adrien said, turning back to Addy. "Rad, you said you could see every system in this building, right? Except for the Nest."

"Yeah, that's right."

"Can you see building controls? Like heating and cooling and fire?"

Rad delayed his response while he tapped a few icons. "Yeah. They're right here. Why?"

"Get into the fire system and look for something called 'Fire Suppressant' or something like that."

Again Rad went silent. "Okay. I got it. But you don't want to set

273

off that stuff, do you? I mean, it'll kill everybody in the building. That's the stuff they use when everybody's out and the building's about to burn down."

"That's right. It's toxic. But if you look closely, you'll see that the warning and discharge functions are separate."

Rad grinned on the other end. "I got it! I got it! Trigger the alarm, but don't discharge the gas. Everybody will evacuate immediately—including security!"

"But won't the elevators lock down because of the alarm?" Addy asked.

"In most buildings they will," answered Rad. "But this building is brand new—state-of-the-art. The elevator system is on completely separate and protected power circuits and ventilation systems. It's like a fire and smoke fortress. It's safer than the stairs, and a heck of a lot faster at getting folks out of the building. It only cuts off when its containment systems have been breached.

"If this works like I think it will, all secured doors *and elevators* will open automatically!"

"Brilliant, Adrien," said Addy. "But how do you know all this?"

"It's a long story. I'll tell you about it later. Rad, can you do it?"

"Almost done."

"Okay." Adrien turned to Addy. "After he flips the switch, we'll wait for the halls to clear and head up to the Nest. If I'm right, we should be able to walk right in and load the data without so much as a peep from security."

"But what if the Nest network is shut down too?" she asked.

Rad's voice sounded in her ear once again. "It won't be, Addy. That system is independent of the building systems. The Global-cast software will take over if nobody's there to do it manually. It'll carry out its programming regardless.

"Give me just a minute and we'll be ready," the Chief Engineer said.

Meanwhile in the GIS main security room, while Nate and Chief Snead continued to scan the entrance video, Damien pulled away.

"What time is it?" he asked.

Nate looked up to the holodisplay. "About ten 'til five. Why?"

"Chief, you said Walter was a regular here. Where does he work?" Damien asked, hurriedly.

The Chief put Walter's file back up on the holodisplay. "Looks like Assimilation."

"Does that have anything to do with the Globalcast?"

"Yeah, they load the data for the Globalcast, I think."

"What is it, uncle?"

"It's Friday just before five. The Globalcast launches in ten minutes!" He grabbed a plasma rifle from the security locker and ran out of the office. Nate, confused by his uncle's sudden exit, grabbed a rifle himself and followed.

As they ran down the hall toward the elevator, Nate yelled, "But what about the entrance?"

"You idiot," Damien yelled back. "They're already here! It's the Globalcast! They're trying to hack it from inside!"

Just then the hallway lights blinked red and an alarm sounded. "Fire Alert" flashed on the holodisplays along the tops of the walls and a loud voice came from every corner, "Fire Alert. Fire Alert. Evacuate the building immediately. Discharge imminent."

Damien stopped in his tracks and looked around. "It's them. They're making their move," he said to himself, and took off for the stairs.

"Okay, guys. You should be hearing the alarm now," Rad informed them.

As they both looked up to the red lights and flashing alert sign, Addy said to Rad, "It's working." Adrien reached down, took the red drive from the tech station, and slipped it into his pocket.

Outside the supervisor's office, silhouettes of people rolled by as workers sprinted from their offices and cubicles toward the exit.

When the department had cleared, Adrien and Addy eased out of the office, tiptoed to the department door, and listened for activity in the main hallway. When the sound of running and commotion had ceased, they stepped out.

"This way," Addy said, pivoting right.

At the end of the hall, they turned left and headed for the Nest elevator. Just then, Damien and Nate appeared from the stairwell on the other side of Assimilation. Damien looked down the hall just in time to see them turn the corner and disappear. Without hesitation, he drew his gun and fired wildly, burning holes through the back wall and tearing off the corner of the hallway.

Caught completely off guard, Adrien and Addy lifted their hands to block the debris exploding behind them. Addy screamed as Adrien grabbed her hand and jerked her down the hall, his attention completely focused on the elevator an eternal 200 feet away.

"It's open," he yelled back while they sprinted for their lives. He had just gotten the words out when Damien turned the corner and lifted his rifle again.

"Jump!" Adrien barked loudly when the elevator door drew near. As Damien's hot shells shrieked just under and over their airborne bodies, they flew the final ten feet into the cabin and crashed against the back wall.

Adrien screamed, "Elevator close! Elevator close! Down! Down! Down!"

Chapter 63

After what seemed like an hour, the elevator doors finally closed and the metal box descended toward the Nest.

"So much for 'not even a peep'!" Addy blurted out sarcastically from the floor.

Adrien stood and reached down to pull her up. "Okay, so I missed that one."

"You guys alright?" Rad asked loudly in their ears.

"Yeah, for now," replied Addy.

"What happened?"

"They're on to us, Rad. I don't know how," Adrien told him. "We're in the elevator down to the Nest now. Can you disable it when we get to the bottom?"

"The system won't let me, Adrien. You can't freeze an elevator when this type of alarm has been activated."

"Can't you just turn the alarm off and then disable it?" asked Addy.

"Yeah, I could do that. But the system would *still* run the safety protocols for another fifteen minutes just to make sure."

"Okay. We'll have to jam the door with something," Adrien

concluded. "That should buy us the time we need."

When the door finally opened, they stepped out onto a platform that compassed the large, circular elevator shoot. From their position, they saw the numerous tech stations on the floor below, and the rounded, clear glass that made up the back wall.

"Grab one of those chairs," Adrien ordered Addy while he held the elevator door open.

Addy turned left and ran down the platform stairs to the main level. She grabbed a black chair from the nearest station and carried it up the stairs. Adrien quickly lodged it in the opening, the wheels jammed in the frame on one end, the chair back pressed against the closing door on the other.

"That ought to hold," he said. Then they both shot down the stairs and turned left toward the front of the Nest. As they exited the short hallway that separated front from back, they saw the elevated Conductor's station facing the giant holoscreen that covered most of the massive front window. Just behind the Conductor's platform, a set of theatre-style chairs appeared where VIPs watched the Globalcast unfold. And below the Conductor, three rows of tech stations, seven stations in each row, came into view, each separated by a thin aisle and metal rail.

Adrien and Addy ran toward the center station on the front row, the control station.

On the back side of the nest, the elevator door continued banging against the stubborn chair blocking its way. Little by little, the wheel lodged in the frame slipped out of place; suddenly, the entire chair popped out completely, and the door closed.

When they got to the station, Addy sat down while Adrien hovered behind her, watching intently. With a single touch, the screen came alive.

"They didn't log out," she said, stunned.

"Finally, some luck." Adrien pulled the black drive from his pocket and dropped it into the tech station platform when it opened.

"Okay, Rad," Addy said. "We're back on line. The drive is in. I've got a window." She scanned the icons on the display. "There,"— she pointed to the middle of the screen—"Globalcast Launch 4.15.23."

She tapped the screen and the folder opened. After dragging the files from the black drive window into the Globalcast desktop file, she waited for the system to respond. Once again, a message appeared.

"Would you like to replace the files in folder 'Globalcast Launch 4.15.23'?" the message asked.

"This is it," Addy whispered. "If they're going to freak out, this is when they'll do it." She tapped the word "Yes" and waited.

"Transferring data. Replacing Files," the system countered; but this time, no error message.

"I think it's working, Rad," she offered.

And then the elevator chimed.

"Oh, no," Adrien said, mortified.

They both turned to see the determined GSS Director explode through the back hallway and open fire. Adrien threw Addy to the floor just as Damien's fireballs burned through the control station. In short order, the holoscreen disappeared and the entire station erupted with sparks and fire. Pieces of metal and shattered components splashed down all around them.

"What just happened, guys?!" Rad yelled.

"No time now, Rad!" Addy screamed. "We're getting shot at

again!"

Adrien and Addy crawled down the aisle away from Damien's position. As they approached the other side of the Nest, Adrien lifted his head and spotted the door to the outer platform just past the last row of stations.

Turning to Addy, he said, "Listen, here's what we're going to do. I'll get his attention. You slip out the maintenance door just past that last row and wait until I get him around back. Then you make a run for the elevator."

"But what about you?"

"I'll be fine. Don't worry. I'll meet you back at the shop when I get out of here."

Meanwhile, Damien signaled for Nate to take the stairs and follow the elevator platform to the other side to cut them off.

Damien ducked slightly and crept toward the front of the Nest, looking carefully down each row for his targets. When he reached the first row, he saw Addy and Adrien at the other end scurrying to make the corner and hide behind the end station. Before they could make the turn, however, he fired a flurry of shots their way, destroying several more stations in the process.

But he missed them again.

Out of time, Adrien yelled, "Go!" and they both took off running. Just past the elevator stairs, Addy broke off and slipped out the maintenance door onto the cold platform outside.

As Adrien ran past the stairs into the corridor, Nate ran down the elevator stairs and took position in the middle of the hallway behind him. When Adrien turned back to check on Addy, he locked eyes with his old friend and stopped dead.

"Nate? What are you doing here?" Adrien called out with a confused and horrified expression.

"Sorry, Adrien," he offered, evenly.

"But Nate…why?"

"I didn't want to, man. But you forced me," he explained with almost a tinge of remorse. Then he clenched his teeth and spoke with disgust. "You're one of them now," he charged. "One of those superstitious nuts!"

"But I thought I was your friend, your best friend? How could you?"

"You were a good friend, Adrien. But I'm not going to let you take us back 500 years with your lunacy! Sorry, man." Nate stared at him for another second and fired; Adrien jumped out of the way just in time.

Seeing he missed his target, Nate took off after him, but pulled off his pursuit when Damien yelled from behind, "Get the girl! Get the girl! Bach is mine!"

Before Adrien could take cover in the back of the Nest, his father's killer turned the corner and fired. The blast from his rifle tore through Adrien's shoulder like a grinder; he spun violently as he ran, tumbled to the floor, and passed out.

Outside, Addy sprinted around the thin platform surrounding the Nest, trying desperately to escape Nate's fierce pursuit. In her haste, she slipped and fell on the slick metal terrace, banging her chest hard against the short guard rail on the way down.

Nate was in full gallop until he turned the corner and saw Addy lying on the platform. He tried to stop his momentum, but his force of motion was too great; he lost his footing, tripped over Addy, and slammed into the rail's vertical supports. His gun launched off the platform and crashed fifteen stories below.

Back in the Nest, it took only a few seconds for Adrien to come to. When his eyes refocused, his face was pressed against the base of a tech station in the back of the Nest. He knew Damien was only a breath away.

Suddenly an idea came to him. He quickly reached into his pocket for the red drive as Damien came about and drew a bead on his position.

Back in the Resistance datacenter, a window appeared on Rad's screen. "What's this?" he asked. "Adrien, is that you?"

"No time to talk, Rad," Adrien said while Damien fired again. "Just do what you've got to do!" he yelled, then pushed himself up with one arm and bolted down the aisle.

"I'm on it. Just don't get yourself killed, man," Rad replied.

"Doing my best," Adrien answered back.

Out on the platform, Nate threw himself onto Addy. She fought back violently, hitting him incessantly with her small fist. When he pulled back to block the blows, she pushed him off and slipped away. Nate, now furious, roared after her, and in only a few steps grabbed her shoulder and flipped her around to face him.

"I see we're a blond now," he gnarled. "I've always been partial to brunets myself."

"I knew you were a traitor," she barked, ignoring his sarcasm.

"I'm not the traitor, sweetheart. You and your boyfriend, you're the traitors."

"Do you have any idea what they've done?"

He shrugged, "You know, I just don't care."

"I thought he was your friend. I thought you cared about him."

"He *was* my friend, right up to the point where he fell for that ridiculous myth. You guys are all crazy!"

"We're not the ones who are crazy!" she fired back.

"Well, that might be so, sweetheart. But you are the ones *about to die*. So how do you feel about heights?"

Nate grabbed her shoulders and thrust her over the short rail. Addy screamed as she started to fall, and then reached up and caught Nate's shirt with her hand. His eyes exploded with fear when his body jerked toward the open air. In a frantic attempt to save his own life, he clenched the rail with one hand and fought wildly to break her grasp with the other.

Just when he was about to succeed, his footing gave way, and they both flipped over the side.

Chapter 64

Adrien's flight brought him back to the front of the Nest just in time to see Nate and Addy disappear. "Nooooo!" he shrieked at the top of his lungs, and took off for the maintenance door. But before he could make it, Damien popped out from the hallway and blocked his advance.

"Mr. Bach," he said, calmly. "What a pleasure to finally meet you."

Adrien looked back and forth between Damien's gun and the door. But when he fixed in on the Director's eyes, a light went off in his mind.

This man killed my father.

The hair was lighter; the skin was not as smooth; but this was the man in the holofile, the one tagged, "Confirmed Assassin."

Adrien answered through his teeth, "The pleasure's all yours."

Damien waved his gun side to side. "Why don't you back away a bit, Mr. Bach?"

As he drew closer, Adrien eased back to maintain his distance.

"So you killed my father, and now you're going to kill me? Is that it?"

Damien looked surprised. "Well, well. It seems you know more than I gave you credit for. I'm sorry about that, Mr. Bach. It was a necessary evil, I'm afraid." Then his voice thickened. "Your father chose the wrong side."

"The *wrong* side, Addergoole, or just not *your* side?"

"They are one and the same, my young friend. Nature chooses who lives and who dies, and who is *worthy*." As the words came out of his mouth, he thought of Prissy, and for a fleeting moment his determination wavered.

Adrien saw a crack in the hard man's eyes. "Nature? You don't actually believe that, do you? Is a person's life only worth the strength of their chemical bonds, or the magnitude of their luck?"

Damien's eyes lost focus for a moment and his rifle began to fall. But his resolve returned just as fast. "Don't try to confuse your fate with meaningless philosophical questions. Your little game is over." He moved to within arm's length of Adrien. "Get down on your hands and knees, Mr. Bach!" he ordered.

"Don't do this!" Adrien pleaded.

"Shut up!" Damien screamed, nailing Adrien in the face with the butt of his weapon. As he shot to the ground, blood hastened from his cheek causing part of his beard to peel off and hang loosely from his chin. "I said on your hands and knees, Mr. Bach!"

Adrien looked at the debris surrounding him on the floor and then swiveled up to the fuzzy form standing over him. His shoulder and face raged with pain. After he took the position demanded by his soon-to-be executioner, he centered his eyes once more on Damien's angry gaze.

"I pray you will one day understand the value of every life, Mr.

Addergoole…even your own."

"Today is not that day," Damien replied, sarcastically. "Say hello to your father for me."

The GSS Director lifted his rifle and aimed it directly at Adrien's head. With the discipline of a trained and experienced killer, he reached his finger into the trigger slot and slowly squeezed. But just when the plasma round was about to activate inside the chamber, Adrien reached toward the debris beside him, grabbed a bent metal bar, and swung it at Damien's ankles with all the strength remaining in his body.

The blow dropped Damien with the force of a concrete block and slammed his head against the steel bar separating the rows of tech stations. His gun flew out of his hands and bounced to a halt under the control station just behind Adrien. The wounded archaeologist lunged for it, but when it was just within reach, Damien squatted down over him and jerked his upper body off the floor.

Adrien screamed in pain.

Undeterred by the suffering of his enemy, Damien pulled his hand back, bent his fingers down to the first knuckle, and started to thrust them toward Adrien's throat.

But then something unexpected happened—the entire holodisplay lit up with the face of Rene Moreau. Damien's hand froze in midair as he looked in absolute unbelief at the massive image above him.

"My fellow citizens. My name is Rene Moreau. I am the leader of a group called the Resistance. I have something to share with you about your government."

In the bottom, left hand corner of the screen, the words "Transmitting Globally" blinked on and off.

While the astonished GSS Director watched the image on the

screen, Adrien reached back and grabbed the loose rifle. Damien, feeling him move, turned back to finish his stroke, but the instant he glanced down, the butt of his own weapon slammed against his head and knocked him out cold.

Adrien quickly pushed him off, peeled his beard the rest of the way off, and hurried out to the maintenance platform.

"Addy!" he yelled as he slid quickly along the rail looking down for any sign of her.

"Adrien!" she cried from below.

He looked to see her hanging by one hand on a metal cross member beneath the Nest. Behind her, many stories below, the crumbled, bloody impression of Nate lay still on the floor.

Adrien knelt down on the platform and pushed himself though the vertical supports of the walkway railing. "Hold on. I'm coming," he called to her, grimacing with pain. He reached down to a set of bars just below the platform and locked his feet behind the vertical supports now elevated behind him. When he was sure he wouldn't fall, he stretched out as far as he could to save her.

"Hurry, Adrien! I'm slipping!" Her body was swinging back and forth while she struggled to hold on. Her eyes bounced from the floor to the cross member and back again.

His fingers came within inches of her cold hand, but though he pushed as hard as he could, he could not reach her.

"Addy, listen to me!" he yelled to focus her attention. Then calmly he said, "Everything's going to be just fine. What I need you to do is throw your other hand up to me and grab mine. I'll catch you. I promise."

"I don't think I can do it, Adrien," she cried out. "I'll fall!"

"No you won't. You *can* reach me. Okay?"

287

Her fingers slipped on the cold rail. She screamed and started to cry. "Oh, no, Adrien! I'm going to die!"

Through tear-filled eyes, he said, "You're *not* going to die, Addy! You're going to be with me for a long time. So just give me your hand."

"Okay," she finally agreed. She propelled her body to one side and swung her hand up as hard as she could. Adrien reached out and grabbed it as her other hand slipped off the crossbar.

She screamed again.

"I got you, baby!" he yelled, excitedly. She smiled a relieved smile, but immediately her hand started to slip, and her grin turned to pure terror.

And then peace.

"I love you, Adrien. I'm so glad I found you," she said, smiling at him one last time.

As he started to cry, he said, "And I love you, Addy…"

Drops of sweat fell slowly from Adrien's face. He heard himself breathe—in and out… in and out—and felt his neck pulse as blood coursed through his veins. His fingers tingled as her hand slipped from his. Her eyes widened. Her arms and legs waved in the air.

"Nooooo!" he howled.

And then he squeezed his eyes closed, not able to bear what came next.

Chapter 65

Adrien rushed back into the Nest and called the elevator. By the time he reached the first floor, a crowd had gathered just outside the glass doors to the Chamber. He pushed through and ran to Addy.

When he reached her in the middle of the cold floor, he knelt down and tenderly lifted her broken body into his arms.

"Addy, don't leave me. No, no, no," he whimpered as his sobbing overcame him. He pulled her bloody wig off, pushed a strand of sticky hair from her face, and gently stroked her forehead.

But there was nothing he could do. Addy Moreau was dead.

While his mourning continued, he gently laid her head on his good shoulder and rocked her back and forth like a baby. And when reason finally broke through the intense anguish and tears, he looked heavenward and let out in one long scream: "Whyyyyy?! Did you bring me here just for this?!" His roar bounced from wall to wall and floor to floor until it eventually overtook the lofty ceiling above, willing itself, as it were, to reach the very feet of the Maker himself.

Anger, rage, betrayal, abandonment—his head was a confusing con-

289

coction of strident emotions. How cruel was this deity? And how unfair! How the Maker could bring him so close to happiness and snatch it from him in such a heartless turn, Adrien would never understand.

This can't be happening *again*, he thought. To lose both of them in this way was simply too much to bear; the agony overwhelmed him. If only he had let himself fall into that canyon on that cold, rainy night!

This was it. He had had enough. He would not survive this day.

And then the door opened in the distance.

Adrien turned to see three men walking into the room, one in front, two behind. Though he expected security uniforms and rifles—and possibly the angry Damien Addergoole himself—these men were dressed like regular people, work boots, pants, and short, collarless jackets. The one in the front was young and thin, with dark, flowing hair and a goatee; the two behind—one with light skin; the other, dark—were taller, thick and strong, intimidating in stature and presence.

As they came closer, the young man in front came more into focus. Adrien recognized him. He was the man from Sauveur's, the one with the ancient Persian coins. What was he doing—? But his thought was cut short by an even more profound realization: He was *also* the man who called out to him at the site the night he almost jumped, the man who saved his life.

But how could this be? His mind must be playing tricks on him, his emotions muddling his senses.

As the man drew near, the commanding duo fell back and took positions on each side. Like personal bodyguards, they crossed their hands at their belts and stood silently.

The stranger came up to Adrien and knelt down. Adrien's bloodshot eyes looked at him intently, and, at least for the moment, his tears ceased.

"Who are you?" he asked, his voice raspy from crying. "What are you doing here?"

The man didn't answer; he simply stared into Adrien's eyes. To the heartbroken archaeologist, his were the kindest, most loving, most powerful eyes he had ever seen. Simply gazing at him sent a chill down Adrien's spine and filled his frigid body with warmth.

"I am the one in the books," he finally answered.

Adrien's mouth dropped open and his entire upper body pulled back in shock at his frightening announcement. Then it all made sense. Now he knew why he didn't recognize the man at the ravine and why he never saw him again in that desert—because he *wasn't* a part of his GSO team at all. He came for that moment only, to save Adrien's life and disappear.

And how else could he explain Sauveur's? How the stranger seemed to know so much, and why when he said, "Perhaps you should not look within yourself for the capacity to accomplish this task…but to your wise and loving king," it was as if he had full view into Adrien's very soul.

Yes, this man's claim was true. Adrien Bach was now in the personal presence of the Maker himself, the one who made the worlds.

His cold mental deductions quickly translated into lively fear and apprehension. He bowed his head and said, "Forgive me. I didn't know."

Laying his hand on Adrien's head, the Maker replied, "Do not fear, my son. I come today as your friend and helper."

Adrien, wondering just what he meant, looked up to him and then down to Addy in his arms.

"Lay her down and step back," he ordered.

Then the two men behind him started to move.

As Adrien stepped slowly backward, he pointed and asked, "Who are they?"

"They are my Strong Ones," he answered, without raising his eyes from Addy. "They have been with me since the beginning."

Suddenly, the Chamber filled with light so powerful its entire form—its boundaries and lines and colors; the Nest, the door, the marble floor—was lost to the brightness. Like lively snowflakes, sparkling embers danced in the air all around them. And the Strong Ones changed.

Their street clothes became majestic, silver capes of silk. From their backs great crimson wings with long, thick feathers emerged and spread out across the room while their bodies gently lifted off the ground. Like a million tiny rockets, light blasted from all around them.

And then the Maker changed. His dark hair and goatee became ashen gray, and his common clothing was replaced by a pure white robe with glistening gold tassel; a blood red sash fastened loosely at his waist. And his skin, unlike only seconds before, now glowed as if it actually radiated light rather than merely reflecting it.

The full message of his presence was a living paradox—innocent, yet ancient; gentle, yet austere; the most approachable man in the world, yet the most holy being in the universe.

When his transformation was complete, he touched Addy with one hand, lifted the other toward the heavens, and cried out, "I say to you…arise!"

Whereas Adrien's scream had echoed slowly into the empty spaces of the Chamber high above, this voice—the Maker's voice—dispersed like thunder, shaking the entire room as if by an earthquake.

As those explosive words hung in the air, melodic voices erupted from the heavens, and the two angels stirred the air with their wings and lifted their deep voices in song.

In all his life Adrien Bach had never experienced a scene so glorious, so magnificent, so breathtaking as what was unfolding before him. His heart exploded with joy and power as he fell to his knees, tears rolling from his eyes.

Addy's arm began to twitch, her eyes blinked open, and her head lifted slowly off the floor. She smiled, her eyes now fixed on her Maker. The blood and bruises that had stained her satin hair and marred her soft skin were now gone. And her cheeks, again infused with life, were full and bright once more.

"It was you," Adrien whispered to the Maker. "Rene was wrong. It was never me who was coming to help—it was always *you*. You're the one they've been waiting for."

The Maker turned and looked at him in silent affirmation. Then he took Addy's hand, helped her to her feet, and turned back to Adrien.

"She is alive, my son," he called out in the most serene voice imaginable. "*And she is yours.*"

Adrien and Addy ran to each other and embraced in the presence of the white-robed Deity. And as they did, the entire Chamber filled with the visible presence of hundreds of angels singing of the greatness and tender mercy of their Maker.

And he smiled over them all.

When their joyful reunion was complete, they turned, walked back to the Maker, and knelt down before him. As they bowed their heads, he lifted his hands and touched them both on the shoulders.

To Adrien he said, "I have put you through many things, my dearest Adrien. But I have done it to bring about a good you could not before imagine, and even now you cannot fully understand. I hope you now see that though my ways are often severe, I richly reward those I love and those who serve me.

"You are my chosen one now. The work you started today is not yet finished. When the time is right, I will show you what else you must do for me. But for now, rejoice with the one I have provided for you. She is yours."

As wet tears of joy cascaded down his cheeks, he bowed and said, "Yes, my king," and turned to kiss Addy once again.

When their lips touched, time seemed to stand still all around them. The sounds of the angels faded to no more than a whisper, and their movements slowed to almost perfect stillness. As he closed his eyes, he felt as if he and Addy were gently spinning in the middle of the crowded room. It was like being taken up into peace itself. Though only a moment had passed, it seemed like an eternity.

When their lips parted, the heavenly spectacle surrounding them began to fade, and time reclaimed its normal rhythm. The light dimmed and slowly disappeared, and the angel's wings folded away. In only a few seconds, everything looked just the way it did before. Even the glorious Maker once again took the form of a humble man.

Adrien looked out beyond the doors to the crowd outside. "Security is back," he said. "We'll never get past them now."

"You just stay with me," the Maker answered, "and you will be fine."

So Adrien and Addy followed him out, the mighty angels behind them, and not a soul laid a hand on them.

As they were just about to walk out of the building, Adrien looked to his left and saw Damien Addergoole staring at them from a distance, his head bleeding, a white rag hanging from his hand. In the background, a group of soldiers approached him, rifles raised.

But Damien didn't move, nor did he say a word. He just watched them all walk out the front door together. And then the soldiers grabbed him, and took him away.

Chapter 66

Munich, Germany
Friday, April 15
4:59 PM, Local/4:59 PM, Paris

Jack sat in the cold, gray cell, shoulder to shoulder with nearly fifty other men. He had no idea where he was, and he barely remembered being thrust into that ominous PAV one dark night over a week ago. His right eye was almost completely swollen shut, and his short bangs were filled with sweat and blood.

At the other end of the long cell, a holodisplay dropped down from the ceiling. His good eye opened when he heard the feminine voice announce, "Welcome to your G-CoN Globalcast." Given his present situation, he couldn't help but chuckle at the presumption of his captors.

His amused look became one of shock and amazement when Rene Moreau's face filled the screen and his words began to echo through the crowded dungeon. As Rene revealed more and more of the truth about the G-CoN, America, and the Maker, the men sleeping on the floor or simply ignoring another dose of the G-CoN's propaganda quickly took notice.

"Hey," Jack said, poking the old man lying on the floor beside him. "Mr. Harris, wake up. You've got to see this." His former neighbor lifted his head off his ragged coat and turned to watch the bright display.

When Rene finished his long speech and vanished from sight, a tear formed in Jack's eye and he started to laugh. He cackled and roared on and on until he simply could laugh no more.

"I can't believe it," he finally said. "You were right, Grandma. You were absolutely right. Somebody exposed them all right. But in your wildest dreams I'll bet you'd never have guessed it would be Uncle Rene who did it."

Chapter 67

Vallée Blanché
Chamonix France
Sunday, April 17
9:41 AM, Local/9:41 AM, Paris

Adrien Bach was on his knees again. Behind his humbled frame was a cold, forbidding landscape of deep snow, jagged slate-gray rocks, and glistening walls of ice. But on this morning, it was not what was behind him that secured his attention—it was the empty space before him.

The open, icy crevasse was clearly visible in the morning sun. In the two years since he had seen it last, he had not forgotten a single detail.

He looked into the hole and remembered the tragic moment that started his life on the wild and winding path that now brought him back again. And he allowed the memory of what had taken place since that fateful day to heal his deep wounds and give meaning to all he had suffered.

As the full picture of these events settled upon him, he wiped a small tear from his cheek and did something he never thought he could do in this place—he smiled.

"Goodbye, Sophie," he said into the mouth of the cavern. "I did what you said. I boxed up our love and put it in a secret place. And now I must move on. I love you, Sophie. I will *always* love you."

297

With those words, he reached out into the bright opening and let the shiny gold band slip through his fingers and fall end over end into the darkness below. When the scene was etched forever in his mind, he stood and walked back to Addy and Journey who waited patiently for him only a few steps behind.

"It's done," he said to Addy, relieved, and breathed out a sigh. "It's finally done."

While they stood together and stared out into the valley below, Adrien's eyes were drawn high above, to a distant image of Sophie standing in the clouds. She smiled down upon him and blew a kiss, and then she turned to the Maker and walked with him into the heavens.

As she slipped into the bright light of the sky above, he knew the dark hand might yet find him again, but he also knew he would inevitably survive and prosper, for he was a chosen vessel of the Maker.

And so with that hopeful thought anchored in his heart, he kissed his new love, and turned and walked away.

THE END

Not long after...

The back of the transport opened just above the eco-garden at 1281 Rue de Salut. Right away the soldiers leapt into action, dropped down to the terrace below by automatic nylon cables. One man served as a lookout as the other three made their way down the gravel path past trees and plants to the entrance at the center of the roof.

When Othman arrived, he nodded to the soldier nearest the door who then waved a thin, red medallion over the access port. The door opened and one by one the assassins entered with the stealth of bats in the night.

In the stairwell, Othman's team gathered just inside the door to the eighteenth floor. He spoke into his comm-port, "Team two, have you secured the lobby and security stations?"

Two hundred feet below, Captain Jaeger replied, "Yes, lobby has been neutralized. Security is down. Exits are sealed."

"Very well. We're moving in to main target areas. Kill anyone who tries to leave."

"Got it," Jaeger confirmed.

Othman opened the door and stepped out into the main hall

followed by the rest of his team. With their rifles drawn and ready, they crept down the long corridor toward the Resistance offices. As they passed a breakroom on their left, Othman pointed without looking and a single trooper peeled off to attack. Screams echoed behind them as the soldier destroyed his targets.

Next they passed a large meeting room. With another quick motion, a lone soldier paused at the entrance, and rushed the room. Bright light flashed from the doorway when his deadly head shots found their mark.

At the end of the hallway, they stopped just outside the main work spaces, and then invaded, firing at point blank range. Clerks and techs, men and women, young and old—no one was spared.

Without delay they regrouped for the last push into the datacenter. All four assassins crept up alongside the main door. As they settled into position, they heard sounds coming from inside.

Othman whispered, "I'll go in first. You three spread out left and right and eliminate the targets."

The men nodded back to their leader. Then he counted down with his fingers, pushed through the door, and ran straight ahead. As his men fanned out and cut down the remaining targets on each side of the room, he pressed ahead to the last living person at the Resistance headquarters.

The frenzy of the attack now over, he slowed down to enjoy his last kill. He lifted his rifle to the final target of his mission. "Director Addergoole sends his regards," he said, and then he fired a single round into the head of Rene Moreau.

More about

The Maker

Table of Contents

Can I talk to you for a moment?

I hope you have enjoyed this story, because I certainly have enjoyed writing it. It brought together so much of my life— my experiences, my passions, my pain—and in some sense gave them all more meaning. And the funniest part is, I never considered myself an author. I never received high marks in English in high school or college (in fact I failed it in the eleventh grade), and until about a year ago never dreamed I would write a novel. But here we are, and I'm very thankful for the opportunity.

I want you to know I wrote this story for you. I wrote it because I care about your troubles. I've been there. I know what it's like to be Adrien Bach—at the end of your way, ready to throw in the towel and give up. The dark hand Adrien battles throughout this story is *my* dark hand. I've been through many deep trials and periods of emotional pain in my life. Early on it was with my father. And then it was a big breakup with my girlfriend in high school. And then it was a terrible job situation. And then…well, I'll spare you the details. One day a couple of years ago, I was trying to tell my wife how I felt inside; I was trying to describe to her what I was experiencing. Finally, I said, "It's like this dark hand that reaches up from the floor and pulls me down into the darkness."

Even as you struggle, I want you to see there is hope. But not a false hope that relies on pixie dust or fairy tales or some impersonal presence. There is hope because there is someone out there, someone who made us all, someone who cares for us and is willing to act on our behalf. And I want you to know that person.

But I also wrote this story because I wanted to give you something to think about. I wanted to put things to you in such a way that you could hear them as if you'd never heard them before. So I wrote a story that was only a fraction of a degree from reality to help you see reality without the biases and filters instilled in us by our culture.

As you've read this book, maybe you've wondered who the Maker is and what, if anything, the two books Adrien found symbolize. Maybe you're asking yourself what I'm trying to say with this story. What exactly do I want you to walk away with when you're done? What themes am I trying to emphasize?

If you're willing to journey with me for a while longer, I'd like to take a few pages to answer those questions and, in the process, introduce you to a book and a person who can bring real hope into your life.

Here's what I'd like to do in the pages that follow:

1. Share the various connections to reality in *The Maker* (Supplement 1).

2. Reveal the central themes from *The Maker* (Supplement 2).

3. Address common spiritual questions in a section called "The Spiritual Top 40" (Supplement 3).

4. List resources for further study (Supplement 4).

5. Provide questions for studying *The Maker* as a group (Supplement 5).

Supplement 1
The Maker: Connections to Reality

If you're wondering if there are any correlations between this story and real life, let me relieve you of your curiosity—yes, there are. Here are the four most important ones (you can draw others as you see fit):

Connection 1: The Maker is God.

He's God, but not just any god. He's the God of the ancient Christian writings—the God of the Bible. Please don't stop listening because I said *Christian* or *Bible*. I know all the baggage those words come with in our culture. Please give me the opportunity to address some of those issues in future pages. For now, just understand that the Maker in the story is the God of the Bible.

Here are some passages from the Bible that refer to God as our Maker:

• "Come, let us bow down in worship, let us kneel before *the Lord our Maker;* for he is our God and we are the people of his pasture, the flock under his care." Psalm 95:6-7[1]

• "Rich and poor have this in common: *The Lord is the Maker* of them all." Proverbs 22:2

• "I, even I, am he who comforts you. Who are you that you fear mortal men, the sons of men, who are but grass, that you *forget the Lord your Maker,* who stretched out the heavens and laid the foundations of the earth." Isaiah 51:13

Connection 2: The Maker is Jesus Christ, the second person of the Trinity.

The parallels are obvious in retrospect, aren't they? At the end of the book, the Maker comes in and resurrects Addy from the dead. There are many hints that this is Christ: He wears a white robe with a blood red sash, and he commands Addy with the same type of language Christ himself used in Mark 12:41 to raise Jairus' daughter.[2]

Connection 3: *The Writings of the Maker* **is the Bible.**

I used a different arrangement of the content and reworded some passages for effect, but this fictional document is meant to point back to the Bible itself. This book, the Bible, is the most well-preserved, logical, scientifically accurate, powerful account of the truth about God, man, and life the world has ever known.

Connection 4: *The Evidence for the Maker* **represents the many thousands of volumes that have been written to affirm the truths taught in the Bible.**

From books written about the resurrection of Jesus, to the account of creation, to the nature of truth itself, the Bible's claims have been successfully defended at every point. (For more information about these books, see Supplement 4.)

Supplement 2
The Maker: Central Themes

So, what do I want you to take away from this story? What thoughts do I want to leave with you? I'll list the five most important below.

Theme 1: Hope

1. Life is full of dark times, but there is hope. You saw in the life of Adrien Bach a man who did not want to go on, a man whose life brought him one hammer blow after another until he was completely broken. This life has a way of doing that to all of us. But there is a way to overcome it and find victory. The word *hope* means "an expectation of future good." Isn't that what you want for your life? You want tomorrow to be better than today; you want that problem to be fixed, that pain to go away. No matter how low you are, or how broken, this is not the end. Just as Adrien found hope he did not expect from a source he never anticipated, so there is hope for you if you are willing to receive it. (I'll tell you how to find it soon.)

2. There is no hope without the personal, good, all-powerful God

309

of the Bible. Think about it for a minute. If there is no God—the God of the Bible, that is: personal, good, and all-powerful—what hope is there? If God isn't out there, or if he isn't strong enough, or good enough, or interested enough to help, why should we expect good in the future? Who's going to bring your dead child back, or make all the wrongs right? And if God is not a person at all, but merely a "force," "entity," or "presence," how can it help us? If the trees are god, and I am god, then I'm sunk because trees can't help me—and I'm the one that got myself into this mess to start with. The point is, your road to hope begins by understanding and acknowledging that there is no hope unless the Bible's God is real.

3. This life is more than just a series of chemical reactions. At some point, you need to decide what kind of a person you're going to be. There are many in this world who tell us we're nothing more than randomly placed chemicals operating according to mind-less physical laws. Do you really believe that? Is a rose nothing more than chance and time? How about love? What about that feeling you get when you stare out into the ocean, across a great plain, or into a valley from some fabulous mountain peak? And what about you? Are *you* nothing more than a mass of cells and tissue, destined for nothing more than being recycled into some other mass of cells and tissues? All the wonders of this life witness in our hearts that there is something more to our existence than what science claims to have found.

4. There is a purpose for your life. Adrien realized that if the universe has a designer then everything in it must have a purpose—including you and me. We are God's most precious creation; every life to him is invaluable. We were created to know him and carry out his important work on the earth. While ultimately everyone has a different task to perform, *we all have a purpose*, and by fulfilling that purpose we find our greatest joy and meaning in life. In time, as you walk with God, he will reveal your purpose to you.

Theme 2: Trials

1. Coming to the God of the Bible does not mean trials go away. You must understand that trials are one of God's greatest tools, both before we come to believe in him and after. Some today promise that if you just believe in Jesus, all your troubles will go away. But notice that even after Adrien put his trust in the Maker, one of his most difficult trials was still before him—Addy's death. Even though the Maker raised her from the dead, he did not promise Adrien that no more trials would come his way. And near the very end of the last chapter, Adrien realizes that the dark hand might indeed come back, but the Maker would cause him to survive and prosper through it all.

2. God has a good purpose for every trial. God brings trials. They aren't just bad luck he uses for good; they are events he orchestrates in order to bring about a greater good otherwise not possible. Let me be clear—I'm not saying God *does* evil, or *creates* cancer. But his control over the universe is so great that these things could not happen without his express permission. There's a great example of this in the Bible. A man named Joseph was attacked by his brothers, sold as a slave, thrown in jail, and betrayed. Finally, God brought him out of all this and made him a very powerful man in Egypt. When he finally saw his brothers again after so many years, what did he say? Did he blame them or the slave traders or the jailor? No. This is what he said, "And now, do not be distressed and do not be angry with yourselves for selling me here, because it was to save lives that *God sent me* ahead of you" (Genesis 45:5). God is sending you through your trials too, not to destroy you, but to bring about good in your life.

3. Trials are meant to open our eyes. Adrien's difficulty had one critical effect: it humbled him. You can't be taught until you humble yourself. We think we know everything these days. We've got science and HD TVs and smart phones. We think we've got life all figured out, and then when our ways are done, so many times we have a big mess. God allows us to get into impossible situations so we will finally listen to him. This is what happened with me. I thought I had it all figured out. I was going to be rich. I didn't need that God stuff; that was just a bunch of nonsense to me. But God cooked up a trial for me that made me seek wisdom in a place I never thought I would look for it—the Bible.

So, are you humbled yet?

Theme 3: Evolution

1. Evolution leads to hopelessness, oppression, and evil. Beliefs inevitably lead to actions. Today, we are heading more and more toward a world where evolution reigns supreme. Adrien's world, though it may seem a stretch, is not at all improbable. The logical end of our beliefs—that we are just evolved animals with no ultimate accountability for our actions—is a godless (evolution says there is no

God), oppressive (that's what survival of the fittest is all about), and evil (no moral absolutes or accountability) worldview.

I know some of you will doubt me when I say this, but the reason western nations still have a measure of charity, benevolence, and mercy is because of the remnants of Christian virtue still alive in their cultures. As time goes by, however, and the basis for that virtue is slowly eliminated (that is, the authority and importance of the Bible as viewed by the culture at large), those virtues will be replaced with the true products of the evolutionary worldview.

2. Evolution does not disprove the Bible. Through the study of *The Evidence for the Maker*, Adrien began to see that the scientific "evidence" he was taught all his life was only one side of the story. The serious problems with the scientific theories of our origins never saw the light of day.

The science discussed in Adrien's conversation with Serena is true. The Big Bang doesn't ultimately answer how the universe came into existence. Natural selection doesn't explain many of the complex biological machines we see in nature (the concept is called *Irreducible Complexity*), and there is no known natural process that can cause information to arise out of matter, the information that must be added to our DNA for life to evolve. Finally, evolution doesn't explain the most basic assumptions we have to make even to do science, like the uniformity of nature, the existence of immaterial laws of logic, and the reliability of our senses.

The Bible explains what we see in the real world better, and it explains how we can do science in the first place.

Theme 4: God

1. God must exist because nothing can make itself. Every effect must have a cause. It's the most basic principle of existence, and we all use it every day, even if we can't articulate it as such. Our universe—this massive, beautiful, amazing universe—must have a cause. It can't make itself. It's impossible. So ultimately something (and I will argue some*one*) had to bring it into existence.

As Adrien learned from *The Evidence for the Maker*, we can learn things about the cause by studying the effect (we can learn things about the carmaker by studying the car itself). The cause of the universe must be powerful because the universe is so incredibly large; the cause must be intelligent because the universe demonstrates such great complexity in its design; the cause must be moral because every human being has a moral sense inside, a conscience.

2. God was not made—he simply exists. But this leads us to another question. If God made the world, who made God? No one. He simply exists. As Adrien suggested, it is logically necessary because we can't go back in time forever. At some point, someone simply has to exist; someone must have the power of life within themselves. Interestingly, the first name God gives himself in the Bible (Exodus 3:14) is I AM which means in Hebrew "the Existing One."

3. God must be a person, with a will, character, and personality. All of this leads us inescapably to the conclusion that God cannot be an impersonal force (like *Star Wars*) or a mindless energy that pulses through all of creation. In other words, by virtue of having intelligence, morality, and creativity (demonstrated also through the design in the universe), God must be a distinct person. God cannot be "in all of us" as an impersonal force, spirit, or presence as some claim, but must be "separate from us" as he is a unique person. This is what the Bible has always taught about God.

Theme 5: Reconciling with Our Maker

1. God is our source of life: moral, physical, and spiritual. Though God is separate and distinct from his creation, his nature and power cannot be separated from what he has made. We rest upon him as the foundation of our existence. Think of it as a house with a foundation and a structure built on top of that foundation. The structure follows the pattern of the foundation. When it runs straight, the structure runs straight; when it turns outward, the structure turns outward. Also, the foundation upholds the structure. It is the power for the structure to exist.

So it is with God and the universe. His mind and nature form the outline of our existence (logic, morality, uniformity); his power upholds our existence (moral, physical, and spiritual).

2. Mankind's relationship with God is broken. The relationship with our source of life has been broken. God has pulled away from the universe because of man's rejection of him. The Christian writings tell us about a test of our father and mother, Adam and Eve. These were real people made directly by God at the beginning of time. God made Adam our representative; so what he did counts for us because the entire human race was legally bound to him when he acted.

The test was simple. "Do not do this," God said. "Do not eat from this tree." Why did God test him? God has a will and has the right, as Creator, to do what he wishes with his creation. Adam disobeyed God, and in response God pulled back his sustaining power (moral, physical, and spiritual). On that day, death became a reality in creation. Since then, every person has been born with an inner pressure to do evil, a fallen nature. Furthermore, each of us has acted on that nature thousands of times, creating for ourselves a massive moral debt to God that we can never repay.

3. The way back into the right relationship with God is open to all. The penalty for each of us is eternal separation from God, what the Bible calls Gehenna. Whereas now, we are only partially separated from God's life, after the Final Judgment, those who have no other way to pay for their sins will be completely removed from God forever. This is what the Bible calls hell.

But God does not desire this for us; he loves us in spite of our hatred of him. He sent his son, Jesus Christ, to pay the entire debt for each of us so that we can be forgiven and our relationship with God restored. Now he sends word out to everyone that he is willing to forgive if we do the following things.

First, *repent of your sins.* This means to mourn them and turn from them. Second, *put your total trust in the life and sacrifice of Jesus Christ as the payment for your sins.* In this step, you transfer your trust from yourself (I'm a good person) or any other means of being right with God (penance, good deeds, special prayers, other gods, and so on) to the person of Jesus Christ alone. Finally, *you must give your life to Christ to serve and obey him faithfully until you die.* This does not earn your salvation (it's a free gift) or mean that you must be perfect (no one can be). It demonstrates that your repentance and faith were real in the first place. If you truly mourn your sins, how can you go on living a disobedient life?

You're first step to hope starts with these three actions. It is my prayer that you will stop right now and pray to God, repenting of your sins, trusting in Christ for forgiveness, and committing to serve him the best you can for the rest of your life.

Supplement 3
The Spiritual Top 40:
40 Common Spiritual Questions and Answers

In addition to the issues *The Maker* takes up directly and those I've talked about in the supplemental material thus far, there are other questions that frequently come up when discussing matters such as these. In this section, I'll list forty common spiritual questions and claims and give brief answers to each.

Following is a listing of the six categories and the specific questions in each category as well as its associated page number.

God Questions

Bible Questions

1. The Bible is full of contradictions and errors.	328
2. The Bible was written by man--how can anyone trust it?	329
3. God commanded genocide in the Old Testament.	330
4. The Bible promotes slavery.	331
5. The Old Testament and New Testament describe different Gods.	332
6. What about the other gospels?	333
7. The Ten Commandments were copied from other cultures.	334
8. Isn't the Bible open to interpretation?	335
9. The Bible is homophobic.	336

Jesus Questions

1. How do we even know Jesus existed?	337
2. Jesus never claimed to be divine.	338
3. Jesus was a good teacher, but not God.	339
4. What about all those who don't hear about Jesus?	340
5. Jesus was never resurrected.	340
6. The story of Jesus was influenced by earlier myths and religious accounts.	341
7. Christ is your "indwelling divinity" or your "God-essence."	342

Science Questions

1. Miracles are scientifically impossible.	344

2. The Genesis creation account was taken from other cultures.	345
3. There is no evidence of a global flood.	346
4. Great scientists, like Galileo, have been persecuted by the church.	347
5. Scientific dating methods have proven the Bible isn't true.	348
6. The fossil record proves the Bible is wrong.	348
7. What about the dinosaurs?	349

Truth Questions

1. No one has all the truth.	351
2. All paths lead to the same God.	352
3. What about Islam and Buddhism?	353
4. There is no absolute truth.	354
5. We should tolerate everyone's beliefs.	355

Church/Christianity Questions

1. "Christians" do as much evil as anybody else.	356
2. You don't have to go to church to be a good person.	357
3. Why are there so many churches and denominations?	358
4. Why are some groups called "cults"?	359
5. Christianity developed from other religions and their teachings.	360
6. The true meaning of Christianity is found in hidden meaning, symbols, and sects.	361

God Questions

1. How can I know who God is and what he is like?

As I've said already, there are certain things we can learn about God just by peering out our kitchen window. We can know God is powerful because the creation is so immense; we can know God is super-intelligent because the world demonstrates such intricate and complicated design; and we can know God is moral because of our inner sense of right and wrong. Interestingly enough, the Bible tells us we can deduce things about God based on his creation:

> For since the creation of the world God's invisible qualities—his eternal power and divine nature—have been clearly seen, being understood from what has been made, so that men are without excuse.
> Romans 1:20

However, there are important limits to what creation can tell us about our Maker, just as there are limits to what a car can tell us about the engineer who designed it. For us to know more personal things about God—what he likes and dislikes, what causes him pain, his gender, his knowledge of the past, his plans for the future—he must tell us directly. In other words, there are some things we simply cannot know about God unless he tells us himself.

So, has God told us any of these things? Yes. The Bible claims to be a record of what God has said about himself. "All Scriptures is God-breathed" is its profound claim (2 Timothy 3:16).

I know what's going through your head right now: But the Bible was written by men. What about the other gospels? What about the errors and contradictions? All of these are good questions, and, thankfully, there are good answers coming. Just keep reading.

2. Why does God let people suffer?

To understand why death and suffering exist, you must understand two simple truths:

1. We have been separated from God, our source of life, allowing death to enter.

2. Our separation is not based on God's choice, but ours.

As I stated in Theme 5: Reconciling with Our Maker, our father, Adam, refused the Creator's command and brought death to all creation.

You might ask why God would allow us to suffer death in the first place. Why didn't he stop Adam or rescind his sentence? At some level, the answer is a mystery; I can't say for sure, and I'm not sure the Bible does either. However, there are a few things I can say for certain.

First, God allowed it to fulfill his ultimate purpose in creating. His ultimate purpose was not to provide us with a "cushy pillow life," but to demonstrate the full glory of his nature. Evil, death, and suffering demonstrate, among other things, the excellencies of his justice, mercy, patience, and grace.

Second, God allowed it to bring about a good otherwise not possible. The Bible is replete with examples of this. In Theme 2: Trials, I gave the illustration of Joseph. An even more powerful example is the death of Jesus Christ.

Finally, God has done more about it than anyone. He limits evil and suffering now, he commands his people to labor to meet the needs of those who are hurting, and he died so it could be fully and finally eliminated (Jesus Christ on the cross). Perhaps best of all, one day he promises no more (Revelation 21:4)!

3. God wouldn't send anyone to hell.

Here are a few things to think about when considering this question.

In the first place, why wouldn't God send anyone to hell? Whether by execution or life in prison, we punish criminals severely when their crimes justify it. Why can't God?

Second, don't place your own sense of morality above your Creator's. Be very careful when you think of elevating your changing, culturally-influenced, and often corrupt moral compass over the unchanging, independent, pure moral nature of God.

Finally, to grasp the reasonableness of hell, you must understand the holiness of God. *Holy* means "separate or transcendent." God's nature—his sense of morality, justice, and judgment—is infinitely higher than ours. He's on another level altogether. We're like pee-wee league football, and he's the best team in the NFL.

To us, a moral slip isn't that big a deal. After all, we can honestly say we've been there before, or at least as sinners, we can understand. Only the most heinous of crimes move us. But God's moral sensitivity is not so numb. He has never sinned; he is completely pure; he is infinitely offended with each moral lapse.

One famous confession says this: "The Lord our God is… infinite in being and perfection…who only hath immortality, dwelling in the light which no man can approach unto; who is immutable, immense, eternal, incomprehensible, almighty, every way infinite, most holy, most wise, most free, most absolute."[3]

A proper understanding of hell is required for a proper understanding of God.

4. Hasn't science disproved God?

Science can't possibly disprove God. As Adrien learned, to say for certain there is no God, you'd have to be everywhere in the universe at the same time—you'd have to be God to say he didn't exist!

Furthermore, scientists must assume the biblical God exists (even if they don't believe in him) and operates as the Bible says in order to do science at all.[4] Uniformity of nature, laws of logic, and the reliability of our senses (to name a few) are all *assumed* when science is performed, but evolutionary theory does not explain why these exist in the first place. How can uniformity come out of chance and chaos (ever seen an explosion produce order)? How do *im*material laws of logic exist in a material-only universe? And how can we be sure our senses are reliable if we evolved by chance (maybe yours are and mine aren't)?

However, the biblical worldview explains why these three things exist. The universe is uniform because the Creator made it that way in the beginning and promises to sustain it (Genesis 1:1, Hebrews 1:3, Numbers 23:19, Psalm 139:7-8); laws of logic reflect the way God thinks (Genesis 1:26, Ephesians 5:1, 2 Timothy 2:13, Colossians 2:3); and our senses are reliable because the Creator made them for the very purpose of understanding the universe he had created (Genesis 1:28).

The universe cannot be separated from God. It relies on his nature to exist. He is the foundation, and the creation is the house. His mind and nature form the outline of our existence (logic, morality, uniformity); his power upholds our existence (moral, physical, and spiritual).

5. Is God a she?

As stated in answer to God Question 1, there are some things we cannot know about God unless he tells us directly. In terms of gender, the Bible (which claims to be God telling us about himself) clearly states that God is masculine, a "he."

This doesn't mean that being female is less "godly." After all, God created women and loves and values them just as he does men. And he gave them uniquely feminine qualities, qualities that flow from his perfect nature, though he is distinctly masculine.

This question touches on the whole concept of God's nature. In addition to those who teach that God is a "she," there are those who teach that God is in all of us and in nature. God, in their view, is "mother earth," or some kind of combined, mindless consciousness of man, animal, and the natural world. God is not a person, with a personality and a will, but a presence in us all.

What I ask of those who hold this view is to show me your proof that God has these kinds of attributes. You have to have a reason for your beliefs. You can't just believe something because you believe it. That's irrational and absurd—that's not only *blind* faith, it's *ignorant* faith (no offense intended). Why? Because you can never know you're right. You can't say your belief is any more valid than believing in fairies or pixie dust.

In fact, the evidence shows the opposite. The same reasoning we use every day tells us that God must have a mind and a will, and that he cannot be a part of creation (see God Question 1).

6. You don't have to believe in God to believe in right and wrong.

No, you don't. Everybody believes in right and wrong, even terrorists. In fact, this is one of the ways we can know God exists and is a moral being.

The question isn't whether or not you *can* believe in right and wrong, but how do you *justify* your belief. For example, when you say, "Murder is wrong," how do you know? *Why* is murder wrong?

You could say because most people say it is, but there have been times when most people believed it was wrong to free slaves. You could say this is what you were taught growing up, but why does that matter? Maybe your parents were wrong. You could say because the law says so, but laws have been passed that legalized slavery, something we now believe to be wrong.

You could say that it inhibits our evolution. But are you sure? How does keeping a child with a developmental disorder alive move us down the path of evolutionary excellence? And what about survival of the fittest? Take a long, hard look into those words before you say anything is wrong. If it promotes my survival, why shouldn't it be right? I survive. You die. Evolution at work.

There must be a final, absolute standard for us to make claims about right and wrong. And the only absolute standard is God. God, our Creator, exercising his absolute right, declares it to be so. In the case of murder, God made us in his image and therefore murder is wrong.

Bible Questions

1. The Bible is full of contradictions and errors.

First, I'd like to ask you to name an error or contradiction in the Bible. Please be specific. Okay, now name another. Can you think of a third?

Undoubtedly, some of you can name specifics, but many people who make this charge cannot. They are simply repeating what they have heard in the culture all their lives, but have never really investigated and confirmed for themselves. They simply assume the Bible is wrong from the outset. And that's my point.

As you work through the answers in this part of the book, challenge yourself to acknowledge the biases you have, even if you haven't recognized them as such before. Labor to give the arguments made in this book a fair hearing and not just assume they're wrong because you've already concluded the Bible isn't true.

Regarding specific alleged contradictions and errors, let me briefly address two so you can see that there are solid answers to common complaints.

The existence of Nazareth, Jesus' hometown. Some have charged that Nazareth never existed in the time of Jesus. However, a list of priests relocating after the fall of Jerusalem in A. D. 70 was found. One of them is listed as having settled in Nazareth.[5]

The existence of the Hittite people from the Old Testament. Critics have disputed the existence of this ancient people group. But the discovery of the Hittite library in Turkey in 1906 dismantled this claim.[6]

2. The Bible was written by man—how can anyone trust it?

This question assumes that God cannot produce something reliable if humans are involved. This is irrational. When you come to see that God must be, and that he must have a super-intelligent mind, a free and creative will, and immense power—just as the Bible says—then concluding he cannot manage human beings in the writing and preservation of a single book becomes absurd.

How exactly was the Bible written? First, God used men to write down the words, but not as puppets on a string. He used their personalities, passions, experiences, and ideas in creating his "Word." However, he oversaw the process in such a way that what was produced in the end was exactly what he wanted. This process is called *inspiration*.

Furthermore, the evidence doesn't support the charge that the Bible is untrustworthy. The Bible is the most well-documented book of all antiquity. The New Testament alone has more supporting manuscripts in the original language than any other book in the world (over 5,000).[7] The closest competitor is Homer's *Iliad* with 643.[8]

Not only this, but the Bible is the most well-preserved book we have today. The Dead Sea Scrolls are a large collection of ancient writings found in caves near the Dead Sea. More than 200 biblical manuscripts were found there, all approximately 1,000 years older than any previously discovered.[9] The comparison of these copies with ones dated much later reveals that in spite of repeated copying through the centuries, the biblical texts remained almost identical.

Bottom line: you can trust the Bible.

3. God commanded genocide in the Old Testament.

Many refuse to believe in the God of the Bible because they do not approve of God's command to kill the nations of Canaan (the Canaanites, also referred to generally as the Amorites) during the Old Testament period. In their minds, either God is an evil tyrant, or the Jews simply made him up to justify their warmongering. Let me give you a few things to think about here.

First, God's destruction of the Canaanites was not arbitrary, but was a direct result of their extreme wickedness, which included child sacrifice (Deuteronomy 12:29-31, Psalm 106:34-38).

Second, God did not carry out his judgment until their evil had reached its full measure; he even made the Jews wait 400 years to take the land so his punishment would be justified (Genesis 15:16).

Third, the sin of the Canaanites was further multiplied because they had the knowledge of the true God in their history. Canaan, the father of the Canaanites, was Noah's grandson (Genesis 9:18, 10:15-18). As Americans, we should take this example to heart.

Fourth, God has the authority to take life. It is not unrighteous for the giver of life to take it when he sees fit. At the end of time, he will take many lives for the same reason he took the Canaanite's—immorality.

Finally, regarding the slaughter of innocent children, remember, "Death is not the ultimate destiny of the human race, nor is it the greatest evil. Someday God will give a full explanation, which is something only He can do."[10]

4. The Bible promotes slavery.

Why doesn't the Bible outlaw slavery altogether? Here are a few things to consider:

1. Our impression of slavery—from American history—is not the same as the ancient practice. When we think of slavery, we think of people who were kidnapped and sold into lifelong cruelty. On the whole this was outlawed by ancient governments, and expressly forbidden by the Bible (Exodus 21:12-27).[11]

2. Slavery in the Roman Empire was frequently a road to freedom and a better life. "Life in slavery, at least with a decent master, could be more predictable and less demanding than the life of a poor free person. Since Romans often freed their salves, and since freed slaves of Roman citizens typically received Roman citizenship, one could improve his social status through enslavement."[12]

3. God limited the abuses of slavery. The Bible protected slaves from prostitution, abuse, and murder (Exodus 21:7-12, 26-27). Kidnapping a free person for slavery was punishable by death (Exodus 21:16), and denounced by Paul as evil (1 Timothy 1:10).

4. God took a wise, long-term approach to slavery's eradication. God laid the foundation for slavery's demise by teaching that owners and slaves are brothers (Philemon), and both the slave and free man are the same to him (Galatians 3:28). Given the economic situation of the first century, immediate and full eradication might have brought about greater suffering than the institution of slavery itself.

5. The Old Testament and New Testament describe different gods.

There's a popular notion that as humanity's view of God evolved, so the description of the biblical God evolved with it. In days past, humans saw God as vengeful, harsh, and cruel—so the God of the Old Testament was written that way—but as time went by they began to conceive of God as more loving, patient, and merciful—hence the loving God of the New Testament. However, when you look at the data, there is clearly only one God whose nature and actions are consistent in both testaments.

The severe God of the New Testament. While certainly loving, the God of the New Testament executed Ananias and Sapphira for lying to him (Acts 5:1-11); put to death a political leader, Herod, for refusing to give him glory (Acts 12:19-23); and promised a "bed of suffering" for those who caused his people to sin and "intense suffering" for those of his people who practiced evil (Revelation 2:22-23).

The loving God of the Old Testament. While certainly severe, the God of the Old Testament spared an entire city out of concern for its children and animals (Jonah 4:10-11); instructed his followers to leave part of their harvest for the "alien, the fatherless, and the widow" (Deuteronomy 24:19); and destroyed his own people for refusing to seek justice, encourage the oppressed, and defend the fatherless and widows (Isaiah 1:17).

6. What about the other gospels?

We live in a conspiracy theory culture where even the Bible does not escape the eye of the cynic. They charge that a host of legitimate descriptions of Jesus' life—other gospels—were kept out of the New Testament (NT) by power-hungry church leaders.

First, the books to be included in the NT were determined by the early churches, not by any official Council (such as the Council of Nicaea). The list of twenty-seven books in our modern NT was already accepted by the people of God by the end of the first century, long before any church councils ever met.[13]

Second, books were kept out not for political reasons but because of who wrote them and what they taught.[14] The first requirement was that each book be written by an apostle or close associate. Books written under a pseudonym or too late to meet this requirement were rejected. Furthermore, many books were disqualified because of their teachings. A host of the rejected gospels were written by a group called the Gnostics. Here's what they believed:

[Gnostics] regard this world as the creation of a series of evil archons or powers who wish to keep the human soul trapped in an evil physical body...preaches a hidden wisdom...only to a select group as necessary for salvation and escape from this world.[15]

From what you know about the NT, I'm sure you can see why they would have excluded teachings like this.

There is no conspiracy. The early Christians acted wisely and with integrity when filtering God's writings from fakes and frauds.

7. The Ten Commandments were copied from other cultures.

Some charge that the Ten Commandments (TC) are not original to the Jews but were copied from either the Egyptian Book of the Dead (BOD), an ancient guide for the afterlife, or Hammurabi's Code, an ancient law code.

When you hear this type of claim, remember that the differences are often far greater than the likenesses. Critics take loose similarities and act as if they are word-for-word replicas.

Furthermore, God has given us all the same moral code written on our hearts, the conscience. Therefore, it would not be surprising to see moral directives reflect some of the same tenets at different times and in different cultures.

Chapter 125 of the BOD tells the dead person to make forty-two moral declarations when they encounter the gods in the afterlife.[16] Some of the statements are similar to the Bible, like, "I have not killed." But there is much more different about them than the same. Consider the following comparisons and questions:

- The BOD is a confession to make after one dies; the TC are instructions for living.
- The BOD has forty-two directives; the TC have only ten.
- The BOD does not contain any mention of the first four commandments.
- The basic language and words used by the BOD and TC are not the same.
- Why didn't the Jews just copy the entire document as is, since they lived in Egypt for the previous 400 years?
- Why did the Jews choose only one God when the BOD mentions forty-two?

• Why didn't the Jews use all negative statements like the BOD?

• Why did the Jews, whose first commandment forbids worship of multiple gods, copy from a document that refers to "two and forty gods" and uses the word *gods* eight times?

8. Isn't the Bible open to interpretation?

How do you understand the newspaper? How do you know the reporter is talking about a real flood in Iowa? Maybe he means it metaphorically. It's not a real flood; it's a flood of emotion, or a flood of corn, or a flood of political activism. Maybe he doesn't mean that at all. Who knows? You decide what you want him to mean and I'll decide what I want him to mean.

Yes, that makes absolutely no sense. Why? Because we know the reporter had an intent when he wrote, a meaning, and we know we can understand that meaning if we pay attention to the context (the words used before and after, the historical setting, the type of literature used, the recipient of the message, and other clues).

The Bible is no different. The Bible was written by authors who had a message to communicate, a message they wanted us to understand. And we can understand that message by paying attention to the context.

It may sound complicated, but we do it every day. We know when someone is kidding or serious; we know when they are telling us the history of Rome or giving us directions to the grocery store.

So what happens when we stop trying to understand the author's meaning, when we let the reader or hearer decide for themselves? The instant we do this we make communication impossible because then any statement can mean *anything at all*, and when this happens it really means *nothing at all*.

9. The Bible is homophobic.

I assume by this you mean the Bible promotes violence and hatred toward homosexuals.

First of all, it is not hatred to declare an action to be morally wrong. If I say prostitution is wrong, does that mean I hate all prostitutes? No, of course not.

Second, you need to study the true intentions of this movement. We are told it is simply to give homosexuals "rights." But this isn't the full story. Search for "1972 Gay Rights Platform" on the Internet and read the stated goals of this movement. Pay special attention to #3, 6, 7, and 8 from the state law section.

Third, the Bible does not condone violence toward or hatred for homosexuals. Jesus showed compassion to all types of sinners, including prostitutes and adulterers. Furthermore, he died to save people caught in sexual oppression. While I have never struggled with homosexual feelings, I have had sex before marriage and wrestled with pornography on and off for years. Yet God loves me and continues to help me overcome my struggles.

Finally, you need to understand that the Bible is clear that this desire and act are sinful. Critics often poke fun at Leviticus which says that homosexuality and eating shellfish are "detestable" before God (11:9-12). But what many don't know is that shellfish have more parasites than fish with fins, so they're a greater health risk. God promised to protect the Israelites from disease. This is how he did it.

Just like disease, moral sickness can also destroy a nation. Homosexuality, bestiality, adultery, and prostitution are forbidden, not out of hatred, but in order to protect the health of the community.

Jesus Questions

1. How do we know Jesus even existed?

Let's not discount the New Testament itself as eyewitness proof of Jesus' existence. It records the words of many different authors, written at different times in different places. Their testimony is found in the most well-preserved collection of documents of all antiquity, the New Testament.

Outside the New Testament, here are several non-Christian accounts of the existence of a man named Jesus in the first century[17]:

• Cornelius Tacitus (A.D. 55-120), a famous Roman historian, wrote in *Annals*, "Christus [a common misspelling of Christ], the founder of the name, was put to death by Pontius Pilate, procurator of Judea in the reign of Tiberius..."

• Lucian of Samosata, a Greek artist of the late second century, wrote, "The Christians, you know, worship a man to this day— the distinguished personage who introduced their novel rites, and was crucified on that account..."

• Suetonius, a Roman historian, wrote in *Life of Claudius*, "As the Jews were making constant disturbances at the instigation of Chrestus [another spelling of Christ], he [Claudius] expelled them from Rome."

• Pliny the Younger, governor of Bithynia in Asia Minor, wrote to Emperor Trajan in A.D. 112 concerning the number of Christians he was putting to death. At one point he said he "made them curse Christ, which a genuine Christian cannot be induced to do."

Note that these sources mention Jesus' death under Pontius Pilate, his crucifixion, and the loyalty of his followers, all key New Testament teachings.

2. Jesus never claimed to be divine.

Where's the proof that Jesus himself claimed to be God? There are several direct and indirect ways to show that Jesus did indeed believe he was God in human form.

1. He accepted worship (Matthew 28:9). A good Jew knew that only God could rightly accept worship. Yet many times Jesus was worshipped by his followers, but he never turned them away.

2. He forgave sins (Mark 2:5-12).[18] In this passage in Mark, Jesus forgives the sins of a sick man. The Jewish religious leaders quickly recognize the implication. "Why does this fellow talk like that?" they pondered. "Who can forgive sins but God alone?" But Jesus didn't back down.

3. He claimed the title Son of Man (Mark 2:10, Daniel 7:13-14).[19] Many people think the reference "Son of Man" has to do with Jesus' humanity, but it doesn't. By taking this name for himself, Jesus was reaching back into the Old Testament to the book of Daniel and grabbing a title of God from one of Daniel's great visions.

4. He claimed the title I AM (John 8:58, Exodus 3:14). Finally, Jesus claimed another title reserved only for God. In fact, when Jesus told the Jewish leaders that he was I AM, he was taking the first name God gave himself when he appeared to the Jewish people. When Moses asked God what his name was, he said, "I AM who I AM. This is what you are to say to the Israelites, 'I AM has sent me to you'" (Exodus 3:14).

3. Jesus was a good teacher, but not God.

Think about what you're saying. In the last question, I showed you how Jesus himself clearly claimed to be God. In the last 2,000 years, millions of people have given up everything—some life itself—to follow him. But if he wasn't what he claimed, then he was a liar and a deceiver. How can he then be a *good* teacher?

Most people say this as a form of religious political correctness. They know many people hold Jesus in high esteem so they don't want to completely dismiss him. Instead, they cleverly accept and reject him at the same time with this spiritual double talk.

Let me ask you a question: Why is it so unacceptable to you that Jesus is actually God? It might be that if he is, the religion you've followed all your life is wrong, and you can't accept that. Or maybe your parents or friends will turn away from you if you follow this Jesus guy.

But for many of you, these issues are only secondary. The real reason is if Jesus is God, then his words have authority over your life. God is real and he has a moral standard, and you hate that thought. You like running your own life and deciding for yourself what is right and wrong.

But is your life really going so well? Is following your "heart" really satisfying you? Is porn and greed and conflict really such a great path? You might just find that following Jesus Christ is the most liberating thing you've ever done.

4. What about all those who don't hear about Jesus?

This is a fairness question. If Jesus is the only way to God, what about all those who haven't heard about him? Will they just be condemned to hell never having had a chance?

First, nobody is innocent. Whether we hear about Jesus or not, we have all violated God's moral standard and are guilty.

Second, the gospel has been preached all over the world for 2,000 years. Ninety-eight percent of the world's population has access to the Bible in their own language.[20]

Third, if someone wants to find the true God, he will get the message to them. For an example of this, see the story of Cornelius in Acts 10.

Fourth, Christians believe that children who die are taken into God's grace automatically, forgiven of their sins, and given eternal life. The Bible gives us a beautiful picture of this in the Old Testament. After the death of King David's newborn son, he said these words, "*I will go to him*, but he will not return to me" (2 Samuel 12:23).

Finally, if you live in America (and especially if you are reading this book), you do not have this excuse. You have heard, many times perhaps, and now the ball is in your court. Remember the steps: 1) repent of your sins, 2) trust that only Christ's death can save you, and 3) commit to serve Christ with the rest of your life.

5. Jesus was never resurrected.

If Jesus wasn't resurrected, he can't be God or the Savior of mankind, and Christianity becomes a crumbling house of cards. However, if he was…well, you know what that means.

As you can imagine, every aspect of the resurrection account has been criticized, yet millions still believe. Why? Because the critiques don't overcome the powerful evidence and reasoning that supports his resurrection.

Here are brief answers to the top three claims:

1. Jesus never died. He was scourged, a cruel, bloody beating which made him too weak to carry his own cross (Mark 15:21). Just after he died, soldiers pierced his side with a spear, releasing blood and water, a clear sign of death (John 19:34). Pilate even sent soldiers to confirm he was dead (Mark 15:44).

2. The disciples stole the body. If so, the body was never found though his enemies certainly would have searched for it. All they would have had to do to kill Christianity forever was to produce the body. Yet they never could. Furthermore, Pilate set a guard to make sure this couldn't happen (Matthew 27:62-66).

3. The disciples made it up. After this deception, they knowingly taught and died for a lie. You may die for a lie you believe to be true, but you would never die for a lie you know to be a lie. "And they were willing to spend the rest of their lives proclaiming this, without any payoff from a human point of view.... They faced a life of hardship. They often went without food, slept exposed to the elements, were ridiculed, beaten, imprisoned. And finally, most of them were executed in tortuous ways."[21]

6. The story of Jesus was influenced by earlier myths and religious accounts.

People around the world claim that the story of Jesus was manufactured by borrowing from world religions and myths that predated him. From

Buddhism, to Zoroastrianism, to Greek mythology, Christianity came about by combining elements of various other faith accounts to create the Jesus fable.

In all cases, you'll find these common flaws in their logic:

• The assumption that the New Testament is wrong. The critics' bias precludes any possibility other than this.

• The assumption that the New Testament authors were liars, in spite of their clear teaching to the contrary. Why build a religion of truth-telling on a foundation of lies and deceit?

• The assumption of the evolution of the "god concept." We start by assuming we are evolving, building on what was developed in the past, and forming a better god along the way.

• The assumption that similarity equals progeny. The critic assumes that if there are any similarities, Christianity must find its partial or full origin in the similar religion or myth. However, in the process, glaring dissimilarities are overlooked.

As an illustration of this last point, consider Asclepius, the Greek god of healing and medicine. One website claims Jesus was virtually identical to Asclepius, but ignores the marked differences.[22] His mother, Coronis, was a mortal who slept with Apollo. When she was unfaithful, she was murdered by Artemis, Apollo's sister, and placed on a funeral pyre. At the last minute, Apollo saved his unborn son and gave him to a centaur named Chiron who became his tutor.[23]

This kind of absurd comparison is common with these types of claims.

7. Christ is your "indwelling divinity" or "God-essence."[24]

The view of Jesus has changed so much that he isn't even a real person anymore, only a state of mind, a "vehicle to pure consciousness."[25] Is this so? Did the Bible get it wrong?

If this is the real Jesus, I'd like to see the evidence. What proof is there that Jesus isn't who the gospels say he is? In the writings that offer this theory, not a single shred of evidence is given, except a list of statements of the historical Jesus taken out of context.

For example, one author says Christ is not eternal because "there is no past or future in Christ."[26] As proof for this, he quotes Christ's statement in John 8:58, "Before Abraham was, I am," and then says, "He did not say: 'I already existed before Abraham was born.'"[27] Yet, when you read the actual account, this is exactly what Jesus was saying.

In verse 56, Jesus had just said that Abraham saw his (Jesus') entrance into the world. The Jews then asked how he could know what Abraham saw since he was too young to have even met Abraham. Jesus answered with the statement, "I AM," taking the name God gave himself in Exodus 3:14. This name means, "The Existing One."

Moreover, the actual evidence militates against this view of Jesus. From the context of his words, to the eyewitnesses of his death and resurrection—the proof points away from the "Christ-essence" theory. Furthermore, the absurdity of the teachings that accompany this view of Christ—pain, problems, and death as illusions, for example[28]—seriously damage the credibility of this teaching.

Science Questions

1. Miracles are scientifically impossible.

Many miracles require the suspension of the normal principles of nature in order to occur, but not all do. The parting of the Rea Sea was caused when "the Lord drove the sea back with a strong east wind and turned it into dry land" (Exodus 14:21). Here the timing of events and the direct cause of the wind were divinely ordered for a purpose.

In this case, science can offer no criticism because the miracle was accomplished within the normal workings of nature.

However, there are miracles that come about against the laws of nature, like the Resurrection, and come under fire by the scientific community. Below is a listing and response to common criticisms:

1. Physical laws cannot be broken. Physical laws only describe how the universe normally operates. If there is a supernatural Creator who brought those laws into existence, what is to preclude him from suspending them for a specific reason? Nothing.

2. No one has seen a miracle. Of course, the Bible is a book documenting eyewitness accounts to specific miracles by God. But what most people mean here is *I've* never seen a miracle. By definition, miracles are rare, so it is no surprise that most of us haven't seen one. As someone has said, I've never seen the dark side of the moon either, but that doesn't mean it doesn't exist.

3. There is no God. More times than not, this is the real issue for most people. Before they even consider the evidence for miracles, they've already concluded they can't happen because there is no God to perform them. But if God is real...

2. The Genesis creation account was taken from other cultures.

Is Genesis 1-11 another story borrowed from other cultures? Let's look at two key parts of the Genesis account, creation and the flood, and analyze these claims.

The Creation. Similar stories from the Near East, like the Babylonian and Sumerian creation accounts, are said to be the basis for the Genesis story. However, these accounts don't explain creation as the act of a single, infinite God, but as a result of a battle between many limited gods. Also, per these accounts, humanity was created by mixing an evil god's blood with clay.

The Genesis account by comparison is simple and less mythological.[29] "In the Ancient Near East," notes Josh McDowell, "the rule is that simple accounts or traditions give rise (by accretion and embellishment) to elaborate legends, but not the reverse."[30]

The Flood. The Greeks, Hindus, Chinese, Mexicans, Algonquins, and Hawaiians have stories of an ancient, global flood. But, like the creation account, their renditions are less believable and more mythological in nature. Also, only Genesis gives the year of the flood and a chronology of Noah's life. The Babylonian account contains a cube-shaped ship (which would have been very unstable in the raging seas), and other pagan accounts have the rainfall lasting only seven days and the waters subsiding in only one day.[31]

"Another striking difference between Genesis and the other versions is that in these accounts the hero is granted immortality and exalted. The Bible moves on to Noah's sin. Only a version that seeks to tell the truth would include this realistic admission."[32]

3. There is no evidence of a global flood.

Here are six evidences of a global flood as presented by Answers in Genesis[33]:

1. Fossils of sea creatures high above sea level. Fossilized sea creatures appear in rock layers on every continent, including the Grand Canyon (over a mile above sea level) and the Himalayas.

2. Rapid burial of plants and animals. Graveyards of well preserved fossils exist all over the world. Billions of nautiloids fossils (squid-like creatures with a shell[34]) are found in the Redwall Limestone of the Grand Canyon. Other examples include the chalk and coal beds of Europe and the United States. The quality of the fossils is evidence of rapid burial.

3. Rapidly deposited sediment layers spread across vast areas. Rock layers that extend across and even between continents and physical characteristics in those strata indicate the material was laid down rapidly.

4. Sediment transported long distances. Some of the sediment in those widespread rock layers, like the sand from the Coconino Sandstone of the Grand Canyon, had to be eroded and carried long distances by fast moving water.

5. Rapid or no erosion between strata. Contrary to the teaching of evolutionary geology, no slow and gradual erosion has been found between rock layers. In fact, the opposite has been observed: rapid erosion between strata.

6. Many strata laid down in rapid succession. Rocks don't normally bend, but break as they become hard and brittle. In many places, however, we find rock layers that bent without cracking or splintering showing the layers were laid down rapidly and flexed while still soft.

4. Great scientists, like Galileo, have been persecuted by the church.

The supposed persecution of Galileo is said to demonstrate the intolerance of the Christian community to scientific progress. Interestingly, however, the facts of the case show the opposite.

In his book, *What's so great about Christianity?*, Dinesh D'Souza takes up the issue and gives a rarely heard historical account.[35] Here is a summary of his findings.

• The issue of whether the earth revolved around the sun or the sun revolved around the earth (heliocentricity or geocentricity) was not settled at the time.

• The pope admired and supported Galileo, as did the head of the Inquisition, Cardinal Bellarmine.

• Given the unproven nature of Galileo's theory and the serious scriptural considerations, Bellarmine issued an injunction that Galileo was not to teach or promote heliocentrism, to which Galileo agreed.

• Later Galileo renewed his public teaching and promotion of heliocentrism and published a book supporting it.

• In his book, Galileo made several critical mistakes: 1) his proofs were wrong, 2) he embarrassed the pope by creating a simpleton character obviously intended to represent the pope, and 3) he taught that the Bible was mostly allegorical and must be continually reinterpreted.

• In the end, he was not found guilty of heresy, but of failing to keep his agreement with Bellarmine and was sentenced to house arrest.

• Galileo was never placed in a dungeon or tortured in any way.

5. Scientific dating methods prove the Bible is not true.

The Bible teaches only thousands of years (about 6,000). Secular science teaches billions (about 14 billion). They both can't be true. So, is the world really billions of years old or only thousands?

There are many physical processes that can be used to calculate the age of the world, most of which contradict secular science. If we measure the amount of salt in the sea and calculate the net increase in saltiness per year, we can work backward and determine the maximum possible age of the oceans (not the actual age), sixty-two million years, many times less than the billions reported in science textbooks.[36]

Radiometric dating (RD), a method of dating rocks from lava flows that supposedly lock down the billions of years dates, are based on unproven assumptions: 1) that all the starting conditions are known, 2) that the decay rate of the radioisotopes hasn't changed, and 3) that the system is closed, allowing no addition or deletion of material. And all of this *over millions or billions of years!*[37]

Furthermore, RD methods are not always accurate for rocks of known ages, and different methods often disagree when dating the same sample.[38]

Ultimately, the best way to determine the age of the earth is to ask an eyewitness: God. He was there when the world and life were created. So, the ultimate question is who are you going to trust—man or God?

6. The fossil record proves the Bible is wrong.

The fossil record is another central pillar in the argument for the evolution of life (an argument against the validity of the Bible).

But it is not the only valid theory that explains the evidence. There is also Noah's flood.

You must understand that what we *actually see* in the fossil record is simply *the order of burial* of certain plants and animals. What we *conclude* from that order—that it represents the order of the evolution of life—is our *interpretation* of what we see. Contrary to popular notions, the fossil record as interpreted by evolutionists is fraught with problems. Here are a few:

• "The impeccable state of preservation of most fossils requires the animals and plants to have been very rapidly buried."[39] Plants or animals buried slowly over long periods would be destroyed by scavengers and bacteria.[40]

• Large fossil graveyards found all over the world cannot be explained by slow, gradual processes. "The Redwall Limestone of the Grand Canyon contains…marine creatures buried by fast-moving slurry that involved 24 cubic miles of lime, sand, and silt. No river or lake today can account for the scale of these graveyards."[41]

• Polystrate fossils (fossils that cut vertically through many geologic layers), like the trees at Joggins, Nova Scotia, are not easily explained by slow, gradual fossilization.[42]

The biblical flood of Noah, however, provides a better explanation for rapid burial and fossilization, massive fossil graveyards, and polystrate fossils.

7. What about the dinosaurs?

Kids love the dinosaurs. A dinosaur coloring book, toy, or movie is a great way to keep them occupied…for hours. But the subject of dinosaurs is more than just kid stuff; it has serious implications on the history of our world and even on faith itself. Perhaps more than anything else, the secular history of the dinosaurs suggests to the world that the Bible is outdated and irrelevant.

The age of the dinosaurs is based on the radiometric dating of rock layers in the vicinity of dinosaur fossils. Therefore, the "certain" age of dinosaurs is subject to the same weaknesses as the fossil record and scientific dating methods, an uncertain foundation to say the least (see Science Question 5 and 6).

So how does the Bible explain the dinosaurs? Here are a few key elements[43]:

- Formed: God created them on Day 6 along with the other land animals and man (Genesis 1:24-26).
- Fell: They suffered the effects of Adam's fall and the curse placed upon creation (Romans 8:20-22).
- Flood: They endured the catastrophic global flood of Noah, although one pair of each kind of dinosaur was saved aboard the Ark (Genesis 6:19-20).[44]
- Faded: After the flood, they spread out to repopulate the earth, but over time became extinct like many other animals in the harsh post-flood world.

Why doesn't the Bible use the word *dinosaur?*

- The word was not invented until 1841 by Sir Richard Owen.
- The dinosaur issue—so fascinating to us—was not an important issue to them.
- The Bible clearly describes a large dinosaur in Job 40:15-19.

Truth Questions

1. No one has all the truth.

I had a great conversation with a woman on an airplane one day. We talked about spiritual things for an hour and covered every conceivable topic. At one point she said this, "No one has all the truth." At the time I wasn't sure exactly how to respond. But as I thought about it later, a few key things came to mind.

First, if no one has all the truth, how do you know your statement is true? Maybe it is a part of the truth that no one can know. This statement is self-refuting: if it's true, it can't be true.

Second, although this nice lady was certain I didn't have all the truth, she certainly held some strong views herself on most major spiritual issues. She was *certain* God was not personal or knowable. She was *certain* there was no heaven or hell. She was *certain* the Bible was not God's Word to mankind. She was *certain* Jesus was not divine and she was *certain* he was never resurrected from the dead.

For someone who didn't believe anyone can know all the truth, she sure did know a lot of the core truths of life!

The point is, we all have a core set of beliefs about life, God, and spiritual things. No one really believes "no one has all the truth"— we each believe we have it! But because we (my airplane friend and I) believe things that contradict—about the Resurrection, for example—one of us is right and one wrong. Of that we both can be certain.

2. All paths lead to the same God.

If there's one thing I could encourage you to do through this book, it would be to learn how to think critically. I don't mean be a critical person, always criticizing others, but to discern good thinking from bad, logical arguments from illogical ones.

This is one of those illogical ones.

Let's say you want to go from Raleigh, NC, to Washington, DC, so you ask two people for directions. One guy says to take I-95 north and another guy says take I-95 south. Now, just in case you're not familiar with the geography of the East Coast, if you follow I-95 south from Raleigh, you'll end up in Miami! You've got to go north to make it to DC. Both of these directions can't be right—lead you to the same place—because they contradict each other. And a contradiction can never be true.

In a similar way, when we say that all paths lead to the same God, we're saying a contradiction can be true. When you analyze the core teachings of the world's religions, you find they continually contradict each other. For example, Christianity claims Jesus Christ was physically resurrected from the dead. Islam says the opposite. Because these contradict, one has to be right and the other wrong, but both cannot be true.

The real problem here—one you've got to get over—is not wanting to believe that some people are right and some are wrong. It doesn't mean they're stupid, or should be hated or oppressed, or that God doesn't care for them. It simply means they're wrong.

3. What about Islam and Buddhism?

Two of the world's largest religions, other than Christianity, are Islam and Buddhism. What do these teach and how are they different from Christianity?

Islam, meaning "submission," is a religion developed from the teachings of Muhammad, an Arab born in Mecca in A.D. 570. It has two major schools, Sunnite, by far the largest, and Shi'ite. Islam teaches a single god, but not a Trinity, rejects the Bible as a source of reliable revelation from God, denies Jesus is the Son of God, and declares salvation can be found only by accomplishing the Five Pillars of the Faith.[45]

Buddhism was developed from Siddhartha Gautama, a rich nobleman of the fifth century B.C. Buddhists seek to escape the cycles of rebirth by experiencing Nirvana, a state without suffering. Nirvana is accomplished by following the Eightfold path: Right belief, resolve, word, act, life, effort, thinking, and meditation. There is no personal God in Buddhism, and, of course, no personal Savior.[46]

In terms of deciding which is true, I turn you back to the law of contradiction. The major teachings of each religion contradict the major teachings of Christianity (nature of God, method of salvation, nature and role of Jesus Christ, the Bible). Therefore, on the issues in question, one must be wrong and one right. For example, Buddhism says God is not personal; Christianity says he is. One is right and the other is wrong.

4. There is no absolute truth.

Let me give you three weaknesses of believing this statement.
1. It is self-refuting. This statement is itself an absolute statement.
When you say it, you are presenting it as truth, making the claim
invalid in the process. Here are few other statements that do this:
  • "No one can know the truth." So how can you know what
  you just said is true?
  • "You can't know you're right and others are wrong." And
  how do you *know* that?
2. It is unlivable. Another major problem is that you can't be
consistent with this view in real life. When someone says they
don't believe in absolutes, ask them if they believe genocide is
ever right. "Of course not," they'll reply.
3. It undermines my ability to know anything. In spite of
the self-refuting nature of this claim, if I insist on holding to
it anyway (which many do), I am accepting a contradiction
as part of my worldview. When I do that, I can never actually know anything, because then any claim made by anyone
can mean absolutely anything, no matter how absurd.[47]
The bottom line is that we all hold absolute beliefs in some respect
for moral and spiritual things. We just differ on which truths we want
to believe. So how do we decide between opposing views? There must
be an absolute standard by which we can measure our beliefs. The
Bible gives us that standard, the Word of the eternal, foundation of
all existence, God.

5. We should tolerate everyone's beliefs.

It depends on what you mean by this. If you mean we should allow others to believe what they want without fear of mistreatment or oppression, yes.

However, if you mean I must allow others to do whatever they want regardless of the costs to individual human beings and society overall, no. If tolerance means I have to say everyone is right, give up my freedom to call someone out for promoting lies, and cease all efforts to show others the light of the Bible and Jesus of Nazareth, no. If tolerance means I have to allow false teachings to spread about the Bible, God, and Christianity, watch quietly as others rewrite history and lay the intellectual foundation to take away my rights, no.

I'm afraid this is what most people mean when they talk about tolerance. These are not the words they use, but this is what they say by their actions. What it really means is that I, as a Christian, must tolerate everybody else's views—no matter how crude or offensive—and keep my mouth shut. All the while people from every angle criticize, mock, and labor to destroy everything I believe in and hold dear.

If you are a non-Christian, I ask you to step back and listen as if you were. Count how many times the name Jesus is used as an expletive on television each night. Hear as the Bible is taunted and attacked by a constant procession of supposed "historical" or "scientific" television shows. Notice how my faith is chiseled off monuments and shoved out of classrooms. Then you tell me, who's really the intolerant lot in America?

Church/Christianity Questions

1. "Christians" do as much evil as anybody else.

Many misunderstand what it means to be a real Christian. It doesn't mean we become perfect and never sin again. It means we have repented of our sins, trusted in the sacrifice of Jesus as payment for our sins, and now vow to live for Christ until we die. However, we retain our sin nature and war with it for the rest of our lives.

Furthermore, much of the evil done in the name of Christ in the past was not done by genuine Christians, but by governments falsely flying the Christian flag. This is nothing new and is not unique to Christianity.[48]

"Religious" people—religious *hypocrites* to be more accurate—have always plagued the earth. Even during the time of Jesus, they were a thorn in humanity's side. Jesus reserved his harshest words for the "scribes and Pharisees." But then, as now, those on the outside could tell the difference.

Also realize you live in a culture blessed by the benevolent, sacrificial work of genuine Christians. "Almost every one of the first 123 colleges and universities in the United States has Christian origins."[49] Furthermore, in America "the first hospitals were started largely by Christians." Think of the names, Baptist Hospital, Methodist Hospital, St Luke's Presbyterian.[50] And don't forget the Salvation Army, Red Cross, and YMCA (Young Men's Christian Association), among others.

2. You don't have to go to church to be a good person.

This statement is due to a misunderstanding of 1) why Christians go to church and 2) what it takes to be right with God.

Church. Christians don't go to church because they think it will make them better than everybody else, because it's the only way to foster moral improvement, or because it makes them right with God. Christians meet with other Christians each week to worship Jesus Christ, experience the love of brothers and sisters, and be transformed by learning the Word of God.

Right with God. We all know that some level of goodness is required to be accepted by our Maker. In our culture, we all believe we've attained that level of goodness. We look around at everybody else and say, "I'm not that bad." But God doesn't compare us to each other to determine our goodness—he compares us to himself.

To be right with God, you must be morally perfect, without a single strike on your record. If you commit five sins a day (which is pretty good) and live seventy years, you'll have more than 100,000 sins to account for on Judgment Day. Because of this, each of us is on the wrong side of an eternal, righteous, all-powerful God who has declared us all guilty.

There's only one escape, but it's freely available to all. Repent of your sins, trust that Jesus Christ died in your place, and commit to live the rest of your life to serve him. When you do this, your debt is wiped away and you are right with God forever.

3. Why are there so many churches and denominations?

Presbyterian, Baptist, Methodist, Lutheran, Pentecostal, Non-denominational. It's confusing, isn't it? So why all the differences and what does it mean to me?

There are several reasons different denominations exist. Let me list and explain a few:

• Different practices: In some churches, the minister wears a robe; in others, a suit; still others, a Hawaiian shirt. Some churches use a band, others a choir, others no music at all.

• Different teachings: Some teach baptism by immersion and others by sprinkling. Some believe sign gifts are still active, others believe they have ceased. Some hold to independent churches while others teach a hierarchical form of church government.

• Conflict: As I said earlier, Christians are sinners too. Sometimes folks just get mad and set out on their own. God hates conflict, but he turns it for good.

As someone considering a life of following Jesus Christ (at least, I hope you are), what recommendations do I have for you regarding visiting or joining a church?

1. The church must believe and teach the Christian Bible as their sole authority.[51] This precludes cults like Mormons, Jehovah's Witnesses, and others, as well as the Catholic Church.

2. The church must believe that Jesus is the lone instrument for salvation from sin. No church that believes in multiple paths to God or salvation through any type of good works should be considered.

3. The church must teach and practice strong biblical morality. The

church should preach moral change—not perfection—as an absolute requirement of genuine Christianity.

4. Why are some groups called "cults"?

In Walter Martin's famous book, *Kingdom of the Cults*, he defines a cult as "a group of people gathered about a specific person or person's *misinterpretation* of the Bible"[52] [emphasis original]. The term, though it has a negative connotation in the culture, is not intended to be disrespectful or insulting.

Cults have several important characteristics. First, they appeal to an authority other than the Bible itself. The Mormon's have Joseph Smith's *Book of Mormon*; Christian Scientists have Mary Baker Eddy's *Science and Health with Key to the Scriptures*.[53] Second, they use Scripture frequently but almost always out of context. Finally, they change the meaning of common Christian terms but use them as if they had not.

So what's the problem? Don't they have the right to believe whatever they want? Of course, they do. But you have the right to know what they believe and the results of following in their spiritual footsteps. The central problem is this: If the Bible, understood in its original context as intended by its original authors, is the truth from God about himself, heaven and hell, salvation, and righteous living, then any deviation from that—and modern cults deviate greatly—jeopardizes not only your ability to live right in the sight of God, but also your eternal destiny.

Inasmuch as cults misrepresent the true teachings of Scripture, they turn their adherents from the life of God in every sense.

5. Christianity developed from other religions and their teachings.

While it makes for a good story, Christianity was not developed by taking bits and pieces of other religions and myths and creating the Jesus narrative. In general, attempts to do this make the following errors:

- Assume the Bible is wrong with very little research into the questions raised.
- Take for granted that the biblical authors were liars, in spite of their clear teaching to the contrary.
- Assume the evolution of history and the "god concept."
- Assume that if any similarities exist, Christianity must have borrowed from that source.
- Ignore glaring dissimilarities between accounts.

Here are a few biblical elements that are often accused of being borrowed:[54]

- The Genesis creation account. Other accounts describe creation as the result of a battle between limited gods, and man's creation by mixing clay with the blood of an evil god.
- The Genesis flood. Only Genesis gives dates, chronology, and a realistic account of the hero.
- The Ten Commandments. Egyptian *Book of the Dead* (BOD) has forty-two commands whereas Genesis has only ten. The BOD has forty-two gods whereas Genesis has only one.
- The life of Jesus. As an example, Asclepius, Greek god of healing, a supposed source for Jesus' life, was born of a sexual relationship between his human mother and Apollo, was pulled from his mother's womb on a funeral pyre, and was given to a centaur named Chiron who became his tutor.

6. The true meaning of Christianity is found in hidden meanings, symbols, and sects.

Our culture is obsessed with what may be hidden, locked away, or kept secret. Consequently, we discount anything that comes from the past as suspect, a bold attempt by the powers-that-be to control and manipulate us. From Dan Brown's novels, to the *National Treasure* movies, to groups seeking meaning in hidden patterns of biblical numbers—the evidence of our paranoia is all around us. Where will it end?

The cause of this fear is not increasing evidence that the truth has been hidden from us, but that our culture has lost something foundational—we've lost trust.

We've lost trust in our fellow man because he has grown more and more untrustworthy. He swindles us; he deceives us; he lies.

We've lost our trust in God. We're not sure who he is anymore. Some people say he's not even there, others say he's not involved, others say he's a mindless presence in us all. We don't know him anymore, so we don't know how to trust him.

This lack of trust of both God and man can ultimately be traced back to our rejection of the Bible. As we have freed ourselves of its moral wisdom, we have lost our integrity and trustworthiness; as we have ignored the clear portrait of the God it reveals, we have lost the rock and anchor of our lives.

In spite of what you fear, the true meaning of Christianity is not hidden from you. Open the Bible and read for yourself. The God of light, who wrote it, has designed it for all to understand.

Notes

[1] All scripture quotations, unless otherwise indicated, are taken from the Holy Bible, New International Version (NIV). Copyright 1973, 1978, and 1984.

[2] The New King James Translation (NKJV) translates Jesus' words here as, "Little girl, I say to you, arise!" Copyright 1982 by Thomas Nelson, Inc.

[3] *1689 London Baptist Confession.* "Chapter 2: Of God and the Holy Trinity." Internet. Available at: www.vor.org/truth/1689. Accessed March 30, 2010.

[4] Jason Lisle, *The Ultimate Proof of Creation* (Green Forest, AK: Master, 2009), 38-43.

[5] Lee Strobel, *The Case for Christ* (Grand Rapids: Zondervan, 1998), 138.

[6] Josh McDowell, *The New Evidence that Demands a Verdict* (Nashville: Thomas Nelson, 1999), 94.

[7] McDowell, 34.

[8] McDowell, 34.

[9] Randall Price, *The Stones Cry Out: What Archaeology Reveals About the Truth of the Bible* (Eugene, Oregon: Harvest House, 1997), 278.

[10] Donald H. Madvig, "Joshua," *The Expositor's Bible Commentary, Volume 3*, Frank E. Gaebelein, General Editor (Zondervan: Grand Rapids, 1992), 247. Each point in this section comes from this source.

[11] A. Rupprecht, "Slavery," in *The Zondervan Pictorial Encyclopedia of the Bible*, Volume 5, Merrill C. Tenney, General Editor (Grand Rapids: Zondervan, 1976), 456.

[12] James S. Jeffers, *The Greco-Roman World of the New Testament Era* (Downers Grove, IL: InterVarsity Press, 1999), 222.

[13] Erwin Lutzer, *The DaVinci Deception* (Carol Stream, IL: 2006), 92.

[14] Ibid, 96.

[15] "Gnostic, Gnostic Gospels, and Gnosticism," available from http://www.earlychristianwritings.com/ gnostics.html; Internet; accessed August 29, 2008.

[16] *The Book of the Dead*, "Chapter 125: The Judgment of the Dead," available at http://www.wsu.edu/~dee/EGYPT/ BOD125.HTM; internet; accessed May 11, 2010.

[17] The points and quotations listed here are taken from Josh McDowell, *The New Evidence That Demands a Verdict* (Nashville: Thomas Nelson, 1999), 120-123.

[18] Strobel, 212.

[19] Ibid, 183.

[20] "Bible translations," available at: http://en.wikipedia.org/wiki/ Bible_translations; Internet; accessed April 27, 2010.

[21] Lee Strobel quoting J. P. Moreland in *The Case for Christ* (Grand Rapids: Zondervan, 1998), 333.

[22] "Original or a copy?" available at http://www.bandoli.no/ nooriginaljesus.htm; Internet; accessed April 27, 2010

[23] Ron Leadbetter, "Asclepius," available at http://www.pantheon. org/articles/a/asclepius.html; Internet; accessed April 27, 2010.

[24] Eckhart Tolle, *The Power of Now* (Novato, CA: Namaste Publishing and New World Library, 1999), 104.

[25] Ibid.

[26] Ibid.

[27] Ibid.

[28] Ibid, 38, 64, and 143.

[29] McDowell, 101.

[30] Ibid.

[31] Ibid, 104-105.

[32] Ibid, 105.

[33] "Worldwide Flood, Worldwide Evidence," available at http:// www.answersingenesis.org/get-answers/features/worldwide-flood-evidence; Internet; accessed April 27, 2010.

[34] Roger Patterson, *Evolution Exposed: Earth Science* (Hebron,

KY: Answers in Genesis, 2008), 150.

[35] Dinesh D'Souza, *What's so great about Christianity?* (Carol Stream, IL: Tyndale, 2007), 103-113. Others have labored along the same lines. I refer you to "The Galileo affair: history or heroic hagiography?" by Thomas Schirrmacher, available at: http://www.answersingenesis.org/tj/v14/i1/galileo.asp; Internet; accessed April 27, 2010.

[36] Don Batten, ed., *The Revised and Expanded Answers Book* (Green Forest, AK: Master Books, 2003), 83-86.

[37] Ibid.

[38] For a thorough study of the dating methods issue, visit http://www.answersingenesis.org/get-answers/topic/radiometric-dating.

[39] Ken Ham, general editor, *The New Answers Book 2* (Green Forest, AK: 2008), 342.

[40] Patterson, 150.

[41] Ibid.

[42] Ibid, 152.

[43] This teaching is taken from Answers in Genesis. For a detailed study visit http://www.answersingenesis.org/get-answers/topic/dinosaurs.

[44] Visit Answers in Genesis for a full discussion of Noah's Ark: http://www.answersingenesis.org/get-answers/topic/noahs-ark.

[45] Walter Martin, *The Kingdom of the Cults* (Minneapolis: Bethany House, 2003), 436-448.

[46] Martin, 300-303.

[47] Lisle, 137-138.

[48] For a full treatment of this subject and well known Christian sins, see chapter 14 of D. James Kennedy and Jerry Newcombe's book, *What if Jesus had never been born?* (Nashville: Thomas Nelson, 1994), 205-223.

[49] Ibid, 52.

[50] Ibid, 147.

[51] This would include belief in one God, the Trinity, Jesus' divinity, and other historic, conservative Christian teachings.

[52] Martin, 18. I recommend this work for an in-depth study of this entire subject.

[53] Ibid, 38.

[54] These have been addressed separately as Bible Question 7, Jesus Question 6, and Science Question 2.

Supplement 4
Recommended Resources

Here are some resources I recommend for further study.

General Questions and Answers (DVD):
• *Respond: Apologetics Course*, produced by Evidence America, www.evidenceamerica.org.

General Questions and Answer (Book):
• *The New Evidence that Demands a Verdict*, Josh McDowell, Nashville: Thomas Nelson, 1999.
• *Reasons We Believe: 50 Lines of Evidence that Confirm the Christian Faith*, Nathan Busenitz, Wheaton, IL: Crossway Books, 2008.
• *Baker Encyclopedia of Christian Apologetics*, Norman Geisler, Grand Rapids: Baker Books, 1999.
• *The Evidence Bible*, Ray Comfort, Orlando: Bridge-logos, 2003.

Science and Evolution:
• Answers in Genesis Ministries: www.answersingenesis.org.
• *The New Answers Book*, Ken Ham, editor, Green Forest, AK: Master Books, 2006.
• *The New Answers Book 2*, Ken Ham, editor, Green Forest, AK: Master Books, 2008.
• *Refuting Evolution*, Jonathan Sarfati, Green Forest, AK: Master

Books, 1999.
• *The Stones Cry Out*, Randall Price, Eugene, OR: Harvest House, 1997.

Document Issues:
• *The Da Vinci Deception*, Erwin Lutzer, Carol Stream, IL: Tyndale House, 2004.
• *The Case for Christ*, Lee Strobel, Grand Rapids: Zondervan, 1998.
• *Baker Encyclopedia of Christian Apologetics*, Norman Geisler, Grand Rapids: Baker Books, 1999.

God Questions:
• *World's Apart: A Handbook on Worldviews*, Norman Geisler and William D. Watkins, Grand Rapids: Baker, 1989.
• *Baker Encyclopedia of Christian Apologetics*, Norman Geisler, Grand Rapids: Baker Books, 1999.
• *The God Question: An Invitation to a Life of Meaning*, J. P. Moreland, Eugene, OR: Harvest House, 2009.
• *Discovering the God Who Is*, R. C. Sproul, Ventura, CA: Gospel Light, 2008.

Bible Questions:
• *When Skeptics Ask: A Handbook on Christian Evidences*, Norman Geisler and Norman Brooks, Grand Rapids: Baker Books, 2008.
• *When Critiques Ask: A Popular Handbook on Bible Difficulties*, Norman Geisler and Thomas Howe, USA: Victor Books.

Jesus Questions:
• *Jesus Among Other Gods*, Ravi Zacharias, Nashville: Thomas Nelson, 2000.
• *The Case for Christ*, Lee Strobel, Grand Rapids: Zondervan, 1998.
• *The Case for the Resurrection of Jesus*, Gary Habermas and Michael

Licona, Grand Rapids: Kregel, 2004.

Truth Questions:
• *How do you know you're not wrong?* Paul Copan, Grand Rapids: Baker, 2005.
• *The New Evidence that Demands a Verdict*, Josh McDowell, Nashville: Thomas Nelson, 1999.
• *Introduction to Philosophy: A Christian Perspective*, Norman Geisler and Paul Feinberg, Grand Rapids: Baker, 1980.

Christianity vs. Other Faith Systems:
• *Handbook of Today's Religions*, Josh McDowell and Don Stewart, Nashville: Thomas Nelson, 1993.
• *The Kingdom of the Cults*, Walter Martin, Minneapolis: Bethany Books, 2003.
• *Answering Islam: The Crescent in Light of the Cross*, Norman Geisler and Abdul Saleeb, Grand Rapids, Baker: 2002.
• *Oprah, Miracles, and the New Earth: A Critique*, Erwin Lutzer, Chicago: Moody, 2009.

Web Sites:
Evidence America, www.evidenceamerica.org
Answers in Genesis, www.answersingenesis.org
Norman Geisler, www.normangeisler.net
Gary Habermas, www.garyhabermas.com
Erwin Lutzer, www.moodychurch.org/radio
Ravi Zacharias, www.rzim.org
Lee Strobel, www.leestrobel.com
Randall Price, www.worldofthebible.com

Supplement 5
Group Study Discussion Questions

This supplement lists questions for discussion in group study situations. There are two sets listed based on the group studying the book. The first is for a group of Inquirers. These are people who are interested in learning more but are not believers in the God of the Bible and have not put their trust in Christ. The second is for a group of Followers. These folks have put their faith in Christ and are presently following him. The reason for two sets is that each group will look at the information differently and, ultimately, will be striving to learn different things from the material.

Questions for Inquirer's Group Study

Study Session 1: Prologue–Chapter 6

1. Have you ever been in Adrien's situation before (chapter 1), where the only way you could see out was suicide? How did you feel at that time?

2. What kept you from acting on your impulse to take your life? Do you see this (being kept from acting) as just a coincidence or

do you look back and see "someone looking out for you"?

3. Can you see any symbolism in the picture painted in chapter 1 of Adrien on his knees at the edge of the ravine? What specific things in this setting do you see as having a deeper meaning (rain, darkness, etc.)? Why?

4. What is hope to you? What do you hope for? List at least three things.

5. Where do you find hope? Will those things in which you find your hope really give you what you hope for? Why or why not?

6. Have you ever thought about asking God for his help? Reflect on these words from the Bible, "Cast all your anxiety on him because he cares for you" (1 Peter 5:7). Do you think God has the power to bring about what you hope for? Why or why not?

Study Session 2: Chapters 7-13

1. Have you ever asked yourself the question Adrien asked at the end of chapter 7: "What if they were right?" In other words, as you struggle through life, have you ever wondered if the Bible is actually true, and if there is a God out there who knows, cares, and is willing to act to help you? Why or why not?

2. Do you think Damien's view of some people as "the defaveur of all nature" (disfavored) is right? Did you realize this concept comes from Charles Darwin's original writing about evolution, *On the Origin of*

Species by Means of Natural Selection, or the Preservation of Favoured Races in the Struggle for Life? From this example, can you see that ideas have consequences?

3. Are you or have you ever been at the point in your life where, like Addy in chapter 10, you want more for your life than your present circumstances? As you grow older, do you feel like you've lost the true purpose for your life?

4. Can you relate to Adrien's work situation (chapter 11), where the trouble in his life caused him to lose his standing at work and led to his demotion? How did this make you feel? How have you dealt with it?

5. Listen to these words, "'For I know the plans I have for you,' declares the Lord, 'plans to prosper you and not to harm you, plans to give you hope and a future'" (Jeremiah 29:11). What would you think if I told you that God made you for a specific purpose? Would you like to know what it is? Why or why not?

Study Session 3: Chapter 14-20

1. Do you think science is right, that we are nothing more than randomly placed chemicals and that there is no ultimate meaning to our lives? Why or why not? How should your answer affect how you treat and value others?

2. Name one or two things you learned from chapter 18 that you didn't know before. What is significant about the things you learned?

3. What did you think about Adrien's explanation in chapter 19 about how we can know God exists and how we can learn certain things about him from the world he created? (See also God Question 1.)

4. Were you surprised to learn that God was not created but has always existed? Do you see why this must be so because, as Adrien argued at the end of chapter 19, an infinite regression (going back in time forever) is impossible?

5. Did you realize that scientists must have faith in order to do science at all as Adrien suggested in chapter 20? The basic assumptions they must make to do the first experiment cannot be proven, but must be taken on faith. What do you think of this? (See also God Question 4.)

6. Does the fact that the Bible taught thousands of years ago that God must be self-existing give it more credibility to you? Here's an example: "Before the mountains were born or you brought forth the earth and the world, from everlasting to everlasting you are God" (Psalm 90:2). Why or why not?

Study Session 4: Chapter 21-27

1. What's starting to go wrong for Damien in chapter 23? What two things are at odds in his heart?

2. How does growing older and learning the harsh realities of life affect the way we view the world when we were younger? Did you believe things about life when you were young that you don't believe now because of your experience? If so, what is one example?

3. What do you think Adrien meant when he said in chapter 25, "I'm a man of science. These aren't my kind of questions"? Do you think this way? How about someone you know? Does saying this really excuse us from considering the deep questions of life, like its ultimate meaning?

4. How has modern science discouraged us from even discussing faith in our society? Is this a good thing? Has this brought us more or less hope? Why or why not?

5. Read and discuss God Question 4. Based on the arguments presented, do you agree with the conclusion of the first sentence, "Science can't possibly disprove God"?

6. Consider these words of Jesus, "I am the resurrection and the life. He who believes in me will live, even though he dies; and whoever lives and believes in me will never die. Do you believe this?" (John 11:25-26). If this statement is true, how can we have hope even in the face of great sickness and tragic death?

Study Session 5: Chapters 28-34

1. What did Banan mean when he said in chapter 31, "All of our problems in life—death, depression, hopelessness, evil—stem from our broken relationship with the Maker. He is the source of life in every sense: moral, physical, emotional.... So if we were separated from him in any way, obviously, life in every sense would suffer?" (See also God Question 2.)

2. Have you ever thought about how the terrorists try to justify their actions, showing even they have an inner moral compass given to them by their Creator?

3. Have you ever broken God's moral code through the actions Banan mentions in chapter 31: lying, pride, deceit, greed, murder, adultery, pornography, lust, or denying his existence? If you met God today, how would you make up for your wrongs?

4. What does Banan mean when he says in chapter 32 that God does not want to sentence us to Gehenna, the place of eternal darkness, but is forced to? (See also God Question 3.)

5. Describe in your own words the illustration Banan gives in chapter 32 of the judge hearing the capital murder case. Is this a moving picture to you? Why or why not?

6. What are the steps to eternal salvation that Banan lays out in these words in chapter 32: "We can acknowledge his reality, mourn our crimes against him, trust that he died for us, and use the rest of our lives to serve him"? (See also Theme 5: Reconciling with Our Maker from Supplement 2.) Would you like to take these steps now?

Study Session 6: Chapters 35-41

1. Can you see how nature would have taken on a different meaning to Adrien (chapter 36) now that he saw it as an expression of God's personality and nature instead of the result of mindless physical processes? Why or why not? In which way do you view nature?

2. Do you think praying would seem strange to you as it did to Adrien in chapter 36? Why does the idea sometimes seem uncomfortable? When you think of it as simply a form of communication between you and God, should it really seem that strange?

3. Meditate on Adrien's words from chapter 36, "I am not random either. I have been made for a purpose." Apply those words to your life. What feelings do they give you? Do you like them? Why or why not?

4. Have you ever found yourself in a situation you didn't know how to get out of like the Resistance at the end of chapter 37? What was it and how did it make you feel? Have you ever thought about approaching it as Rene suggested, by formulating the best plan you could and then trusting God to do the rest? How would this affect your anxiety level if you did?

5. At the end of chapter 37, Leroux, one of the Council members, said, "Yes, there are more with us than there are with them!" If the God described in the Bible (all-powerful, all-knowing, loving, and willing to help) is on your side, how does that make you a majority no matter who or what you face?

6. How would it make you feel if you believed the following words in the Bible were actually true and applied to you: "God is our refuge and strength, an ever-present help in trouble. Therefore we will not fear, though the earth give way and the mountains fall into the heart of the sea" (Psalm 46:1-2)?

Study Session 7: Chapter 42-48

1. How is a person who believes in evolution forced into the dilemma Damien faced with Prissy in chapter 46? How does one reconcile love for family and friends and desire for hope in the future with the cold phrase "survival of the fittest"?

2. Did you notice Damien's inconsistency when just after he learns of Prissy's diagnosis, he says after hearing of Seger's death, "Rejoice, Mr. Richter. Our gene pool has been purified." Why do people allow wild contradictions like that to exist in their thinking?

3. Take some time to think about Rene's words about America at the beginning of chapter 42: "But, as time when by, America's power faded while her enemies grew stronger. Eventually, in spite of the Maker's influence, her greed, arrogance, and corruption led to her military and economic collapse." First, do you believe America has been positively influenced by the God of the Bible (see the last part of Church/Christianity Question 1)? Secondly, how is our greed, arrogance, and corruption leading to our demise? Are these acts condoned or condemned in the Bible?

4. In chapter 44, Adrien said, "And, as I am starting to understand, what appears to me as chaos and randomness is to the one above all according to plan." Do you believe that the God described in the Bible could actually control all of life and work it all for good, even the worst tragedies and problems? (See God Question 2.) How would it change your view of life's troubles if this were true?

5. Can you relate to Adrien's feelings of inadequacy expressed in chapter 48? Why do you think he felt this way?

6. Saint Paul said this, "I have learned the secret of being content in any and every situation, whether well fed or hungry, whether living in plenty or in want. I can do everything through him [Jesus Christ] who gives me strength" (Philippians 4:12-13). Regarding the confidence to take on the hard tasks of life, how would looking to Christ for the strength to perform them (as Paul did), instead of to ourselves, change our confidence level? How does God have more of what we need than we do?

Study Session 8: Chapters 49-55

1. Summarize the lesson(s) Adrien learned from the stranger at Sauveur's in chapter 50? Is there anything you can learn from him that you can apply to your life? If so, what?

2. Do you think Adrien's desire to go for a walk and his ultimate arrival at Sauveur's in chapter 50 was purely coincidence, or was he led there by the Maker for a specific reason? Can you see your life being led in the same way, by a God who cares for you and is speaking to you even through the events of your life? Why or why not?

3. In the beginning of chapter 52, what outlets did Damien chose for his sorrow over Prissy's situation? What other destructive outlets do

people chose when in Damien's situation? Have you ever chosen these same outlets when trouble came into your life? What was the result?

4. How does Damien's approach from question 1 above compare to the approach of the man in these words, "I lift up my eyes to the hills—where does my help come from? My help comes from the Lord, the Maker of heaven and earth"? What benefits would there be in turning to an infinite, loving God in our times of trouble instead of the solutions so common in our culture?

5. How much did guilt over Sophie's death affect Adrien's struggle to love Addy as demonstrated in chapter 54? Does guilt affect the decisions you make today? How so? How would God's forgiveness free you to live your life without the constant baggage of the past?

6. Regarding finding freedom from guilt for past sins, consider this passage, "As far as the east is from the west, so far has he removed our transgressions [sins] away from us" (Psalm 103:12). How far is the east from the west? What is God saying here? If God can put our sins away like this, why should we continue to hold on to them through guilt?

Study Session 9: Chapter 56-62

1. What were the images on the holopad Adrien found in his apartment (chapter 56)? Why was it so important to him to risk going back just to get them?

2. Does your past have a powerful influence over you? In what

ways is this good? In what ways is this bad?

3. How can God help us overcome the parts of our past that trouble us? (See Supplement 2, Theme 2: Trials, for some ideas.)

4. What do you believe happens to us after we die? What is the afterlife like to you? What do you want it to be like?

5. What are some of the ways taught in our culture that we can have a positive afterlife? In other words, what are some of the ways we are taught we can make it to heaven?

6. Hear these words of Jesus, "Do not let your hearts be troubled. Trust in God; trust also in me. In my Father's house are many rooms; if it were not so, I would have told you. I am going there to prepare a place for you. And if I go and prepare a place for you, I will come back and take you to be with me that you also may be where I am" (John 14:1-3). In Jesus' thinking, should we be troubled or worried about the afterlife? Why or why not? Who is responsible for preparing our place in heaven? Based on Supplement 2, Theme 5: Reconciling with Our Maker, how do we enter the place Jesus is describing?

7. Read Jesus Question 5. Do you think Jesus was really resurrected from the dead? What does it mean to humanity in general and you in particular if he was?

Study Session 10: Chapter 63-Epilogue

1. Have you ever been betrayed by someone like Adrien was by Nate in chapter 63? Share one of your experiences with the group. How did it make you feel?

2. Have you ever thought about how Jesus Christ was betrayed by those close to him? (Read Matthew 26:14-16 and 47-50.) How was his betrayal worse than yours? Why did he allow himself to be betrayed in this way?

3. Why did Damien continue his efforts to kill Adrien even after he realized the inconsistency of his words in chapter 64, "Nature chooses who lives and who dies, and who is worthy"? What does this tell us about humanity?

4. Have you ever felt like God had abandoned you as Adrien felt in the beginning of chapter 65? Have you ever asked, "Why? Did you bring me here just for this?" Share a situation from your life with the group.

5. Looking back on your struggle, can you see God's hand in your life as Adrien did when he realized the Maker was there all along, guiding the situation (appearances at the ravine, at Sauveur's, and finally at GIS)? What are they?

6. Ponder the Maker's comments at the end of chapter 65: "I have put you through many things, my dearest Adrien. But I have done it to bring about a good you could not before imagine, and even now you cannot fully understand." What good could God be doing through your situation? List at least three things.

Questions for Follower's Group Study

Study Session 1: Prologue-Chapter 6

1. Have you ever been as dark as Adrien was in chapter 1? Have you been this dark since you've become a Christian? Share your story with the group.

2. Is it okay for a Christian to go through periods of difficulty, darkness, and depression? Why or why not?

3. Adrien suffered from an extreme loss of hope. What is hope to you? As a Christian, where should we find our hope for not only eternal life, but also everyday living? How do trials show weaknesses in our hope in God?

4. Is it ever God's will that we suffer? Why or why not?

5. According to the following passages, what are some of God's purposes in sending us through trials? A. Psalm 119:67 and 71, B. 2 Corinthians 1:3-4, and C. 2 Corinthians 1:8-9.

6. Regarding the trials you are enduring now, are you trying to hide them from others as Adrien was trying to hide his in chapter 5? Is it God's will that we struggle alone, or has he given us each other to help us when we are in need (Proverbs 17:17 and Galatians 6:2)?

Study Session 2: Chapters 7-13

1. Why do some people in our culture believe the Bible is a fairy tale, like Nate in chapter 7? From Nate's perspective as an archaeologist and scientist, why would he believe something like this? Has the church done enough to show people like Nate that the Bible is true?

2. When was the last time you heard a Sunday sermon or Sunday school lesson on the scientific aspects of the Bible (like creation, evolution, Noah's flood, or archaeology)? Do you think people have these questions today that are keeping them from believing? What kinds of questions do they have?

3. Consider this statement: "Why would you accept the Jesus of the Bible if you have rejected the Bible of Jesus?" How is the Jesus of the Bible different from common perceptions of Jesus in the culture? Can you really accept the Jesus of the Scriptures if you believe the Bible is fairy tales, like Nate? Why or why not?

4. Look up the following texts and answer this question: Does the Bible give evidence that what it teaches is true? A. Joshua 4:1-9, B. John 10:38, and C. 1 Corinthians 15:3-6. If the Bible does, why don't we?

5. Read Science Question 1 about miracles. Discuss the two types of miracles mentioned (those which suspend the laws of nature and those which don't). Discuss the three criticisms and responses listed in the second half of the article. Are these strong arguments? Why or why not?

Study Session 3: Chapters 14-20

1. Adrien asked Nate in chapter 14, "Why are we here?" Do you think people in our culture are asking this kind of powerful question? Why are they asking it? What is the Bible's answer?

2. In chapter 14, how did Adrien try to show Nate that there must be more to life than just "random chemical reactions"? What arguments did he use, and what was Nate's response? Could we use his arguments with our friends?

3. If you had to explain to Adrien why people die, like Sophie (chapter 15-16), what would you say? (See God question 2 and study Genesis 3:17-19.)

4. What were the reasons for the stars as revealed to Adrien in chapter 18? (Look up these reasons in Genesis 1:14-19 and Psalm 8:3-4.) How does this differ from what secular science teaches? Do these two views (Bible versus science) conflict?

5. According to Adrien in chapter 19, A. Can science say there is no God?, B. Does the Big Bang really explain where we came from?, and C. Who made God?

6. What can we learn about God from the universe itself, per Adrien in chapter 20?

Study Session 4: Chapters 21-27

1. As Christians, are we ever tempted to get discouraged because of our circumstances? Why? Does it help us to have other Christians who have strong faith around us when we're feeling this way (like Rene and the lady who stood to sing in chapter 21)? How does this help us?

2. What caused Damien's hard shell to start to crack in chapter 23? What can we learn about this for our evangelism? In other words, when people encounter a great trial, could it be an open door for us to share God's truth? (Look through Matthew chapter 8 for the many examples of how those who were suffering were much more willing to hear Jesus' message than those who were not.)

3. What two things are at odds in Damien's heart in chapter 23? Why is he struggling? How can we use the truth behind this struggle to challenge those who believe in evolution today?

4. Read Theme 3: Evolution. Why does evolution ultimately lead to hopelessness, oppression, and evil? How is the Bible's message different?

5. What do you think Adrien meant when he said in chapter 25, "I'm a man of science. These aren't my kind of questions"? How would you respond to someone who said this to you?

Study Session 5: Chapters 28-34

1. What did Banan mean when he said in chapter 31, "All of our problems in life—death, depression, hopelessness, evil—stem

from our broken relationship with the Maker. He is the source of life in every sense: moral, physical, emotional.... So if we were separated from him in any way, obviously, life in every sense would suffer?" (See also God Question 2.)

2. Have you ever thought about how terrorists try to justify their actions? What does this tell us about A. God's existence and B. God's character?

3. What does Banan mean when he says in chapter 32 that God does not want to sentence us to Gehenna, the place of eternal darkness, but is forced to? (See also God Question 3.)

4. Describe in your own words the illustration Banan gives in chapter 32 of the judge hearing the capital murder case. Would this be a good example to use with a non-Christian? Why or why not?

5. What are the steps to eternal salvation that Banan lays out in these words in chapter 32: "We can acknowledge his reality, mourn our crimes against him, trust that he died for us, and use the rest of our lives to serve him"? (See also Theme 5: Reconciling with Our Maker from Supplement 2.) Are all of these steps essential biblically (see Hebrews 11:6, Mark 1:15, Romans 3:22-23, and Luke 14:25-33)?

Study Session 6: Chapters 35-41

1. In chapter 36, Adrien goes for a walk and contemplates the purpose of his existence. How do people who do not believe in the God of the Bible determine why they exist? What reasons do they come up with? Will these things ultimately satisfy them? Why or why not?

2. Is Christ's ultimate purpose that we go to church every Sunday and sit on a pew or huddle in a Sunday school class? Look up these verses and discuss some of the more important things God has in mind for us: A. Ephesians 6:19-20, B. James 1:27, and C. Philippians 3:10.

3. Is the natural world—which Adrien loved so much—more valuable than human beings? Why or why not? Is our culture getting the two mixed up, placing more value on the environment than the people? How can we help them see things from God's point of view?

4. In chapter 37, the Resistance team discusses the death of Walter from chapter 35. Like Addy and Rene, do well-meaning Christians make mistakes in the Lord's work sometimes? What kinds of mistakes have you made personally or seen others make while trying to serve the Lord? When we do make a mistake, what is the correct response (see Rene's response in chapter 37)?

5. In chapter 39, Luciana talks about the Global Government's attempt to control the minds of the people. Why is this so important to Satan and those who serve him? Does God seek to control our minds as well (see Romans 12:1-2)? What can we do to give our minds over to the Spirit's control?

Study Session 7: Chapters 42-48

1. Take some time to think about Rene's words about America at the beginning of chapter 42: "But, as time when by, America's power faded while her enemies grew stronger. Eventually, in spite of the

Maker's influence, her greed, arrogance, and corruption led to her military and economic collapse." First, how is our greed, arrogance, and corruption leading to our demise? Are these acts condoned or condemned in the Bible? Second, how does the church demonstrate these same sins—greed, arrogance, and corruption?

2. In chapter 44, Adrien said, "And, as I am starting to understand, what appears to me as chaos and randomness is to the one above all according to plan." Do you believe that God brings about all the events of your life, even the worst trials? (See God Question 2.) What are the consequences if God does not control all aspects of our trials?

3. In chapter 44, Adrien addresses the Resistance regarding his experience with the Maker. Do you think he thought of himself as serving his purpose by sharing with them on that night? From the bigger picture perspective, do you think he really was serving his purpose? How can we apply his experience to our own?

4. How is a person who believes in evolution forced into the dilemma Damien faced with Prissy in chapter 46? How does one reconcile love for others and a desire for hope in the future with the cold phrase "survival of the fittest"?

5. Can you relate to Adrien's feelings of inadequacy expressed in chapter 48? Why do you think he felt this way? Do Christians feel this way sometimes? Why do we not have an excuse to feel like this (Philippians 4:12-13)?

Study Session 8: Chapters 49-55

1. Summarize the lesson(s) Adrien learned from the stranger at Sauveur's in chapter 50? Is there anything you can learn from him that you can apply to your life? If so, what?

2. Do you think Adrien's desire to go for a walk and his ultimate arrival at Sauveur's in chapter 50 was purely coincidence, or was he led there by the Maker for a specific reason? Can you see your life being led in the same way, by a God who cares for you and is speaking to you even through the events of your life? Why or why not?

3. In the beginning of chapter 52, what outlets did Damien chose for his sorrow over Prissy's situation? What other destructive outlets do people chose when in Damien's situation? Have you ever chosen these same outlets when trouble came into your life? What was the result?

4. How does Damien's approach from question 1 above compare to the approach of the man in these words, "I lift up my eyes to the hills—where does my help come from? My help comes from the Lord, the Maker of heaven and earth"? Why do Christians not always turn to the Maker of heaven and earth in their time of trouble?

5. How much did guilt over Sophie's death affect Adrien's struggle to love Addy as demonstrated in chapter 54? Does guilt affect the decisions you make today? How so? How should God's forgiveness

through Christ free us to live our lives without the constant baggage of the past?

Study Session 9: Chapters 56-62

1. What were the images on the holopad Adrien found in his apartment (chapter 56)? Why was it so important to him to risk going back just to get them?

2. Does your past have a powerful influence over you? In what ways is this good? In what ways is this bad?

3. How can God help us overcome the parts of our past that trouble us? What things can we do to overcome our past, and what things must we rely on God to do?

4. In chapter 56, Nate comes back into Adrien's life in an attempt to sabotage his work. Do you believe Satan will send someone into your life to prevent you from serving the Lord? Take a few moments and think about the people in your life now. Which of them is steering you from Christ? What should you do about it? How can we better discern the intent and effect of others in our lives?

5. How do you think the image inside the Chamber—the Nest high above the massive image of the world map on the floor—illustrates Satan's attempt to dominate the world? How do we, as Christians, defeat him? What specific things should we be doing to ensure our victory?

Study Session 10: Chapter 63-Epilogue

1. Have you ever been betrayed by someone like Adrien was by Nate in chapter 63? Share one of your experiences with the group. How did it make you feel?

2. Have you ever thought about how Jesus Christ was betrayed by someone close to him? (Read Matthew 26:14-16 and 47-50.) How was his betrayal worse than yours? Why did he allow himself to be betrayed in this way?

3. Why did Damien continue his efforts to kill Adrien even after he realized the inconsistency of his words in chapter 64, "Nature chooses who lives and who dies, and who is worthy"? What does this tell us about humanity?

4. Have you ever felt like Adrien in the beginning of chapter 65, like God had abandoned you? Have you ever asked, "Why? Did you bring me here just for this?" Share a situation from your life with the group.

5. Looking back on your struggle, can you see God's hand in your life as Adrien did when he realized the Maker was there all along, guiding the situation (appearances at the ravine, at Sauveur's, and finally at GIS)? How was God there in your situation?

6. In chapter 65, the Maker resurrects Addy from the dead. Read Jesus Question 5. Summarize the objections people have to his resurrection and the answers for each objection.

Thanks and Appreciation

First, I'd like to acknowledge Yeshua, my God, who chose me to suffer so I could experience the indescribable joy of bringing this story to life. Not only this, but he also constantly poured his creativity and ideas into my mind from the very beginning of this effort.

Second, I'd like to thank my wife, Dana, for the invaluable guidance she gave me during this project through her hours of patient listening and encouragement.

And then I must remember my little critters—Madi, Asa, Corbin, and Silas—who interrupted my writing many times to give me warm hugs and precious smiles.

Finally, I'd like to thank my fellow laborers on this project. My deepest appreciation to Chris Vestal for his creativity on the cover (among other things). And a big thanks to Chris Applegate, Tiffany Dorrin, Lisa Lockey, Gerald Long, Gary Menting, and Kyle Valaer for their marvelous editing work.

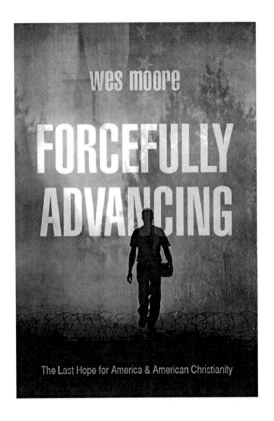

Learn how to share your faith

Forcefully Advancing:
The Last Hope for America
and American Christianity

by Wes Moore

www.forcefullyadvancingthebook.com

Learn answers to faith questions
DVD or online course

by Wes Moore
www.evidenceamerica.org

Learn more about Wes Moore

To learn more about Wes Moore:

Visit www.themakernovel.com

E-mail him at wes@themakernovel.com

LaVergne, TN USA
06 July 2010
188318LV00001BC/2/P